William George Waters

Jerome Cardan

A biographical study

William George Waters

Jerome Cardan
A biographical study

ISBN/EAN: 9783337384081

Printed in Europe, USA, Canada, Australia, Japan

Cover: Foto ©Raphael Reischuk / pixelio.de

More available books at **www.hansebooks.com**

JÉROME CARDAN

A BIOGRAPHICAL STUDY

W. G. WsATERS

"To be content that times to come should only know there was such a man, not caring whether they knew more of him, was a frigid ambition in Cardan."—Sir Thomas Browne.

LAWRENCE & BULLEN, Limited,
16 Henrietta Street, Covent Garden,
London, MDCCCXCVIII.
1 8 9 8

PREFACE

No attempt is made in the following pages to submit to historical treatment the vast and varied mass of printed matter which Cardan left as his contribution to letters and science, except in the case of those works which are, in purpose or incidentally, autobiographical, or of those which furnish in themselves effective contributions towards the framing of an estimate of the genius and character of the writer. Neither has it seemed worth while to offer to the public another biography constructed on the lines of the one brought out by Professor Henry Morley in 1854, for the reason that the circumstances of Cardan's life, the character of his work, and of the times in which he lived, all appeared to be susceptible of more succinct and homogeneous treatment than is possible in a chronicle of the passing years, and of the work that each one saw accomplished. At certain junctures the narrative form is inevitable, but an attempt has been made to treat the more noteworthy episodes of Cardan's life and work, and the contemporary aspect of the republic of letters, in relation to existing tendencies and conditions, whenever such a course has seemed possible.

Professor Morley's book, *The Life of Girolamo Cardano, of Milan, physician*, has been for some time out of print. This industrious writer gathered together a large quantity of material, dealing almost as fully with the more famous of the contemporary men of mark, with whom Cardan was brought into contact, as with Cardan himself. The translations and analyses of some of Cardan's more popular works which Professor Morley gives are admirable in their way, but the space they occupy in the biography is somewhat excessive. Had sufficient leisure for revision and condensation been allowed, Professor Morley's book would have taken a high place in biographical literature. As it stands it is a noteworthy performance ; and, by reason of its wide and varied stores of information and its excellent index, it must always prove a valuable magazine of *mémoires pour servir* for any future students who may be moved to write afresh concerning the life and work of the great Milanese physician.

An apology may be needed for the occurrence here and there of passages translated from the *De Vita Propria* and the *De Utilitate ex Adversis capienda*, passages which some readers may find too frequent and too lengthy, but contemporary opinion is strongly in favour of letting the subject speak for himself as far as may be possible. The date and place of Cardan's quoted works are given in the first citation therefrom ; those of his writings which have not been available in separate form have been consulted in the collected edition of his works in ten volumes, edited by Spon, and published at Lyons in 1663.

The author desires to acknowledge with gratitude the valuable assistance in the way of suggestion and emendation which he received from Mr. R. C. Christie during the final revision of the proofs.

London, October 1898.

JEROME CARDAN

CHAPTER I

LIKE certain others of the illustrious personages who flourished in his time, Girolamo Cardano, or, as he has become to us by the unwritten law of nomenclature, Jerome Cardan, was fated to suffer the burden and obloquy of bastardy.[1] He was born at Pavia from the illicit union of Fazio Cardano, a Milanese jurisconsult and mathematician of considerable repute, and a young widow, whose maiden name had been Chiara Micheria, his father being fifty-six, and his mother thirty-seven years of age at his birth. The family of Fazio was settled at Gallarate, a town in Milanese territory, and was one which, according to Jerome's contention, could lay claim to considerable antiquity and distinction. He prefers a claim of descent from the house of Castillione, founding the same upon an inscription on the apse of the principal

---

[1] Bayle is unwilling to admit Cardan's illegitimate birth. In *De Consolatione*, Opera, tom. i. p. 619 (Lyons, 1663), Cardan writes in reference to the action of the Milanese College of Physicians: "Medicorum collegium, suspitione obortâ, quòd (tam malè à patre tractatus) spurius essem, repellebat." Bayle apparently had not read the *De Consolatione*, as he quotes the sentence as the work of a modern writer, and affirms that the word "suspitio" would not have been used had the fact been notorious. But in the *Dialogus de Morte*, Opera, tom. i. p. 676, Cardan declares that his father openly spoke of him as a bastard.

B

church at Gallarate.[1]   He asserts that as far back as
1189 Milo Cardano was Governor of Milan for more
than seven years, and according to tradition Franco
Cardano, the commander of the forces of Matteo
Visconti,[2] was a member of the family.   If the claim of
the Castillione ancestry be allowed the archives of the
race would be still farther enriched by the name of Pope
Celestine IV., Godfrey of Milan, who was elected Pope
in 1241, and died the same year.

Cardan's immediate ancestors were long-lived.   The
sons of Fazio Cardano, his great-grandfather, Joanni,
Aldo, and Antonio, lived to be severally ninety-four,
eighty-eight, and eighty-six years of age.   Of these
Joanni begat two sons: Antonio, who lived eighty-eight
years, and Angelo, who reached the age of eighty-six.
To Aldo were born Jacopo, who died at seventy-two;
Gottardo, who died at eighty-four; and Fazio, the father
of Jerome, who died at eighty.[3]

Fazio, albeit he came of such a long-lived stock, and
lived himself to be fourscore, suffered much physical
trouble during his life.   On account of a wound which
he had received when he was a youth, some of the
bones of his skull had to be removed, and from this
time forth he never dared to remain long with his head
uncovered.   When he was fifty-nine he swallowed a
certain corrosive poison, which did not kill him, but
left him toothless.   He was likewise round-shouldered,
a stammerer, and subject to constant palpitation of the

---

[1] *De Utilitate ex adversis Capienda* (Franeker, 1648), p. 357.

[2] Matteo Visconti was born in 1250, and died in 1322.   He was
lord of Novara Vercello Como and Monferrato, and was made
Vicar Imperial by Adolphus of Nassau.   Though he was worsted
in his conflict with John XXII. he did much to lay the foundations
of his family.

[3] *De Vita Propria* (Amsterdam, 1654), ch. i. p. 4.

heart; but in compensation for these defects he had eyes which could see in the dark and which needed not spectacles even in advanced age.

Of Jerome's mother little is known, Her family seems to have been as tenacious of life as that of Fazio, for her father Jacopo lived to be seventy-five years of age. Of his maternal grandfather Jerome remarks that he was a highly skilled mathematician, and that when he was about seventy years of age, he was cast into prison for some offence against the law. He speaks of his mother as choleric in temper, well dowered with memory and mental parts, small in stature and fat, and of a pious disposition,[1] and declares that she and his father were alike in one respect, to wit that they were easily moved to anger and were wont to manifest but lukewarm and intermittent affection for their child. Nevertheless they were in a way indulgent to him. His father permitted him to remain in bed till the second hour of the day had struck, or rather forbade him to rise before this time—an indulgence which worked well for the preservation of his health. He adds that in after times he always thought of his father as possessing the kindlier nature of the two.[2]

It would seem from the passage above written, as well as from certain others subsequent, that Jerome had little affection for his mother; and albeit he neither chides nor reproaches her, he never refers to her in terms so appreciative and loving as those which he uses in lamenting the death of his harsh and tyrannical father.

[1] Cardan makes a statement in *De Consolatione*, Opera, tom. i. p. 605, which indicates that her disposition was not a happy one. "Matrem meam Claram Micheriam,.juvenem vidi, cum admodum puer essem, meminique hanc dicere solitam, Utinam si Deo placuisset, extincta forem in infantia."

[2] *De Vita Propria*, ch. i. p. 4.

In the *Geniturarum Exempla*[1] he says that, seeing he is writing of a woman, he will confine his remarks to saying that she was ingenious, of good parts, generous, upright, and loving towards her children. Perhaps the fact that his father died early, while his mother lived on for many years, and was afterwards a member of his household—together with his wife—may account for the colder tone of his remarks while writing about her. She was the widow of a certain Antonio Alberio,[2] and during her marriage had borne him three children, Tommaso, Catilina, and Joanni Ambrogio ; but when Jerome was a year old all three of these died of the plague within the space of a few weeks.[3] He himself narrowly escaped death from the same cause, and this attack he attributes to an inherited tendency from his mother, she having suffered from the same disease during her girlhood. There seems to have been born to Fazio and Chiara another son, who died at birth.[4]

Jerome Cardan was born on September 24, 1501, between half-past six o'clock and a quarter to seven in the evening. In the second chapter of his autobiography he gives the year as 1500, and in *De Utilitate*, p. 347, he writes the date as September 23, but on all other occasions the date first written is used. Before he saw the light malefic influences were at work against him. His mother, urged on no doubt by the desire to conceal her shame, and

---

[1] *Geniturarum Exempla* (Basil, 1554), p. 436.

[2] *De Rerum Varietate* (Basil, 1557), p. 655.

[3] *De Utilitate*, p. 347. There is a passage in *Geniturarum Exempla*, p. 435, dealing with Fazio's horoscope, which may be taken to mean that these children were his. "Alios habuisse filios qui obierint ipsa genitura demõstrat, me solo diu post etiã illius mortē superstite."

[4] With regard to the union of his parents he writes: "Uxorem vix duxit ob Lunam afflictam et eam in senectute."—*Geniturarum Exempla*, p. 435.

persuaded by evil counsellors, drank a potion of abortive drugs in order to produce miscarriage,[1] but Nature on this occasion was not to be baulked. In recording the circumstances of his birth he writes at some length in the jargon of astrology to show how the celestial bodies were leagued together so as to mar him both in body and mind. "Wherefore I ought, according to every rule, to have been born a monster, and, under the circumstances, it was no marvel that it was found necessary to tear me from the womb in order to bring me into the world. Thus was I born, or rather dragged from my mother's body. I was to all outward seeming dead, with my head covered with black curly hair. I was brought round by being plunged in a bath of heated wine, a remedy which might well have proved hurtful to any other infant. My mother lay three whole days in labour, but at last gave birth to me, a living child."[2]

The sinister influences of the stars soon began to manifest their power. Before Jerome had been many days in the world the woman into whose charge he had been given was seized with the plague and died the same day, whereupon his mother took him home with her. The first of his bodily ailments,—the catalogue of the same which he subsequently gives is indeed a portentous one,[3]—was an eruption of carbuncles on the face in the form of a cross, one of the sores being set on the tip of

---

[1] " Igitur ut ab initio exordiar, in pestilentia conceptus, matrem, nondum natus (ut puto) mearum calamitatum participem, profugam habui."—*Opera*, tom. i. p. 618.

"Mater ut abortiret medicamentum abortivum dum in utero essem, alieno mandato bibit."—*De Utilitate*, p. 347.

[2] *De Vita Propria*, ch. ii. p. 6.

[3] In one passage, *De Utilitate*, p. 348, he sums up his physical misfortunes: " Hydrope, febribus, aliisque morbis conflictatus sum, donec sub fine octavi anni ex dysenteria ac febre usque ad mortis limina perveni, pulsavi ostium sed non aperuere qui intro erant."

the nose; and when these disappeared, swellings came. Before the boy was two months old his godfather, Isidore di Resta of Ticino, gave him into the care of another nurse who lived at Moirago, a town about seven miles from Milan, but here again ill fortune attended him. His body began to waste and his stomach to swell because the nurse who gave him suck was herself pregnant.[1] A third foster-mother was found for him, and he remained with her till he was weaned in his third year.

When he was four years of age he was taken to Milan to be under the care of his mother, who, with her sister, Margarita, was living in Fazio's house; but whether she was at this time legally married to him or not there is no evidence to show. In recording this change he remarks that he now came under a gentler discipline from the hands of his mother and his aunt, but immediately afterwards proclaims his belief that the last-named must have been born without a gall bladder, a remark somewhat difficult to apply, seeing he frequently complains afterwards of her harshness. It must be remembered, however, that these details are taken from a record of the writer's fifth year set down when he was past seventy.[2] He quotes certain lapses from kindly usage, as for instance when it happened that he was beaten by his father or his mother without a cause. After much chastisement he always fell sick, and lay some time in mortal danger. "When I was seven years old my father and my mother were then living apart—my kinsfolk determined, for some reason or other, to give over beating me, though perchance a touch of the whip

---

[1] "Inde lac praegnantis hausi per varias nutrices lactatus ac jactatus."—*De Utilitate*, p. 348.

[2] The *De Vita Propria*, the chief authority for these remarks, was written by Cardan in Rome shortly before his death.

might then have done me no harm. But ill-fortune was ever hovering around me; she let my tribulation take a different shape, but she did not remove it. My father, having hired a house, took me and my mother and my aunt to live with him, and made me always accompany him in his rounds about the city. On this account I, being taken at this tender age with my weak body from a life of absolute rest and put to hard and constant work, was seized at the beginning of my eighth year with dysentery and fever, an ailment which was at that time epidemic in our city. Moreover I had eaten by stealth a vast quantity of sour grapes. But after I had been visited by the physicians, Bernabo della Croce and Angelo Gyra, there seemed to be some hope of my recovery, albeit both my parents, and my aunt as well, had already bewept me as one dead.

"At this season my father, who was at heart a man of piety, was minded to invoke the divine assistance of San Girolamo (commending me to the care of the Saint in his prayers) rather than trust to the working of that familiar spirit which, as he was wont to declare openly, was constantly in attendance upon him. The reason of this change in his treatment of me I never cared to inquire. It was during the time of my recovery from this sickness, that the French celebrated their triumph after defeating the Venetians on the banks of the Adda, which spectacle I was allowed to witness from my window.[1] After this my father freed me of the task of going with him on his rounds. But the anger of Juno was not yet exhausted; for, before I had fully recovered

---

[1] The illness would have occurred about October 1508, and the victory of the Adda was on May 14, 1509. This fact fixes his birth in 1501, and shows that his illness must have lasted six or seven months.

my health, I fell down-stairs (we were then living in the
Via dei Maini), with a hammer in my hand, and by this
accident I hurt the left side of my forehead, injuring the
bone and causing a scar which remains to this day.
Before I had recovered from this mishap I was sitting
on the threshold of the house when a stone, about as
long and as broad as a nut, fell down from the top of a
high house next door and wounded my head just where
my hair grew very thickly on the left side.

"At the beginning of my tenth year my father changed
this house, which had proved a very unlucky one for me,
for another in the same street, and there I abode for
three whole years. But my ill luck still followed me,
for my father once more caused me to go about with
him as his *famulus*, and would never allow me on any
pretext to escape this task. I should hesitate to say
that he did this through cruelty; for, taking into consideration what ensued, you may perchance be brought
to see that this action of his came to pass rather through
the will of Heaven than through any failing of his own.
I must add too that my mother and my aunt were fully
in agreement with him in his treatment of me. In after
times, however, he dealt with me in much milder fashion,
for he took to live with him two of his nephews, wherefore my own labour was lessened by the amount of
service he exacted from these. Either I did not go out
at all, or if we all went out together the task was less
irksome.

"When I had completed my sixteenth year—up to
which time I served my father constantly—we once more
changed our house, and dwelt with Alessandro Cardano
next door to the bakery of the Bossi. My father had
two other nephews, sons of a sister of his, one named
Evangelista, a member of the Franciscan Order, and

nearly seventy years of age, and the other Otto Cantone, a farmer of the taxes, and very rich. The last-named, before he died, wished to leave me his sole heir ; but this my father forbad, saying that Otto's wealth had been ill gotten; wherefore the estate was distributed according to the directions of the surviving brother." [1]

This, told as nearly as may be in his own words, is the story of Cardan's birth and childhood and early discipline, a discipline ill calculated to let him grow up to useful and worthy manhood. It must have been a wretched spring of life. Many times he refers to the hard slavery he underwent in the days when he was forced to carry his father's bag about the town, and tells how he had to listen to words of insult cast at his mother's name.[2] Like most boys who lead solitary lives, unrelieved by the companionship of other children, he was driven in upon himself, and grew up into a fanciful imaginative youth, a lover of books rather than of games, with an old head upon his young shoulders. After such a training it was only natural that he should be transformed from a nervous hysterical child into an embittered, cross-grained man, profligate and superstitious at the same time. Abundant light is thrown upon every stage of his career, for few men have left a clearer picture of themselves in their written words, and nowhere is Cardan, from the opening to the closing scene, so plainly exhibited as in the *De Vita Propria*, almost the last work which came from his pen. It has been asserted that this book, written in the twilight of senility by an old man with his heart cankered by misfortune and ill-usage, and his brain upset by the dread of real or fancied assaults of foes who lay in wait for him at every turn, is no trustworthy guide, even when bare facts are in

[1] *De Vita Propria*, ch. iv. p. 11.   [2] *Opera*, tom. i. p. 676.

question, and undoubtedly it would be undesirable to trust this record without seeking confirmation elsewhere· This confirmation is nearly always at hand, for there is hardly a noteworthy event in his career which he does not refer to constantly in the more autobiographic of his works. The *De Vita Propria* is indeed ill arranged and full of inconsistencies, but in spite of its imperfections, it presents its subject as clearly and effectively as Benvenuto Cellini is displayed in his own work. The rough sketch of a great master often performs its task more thoroughly than the finished painting, and Cardan's autobiography is a fragment of this sort. It lets pass in order of procession the moody neglected boy in Fazio's ill-ordered house, the student at Pavia, the youthful Rector of the Paduan Gymnasium, plunging when just across the threshold of life into criminal excess of Sardanapalean luxury, the country doctor at Sacco and afterwards at Gallarate, starving amongst his penniless patients, the University professor, the famous physician for whose services the most illustrious monarchs in Europe came as suppliants in vain, the father broken by family disgrace and calamity, and the old man, disgraced and suspected and harassed by persecutors who shot their arrows in the dark, but at the same time tremblingly anxious to set down the record of his days before the night should descend.

Until he had completed his nineteenth year Jerome continued to dwell under the roof which for the time being might give shelter to his parents. The emoluments which Fazio drew from his profession were sufficient for the family wants—he himself being a man of simple tastes; wherefore Jerome was not forced, in addition to his other youthful troubles, to submit to that *execrata paupertas* and its concomitant miseries which vexed him in later years. To judge from his conduct in the matter of Otto Cantone's estate, Fazio seems to have been as great a despiser of wealth as his son proved to be afterwards. His virtue, such as it was, must have been the outcome of one of those hard cold natures, with wants few and trifling, and none of those tastes which cry out daily for some new toy, only to be procured by money. The fact that he made his son run after him through the streets of Milan in place of a servant is not a conclusive proof of avarice ; it may just as likely mean that the old man was indifferent and callous to whatever suffering he might inflict upon his young son, and indisposed to trouble himself about scarching for a hireling to carry his bag. The one in-dication we gather of his worldly wisdom is his dissatis-faction that his son was firmly set to follow medicine rather than jurisprudence, a step which would involve the loss of the stipend of one hundred crowns a year which he drew for his lectureship, an income which he had hoped might be continued to a son of his after his death.[1]

Amidst the turmoil and discomfort of what must at the best have been a most ill-regulated household, the boy's education was undertaken by his father in such odds and ends of time as he might find to spare for the task.[2] What with the hardness and irritability of the teacher, and the peevishness inseparable from the

[1] "Quod munus profitendi institutiones in urbe ipsa cum honor-ario centum coronatorum, quo jam tot annis gaudebat, non in me (ut speraverat) transiturum intelligebat."—*De Vita Propria*, ch. x. p. 35.

[2] "Pater jam antè concesserat ut Geometriæ et Dialecticæ operam darem, in quo (quanquam præter paucas admonitiones, librosque, ac licentiam, nullum aliud auxilium præbuerit) eas tamen ego (succicivis temporibus studens) interim feliciter sum assecutus."—*De Consolatione*, Opera, tom. i. p. 619.

pupil's physical feebleness and morbid overwrought mental habit, these hours of lessons must have been irksome to both, and of little benefit. " In the meantime my father taught me orally the Latin tongue as well as the rudiments of Arithmetic, Geometry, and Astrology. But he allowed me to sleep well into the day, and he himself would always remain abed till nine o'clock. But one habit of his appeared to me likely to lead to grave consequences, to wit the way he had of lending to others anything which belonged to him. Part of these loans, which were made to insolvents, he lost altogether ; and the residue, lent to divers persons in high places, could only be recovered with much trouble and no little danger, and with loss of all interest on the same. I know not whether he acted in this wise by the advice of that familiar spirit [1] whose services he retained for eight-and-thirty years. What afterwards came to pass showed that my father treated me, his son, rightly in all things relating to education, seeing that I had a keen intelligence. For with boys of this sort it is well to make use of the bit as though you were dealing with mules. Beyond this he was witty and diverting in his conversation, and given to the telling of stories and strange occurrences well worth notice. He told me many things about familiar spirits, but what part of these were true I know not ; but assuredly tales of this sort, wonderful in themselves and artfully put together, delighted me marvellously.

[1] " Facius Cardanus dæmonem ætherium, ut ipse dicebat, diu familiarem habuit ; qui quamdiu conjuratione usus est, vera illi dabat responsa, cùm autem illam exussisset, veniebat quidem, sed responsa falsa dabat. Tenuit igitur annis, ni fallor, vinginti octo cum conjuratione, solutum autem circiter quinque."—*De Varietale*, p. 629.

In the *Dialogus Tetim* (*Opera*, tom. i. p. 672), Cardan writes : " Pater honeste obiit et ex senio, sed multo antea eum Genius ille reliquerat."

"But what chiefly deserved condemnation in my father was that he brought up certain other youths with the intention of leaving to them his goods in case I should die; which thing, in sooth, meant nothing less than the exposure of myself to open danger through plots of the parents of the boys aforesaid, on account of the prize offered. Over this affair my father and my mother quarrelled grievously, and finally decided to live apart. Whereupon my mother, stricken by this mental vexation, and troubled at intervals with what I deem to have been an hysterical affection, fell one day full on the back of her neck, and struck her head upon the floor, which was composed of tiles. It was two or three hours before she came round, and indeed her recovery was little short of miraculous, especially as at the end of her seizure she foamed much at the mouth.

"In the meantime I altered the whole drift of this tragedy by a pretended adoption of the religious life, for I became for a time a member of the mendicant Franciscan brotherhood. But at the beginning of my twenty-first year[1] I went to the Gymnasium at Pavia, whereupon my father, feeling my absence, was softened towards me, and a reconciliation between him and my mother took place.

"Before this time I had learnt music, my mother and even my father having secretly given me money for the same; my father likewise paid for my instruction in dialectics. I became so proficient in this art that I taught it to certain other youths before I went to the University. Thus he sent me there endowed with the means of winning an honest living; but he never once

---

[1] There is a discrepancy between this date and the one given in *De Vita Propria*, ch. iv. p. 11. "Anno exacto XIX contuli me in Ticinensem Academiam."

spake a word to me concerning this matter, bearing himself always towards me in considerate, kindly, and pious wise.

" For the residue of his days (and he lived on well-nigh four more years) his life was a sad one, as if he would fain let it be known to the world how much he loved me.[1] Moreover, when by the working of fate I returned home while he lay sick, he besought, he commanded, nay he even forced me, all unwilling, to depart thence, what though he knew his last hour was nigh, for the reason that the plague was in the city, and he was fain that I should put myself beyond danger from the same. Even now my tears rise when I think of his goodwill to-wards me. But, my father, I will do all the justice I can to thy merit and to thy paternal care ; and, as long as these pages may be read, so long shall thy name and thy virtues be celebrated. He was a man not to be cor-rupted by any offering whatsoever, and indeed a saint. But I myself was left after his death involved in many lawsuits, having nothing clearly secured except one small house." [2]

Fazio contracted a close intimacy with a certain Galeazzo Rosso, a man clever as a smith, and endowed with mechanical tastes which no doubt helped to secure him Fazio's friendship. Galeazzo discovered the prin-ciple of the water-screw of Archimedes before the descrip-tion of the same, written in the books of the inventor, had been published. He also made swords which could be bent as if they were of lead, and sharp enough to cut iron like wood. He performed a more wonderful feat

---

[1] " Inde (desiderium augente absentiâ) mortuus est, sæviente peste, cùm primum me diligere cœpisset."—*De Consolatione*, Opera, tom. i. p. 619.

[2] *De Utilitate*, p. 348.

in fashioning iron breast-plates which would resist the impact of red-hot missiles. In the *De Sapientia*, Cardan records that when Galeazzo perfected his water-screw, he lost his wits for joy.

Fazio took no trouble to teach his son Latin,[1] though the learned language would have been just as necessary for the study of jurisprudence as for any other liberal calling, and Jerome did not begin to study it systematically till he was past nineteen years of age. Through some whim or prejudice the old man refused for some time to allow the boy to go to the University, and when at last he gave his consent he still fought hard to compel Jerome to qualify himself in jurisprudence ; but here he found himself at issue with a will more stubborn than his own. Cardan writes : " From my earliest youth I let every action of mine be regulated in view of the after course of my life, and I deemed that as a career medicine would serve my purpose far better than law, being more appropriate for the end I had in view, of greater interest to the world at large, and likely to last as long as time itself. At the same time I regarded it as a study which embodied the nobler principles, and rested upon the ground of reason (that is upon the eternal laws of Nature) rather than upon the sanction of human opinion. On this account I took up medicine rather than jurisprudence, nay I almost entirely cast aside, or even fled from the company of those friends of mine who followed the law, rejecting at the same time wealth and power and honour. My father, when he heard that I had abandoned the study of law to follow philosophy, wept in my presence, and grieved amain that I would not settle down to the study of his

---

[1] " Nimis satis fuit defuisse tot, memoriam, linguam Latinam per adolescentiam."—*De Vita Propria*, ch. li. p. 218.

own subject. He deemed it the more salutary discipline
—proofs of which opinion he would often bring forward
out of Aristotle—that it was better adapted for the
acquisition of power and riches ; and that it would help
me more efficiently in restoring the fortunes of our
house. He perceived moreover that the office of teaching in the schools of the city, together with its accompanying salary of a hundred crowns which he had
enjoyed for so many years, would not be handed on to
me, as he had hoped, and he saw that a stranger would
succeed to the same. Nor was that commentary of his
destined ever to see the light or to be illustrated by my
notes. Earlier in life he had nourished a hope that his
name might become illustrious as the emendator of the
'Commentaries of John, Archbishop of Canterbury on
Optics and Perspective.'[1] Indeed the following verses
were printed thereanent :

> ' Hoc Cardana viro gaudet domus : omnia novit
> Unus : habent nullum saecula nostra parem.'

"These words may be taken as a sort of augury re-
ferring rather to certain other men about to set forth to do
their work in the world, than to my father, who, except
in the department of jurisprudence (of which indeed

---

[1] John Peckham was a Franciscan friar, and was nominated to
the see of Canterbury by Nicholas III. in 1279. He had spent
much time in the convent of his Order at Oxford, and there is a
legend connecting him with a Johannes Juvenis or John of London,
a youth who had attracted the attention and benevolence of Roger
Bacon. This Johannes became one of the first mathematicians
and opticians of the age, and was sent to Rome by Bacon, who
entrusted to him the works which he was sending to Pope Clement
IV. There is no reason for this view beyond the fact that both
were called John, and distinguished in the same branches of learning. The *Perspectiva Communis* was his principal work ; it does
not deal with perspective as now understood, but with elementary
propositions of optics. It was first printed in Milan in or about 1482.

rumour says that he was a master), never let his mind take in aught that was new. The rudiments of mathematics were all that he possessed, and he gathered no fresh knowledge from the store-houses of Greek learning. This disposition in him was probably produced by the vast multitude of subjects to be mastered, and by his infirmity of purpose, rather than by any lack of natural parts, or by idleness or by defect of judgment; vices to which he was in no way addicted. But I, being firmly set upon the object of my wishes, for the reasons given above, and because I perceived that my father had achieved only moderate success—though he had encountered but few hindrances—remained unconvinced by any of his exhortations."[1]

[1] *De Vita Propria*, ch. x. p. 34. A remark in *De Sapientia*, Opera, tom. i. p. 578, suggests that Fazio began life as a physician : " Pater meus Facius Cardanus Medicus primò, inde Jurisconsultus factus est."

CHAPTER II

THE University of Pavia to which Jerome now betook himself was by tradition one of the learned foundations of Charlemagne.[1] It had certainly enjoyed a high reputation all through the Middle Ages, and had recently had the honour of numbering Laurentius Valla amongst its professors. In 1362, Galeazzo Visconti had obtained a charter for it from the Emperor Charles IV., and that it had become a place of consequence in 1400 is proved by the fact that, besides maintaining several professors in the Canon Law, it supported thirteen in Civil Law, five in Medicine, three in Philosophy, and one each in Astrology, Greek, and Eloquence. Like all the other Universities of Northern Italy, it suffered occasional eclipse or even extinction on account of the constant war and desolation which vexed these parts almost without intermission during the years following the formation of the League of Cambrai. Indeed, as recently as 1500, the famous library collected by Petrarch, and presented by Gian Galeazzo Visconti to the University, was carried off by the French.[2]

---

[1] Pavia, like certain modern universities, did not spend all its time over study. "Aggressus sum Mediolani vacationibus quadragenariæ, seu Bacchanalium potius, anni MDLXI. Ita enim non obscurum est, nostra ætate celebrari ante quadragenariam vacationes, in quibus ludunt, convivantur, personati ac larvati incedunt, denique nullum luxus ac lascivæ genus omittunt : Sybaritæ et Lydi Persæque vincuntur." *Opera*, tom. i. p. 118.

[2] These books were taken to Blois. They were subsequently

To judge from the pictures which the Pavian student, writing in after years, gives of his physical self, it may be inferred that he was ill-endowed by the Graces. " I am of middle height. My chest is somewhat narrow and my arms exceedingly thin : my right hand is the more grossly fashioned of the two, so that a chiromantist might have set me down as rude or doltish : indeed, should such an one examine my hand, he would be ashamed to say what he thought. In it the line of life is short, and that named after Saturn long and well marked. My left hand, however, is seemly, with fingers long, tapering, and well-set, and shining nails. My neck is longer and thinner than the rule, my chin is divided, my lower lip thick and pendulous, my eyes are very small, and it is my wont to keep them half-closed, peradventure lest I should discern things over clearly. My forehead is wide and bare of hair where it meets the temples. My hair and beard are both of them yellow in tint, and both as a rule kept close cut. My chin, which as I have said already is marked by a division, is covered in its lower part with a thick growth of long hair. My habit is to speak in a highly-pitched voice, so that my friends sometimes rebuke me thereanent ; but, harsh and loud as is my voice, it cannot be heard at any great distance while I am lecturing. I am wont to talk too much, and in none too urbane a tone. The look of my eyes is fixed, like that of one in deep thought. My front teeth are large, and my complexion red and white : the form of my countenance being somewhat elongated, and my head is finished off in narrow wise at the back, like to a small sphere. Indeed, it was no rare thing for the painters, who came from distant countries to paint

---

removed by Francis I. to Fontainebleau, and with the other collections formed the nucleus of the Bibliothèque Nationale.

my portrait, to affirm that they could find no special characteristic which they could use for the rendering of my likeness, so that I might be known by the same."[1]

After giving this account of his person, Cardan writes down a catalogue of the various diseases which vexed him from time to time, a chapter of autobiography which looks like a transcript from a dictionary of Nosology. More interesting is the sketch which he makes of his mental state during these early years. Boys brought up in company of their elders often show a tendency to introspection, and fall into a dreamy whimsical mood, and his case is a striking example. "By the command of my father I used to lie abed until nine o'clock,[2] and, if perchance I lay awake any time before the wonted hour of rising, it was my habit to spend the same by conjuring up to sight all sorts of pleasant visions, nor can I remember that I ever summoned these in vain. I used to behold figures of divers kinds like airy bodies. Meseemed they were made up of tiny rings, like those in coats of chain-armour, though at this time I had seen nought of the kind. They would rise at the bottom of the bed, from the right-hand corner; and, moving in a semi-circle, would pass slowly on and disappear in the left. Moreover I beheld the shapes of castles and houses, of horses and riders, of plants, trees, musical instruments, theatres, dresses of men of all sorts, and flute-players who seemed to be playing upon their instruments, but neither voice nor sound was heard therefrom. And besides these things I beheld soldiers, and crowds of men, and fields, and certain bodily forms, which seem hateful to me even now: groves and forests,

---

[1] *De Vita Propria*, ch. v. p. 18.

[2] The time covered by this experience was from his fourth to his seventh year.

and divers other things which I now forget. In all this I took no small delight, and with straining eyes I would gaze upon these marvels; wherefore my Aunt Margaret asked me more than once whether I saw anything. I, though I was then only a child, deliberated over this question of hers before I replied, saying to myself: 'If I tell her the facts she will be wroth at the thing—whatever it may be—which is the cause of these phantasms, and will deprive me of this delight.' And then I seemed to see flowers of all kinds, and four-footed beasts, and birds; but all these, though they were fashioned most beautifully, were lacking in colour, for they were things of air. Therefore I, who neither as a boy nor as an old man ever learned to lie, stood silent for some time. Then my aunt said—'Boy, what makes you stare thus and stand silent?' I know not what answer I made, but I think I said nothing at all. In my dreams I frequently saw what seemed to be a cock, which I feared might speak to me in a human voice. This in sooth came to pass later on, and the words it spake were threatening ones, but I cannot now recall what I may have heard on these occasions." [1]

With a brain capable of such remarkable exercises as the above-written vision, living his life in an atmosphere of books, and with all games and relaxations dear to boys of his age denied to him, it was no marvel that Jerome should make an early literary essay on his own account. The death of a young kinsman, Niccolo Cardano,[2] suggested to him a theme which he elaborated in a tract called *De immortalitate paranda*, a work which perished unlamented by its author, and a little later he wrote a treatise on the calculation of the distances between

<hr />

[1] *De Vita Propria*, ch. xxxvii. p. 114; *De Rerum Subtilitate* (Basil, 1554), p. 524. [2] *Opera*, tom. i. p. 61.

the various heavenly bodies.[1]   But he put his mathematical skill to other and more sinister uses than this; for, having gained practical experience at the gaming-tables, he combined this experience with his knowledge of the properties of numbers, and wrote a tract on games of chance.   Afterwards he amplified this into his book, *Liber de Ludo Aleæ.*

With this equipment and discipline Jerome went to Pavia in 1520. He found lodging in the house of Giovanni Ambrogio Targio, and until the end of his twenty-first year he spent all his time between Pavia and Milan.   By this date he had made sufficiently good use of his time to let the world see of what metal he was formed, for in the year following he had advanced far enough in learning to dispute in public, to teach Euclid in the Gymnasium, and to take occasional classes in Dialectics and Elementary Philosophy.   At the end of his twenty-second year the country was convulsed by the wars between the Spaniards and the French under Lautrec, which ended in the expulsion of the last-named and the establishment of the Imperial power in Milan. Another result of the war, more germane to this history, was the closing of the University of Pavia through lack of funds.   In consequence of this calamity Jerome remained some time in Milan, and during these months he worked hard at mathematics; but he was not destined to return to Pavia as a student.   The schools there remained some long time in confusion, so in 1524 he went with his father's consent to Padua.   In the autumn of that same year he was summoned back to Milan to find Fazio in the grip of his dying illness.

---

[1] "Erat liber exiguus, rem tamen probe absolvebat : nam tunc forte in manus meas inciderat, Gebri Hispani liber, cujus auxilio non parum adjutus sum."—*Opera*, tom. i. p. 56.

"Whereupon he, careful of my weal rather than his own, bade me return to Padua at once, being well pleased to hear that I had taken at the Venetian College the Baccalaureat of Arts.[1] After my return to Padua, letters were brought to me which told me that he had died on the ninth day after he had refused nourishment. He died on the twenty-eighth of August, having last eaten on Sunday the twentieth of the month. Towards the close of my twenty-fourth year I was chosen Rector of the Academy at Padua,[2] and at the end of the next was made Doctor of Medicine. For the first-named office I came out the victor by one vote, the suffrages having to be cast a second time ; and for the Doctorate of Medicine my name had already twice come forth from the ballot with forty-seven votes cast against me (a circumstance which forbade another voting after the third), when, at the third trial, I came out the winner, with only nine votes against me (previously only this same number had been cast for me), and with forty-eight in my favour.

"Though I know well enough that affairs like these must needs be of small account, I have set them down in the order in which they came to pass for no other

[1] "Initio multi quidem paupertate aliave causa quum se nolunt subjicere rigoroso examini Cl. Collegii in artibus Medicinae vel in Jure, Baccalaureatus, vel Doctoratus gradum a Comitibus Palatinis aut Lateranensibus sumebant. Postea vero, sublata hac consuetudine, Gymnasii Rector, sive substitutus, convocatis duobus professoribus, bina puncta dabantur, iisque recitatis et diligentis [*sic*] excussis, illis gradus Baccalaureatus conferebatur."—*Gymnasium Patavinum* (1654), p. 200.

[2] He constantly bewails this step as the chief folly of his life : "Stulte vero id egi, quod Rector Gymnasii Patavini effectus sum, tum, cum, inops essem, et in patria maxime bella vigerent, et tributa intolerabilia. Matris tamen solicitudine effectum est, ut pondus impensarum, quamvis aegre, sustinuerim."—*De Utilitate*, p. 350.

reason than that I give pleasure to myself who write these words by so doing: and I do not write for the gratification of others. At the same time those people who read what I write—if indeed any one should ever be so minded—may learn hereby that the beginnings and the outcomes of great events may well be found difficult to trace, because in sooth it is the way of such things to come to the notice of anybody rather than of those who would rightly observe them."[1]

Padua cannot claim for its University an antiquity as high as that which may be conceded to Pavia, but in spite of its more recent origin, there is no little obscurity surrounding its rise. The one fact which may be put down as certain is that it sprang originally from the University of Bologna. Early in the thirteenth century violent discords arose between the citizens of Bologna and the students, and there is a tradition that the general school of teaching was transferred to Padua in 1222. What happened was probably a large migration of students, part of whom remained behind when peace between town and gown in Bologna was restored. The orthodox origin of the University is a charter granted by Frederic II. in 1238. Frederic at this time was certainly trying to injure Bologna, actuated by a desire to help on his own University at Naples, and to crush Bologna as a member of the Lombard League.[2] Padua, however, was also a member of this league, so his benevolent action towards it is difficult to understand. In 1228 the students had quarrelled with the Paduan citizens, and there was a movement to migrate to Vercelli; but, whether this really took place or not, the Paduan school did not suffer: its ruin and extinction

---

[1] *De Vita Propria*, ch. iv. p. 11.
[2] Muratori, *Chron. di Bologna*, xviii. 254.

was deferred till the despotism of the Ezzelini. In 1260 it was again revived by a second migration from Bologna, and this movement was increased on account of the interdict laid by the Pope upon Bologna in 1306 after the expulsion of the Papal Legate by the citizens.

In the early days Medicine and Arts were entirely subordinate to the schools of canon and civil law; but by the end of the fourteenth century these first-named Faculties had obtained a certain degree of independence, and were allowed an equal share in appointing the Rector.[1] The first College was founded in 1363, and after 1500 the number rapidly increased. The dominion of the Dukes of Carrara after 1322 was favourable to the growth of the University, which, however, did not attain its highest point till it came under Venetian rule in 1404. The Venetian government raised the stipends of the professors, and allowed four Paduan citizens to act as *Tutores Studii;* the election of the professors being vested in the students, which custom obtained until the end of the sixteenth century.[2] The Rector was allowed to wear a robe of purple and gold; and, when he retired, the degree of Doctor was granted to him, together with the right to wear the golden collar of the order of Saint Mark.

Padua like Athens humanized its conquerors. It became the University town of Venice, as Pavia was of Milan, and it was for a long time protected from the assaults of the Catholic reaction by its rulers, who

[1] The stipends paid to teachers of jurisprudence were much more liberal than those paid to humanists. In the Diary of Sanudo it is recorded that a jurist professor at Padua received a thousand ducats per annum. Lauro Quirino, a professor of rhetoric, meantime received only forty ducats, and Laurentius Valla at Pavia received fifty sequins.—Muratori, xxii. 990.

[2] Tomasinus, *Gymnasium Patavinam* (1654), p. 136.

possibly were instigated rather by political jealousy of the Papacy as a temporal power, than by any enthusiasm for the humanist and scientific studies of which Padua was the most illustrious home south of the Alps ; studies which the powers of the Church began already to recognize as their most dangerous foes.

Such was the University of Padua at the height of its glory, and it will be apparent at once that Padua must have fallen considerably in its fortunes when it installed as its Rector an obscure student, only twenty-four years of age, and of illegitimate birth, and conferred upon him the right to go clad in purple and gold, and to claim, as his retiring gift, the degree of Doctor and the cross of Saint Mark. In 1508 the League of Cambrai had been formed, and Venice, not yet recovered from the effects of its disastrous wars with Bajazet II., was forced to meet the combined assault of the Pope, the Emperor, and the King of France. Padua was besieged by the Imperial forces, a motley horde of Germans, Swiss, and Spaniards, and the surrounding country was pillaged and devastated by these savages with a cruelty which recalled the days of Attila. It is not wonderful that the University closed its doors in such a time. When the confederates began to fight amongst themselves the class-rooms were reopened, intermittently at first, but after 1515 the teaching seems to have been continuous. Still the prevalent turmoil and poverty rendered it necessary to curtail all the mere honorary and ornamental adjuncts of the schools, and for several years no Rector was appointed, for the good and sufficient reason that no man of due position and wealth and character could be found to undertake the rectorial duties, with the Academy just emerging from complete disorganization. These duties were many and important, albeit the Rector could, if he willed, appoint a deputy, and the calls upon the purse of the holder must have been very heavy. It would be hard to imagine any one less fitted to fill such a post than Cardan, and assuredly no office could befit him less than this pseudo-rectorship.[1] It must ever remain a mystery why he was preferred, why he was elected, and why he consented to serve: though, as to the last-named matter, he hints in a passage lately cited from *De Utilitate*, that it was through the persuasions of his mother that he took upon himself this disastrous honour. Many passages in his writings suggest that Chiara was an indulgent parent. She let Fazio have no peace till he consented to allow the boy to go to college; she paid secretly for music-lessons, so that Jerome was enabled to enjoy the relaxation he loved better than anything else in the world—except gambling; she paid all his charges during his student life at Padua; and now, quite naturally, she would have shed her heart's blood rather than let this son of hers—ugly duckling as he was— miss what she deemed to be the crowning honour of the rectorship; but after all the sacrifices Chiara made, after all the misfortunes which attended Jerome's ill-directed ambition, there is a doubt as to whether he ever was Rector in the full sense of the term. Many times and in divers works he affirms that once upon a time he was Rector, and over and beyond this he sets down in black and white the fact, more than once, that he never told a lie; so it is only polite to accept this

---

[1] Tomasinus writes that the Rector should be "Virum illustrem, providum, eloquentem ac divitem, quique eo pollet rerum usu ut Gymnasi decora ipsius gubernatione et splendore augeantur."— *Gymnasium Patavinum*, p. 54. He likewise gives a portrait of the Rector in his robes of office, and devotes several chapters to an account of his duties.

legend for what it is worth. But it must likewise be
noted that in the extant records of the University there
is no mention of his name in the lists of Rectors.[1]

Jerome has left very few details as to his life at
Padua. Of those which he notices the following are
the most interesting: "In 1525, the year in which I
became Rector, I narrowly escaped drowning in the
Lago di Garda. I went on board the boat, unwillingly
enough, which carried likewise some hired horses; and,
as we sailed on, the mast and the rudder, and one of
the two oars we had with us, were broken by the wind.
The sails, even those on the smaller mast, were split,
and the night came on. We landed at last safe and
sound at Sirmio, but not before all my companions
had given up hope, and I myself was beginning to
despair. Indeed, had we been a minute later we must
have perished, for the tempest was so violent that the
iron hinges of the inn windows were bent thereby. I,
though I had been sore afraid ever since the wind
began to blow, fell to supper with a good heart when
the host set upon the board a mighty pike, but none
of the others had any stomach for food, except the one
passenger who had advised us to make trial of this
perilous adventure, and who had proved to be an able
and courageous helper in our hour of distress.

"Again, once when I was in Venice on the birthday
of the Virgin, I lost some money at dicing, and on the

---

[1] "Ab anno 1509 usque ad annum 1515 ob bellum Cameracense
Gymn. interrmissum fuit."—*Elenchus nominum Patavii* (1706), p.
28. The first names given after this interregnum are Dom. Jo.
Maria de Zaffaris, Rector in Arts, and Dom. Marinus de Ongaris,
Rector in Jurisprudence in 1527.

Papadapoli (*Historia Gymn. Patav.*) gives the name of As-
canius Serra as pro-Rector in 1526: no Rector being mentioned
at all.

day following all that was left me went the same way.
This happened in the house of the man with whom I
was gambling, and in the course of play I noticed that
the cards were marked, whereupon I struck him in the
face with my dagger, wounding him slightly.   Two of
his servants were present at the time ; some spears
hung all ready from the beams of the roof, and besides
this the house door was fastened.   But when I had
taken from him all the money he had about him—his
own as well as that which he had won from me by
cheating, and my cloak and the rings which I had
lost to him the day before—I was satisfied that I had
got back all my possessions.   The chattels I sent home
by my servant at once, but a portion of the money I
tossed back to the fellow when I saw that I had drawn
blood of him.   Then I attacked the servants who were
standing by; and, as they knew not how to use their
weapons and besought my mercy, I granted this on the
condition that they should unlock the door.   Their
master, taking account of the uproar and confusion,
and mistrusting his safety in case the affair should not
be settled forthwith (I suspect he was alarmed about
the marked cards), commanded the servants to open
the door, whereupon I went my way.

"That very same evening, while I was doing my best
to escape the notice of the officers of justice on account
of the wound I had given to this Senator, I lost my
footing and fell into a canal, having arms under my
cloak the while.   In my fall I did not lose my nerve,
but flinging out my right arm, I grasped the thwart of a
passing boat and was rescued by those on board.   When
I had been hauled into the boat I discovered—wonderful
to relate—that the man with whom I had lately played
cards was likewise on board, with his face bandaged by

reason of the wounds I had given him. Now of his own accord he brought out a suit of clothes, fitted for seafaring, and, having clad myself in them, I journeyed with him as far as Padua." [1]

Cardan's life from rise to set cannot be estimated otherwise than an unhappy one, and its least fortunate years were probably those lying between his twenty-first and his thirty-first year of age. During this period he was guilty of that crowning folly, the acceptance of the Rectorship of the Gymnasium at Padua, he felt the sharpest stings of poverty, and his life was overshadowed by dire physical misfortune. He gives a rapid sketch of the year following his father's death. " Then, my father having breathed his last and my term of office come to an end, I went, at the beginning of my twenty-sixth year, to reside at Sacco, a town distant ten miles from Padua and twenty-five from Venice. I fixed on this place by the advice of Francesco Buonafidei, a physician of Padua, who, albeit I brought no profit to him—not even being one of those who attended his public teaching —helped me and took a liking for me, being moved to this benevolence by his exceeding goodness of heart. In this place I lived while our State was being vexed by every sort of calamity. In 1524 by a raging pestilence and by a two-fold change of ruler. In 1526 and 1527 by a destructive scarcity of the fruits of the earth. It was hard to get corn in exchange for money of any kind, and over and beyond this was the intolerable weight of taxation. In 1528 the land was visited by divers diseases and by the plague as well, but these afflictions seemed the easier to bear because all other parts were likewise suffering from the same. In 1529 I ventured to return to Milan—these ill-starred troubles being in some

[1] *De Vita Propria*, ch. xxx. p. 79.

degree abated—but I was refused membership by the College of Physicians there, I was unable to settle my lawsuit with the Barbiani, and I found my mother in a very ill humour, so I went back to my village home, having suffered greatly in health during my absence. For what with cruel vexations, and struggles, and cares which I saw impending, and a troublesome cough and pleurisy aggravated by a copious discharge of humour, I was brought into a condition such as few men exchange for aught else besides a coffin." [1]

The closing words of his eulogy on his father tell how the son, on the father's death, found that one small house was all he could call his own. The explanation of this seems to be that the old man, being of a careless disposition and litigious to boot, had left his affairs in piteous disorder. In consequence of this neglect Jerome was involved in lawsuits for many years, and the one afore-mentioned with the Barbiani was one of them. This case was subsequently settled in Jerome's favour.

[1] *De Vita Propria*, ch. iv. p. 13.

CHAPTER III

DURING his life at Padua it would appear that Cardan, over and above the allowance made to him by his mother, had no other source of income than the gaming-table.[1] However futile and disastrous his sojourn at this University may have been, he at least took away with him one possession of value, to wit his doctorate of medicine, on the strength of which he began to practise as a country physician at Sacco. The record of his life during these years gives the impression that he must have been one of the most wretched of living mortals. The country was vexed by every sort of misfortune, by prolonged warfare, by raging pestilence, by famine, and by intolerable taxation;[2] but while he paints this picture of misery and desolation in one place, he goes on to declare in another that the time which he spent at Sacco was the happiest he ever knew.[3] No greater instance of inconsistency is to be found in his pages. He writes : " I gambled, I occupied myself with music, I walked abroad, I feasted, giving

---

[1] " Nec ullum mihi erat relictum auxilium nisi latrunculorum Ludus."—*Opera*, tom. i. p. 619.

[2] From the formation of the League of Cambrai in 1508 to the establishment of the Imperial supremacy in Italy in 1530, the whole country was desolated by the marching and counter-marching of the contending forces. Milan, lying directly in the path of the French armies, suffered most of all.

[3] Compare *De Vita Propria*, chaps. iv. and xxxi. pp. 13 and 92.

scant attention the while to my studies. I feared no hurt, I paid my respects to the Venetian gentlemen living in the town, and frequented their houses. I, too, was in the very flower of my age, and no time could have been more delightful than this which lasted for five years and a half." [1]

But for almost the whole of this period Cardan was labouring under a physical misfortune concerning which he writes in another place in terms of almost savage bitterness. During ten years of his life, from his twenty-first to his thirty-first year, he suffered from the loss of virile power, a calamity which he laments in the following words : "And I maintain that this misfortune was to me the worst of evils. Compared with it neither the harsh servitude under my father, nor unkindness, nor the troubles of litigation, nor the wrongs done me by my fellow-townsmen, nor the scorn of my fellow-physicians, nor the ill things falsely spoken against me, nor all the measureless mass of possible evil, could have brought me to such despair, and hatred of life, and distaste of all pleasure, and lasting sorrow. I bitterly wept this misery, that I must needs be a laughing-stock, that marriage must be denied me, and that I must ever live in solitude. You ask for the cause of this misfortune, a matter which I am quite unable to explain. Because of the reasons just mentioned, and because I dreaded that men should know how grave was the ill afflicting me, I shunned the society of women ; and, on account of this habit, the same miserable public scandal which I desired so earnestly to avoid, arose concerning me, and brought upon me the suspicion of still more nefarious practices :

---

[1] *De Vita Propria*, ch. xxxi. p. 92. In taking the other view he writes : "Vitam ducebam in Saccensi oppido, ut mihi videbar, infelicissime."—*Opera*, tom. i. p. 97.

in sooth it seemed that there was no further calamity left for me to endure." [1]   After reading these words, it is hard to believe that a man, afflicted with a misfortune which he characterizes in these terms, could have been even moderately happy ; much less in that state of bliss which he sits down to describe forty years afterwards.

But the end of his life at Sacco was fated to be happier than the beginning, and it is possible that memories of the last months he spent there may have helped to colour with rosy tint the picture of happiness recently referred to.   In the first place he was suddenly freed from his physical infirmity, and shortly after his restoration he met and married the woman who, as long as she lived with him, did all that was possible to make him happy.   Every momentous event of Cardan's life—and many a trifling one as well —was heralded by some manifestation of the powers lying beyond man's cognition.   In writing about the signs and tokens which served as premonitions of his courtship and marriage, he glides easily into a description of the events themselves in terms which are worth producing.   "In times past I had my home in Sacco, and there I led a joyful life, as if I were a man unvexed by misfortune (I recall this circumstance somewhat out of season, but the dream I am about to tell of seems only too appropriate to the occasion), or a mortal made free of the habitations of the blest, or rather of some region of delight.   Then, on a certain night, I seemed to find myself in a pleasant garden, beautiful exceedingly, decked with flowers and filled with fruits of divers sorts, and a soft air breathed around.   So lovely was it all that no painter nor our poet Pulci, nor any imagination of man could have figured the like.   I was standing in

---

[1] *De Utilitate*, p. 235.

the forecourt of this garden, the door whereof was open, and there was another door on the opposite side, when lo! I beheld before me a damsel clad in white. I embraced and kissed her; but before I could kiss her again, the gardener closed the door. I straightway begged him earnestly that he would open it again, but I begged in vain; wherefore, plunged in grief and clinging to the damsel, I seemed to be shut out of the garden.

"A little time after this there was a rumour in the town of a house on fire, and I was roused from sleep to hurry to the spot. Then I learned that the house belonged to one Altobello Bandarini,[1] a captain of the Venetian levies in the district of Padua. I had no acquaintance with him, in sooth I scarcely knew him by sight. Now it chanced that after the fire he hired a house next door to my own, a step which displeased me somewhat, for such a neighbour was not to my taste; but what was I to do? After the lapse of a few days, when I was in the street, I perceived a young girl who, as to her face and her raiment, was the exact image of her whom I had beheld in my dream. But I said to myself, 'What is this girl to me? If I, poor wretch that I am, take to wife a girl dowered with naught, except a crowd of brothers and sisters, it will be all over with me; forasmuch as I can hardly keep myself as it is. If I should attempt to carry her off, or to have my will of her by stealth, there will of a surety be some tale-bearers about; and her father, being a fellow-townsman and a soldier to boot, would not sit down lightly under such an injury. In this case, or in that, it is hard to say what course I should follow, for

---

[1] He gives a long and interesting sketch of his father-in-law in *De Utilitate*, p. 370.

if this affair should come to the issue I most desire, I must needs fly the place.' From that same hour these thoughts and others akin to them possessed my brain, which was only too ready to harbour them, and I felt it would be better to die than to live on in such perplexity. Thenceforth I was as one love-possessed, or even burnt up with passion, and I understood what meaning I might gather from the reading of my dream. Moreover I was by this time freed from the chain which had held me back from marriage. Thus I, a willing bridegroom, took a willing bride, her kinsfolk questioning us how this thing had been brought about, and offering us any help which might be of service ; which help indeed proved of very substantial benefit.

"But the interpretation of my dreams did not work itself out entirely in the after life of my wife ; it made itself felt likewise in the lives of my children. My wife lived with me fifteen years, and alas ! this ill-advised marriage was the cause of all the misfortunes which subsequently happened to me. These must have come about either by the working of the divine will, or as the recompense due for some ill deeds wrought by myself or by my forefathers." [1]

The dream aforesaid was not the only portent having reference to his marriage. After describing shakings and tremblings of his bed, for which indeed a natural cause was not far to seek, he tells how in 1531 a certain dog, of gentle temper as a rule, and quiet, kept up a persistent howling for a long time ; how some ravens perched on the house-top and began croaking in an unusual manner ; and how, when his servant was breaking up a faggot, some sparks of fire flew out of the same ; whereupon, " by an unlooked-for step I married

[1] *De Vita Propria*, ch. xxvi. p. 68 ; *Opera*, tom. i. p. 97.

a wife, and from that time divers misfortunes have attended me."[1]   Lucia, the wife of his choice, was the eldest daughter of Altobello Bandarini, who had, besides her, three daughters and four sons. Jerome, as it has been already noted, was possessed with a fear lest he should be burdened by his brothers- and sisters-in-law after his marriage ; but, considering that he was a young unknown physician, without either money or patients, and that Bandarini was a man of position and repute, with some wealth and more shrewdness, the chances were that the burden would lie on the other side. Cardan seems to have inherited Fazio's contempt for wealth, or at least to have made a profession thereof ; for, in chronicling the event of his marriage, he sets down, with a certain degree of pomposity, that he took a wife without a dower on account of a certain vow he had sworn.[2] If the bride was penniless the father-in-law was wealthy, and the last-named fact might well have proved a powerful argument to induce Cardan to remain at Sacco, albeit he had little scope for his calling. That he soon determined to quit the place, is an evidence of his independence of spirit, and of his disinclination to sponge upon his well-to-do connections. Bandarini, when this scheme was proposed to him, vetoed it at once. He was unwilling to part with his daughter, and possibly he may have taken a fancy to his son-in-law, for Cardan has left it on record that Bandarini was greatly pleased with the match ; he ended, however, by consenting to the migration, which was not made without the intervention of a warning portent. A short time before the young couple departed, it happened that a tile got mixed with the embers in Bandarini's bed-chamber ; and, in the course of the night, exploded

[1] *De Vita Propria*, ch. xli. p. 149.   [2] *De Utilitate*, p. 350.

with a loud report, and the fragments thereof were scattered around. This event Bandarini regarded as an augury of evil, and indeed evil followed swiftly after. Before a year had passed he was dead, some holding that his death had been hastened by the ill conduct of his eldest son, and others whispering suspicions of poison.

Jerome and his young wife betook themselves to Milan, but this visit seems to have been fully as unprofitable as the one he had paid in 1529. In that year he had to face his first rejection by the College of Physicians, when he made application for admission; and there is indirect evidence that he now made a second application with no better result.[1] In any case his affairs were in a very bad way. If he had money in his pocket he would not keep long away from the gaming-table; and, with the weight of trouble ever bearing him down more and more heavily, it is almost certain that his spirits must have suffered, and that poor Lucia must have passed many an unhappy hour on account of his nervous irritability. Then the gates of his profession remained closed to him by the action of the College. The pretext the authorities gave for their refusal to admit him was his illegitimate birth; but it is not unlikely that they may have mistrusted as a colleague the son of Fazio Cardano, and that stories of the profligate life and the intractable temper of the candidate may have been brought to them.[2] His health suffered

[1] *De Utilitate*, p. 357: "Nam in urbe nec collegium recipere volebat nec cum aliquo ex illis artem exercere licebat et sine illis difficillimum erat." He writes thus while describing this particular visit to Milan.

[2] Ill fortune seems to have pursued the whole family in their relations with learned societies. "Nam et pater meus ut ab eo accepi, diu in ingressu Collegii Jurisconsultorum laboravit, et

from the bad air of the city almost as severely as before, and Lucia, who was at this time pregnant, miscarried at four months, and shortly afterwards had a second misfortune of the same kind. His mother's temper was not of the sweetest, and it is quite possible that between her and her daughter-in-law there may have been strained relations. Cardan at any rate found that he must once more beat a retreat from Milan, wherefore, at the end of April 1533, he made up his mind to remove to Gallarate.

This town has already been mentioned as chief place of the district, from which the Cardan family took its origin. Before going thither Jerome had evidently weighed the matter well, and he has set down at some length the reasons which led him to make this choice. "Thus, acting under the reasons aforesaid (the family associations), I resolved to go to Gallarate, in order that I might have the enjoyment of four separate advantages which it offered. Firstly, that in the most healthy air of the place I might shake off entirely the distemper which I had contracted in Milan. Secondly, that I might earn something by my profession, seeing that then I should be free to practise. Thirdly, that there would be no need for me to pine away while I beheld those physicians, by whom I reckoned I had been despoiled, flourishing in wealth and in the high estimation of all men. Lastly, that by following a more frugal way of life, I might make what I possessed last the longer. For all things are cheaper in the country, since they have to be carried from the country into the town, and many necessaries may be had for the asking.

ego, ut alias testatus sum, bis a medicorum Patavino, toties filius meus natu major, a Ticinensi, uterque a Mediolanensi rejecti sumus."—*Opera*, tom. i. p. 94.

Persuaded by these arguments, I went to this place, and I was not altogether deceived, seeing that I recovered my health, and the son—who was to be reft from me later on by the Senate—was born to me."[1]

Employment at Gallarate was, however, almost as scarce as it had been at Sacco, wherefore Jerome found leisure in plenty for literary work. He began a treatise on Fate; but, even had this been completed, it would scarcely have filled the empty larder by the proceeds of its sale. More profitable was some chance employment which was given to him by Filippo Archinto,[2] a generous and accomplished young nobleman of Milan, who was ambitious to figure as a writer on Astronomy, and, it may be remarked, Archinto's benefactions were not confined to the payment for the hack work which Jerome did for him at this period. Had it not been for his subsequent patronage and support, it is quite possible that Cardan would have gone under in the sea of adversity.

In spite of the cheapness of provisions at Gallarate, and of occasional meals taken gratis from the fields, complete destitution seemed to be only a matter of days, and just at this crisis, to add to his embarrassments—though he longed earnestly for the event—Lucia was brought to bed with her first-born living child on May 14, 1534. The child's birth was accompanied by divers omens, one of which the father describes, finding therein some premonition of future disaster. " I had great fear of his life until the fifteenth day of June, on which day, being a Sunday, he was

[1] *De Utilitate*, p. 358.
[2] He became a priest, and died Archbishop of Milan in 1552. Cardan dedicated to him his first published book, *De Malo Medendi*.

baptized. The sun shone brightly into the bed-chamber : it was between the hours of eleven and twelve in the forenoon ; and, according to custom, we were all gathered round the mother's bed except a young servant, the curtain was drawn away from the window and fastened to the wall, when suddenly a large wasp flew into the room, and circled round the infant. We were all greatly afeard for the child, but the wasp did him no hurt. The next moment it came against the curtain, making so great a noise that you would have said that a drum was being beaten, and all ran towards the place, but found no trace of the wasp. It could not have flown out of the room, because all eyes had been fixed upon it. Then all of us who were then present felt some foreboding of what subsequently came to pass, but did not deem that the end would be so bitter as it proved to be." [1]

The impulse which drives men in desperate straits to seek shelter in the streets of a city was as strong in Cardan's time as it is to-day. At Gallarate the last coin was now spent, and there was an extra mouth to feed. There seemed to be no other course open but another retreat to Milan. Archinto was rich in literary . ambitions, which might perchance stimulate him to find farther work for the starving scholar : and there was Chiara also who would scarcely let her grandchild die of want. The revelation which Cardan makes of himself and of his way of life at this time is not one to enlist sympathy for him entirely ; but it is not wanting in a note of pathetic sincerity. " For a long time the College at Milan refused to admit me, and during these days I was assuredly a spendthrift and heedless. In body I was weakly, and in estate plundered by thieves

[1] *De Vita Propria*, ch. xxxvii. p. 119.

on all sides, yet I never grudged money for the buying of books. My residence at Gallarate brought me no profit, for in the whole nineteen months I lived there, I did not receive more than twenty-five crowns towards the rent of the house I hired. I had such ill luck with the dice that I was forced to pawn all my wife's jewels, and our very bed. If it is a wonder that I found myself thus bereft of all my substance, it is still more wonderful that I did not take to begging on account of my poverty, and a wonder greater still that I harboured in my mind no unworthy thoughts against my forefathers, or against right living, or against those honours which I had won—honours which afterwards stood me in good stead—but bore my misfortunes with mind undisturbed." [1]

Cardan's worldly fortunes were now at their lowest ebb. Burdened with a wife and child, he had found it necessary to return, after a second futile attempt to gain a living by his calling in a country town, to Milan, his " stony-hearted step-mother." If he had reckoned on his mother's bounty he was doomed to disappointment, for Chiara was an irritable woman, and as her son's temper was none of the sweetest, it is almost certain that they must have quarrelled occasionally. It is hard to believe that they could have been on good terms at this juncture, otherwise she would scarcely have allowed him to take his wife and child to what was then the public workhouse of the city ; [2] but this place was his only refuge, and in October 1534 he was glad to shelter himself beneath its roof.

[1] *De Vita Propria*, ch. xxv. p. 67.

[2] The Xenodochium, which was originally a stranger's lodging-house. By this time places of this sort had become little else than *succursales* of some religious house. The Governors of the Milanese Xenodochium were the patrons of the Plat endowment which Cardan afterwards enjoyed.

There was in Cardan's nature a strong vein of melancholy, and up to the date now under consideration he had been the victim of a fortune calculated to deepen rather than disperse his morbid tendencies. A proof of his high courage and dauntless perseverance may be deduced from the fact that neither poverty, nor the sense of repeated failure, nor the flouts of the Milanese doctors, prevailed at any time to quench in his heart the love of fame,[1] or to disabuse him of the conviction that he, poverty-stricken wretch as he was, would before long bind Fortune to his chariot-wheels, and would force the adverse world to acknowledge him as one of its master minds. The dawn was now not far distant, but the last hours of his night of misfortune were very dark. The worst of the struggle, as far as the world was concerned, was over, and the sharpest sorrows and the heaviest disgrace reserved for Cardan in the future were to be those nourished in his own household.

Writing of his way of life and of the vices and defects of his character, he says: "If a man shall fail in his carriage before the world as he fails in other things, who shall correct him? Thus I myself will do duty for that one leper who alone out of the ten who were healed came back to our Lord. By reasoning of this sort, Physicians and Astrologers trace back the origin of our natural habits to our primal qualities, to the training of our will, and to our occupations and conversation. In every man all these are found in proper ratio to the time of life of each individual; nevertheless it will be easy to discern marked variations in cases otherwise similar. Therefore it behoves us to hold fast to some guiding principle chosen out of these, and I on my part

---

[1] "Hoc unum sat scio, ab ineunte ætate me inextinguibili nominis immortalis cupiditate flagrasse."—*Opera*, tom. i. p. 61.

am inclined, as far as it may be allowed, to say with respect to all of them, γνῶθι σεαυτὸν.

"My own nature in sooth was never a mystery to myself. I was ever hot-tempered, single-minded, and given to women. From these cardinal tendencies there proceeded truculence of temper, wrangling, obstinacy, rudeness of carriage, anger, and an inordinate desire, or rather a headstrong passion, for revenge in respect to any wrong done to me ; so that this inclination, which is censured by many, became to me a delight. To put it briefly, I held *At vindicta bonum vita jucundius ipsa.* As a general rule I went astray but seldom, though it is a common saying, ' *Natura nostra prona est ad malum.*' I am moreover truthful, mindful of benefits wrought to me, a lover of justice and of my own people, a despiser of money, a worshipper of that fame which defies death, prone to thrust aside what is commonplace, and still more disposed to treat mere trifles in the same way. Still, knowing well how great may be the power of little things at any moment during the course of an undertaking, I never make light of aught which may be useful. By nature I am prone to every vice and ill-doing except ambition, and I, if no one else does, know my own imperfections. But because of my veneration for God, and because I recognize the vanity and emptiness of all things of this sort, it often happens that, of my own free will, I forego certain opportunities for taking revenge which may be offered to me. I am timid, with a cold heart and a hot brain, given to reflection and the consideration of things many and mighty, and even of things which can never come to pass. I can even let my thoughts concern themselves with two distinct subjects at the same time. Those who throw out charges of garrulity and extravagance by way of contradicting any praise accorded to me, charge me with the faults of others rather than my own. I attack no man, I only defend myself.

"And what reason is there why I should spend myself in this cause since I have so often borne witness of the emptiness of this life of ours? My excuse must be that certain men have praised me, wherefore they cannot deem me altogether wicked. I have always trained myself to let my face contradict my thoughts. Thus while I can simulate what is not, I cannot dissimulate what is. To accomplish this is no difficult task if a man cultivates likewise the habit of hoping for nothing. By striving for fifteen years to compass this end and by spending much trouble over the same I at last succeeded. Urged on by this humour I sometimes go forth in rags, sometimes finely dressed, sometimes silent, sometimes talkative, sometimes joyful, sometimes sad ; and on this account my two-fold mood shows everything double. In my youth I rarely spent any care in keeping my hair in order, because of my inclination for other pursuits more to my taste. My gait is irregular. I move now quickly, now slowly. When I am at home I go with my legs naked as far as the ankles. I am slack in duty and reckless in speech, and specially prone to show irritation over anything which may disgust or irk me."

The above-written self-description does not display a personality particularly attractive. Jerome Cardan was one of those men who experience a morbid gratification in cataloguing all their sinister points of character, and exaggerating them at the same time ; and in this picture, as in many others scattered about the *De Vita Propria,* the shadows may have been put in too strongly.

In the foregoing pages reference was made to certain

acts of benevolence done to Cardan by the family of Archinto. ˙ It is not impossible that the promises and persuasions of his young patron Filippo may have had some weight in inducing Jerome to shift his home once more. Whatever befell he could hardly make his case worse ; but whether Filippo had promised help or not, he showed himself now a true and valuable friend. There was in Milan a public lectureship in geometry and astronomy supported by a small endowment left by a certain Tommaso Plat, and to this post, which happened opportunely to be vacant, Cardan was appointed by the good offices of Filippo Archinto. Yet even when he was literally a pauper he seems to have felt some scruples about accepting this office, but fortunately in this instance his poverty overcame his pride. The salary was indeed a very small one,[1] and the lecturer was not suffered to handle the whole of it, but it was at least liberal enough to banish the dread of starvation, and his duties, which consisted solely in the preparation and delivery of his lectures, did not debar him from literary work on his own account. Wherefore in his leisure time he worked hard at his desk.

Any differences which may have existed between him and his mother were now removed, for he took her to live with him, the household being made up of himself, his wife, his mother, a friend (a woman), a nurse, the little boy, a man- and maidservant, and a mule.[2] Possibly Chiara brought her own income with her, and thus allowed the establishment to be conducted on a more liberal scale. The Plat lectureship would scarcely

---

[1] " Minimo tamen honorario, et illud etiam minimum suasu cujusdam amici egregii praefecti Xenodochii imminuerunt ; ita cum hujus recordor in mentem venit fabellæ illius Apuleii de annonæ Praefecto."—*Opera*, tom. i. p. 64.

[2] *De Utilitate*, p. 351.

have maintained three servants, and Jerome's gains from other sources must have been as yet very slender. His life at this time was a busy one, but he always contrived to portion out his days in such wise that certain hours were left for recreation. At such times as he was called upon to teach, the class-room, of course, had the first claims. After the lecture he would walk in the shade outside the city walls, then return to his dinner, then divert himself with music, and afterwards go fishing in the pools and streams hard by the town. In the course of time he obtained other employment, being appointed physician to the Augustinian friars. The Prior of this Order, Francesco Gaddi, was indeed his first patient of note. He tells how he cured this man of a biennial leprosy after treating him for six months;[1] adding that his labour was in vain, inasmuch as Gaddi died a violent death afterwards. The refusal of the College of Milan to admit him to membership did not forbid him to prescribe for whatever patients might like to consult him by virtue of his Paduan degree. He read voraciously everything which came in his way, and it must have been during these years that he stored his memory with that vast collection of facts out of which he subsequently compounded the row of tomes which form his legacy to posterity. Filippo Archinto was unfailing in his kindness, and Jerome at this time was fortunate enough to attract the attention of certain other Milanese citizens of repute who afterwards proved to be valuable friends ; Ludovico Madio, Girolamo Guerrini a jeweller, Francesco Belloti, and Francesco della Croce. The last-named was a skilled jurisconsult, whose help

---

[1] The following gives a hint as to the treatment followed : " Referant leprosos balneo ejus aquae in qua cadaver ablutum sit, sanari."—*De Varietate*, p. 334.

proved of great service in a subsequent litigation between Jerome and the College of Physicians.

All his life long Cardan was a dreamer of dreams, and he gives an account of one of his visions in this year, 1534, which, whether regarded as an allegory or as a portent, is somewhat remarkable. " In the year 1534, when I was as it were groping in the dark, when I had settled naught as to my future life, and when my case seemed to grow more desperate day by day, I beheld in a dream the figure of myself running towards the base of a mountain which stood upon my right hand, in company with a vast crowd of people of every station and age and sex—women, men, old men, boys, infants, poor men and rich men, clad in raiment of every sort. I inquired whither we were all running, whereupon one of the multitude answered that we were all hastening on to death. I was greatly terrified at these words, when I perceived a mountain on my left hand. Then, having turned myself round so that it stood on my right side, I grasped the vines (which, here in the midst of the mountains and as far as the place wherein I stood, were covered with dry leaves, and bare of grapes, as we commonly see them in autumn) and began to ascend. At first I found this difficult, for the reason that the mountain was very steep round the base, but having surmounted this I made my way upward easily. When I had come to the summit it seemed that I was like to pass beyond the dictates of my own will. Steep naked rocks appeared on every side, and I narrowly escaped falling down from a great height into a gloomy chasm. So dreadful is all this that now, what though forty years have rolled away, the memory thereof still saddens and terrifies me. Then, having turned towards the right where I could see naught but a plain covered with heath, I took that path out of fear, and, as I wended thither in reckless mood, I found that I had come to the entrance of a rude hut, thatched with straw and reeds and rushes, and that I held by my right hand a boy about twelve years of age and clad in a grey garment. Then at this very moment I was aroused from sleep, and my dream vanished.

"In this vision was clearly displayed the deathless name which was to be mine, my life of heavy and ceaseless work, my imprisonment, my seasons of grievous terror and sadness, and my abiding-place foreshadowed as inhospitable, by the sharp stones I beheld : barren, by the want of trees and of all serviceable plants ; but destined to be, nevertheless, in the end happy, and righteous, and easy. This dream told also of my lasting fame in the future, seeing that the vine yields a harvest every year. As to the boy, if he were indeed my good spirit, the omen was lucky, for I held him very close. If he were meant to foreshadow my grandson it would be less fortunate. That cottage in the desert was my hope of rest. That overwhelming horror and the sense of falling headlong may have had reference to the ruin of my son.[1]

"My second dream occurred a short time after. It seemed to me that my soul was in the heaven of the moon, freed from the body and all alone, and when I was bewailing my fate I heard the voice of my father, saying : 'God has appointed me as a guardian to you. All this region is full of spirits, but these you cannot see, and you must not speak either to me or to them. In this part of heaven you will remain for seven thousand years, and for the same time in certain other stars, until

---

[1] *De Vita Propria*, ch. xxxvii. p. 121. This dream is also told in *De Libris Propriis*, Opera, tom. i. p. 64.

you come to the eighth. After this you shall enter the kingdom of God.' I read this dream as follows. My father's soul is my tutelary spirit. What could be dearer or more delightful ? The Moon signifies Grammar; Mercury Geometry and Arithmetic; Venus Music, the Art of Divination, and Poetry; the Sun the Moral, and Jupiter the Natural, World; Mars Medicine; Saturn Agriculture, the knowledge of plants, and other minor arts. The eighth star stands for a gleaning of all mundane things, natural science, and various other studies. After dealing with these I shall at last find my rest with the Prince of Heaven."[1]

[1] *De Vita Propria*, ch. xxxvii. p. 121.

CHAPTER IV

JEROME CARDAN is now standing on the brink of authorship. The very title of his first book, *De Malo Recentiorum Medicorum Medendi Usu*, gives plain indication of the humour which possessed him, when he formulated his subject and put it in writing. With his temper vexed by the persistent neglect and insult cast upon him by the Milanese doctors he would naturally sit down *con amore* to compile a list of the errors perpetrated by the ignorance and bungling of the men who affected to despise him, and if his object was to sting the hides of these pundits and arouse them to hostility yet more vehement, he succeeded marvellously well. He was enabled to launch his book rather by the strength of private friendship than by the hope of any commercial success. Whilst at Pavia he had become intimate with Ottaviano Scoto, a fellow-student who came from Venice, and in after times he found Ottaviano's purse very useful to his needs. Since their college days Ottaviano's father had died and had left his son to carry on his calling of printing. In 1536 Jerome bethought him of his friend, and sent him the MS. of the treatise which was to let the world learn with what little wisdom it was being doctored.[1]

Ottaviano seems to have expected no profit from this

---

[1] *De Libris Propriis*, Opera, tom. i. p. 102.

venture, which was manifestly undertaken out of a genuine desire to help his friend, and he generously bore all the costs. Cardan deemed that, whatever the result of the issue of the book might be, it would surely be to his benefit; he hazarded nothing, and the very publication of his work would give him at least notoriety. It would moreover give him the intense pleasure of knowing that he was repaying in some measure the debt of vengeance owing to his professional foes. The outcome was exactly the opposite of what printer and author had feared and hoped. The success of the book was rapid and great.

Ottaviano must soon have recouped all the cost of publication ; and, while he was counting his money, the doctors everywhere were reading Jerome's brochure, and preparing a ruthless attack upon the daring censor, who, with the impetuosity of youth, had laid himself open to attack by the careless fashion in which he had compiled his work. He took fifteen days to write it, and he confesses in his preface to the revised edition that he found therein over three hundred mistakes of one sort or another. The attack was naturally led by the Milanese doctors. They demanded to be told why this man, who was not good enough to practise by their sanction, was good enough to lay down the laws for the residue of the medical world. They heaped blunder upon blunder, and held him up to ridicule with all the wealth of invective characteristic of the learned controversy of the age. Cardan was deeply humbled and annoyed. "For my opponents, seizing the opportunity, took occasion to assail me through the reasoning of this book, and cried out: 'Who can doubt that this man is mad ? and that he would teach a method and a practice of medicine differing from our own, since he has so many hard things to say of our procedure.' And, as Galen said, I must in truth have appeared crazy in my efforts to contradict this multitude raging against me. For, as it was absolutely certain that either I or they must be in the wrong, how could I hope to win? Who would take my word against the word of this band of doctors of approved standing, wealthy, for the most part full of years, well instructed, richly clad and cultivated in their bearing, well versed in speaking, supported by crowds of friends and kinsfolk, raised by popular approval to high position, and, what was more powerful than all else, skilled in every art of cunning and deceit?"

Cardan had indeed prepared a bitter pill for his foes, but the draught they compelled him to swallow was hardly more palatable. The publication of the book naturally increased the difficulties of his position, and in this respect tended to make his final triumph all the more noteworthy.

It was in 1536 that Cardan made his first essay as an author.[1] The next three years of his life at Milan were remarkable as years of preparation and accumulation, rather than as years of achievement. He had struck his first blow as a reformer, and, as is often the lot of reformers, his sword had broken in his hand, and there now rested upon him the sense of failure as a superadded torment. Yet now and again a gleam of consolation would disperse the gloom, and advise him that the world was beginning to recognize his existence, and in a way his merits. In this same year he received an offer from Pavia of the Professorship of Medicine, but this he re-

---

[1] Besides the *De Malo Medendi Usu*, he published in 1536 a tract upon judicial astrology. This, in an enlarged form, was reprinted by Petreius at Nuremburg in 1542.

fused because he did not see any prospect of being paid for his services. His friend Filippo Archinto was loyal still, and zealous in working for his success, and as he had been recently promoted to high office in the Imperial service, his good word might be very valuable indeed. He summoned his *protégé* to join him at Piacenza, whither he had gone to meet Paul III., hoping to advance Cardan's interests with the Pope; but though Marshal Brissac, the French king's representative,[1] joined Archinto in advocating his cause, nothing was done, and Jerome returned disappointed to Milan.

In these months Cardan, disgusted by the failure of his late attack upon the fortress of medical authority, turned his back, for a time, upon the study of medicine, and gave his attention almost entirely to mathematics, in which his reputation was high enough to attract pupils, and he always had one or more of them in his house, the most noteworthy of whom was Ludovico Ferrari of Bologna, who became afterwards a mathematician of repute, and a teacher both at Milan and Bologna. While he was working at the *De Malo Medendi*, he began a treatise upon Arithmetic, which he dedicated to his friend Prior Gaddi; but this work was not published till 1539. In 1536 he first heard a report of a fresh and important discovery in algebra, made by one Scipio Ferreo of Bologna; the prologue to one of the most dramatic incidents in his career, an incident which it will be necessary to treat at some length later on.

Cardan was well aware that his excursions into astrology worked to his prejudice in public esteem, but in spite of this he could not refrain therefrom. It was during the plentiful leisure of this period that he

---

[1] Cardan writes of Brissac: "Erat enim Brissacus Prorex singularis in studiosis amoris et humanitatis."—*De Vita Propria*, ch. iv. p. 14.

cast the horoscope of Jesus Christ, a feat which subsequently brought upon him grave misfortune ; a few
patients came to him, moved no doubt by the spirit
which still prompts people suffering from obscure
diseases to consult professors of healing who are
either in revolt or unqualified in preference to going
to the orthodox physician.   In connection with this
irregular practice of his he gives a curious story
about a certain Count Borromeo. " In 1536, while I was
attending professionally in the house of the Borromei, it
chanced that just about dawn I had a dream in which I
beheld a serpent of enormous bulk, and I was seized
with fear lest I should meet my death therefrom. Shortly
afterwards there came a messenger to summon me to
see the son of Count Carlo Borromeo. I went to the
boy, who was about seven years old, and found him
suffering from a slight distemper, but on feeling his
pulse I perceived that it failed at every fourth beat.
His mother, the Countess Corona, asked me how he
fared, and I answered that there was not much fever
about him ; but that, because his pulse failed at every
fourth beat, I was in fear of something, but what it
might be I knew not rightly (but I had not then by me
Galen's books on the indications of the pulse).   Therefore, as the patient's state changed not, I determined on
the third day to give him in small doses the drug called
Diarob: cum Turbit: I had already written my prescription, and the messenger was just starting with it to
the pharmacy, when I remembered my dream. 'How
do I know,' said I to myself, 'that this boy may not be
about to die as prefigured by the portent above written ?
and in that case these other physicians who hate me so
bitterly, will maintain he died through taking this drug.'
I called to the messenger, and said there was wanting in

the prescription something which I desired to add. Then
I privately tore up what I had written, and wrote out
another made of pearls, of the horn of unicorn,[1] and
certain gems. The powder was given, and was followed
by vomiting. The bystanders perceived that the boy
was indeed sick, whereupon they called in three of the
chief physicians, one of whom was in a way friendly to
me. They saw the description of the medicine, and
demanded what I would do now. Now although two of
these men hated me, it was not God's will that I should
be farther attacked, and they not only praised the
medicine, but ordered that it should be repeated. This
was the saving of me. When I went again in the evening I understood the case completely. The following
morning I was summoned at daybreak, and found the
boy battling with death, and his father lying in tears.
'Behold him,' he cried, 'the boy whom you declared to
ail nothing' (as if indeed I could have said such a thing);
'at least you will remain with him as long as he lives.'
I promised that I would, and a little later the boy tried
to rise, crying out the while. They held him down, and
cast all the blame upon me. What more is there to say?
If there had been found any trace of that drug *Diarob :
cum Turbit :* (which in sooth was not safe) it would have
been all over with me, since Borromeo all his life would
either have launched against me complaints grave enough
to make all men shun me, or another Canidia, more fatal
than African serpents, would have breathed poison upon
me." [2]

[1] "Mirumque in modum venenis cornu ejus adversari creditur."
—*De Subtilitate*, p. 315. Sir Thomas Browne (*Vulgar Errors*,
Bk. iii. 23) deals at length with the pretended virtues of the horn,
and in the Bestiary of Philip de Thaun (*Popular Treatises on Science
during the Middle Ages*) is given an account of the many wonderful
qualities of the beast.

[2] *De Vita Propria*, ch. xxxiii. p. 105. He also alludes to this case

In this same year, 1536, Lucia brought forth another child, a daughter, and it was about this time that Cardan first attracted the attention of Alfonso d'Avalos, the Governor of Milan, and an intimacy began which, albeit fruitless at first, was destined to be of no slight service to Jerome at the crisis of his fortunes.[1] In the following year, in 1537, he made a beginning of two of his books, which were subsequently found worthy of being finished, and which may still be read with a certain interest: the treatises *De Sapientia* and *De Consolatione*. Of the last-named, he remarks that it pleased no one, forasmuch as it appealed not to those who were happy, and the wretched rejected it as entirely inadequate to give them solace in their evil case. In this year he made another attempt to

in *De Libris Propriis* (Opera, tom. i. p. 65), affirming that the other doctors concerned in the case raised a great prejudice against him on account of his reputation as an astrologer. " Ita tot modis et insanus paupertate, et Astrologus profitendo edendoque libros, et imperitus casu illustris pueri, et modum alium medendi observans ex titulo libri nuper edito, jam prope ab omnibus habebar. Atque hæc omnia in Urbe omnium nugacissima, et quæ calumniis maximè patet."

[1] The founder of this family was Indico d'Avalos, a Spanish gentleman, who was chosen by Alfonso of Naples as a husband for Antonella, the daughter and heiress of the great Marchese Pescara of Aquino. This d'Avalos Marchese dal Guasto was the grandson of Indico. He commanded the advanced guard at the battle of Pavia, and took part in almost every battle between the French and Imperialists, and went with the Emperor to Tunis in 1535. Though he was a brave soldier and a skilful tactician, he was utterly defeated by d'Enghien at Cerisoles in 1544. He has been taxed with treachery in the case of the attack upon the messengers Rincon and Fregoso, who were carrying letters from Francis I. to the Sultan during a truce, but he did little more than imitate the tactics used by the French against himself; moreover, neither of the murdered men was a French subject, or had the status of an ambassador. D'Avalos was a liberal patron of letters and arts, and was very popular as Governor of Milan. He was a noted gallant and a great dandy. Brantôme writes of him—" qu'il était si dameret qu'il parfumait jusqu'aux selles de ses chevaux."—He died in 1546.

gain admission to the College at Milan, and was again rejected ; the issue of the *De Malo Medendi* was too recent, and it needed other and more potent influences than those exercised by mere merit, to appease the fury of his rivals and to procure him due status. But it would appear that, in 1536 or 1537, he negotiated with the College to obtain a quasi-recognition on conditions which he afterwards describes as disgraceful to himself, and that this was granted to him.[1]

Whatever his qualifications may have been, Cardan had no scruples in treating the few patients who came to him. The first case he notes is that of Donato Lanza,[2] a druggist, who had suffered for many years with blood-spitting, which ailment he treated success-fully. Success of this sort was naturally helpful, but far more important than Lanza's cure was the introduc-tion given by the grateful patient to the physician, com-mending him to Francesco Sfondrato, a noble Milanese, a senator, and a member of the Emperor's privy council. The eldest son of this gentleman had suffered many months from convulsions, and Cardan worked a cure in his case without difficulty. Shortly afterwards another child, only ten months old, was attacked by the same complaint, and was treated by Luca della Croce, the procurator of the College of Physicians, of which Sfondrato was a patron. As the attack threatened to be a serious one, Della Croce recommended that another physician, Ambrogio Cavenago, should be called in, but the father, remembering Cardan's cure of Lanza, wished

[1] "Violentia quorundam Medicorum adactus sum anno MDXXXVI, seu XXXVII, turpi conditione pacisci cum Collegio, sed ut dixi, postmodum dissoluta est, anno MDXXXIX et restitutus sum integrè."—*De Vita Propria*, ch. xxxiii. p. 105.

[2] *De Vita Propria*, ch. xl. p. 133.—He gives a long list of cases of his successful treatment in *Opera*, tom. i. p. 82.

for him as well. The description of the meeting of the
doctors round the sick child's bed, of their quotations
from Hippocrates, of the uncertainty and helplessness
of the orthodox practitioners, and of the ready resource
of the free-lance—who happens also to be the teller of
the story—is a richly typical one.[1] " We, the physicians
and the father of the child, met about seven in the
morning, and Della Croce made a few general observations on death, for he knew that Sfondrato was a
sensible man, and he himself was both honoured and
learned. Cavenago kept silence at this stage, because
the last word had been granted to him. Then I said,
' Do you not see that the child is suffering from Opis-
thotonos?' whereupon the first physician stood as one
dazed, as if I were trying to trouble his wits by my
hard words. But Della Croce at once swept aside all
uncertainty by saying, ' He means the backward con-
traction of the muscles.' I confirmed his words, and
added, ' I will show you what I mean.' Whereupon I
raised the boy's head, which the doctors and all the
rest believed was hanging down through weakness, and
by its own weight, and bade them put it into its former
position. Then Sfondrato turned to me, and said, ' As
you have discovered what the disease is, tell us likewise
what is the remedy therefor.' Since no one else spoke,
I turned towards him and—careful lest I should do hurt
to the credit I had gained already,—I said, ' You know
what Hippocrates lays down in a case like this—*febrem
convulsioni*'—and I recited the aphorism. Then I
ordered a fomentation, and an application of lint mois-
tened with linseed-oil and oil of lilies, and gave directions
that the child should be gently handled until such time

[1] There is a full account of this episode in *De Libris Propriis*,
p. 128, and in *De Vita Propria*, ch. xl. p. 133.

as the neck should be restored; that the nurse should eat no meat, and that the child should be nourished entirely by the milk of her breast, and not too much of that; that it should be kept in its cradle in a warm place, and rocked gently till it should fall asleep. After the other physicians had gone, I remember that the father of the child said to me, 'I give you this child for your own,' and that I answered, 'You are doing him an ill turn, in that you are supplanting his rich father by a poor one.' He answered, 'I am sure that you would care for him as if he were your own, fearing naught that you might thereby give offence to these others' (meaning the physicians). I said, 'It would please me well to work with them in everything, and to win their support.' I thus blended my words, so that he might understand I neither despaired of the child's cure, nor was quite confident thereanent. The cure came to a favourable end; for, after the fourteenth day of the fever—the weather being very warm—the child got well in four days' time. Now as I review the circumstances, I am of opinion that it was not because I perceived what the disease really was, for I might have done so much by reason of my special practice; nor because I healed the child, for that might have been attributed to chance; but because the child got well in four days, whereas his brother lay ill for six months, and was then left half dead, that his father was so much amazed at my skill, and afterwards preferred me to all others. That he thought well of me is certain, because Della Croce himself, during the time of his procuratorship, was full of spite and jealousy against me, and declared in the presence of Cavenago and of Sfondrato, that he would not, under compulsion, say a word in favour of a man like me, one whom the College regarded with disfavour. Whereupon Sfon-

drato saw that the envy and jealousy of the other
physicians was what kept me out of the College, and not
the circumstances of my birth. He told the whole
story to the Senate, and brought such influence to bear
upon the Governor of the Province and other men of
worship, that at last the entrance to the College was
opened to me."

Up to the time of his admission to the College,
Jerome had never felt that he could depend entirely
upon medicine for his livelihood. He now determined
to publish his *Practica Arithmeticæ*, the book which he
had prepared *pari passu* with the ill-starred *De Malo
Medendi*. It seems to have been thoroughly revised
and corrected, and was finally published in 1539, in
Milan ; Cardan only received ten crowns for his work,
but the sudden fame he achieved as a mathematician
ought to have set him on firm ground. His friends
were still working to secure for him benefits yet
more substantial. Alfonso d'Avalos, Francesco della
Croce, the jurisconsult whose name has already been
mentioned, and the senator Sfondrato, were doing their
best to bring the physicians of the city into a more
reasonable temper, and they finally succeeded in 1539 ;
when, after having been denied admission for twelve
years, Jerome Cardan became a member of the
College, and a sharer in all the privileges appertaining
thereto.

Though Cardan was now a fully qualified physician,
he spent his time for the next year or two rather with
letters than with medicine. He worked hard at Greek,
and as the result of his studies published somewhat
prematurely a treatise, *De Immortalitate Animorum*,
a collection of extracts from Greek writers which Julius
Cæsar Scaliger with justice calls a confused farrago

of other men's learning.[1] He published also about this period the treatise on Judicial Astrology, and the Essay *De Consolatione*, the only one of his books which has been found worthy of an English translation.[2] In 1541 he became Rector of the College of Physicians, but there is no record of any increase in the number of his patients by reason of this superadded dignity. A passage in the *De Vita Propria*, written with even more than his usual brutal candour, gives a graphic view of his manner of life at this period. "It was in the summer of the year 1543, a time when it was my custom to go every day to the house of Antonio Vicomercato, a gentleman of the city, and to play chess with him from morning till night. As we were wont to play for one real, or even three or four, on each game, I, seeing that I was generally the winner, would as a rule carry away with me a gold piece after each day's play, sometimes more and sometimes less. In the case of Vicomercato it was a pleasure and nothing else to spend money in this wise ; but in my own there was an element of conflict as well ; and in this manner I lost my self-respect so completely that, for two years and more, I took no thought of practising my art, nor considered that I was wasting all my substance—save what I made by play—that my good name and my studies as well would suffer shipwreck. But on a certain day towards the end of August, a new humour seized Vicomercato (either advisedly on account of the constant loss he suffered, or perhaps because he thought his decision would be for my benefit), a determination from which he was

[1] Exotericarum exercitationum, p. 987.
[2] *Cardanus Comforte, translated into Englishe,* 1573. It was the work of Thomas Bedingfield, a gentleman pensioner of Queen Elizabeth.

to be moved neither by arguments, nor adjurations, nor abuse. He forced me to swear that I would never again visit his house for the sake of gaming, and I, on my part, swore by all the gods as he wished. That day's play was our last, and thenceforth I gave myself up entirely to my studies." [1]

But these studies unfortunately were not of a nature to keep the wolf from the door; and Jerome, albeit now a duly qualified physician, and known to fame as a writer on Mathematics far beyond the bounds of Italy, was well-nigh as poor as ever. His mother had died several years before, in 1537; but what little money she may have left would soon have been wasted in gratifying his extravagant taste for costly things,[2] and at the gaming-table. He found funds, however, for a journey to Florence, whither he went to see d'Avalos, who was a generous, open-handed man, and always ready to put his purse at the service of one whom he regarded as an honour to his city and country. There can be little doubt that he helped Cardan liberally at this juncture. The need for a loan was assuredly urgent enough. The recent resumption of hostilities between the French and the Imperialists had led to intolerable taxation throughout the Milanese provinces, and in consequence of dearth of funds in 1543, the Academy at Pavia was forced to close its class-rooms, and leave its teachers unpaid. The greater part of the professors migrated to Pisa; and the Faculty of Medicine, then vacant, was, *pro formâ*, transferred to Milan. This chair was now offered to Cardan. He was in desperate straits—a third

---

[1] *De Vita Propria*, ch. xxxvii. p. 116.

[2] "Delectant me gladii parvi, seu styli scriptorii, in quos plus viginti coronatis aureis impendi: multas etiam pecunias in varia pennarum genera, audeo dicere apparatum ad scribendum ducentis coronatis non potuisse emi."—*De Vita Probria*, ch. xviii. p. 57.

child had been born this year—and, though there must have been even less chance of getting his salary paid than when he had refused it before, he accepted the post, explaining that he took this step because there was now no need for him to leave Milan, or danger that he would be rated as an itinerant teacher. It is not improbable that he may have been led to accept the office on account of the additional dignity it would give to him as a practising physician. When, a little later on, the authorities began to talk of returning to Pavia, he was in no mind to follow them, giving as a reason that, were he to leave Milan, he would lose his stipend for the Plat lectureship, and be put to great trouble in the transport of his household, and perhaps suffer in reputation as well. The Senate was evidently anxious to retain his services. They bade him consider the matter, promising to send on a certain date to learn his decision; and, as fate would have it, the question was conveniently decided for him by a portent.

" On the night before the day upon which my answer was to be sent to the Senate to say what course I was going to take, the whole of the house fell down into a heap of ruins, and no single thing was left unwrecked, save the bed in which I and my wife and my children were sleeping. Thus the step, which I should never have taken of my own free will or without some sign, I was compelled to take by the course of events. This thing caused great wonder to all those who heard of it." [1]

This was in 1544. Jerome hesitated no longer, and went forthwith to Pavia as Professor of Medicine at a salary of two hundred and forty gold crowns per annum; but, for the first year at least, this salary was

[1] *De Vita Propria*, ch. iv. p. 15.

not paid ; and the new professor lectured for a time to empty benches ; but, as he was at this time engaged in the final stage of his great work on Algebra, the leisure granted to him by the neglect of the students must have been most acceptable. He published at this time a treatise called *Contradicentium Medicorum*, and in 1545 his *Algebra* or *Liber Artis Magnæ* was issued from the press by Petreius of Nuremberg. The issue of this book, by which alone the name of Cardan holds a place in contemporary learning, is connected with an episode of his life important enough to demand special and detailed consideration in a separate place.

His practice in medicine was now a fairly lucrative one, but his extravagant tastes and the many vices with which he charges himself would have made short work of the largest income he could possibly have earned, consequently poverty was never far removed from the household. Hitherto his reputation as a man of letters and a mathematician had exceeded his fame as a doctor; for, even after he had taken up his residence as Professor of Medicine at Padua, many applications were made to him for his services in other branches of learning. It was fortunate indeed that he had let his reading take a somewhat eclectic course, for medicine at this time seemed fated to play him false. At the end of 1544 no salary was forthcoming at Pavia, so he abandoned his class-room, and returned to Milan.

During his residence there, in the summer of 1546, Cardinal Moroni, acting on behalf of Pope Paul III., made an offer for his services as a teacher of mathematics, accompanied by terms which, as he himself admits, were not to be despised; but, as was his wont, he found some reason for demur, and ultimately refused the offer. In his Harpocratic vein he argued, " This

F

pope is an old man, a tottering wall, as it were. Why should I abandon a certainty for an uncertainty?"[1] The certainty he here alludes to must have been the salary for the Plat lectureship; and, as this emolument was a very small one, it would appear that he did not rate at a high figure any profits which might come to him in the future from his acceptance of the Pope's offer; but, as he admits subsequently, he did not then fully realize the benevolence of the Cardinal who approached him on the subject, or the magnificent patronage of the Farnesi.[2] It is quite possible that this refusal of his may have been caused by a reluctance to quit Milan, the city which had treated him in such cruel and inhospitable fashion, just at the time when he had become a man of mark. In the arrogance of success it was doubtless a keen pleasure to let his fellow-townsmen see that the man upon whom they had heaped insult after insult for so many years was one who could afford to let Popes and Cardinals pray for his services in vain. But whatever may have been his humour, he resolved to remain in Milan; and, as he had no other public duty to perform except the delivery of the Plat lectures, he had abundant leisure to spend upon the many and important works he had on hand at this season.

Cardan had now achieved European fame, and was apparently on the high road to fortune, but on the

---

[1] " At ego qui, ut dixi, Harpocraticus sum dicebam:—Summus Pont: decrepitus est : murus ruinosus, certa pro incertis derelinquam?"—*De Vita Propria*, ch. iv. p. 15. It is quite possible that Paul III. may have desired to have Cardan about him on account of his reputation as an astrologer, the Pope being a firm believer in the influence of the stars.—*Vide* Ranke, *History of the Popes* i. 166.

[2] " Neque ego tum Moroni probitatem, nec Pharnesiorum splendorem intelligebam."—*De Vita Propria*, ch. iv. p. 15.

very threshold of his triumph a great sorrow and misfortune befell him, the full effect of which he did not experience all at once. In the closing days of 1546 he lost his wife. There is very scant record of her life and character in any of her husband's writings,[1] although he wrote at great length concerning her father; and the few words that are to be found here and there favour the view that she was a good wife and mother. That Jerome could have been an easy husband to live with under any circumstances it is hard to believe. Lucia's life, had it been prolonged, might have been more free of trouble as the wife of a famous and wealthy physician; but it was her ill fortune to be the companion of her husband only in those dreary, terrible days at Sacco and Gallarate, and in the years of uncertainty which followed the final return to Milan. In the last-named period there was at least the Plat lectureship standing between them and starvation; but children increased the while in the nursery, and manuscripts in the desk of the physician without patients, and Lucia's short life was all consumed in this weary time of waiting for fame and fortune which, albeit hovering near, seemed destined to mock and delude the seeker to the end. Cardan was before all else a man of books and of the study, and it is not rare to find that

---

[1] In writing of his own horoscope (*Geniturarum Exempla*, p. 461) he records that she miscarried thrice, brought forth three living children, and lived with him fifteen years. He dismisses his marriage as follows : " Duxi uxorem inexpectato, a quo tempore multa adversa concomitata sunt."—*De Vita Propria*, ch. xli. p. 149. But in *De Rerum Subtilitate*, p. 375, he records his grief at her death :—"Itaque cùm a luctu dolor et vigilia invadere soleant, ut mihi anno vertente in morte uxoris Luciæ Bandarenæ quanquam institutis philosophiæ munitus essem, repugnante tamen natura, memorque vinculi côjugalis, suspiriis ac lachrymis et inedia quinque dierum, a periculo me vindicavi."

one of this sort makes a harsh unsympathetic husband. The qualities which he attributes to himself in his autobiography suggest that to live with a man cursed with such a nature would have been difficult even in prosperity, and intolerable in trouble and privation. But fretful and irascible as Cardan shows himself to have been, there was a warm-hearted, affectionate side to his nature. He was capable of steadfast devotion to all those to whom his love had ever been given. His reverence for the memory of his tyrannical and irascible father had been noted already, and a still more remarkable instance of his fidelity and love will have to be considered when the time comes to deal with the crowning tragedy of his life. If Cardan had this tender side to his nature, if he could speak tolerant and even laudatory words concerning such a father as Fazio Cardano, and show evidences of a love strong as death in the fight he made for the life of his ill-starred and unworthy son, it may be hoped—in spite of his almost unnatural silence concerning her—that he gave Lucia some of that tenderness and sympathy which her life of hard toil and heavy sacrifice so richly deserved ; and that even in the days when he sold her trinkets to pay his gambling losses, she was not destined to weep the bitter tears of a neglected wife. If her early married life had been full of care and travail, if she died when a better day seemed to be dawning, she was at least spared the supreme sorrow and disgrace which was destined to fall so soon upon the household. Judging by what subsequently happened, it will perhaps be held that fate, in cutting her thread of life, was kinder to her than to her husband, when it gave him a longer term of years under the sun.

CHAPTER V

AT this point it may not be inopportune to make a break in the record of Cardan's life and work, and to treat in retrospect of that portion of his time which he spent in the composition of his treatises on Arithmetic and Algebra. Ever since 1535 he had been working intermittently at one or other of these, but it would have been impossible to deal coherently and effectively with the growth and completion of these two books— really the most important of all he left behind him— while chronicling the goings and comings of a life so adventurous as that of the author.

The prime object of Cardan's ambition was eminence as a physician. But, during the long years of waiting, while the action of the Milanese doctors kept him outside the bounds of their College, and even after this had been opened to him without inducing ailing mortals to call for his services, he would now and again fall into a transport of rage against his persecutors, and of contempt for the public which refused to recognize him as a master of his art, and cast aside his medical books for months at a time, devoting himself diligently to Mathematics, the field of learning which, next to Medicine, attracted him most powerfully. His father Fazio was a geometrician of repute and a student of applied mathematics, and, though his first desire was to make his son a jurisconsult, he gave Jerome in early youth a fairly good grounding in arithmetic and geometry, deeming probably that such training would not prove a bad discipline for an intellect destined to attack those formidable tomes within which lurked the mysteries of the Canon and Civil Law. Mathematical learning has given to Cardan his surest title to immortality, and at the outset of his career he found in mathematics rather than in medicine the first support in the arduous battle he had to wage with fortune. His appointment to the Plat lectureship at Milan has already been noted. In the discharge of his new duties he was bound, according to the terms of the endowment of the Plat lecturer, to teach the sciences of geometry, arithmetic, and astronomy, and he began his course upon the lines laid down by the founder. Few listeners came, however, and at this juncture Cardan took a step which serves to show how real was his devotion to the cause of true learning, and how lightly he thought of an additional burden upon his own back, if this cause could be helped forward thereby. Keenly as he enjoyed his mathematical work, he laid a part of it aside when he perceived that the benches before him were empty, and, by way of making his lectures more attractive, he occasionally substituted geography for geometry, and architecture for arithmetic. The necessary research and the preparation of these lectures led naturally to the accumulation of a large mass of notes, and as these increased under his hand Jerome began to consider whether it might not be worth his while to use them in the composition of one or more volumes. In 1535 he delivered as Plat lecturer his address, the *Encomium Geometriæ*, which he followed up shortly after by the publication of a work, *Quindecim Libri Novæ Geometriæ*. But the most profitable labour of these years was that which produced his first important book, *The Practice of Arithmetic and Simple Mensuration*, which was published in 1539, a venture which brought to the author a reward of ten crowns.[1] It was a well-planned and well-arranged manual, giving proof of the wide erudition and sense of proportion possessed by the author. Besides dealing with Arithmetic as understood by the modern school-boy, it discusses certain astronomical operations, multiplication by memory, the mysteries of the Roman and Ecclesiastical Calendars, and gives rules for the solution of any problem arising from the terms of the same. It treats of partnership in agriculture, the Mezzadria system still prevalent in Tuscany and in other parts of Italy, of the value of money, of the strange properties of certain numbers, and gives the first simple rules of Algebra to serve as stepping-stones to the higher mathematics. It ends with information as to house-rent, letters of credit and exchange, tables of interest, games of chance, mensuration, and weights and measures. In an appendix Cardan examines critically the work of Fra Luca Pacioli da Borgo, an earlier writer on the subject, and points out numerous errors in the same. The book from beginning to end shows signs of careful study and compilation, and the fame which it brought to its author was well deserved.

Cardan appended to the Arithmetic a printed notice

[1] It was published at Milan by Bernardo Caluschio, with a dedication—dated 1537—to Francesco Gaddi, a descendant of the famous family of Florence. This man was Prior of the Augustinian Canons in Milan, and a great personage, but ill fortune seems to have overtaken him in his latter days. Cardan writes (*Opera*, tom. i. p. 107) : —"qui cum mihi amicus esset dum floreret, Rexque cognomine ob potentiam appellaretur, conjectus in carcerem, miseré vitam ibi, ne dicam crudeliter, finivit : nam per quindecim dies in profundissima gorgyne fuit, ut vivus sepeliretur."

which may be regarded as an early essay in advertising. He was fully convinced that his works were valuable and quite worth the sums of money he asked for them ; the world was blind, perhaps wilfully, to their merits, therefore he now determined that it should no longer be able to quote ignorance of the author as an excuse for not buying the book. This appendix was a notification to the learned men of Europe that the writer of the *Practice of Arithmetic* had in his press at home thirty-four other works in MS. which they might read with profit, and that of these only two had been printed, to wit the *De Malo Medendi Usu* and a tract on *Simples*. This advertisement had something of the character of a legal document, for it invoked the authority of the Emperor to protect the copyright of Cardan's books within the Duchy of Milan for ten years, and to prevent the introduction of them from abroad.

The Arithmetic proved far superior to any other treatise extant, and everywhere won the approval of the learned. It was from Nuremberg that its appearance brought the most valuable fruits. Andreas Osiander,[1] a learned humanist and a convert to Lutheranism, and Johannes Petreius, an eminent printer, were evidently impressed by the terms of Cardan's advertisement, for they wrote to him and offered in combination to edit and print any of the books awaiting publication in his study at Milan. The result of this offer was the reprinting of *De Malo Medendi*, and subsequently of the tract on Judicial Astrology, and of the treatise *De Consolatione;* the *Book of the Great Art*, the treatises *De Sapientia* and *De Immortalitate Animorum* were published in the

---

[1] There is a reference to Osiander in *De Subtilitate*, p. 523. Cardan gives a full account of his relations with Osiander and Petreius in *Opera*, tom. i. p. 67.

first instance by these same patrons from the Nuremberg press.

But Cardan, while he was hard at work on his Arithmetic, had not forgotten a certain report which had caused no slight stir in the world of Mathematics some three years before the issue of his book on Arithmetic, an episode which may be most fittingly told in his own words. "At this time[1] it happened that there came to Milan a certain Brescian named Giovanni Colla, a man of tall stature, and very thin, pale, swarthy, and hollow-eyed. He was of gentle manners, slow in gait, sparing of his words, full of talent, and skilled in mathematics. His business was to bring word to me that there had been recently discovered two new rules in Algebra for the solution of problems dealing with cubes and numbers. I asked him who had found them out, whereupon he told me the name of the discoverer was Scipio Ferreo of Bologna. 'And who else knows these rules?' I said. He answered, 'Niccolo Tartaglia and Antonio Maria Fiore.' And indeed some time later Tartaglia, when he came to Milan, explained them to me, though unwillingly; and afterwards I myself, when working with Ludovico Ferrari,[2] made a thorough study of the rules aforesaid. We devised certain others, heretofore unnoticed, after we had made trial of these new rules, and out of this material I put together my *Book of the Great Art*."[3]

Before dealing with the events which led to the composition of the famous work above-named, it may

---

[1] November 1536.

[2] Ferrari was one of Cardan's most distinguished pupils. "Ludovicus Ferrarius Bononiensis qui Mathematicas et Mediolani et in patria sua professus est, et singularis in illis eruditionis."—*De Vita Propria*, ch. xxxv. p. 111. There is a short memoir of Ferrari in *Opera*, tom. ix.   [3] *Opera*, tom. i. p. 66.

be permitted to take a rapid survey of the condition
of Algebra at the time when Cardan sat down to write.
Up to the beginning of the sixteenth century the
knowledge of Algebra in Italy, originally derived from
Greek and Arabic sources, had made very little progress,
and the science had been developed no farther than to
provide for the solution of equations of the first or
second degree.[1] In the preface to the *Liber Artis
Magnæ* Cardan writes:—"This art takes its origin
from a certain Mahomet, the son of Moses, an Arabian,
a fact to which Leonard the Pisan bears ample testimony.
He left behind him four rules, with his demonstrations
of the same, which I duly ascribe to him in their proper
place. After a long interval of time, some student,
whose identity is uncertain, deduced from the original
four rules three others, which Luca Paciolus put with
the original ones into his book. Then three more were
discovered from the original rules, also by some one
unknown, but these attracted very little notice though
they were far more useful than the others, seeing that
they taught how to arrive at the value of the *cubus* and
the *numerus* and of the *cubus quadratus*.[2] But in
recent times Scipio Ferreo of Bologna discovered

---

[1] Fra Luca's book, *Summa de Arithmetica Geometria Proportioni é Proportionalita*, extends as far as the solution of quadratic
equations, of which only the positive roots were used. At this
time letters were rarely used to express known quantities.

[2] The early writers on Algebra used *numerus* for the absolute or
known term, *res* or *cosa* for the first power, *quadratum* for the
second, and *cubus* for the third. The signs + and − first appear
in the work of Stifelius, a German writer, who published a book of
Arithmetic in 1544. Robert Recorde in his *Whetstone of Wit*
seems first to have used the sign of equality =. Vieta in France
first applied letters as general symbols of quantity, though the
earlier algebraists used them occasionally, chiefly as abbreviations.
Aristotle also used them in the *Physics.—Libri. Hist. des Sciences
Mathématiques*, i. 104.

the rule of the *cubus* and the *res* equal to the *numerus* ($x^3 + px = q$), truly a beautiful and admirable discovery. For this Algebraic art outdoes all other subtlety of man, and outshines the clearest exposition mortal wit can achieve : a heavenly gift indeed, and a test of the powers of a man's mind. So excellent is it in itself that whosoever shall get possession thereof, will be assured that no problem exists too difficult for him to disentangle. As a rival of Ferreo, Niccolo Tartaglia of Brescia, my friend, at that time when he engaged in a contest with Antonio Maria Fiore, the pupil of Ferreo, made out this same rule to help secure the victory, and this rule he imparted to me after I had diligently besought him thereanent. I, indeed, had been deceived by the words of Luca Paciolus, who denied that there could be any general rule besides these which he had published, so I was not moved to seek that which I despaired of finding ; but, having made myself master of Tartaglia's method of demonstration, I understood how many other results might be attained ; and, having taken fresh courage, I worked these out, partly by myself and partly by the aid of Ludovico Ferrari, a former pupil of mine. Now all the discoveries made by the men aforesaid are here marked with their names. Those unsigned were found out by me ; and the demonstrations are all mine, except three discovered by Mahomet and two by Ludovico." [1]

This is Cardan's account of the scheme and origin of his book, and the succeeding pages will be mainly an amplification thereof. The earliest work on Algebra used in Italy was a translation of the MS. treatise of Mahommed ben Musa of Corasan, and next in order is a MS. written by a certain Leonardo da Pisa in 1202.

---

[1] *Opera*, tom. iv. p. 222.

Leonardo was a trader, who had learned the art during his voyages to Barbary, and his treatise and that of Mahommed were the sole literature on the subject up to the year 1494, when Fra Luca Pacioli da Borgo[1] brought out his volume treating of Arithmetic and Algebra as well. This was the first printed work on the subject.

After the invention of printing the interest in Algebra grew rapidly. From the time of Leonardo to that of Fra Luca it had remained stationary. The important fact that the resolution of all the cases of a problem may be comprehended in a simple formula, which may be obtained from the solution of one of its cases merely by a change of the signs, was not known, but in 1505 the Scipio Ferreo alluded to by Cardan, a Bolognese professor, discovered the rule for the solution of one case of a compound cubic equation. This was the discovery that Giovanni Colla announced when he went to Milan in 1536.

Cardan was then working hard at his Arithmetic—which dealt also with elementary Algebra—and he was naturally anxious to collect in its pages every item of fresh knowledge in the sphere of mathematics which might have been discovered since the publication of the last treatise. The fact that Algebra as a science had made such scant progress for so many years, gave to this new process, about which Giovanni Colla was talking, an extraordinary interest in the sight of all mathematical students ; wherefore when Cardan heard the report that Antonio Maria Fiore, Ferreo's pupil, had been entrusted by his master with the secret of

---

[1] In the conclusion of the Treatise on Arithmetic, Cardan points out certain errors in the work of Fra Luca. Fra Luca was a pupil of Piero della Francesca, who was highly skilled in Geometry, and who, according to Vasari, first applied perspective to the drawing of the human form.

this new process, and was about to hold a public disputation at Venice with Niccolo Tartaglia, a mathematician of considerable repute, he fancied that possibly there would be game about well worth the hunting.

Fiore had already challenged divers opponents of less weight in the other towns of Italy, but now that he ventured to attack the well-known Brescian student, mathematicians began to anticipate an encounter of more than common interest. According to the custom of the time, a wager was laid on the result of the contest, and it was settled as a preliminary that each one of the competitors should ask of the other thirty questions. For several weeks before the time fixed for the contest Tartaglia studied hard ; and such good use did he make of his time that, when the day of the encounter came, he not only fathomed the formula upon which Fiore's hopes were based, but, over and beyond this, elaborated two other cases of his own which neither Fiore nor his master Ferreo had ever dreamt of.

The case which Ferreo had solved by some unknown process was the equation $x^3 + p\,x = q$, and the new forms of cubic equation which Tartaglia elaborated were as follows: $x^3 + p\,x^2 = q$: and $x^3 - p \times 2 = q$. Before the date of the meeting, Tartaglia was assured that the victory would be his, and Fiore was probably just as confident. Fiore put his questions, all of which hinged upon the rule of Ferreo which Tartaglia had already mastered, and these questions his opponent answered without difficulty ; but when the turn of the other side came, Tartaglia completely puzzled the unfortunate Fiore, who managed indeed to solve one of Tartaglia's questions, but not till after all his own had been answered. By this triumph the fame of Tartaglia spread far and wide, and Jerome Cardan, in consequence of the rumours of the Brescian's extraordinary skill, became more anxious than ever to become a sharer in the wonderful secret by means of which he had won his victory.

Cardan was still engaged in working up his lecture notes on Arithmetic into the Treatise when this contest took place ; but it was not till four years later, in 1539, that he took any steps towards the prosecution of his design. If he knew anything of Tartaglia's character, and it is reasonable to suppose that he did, he would naturally hesitate to make any personal appeal to him, and trust to chance to give him an opportunity of gaining possession of the knowledge aforesaid, rather than seek it at the fountain-head. Tartaglia was of very humble birth, and according to report almost entirely self-educated. Through a physical injury which he met with in childhood his speech was affected ; and, according to the common Italian usage, a nickname[1] which pointed to this infirmity was given to him. The blow on the head, dealt to him by some French soldier at the sack of Brescia in 1512, may have made him a stutterer, but it assuredly did not muddle his wits; nevertheless, as the result of this knock, or for some other cause, he grew up into a churlish, uncouth, and ill-mannered man, and, if the report given of him by Papadopoli[2] at the end of his history be worthy of credit, one not to be entirely trusted as an autobiographer in the account he himself gives of his early days in the preface to one of his works. Papadopoli's notice of him states that he was in no sense the self-taught scholar he represented himself to be, but that he was indebted for some portion at least of his training to the

---

[1] Tartaglia, *i. e.* the stutterer.
[2] Papadopoli, *Hist. Gymn. Pata.* (Ven. 1724).

beneficence of a gentleman named Balbisono,[1] who took him to Padua to study. From the passage quoted below he seems to have failed to win the goodwill of the Brescians, and to have found Venice a city more to his taste. It is probable that the contest with Fiore took place after his final withdrawal from his birthplace to Venice.

In 1537 Tartaglia published a treatise on Artillery, but he gave no sign of making public to the world his discoveries in Algebra. Cardan waited on, but the morose Brescian would not speak, and at last he determined to make a request through a certain Messer Juan Antonio, a bookseller, that, in the interests of learning, he might be made a sharer of Tartaglia's secret. Tartaglia has given a version of this part of the transaction; and, according to what is there set down, Cardan's request, even when recorded in Tartaglia's own words, does not appear an unreasonable one, for up

---

[1] " Balbisonem post relatam jurisprudentiæ lauream redeuntem Brixiam Nicolaus secutus est, cæpitque ex Mathematicis gloriam sibi ac divitias parare, æque paupertatis impatiens, ac fortunæ melioris cupidus, quam dum Brixiæ tuetur, homo morosæ, et inurbanæ rusticitatis prope omnium civium odia sibi conciliavit. Quamobrem alibi vivere coactus, varias Italiæ urbes incoluit, ac Ferrariæ, Parmæ, Mediolani, Romæ, Genuæ, arithmeticam, geometricam, ceteraque quæ ad Mathesim pertinent, docuit; depugnavitque scriptis accerrimis cum Cardano ac sibi ex illis quæsivit nomen et gloriam. Tandem domicilium posuit Venetiis, ubi non a Senatoribus modo, ut mos Venetus habet eruditorum hominum studiosissimus, maximi habitus est, at etiam a variis Magnatum ac Principum legatis præmiis ac muneribus auctus sortem, quam tamdiu expetierat visus sibi est conciliasse. Ergo ratus se majorem, quam ut a civibus suis contemneretur, Brixiam rediit, ubi spe privati stipendii Euclidis elementa explanare cœpit; sed quæ illum olim a civitate sua austeritas, rustica, acerba, morosa, depulerat, eadem illum in eum apud omnes contemptum, et odium iterum dejicit, ut exinde horrendus ac detestabilis omnibus fugere, atque iterum Venetias confugere compulsus fuerit. Ibi persenex decessit."—Papadopoli, *Hist. Gymn. Pata.*, ii. p. 210.

to this time Tartaglia had never announced that he
had any intention of publishing his discoveries as part
of a separate work on Mathematics. There was indeed
a good reason why he should refrain from doing this in
the fact that he could only speak and write Italian, and
that in the Brescian dialect, being entirely ignorant of
Latin, the only tongue which the writer of a mathematical work could use with any hope of success.
Tartaglia's record of his conversation with Messer Juan
Antonio, the emissary employed by Cardan, and of all
the subsequent details of the controversy, is preserved
in his principal work, *Quesiti et Inventioni Diverse de
Nicolo Tartalea Brisciano*,[1] a record which furnishes
abundant and striking instance of his jealous and
suspicious temper. Much of it is given in the form of
dialogue, the terms of which are perhaps a little too
precise to carry conviction of its entire sincerity and
spontaneity. It was probably written just after the
final cause of quarrel in 1545, and its main object seems
to be to set the author right in the sight of the world,
and to exhibit Cardan as a meddlesome fellow not to
be trusted, and one ignorant of the very elements of the
art he professed to teach.[2]

The inquiry begins with a courteously worded request
from Messer Juan Antonio (speaking on behalf of Messer
Hieronimo Cardano), that Messer Niccolo would make
known to his principal the rule by means of which he
had made such short work of Antonio Fiore's thirty
questions. It had been told to Messer Hieronimo that
Fiore's thirty questions had led up to a case of the *cosa*

---

[1] This work is the chief authority for the facts which follow.
The edition referred to is that of Venice, 1546. There is also a
full account of the same in Cossali, *Origine dell' Algebra* (Parma,
1799), vol. ii. p. 96.

[2] *Quesiti et Inventioni*, p. 115.

and the *cubus* equal to the *numerus*, and that Messer Niccolo had discovered a general rule for such case. Messer Hieronimo now especially desired to be taught this rule. If the inventor should be willing to let this rule be published, it should be published as his own discovery; but, if he were not disposed to let the same be made known to the world, it should be kept a profound secret. To this request Tartaglia replied that, if at any time he might publish his rule, he would give it to the world in a work of his own under his own name, whereupon Juan Antonio moderated his demand, and begged to be furnished merely with a copy of the thirty questions preferred by Fiore, and Tartaglia's solutions of the same; but Messer Niccolo was too wary a bird to be taken with such a lure as this. To grant so much, he replied, would be to tell everything, inasmuch as Cardan could easily find out the rule, if he should be furnished with a single question and its solution. Next Juan Antonio handed to Tartaglia eight algebraical questions which had been confided to him by Cardan, and asked for answers to them; but Tartaglia, having glanced at them, declared that they were not framed by Cardan at all, but by Giovanni Colla. Colla, he declared, had sent him one of these questions for solution some two years ago. Another, he (Tartaglia) had given to Colla, together with a solution thereof. Juan Antonio replied by way of contradiction—somewhat lamely—that the questions had been handed over to him by Cardan and no one else, wishing to maintain, apparently, that no one else could possibly have been concerned in them, whereupon Tartaglia replied that, supposing the questions had been given by Cardan to Juan Antonio his messenger, Cardan must have got the questions from Colla, and have sent them on to him

(Tartaglia) for solution because he could not arrive at the meaning of them himself. He waved aside Juan Antonio's perfectly irrelevant and fatuous protests—that Cardan would not in any case have sent these questions if they had been framed by another person, or if he had been unable to solve them. Tartaglia, on the other hand, declared that Cardan certainly did not comprehend them. If he did not know the rule by which Fiore's questions had been answered (that of the *cosa* and the *cubus* equal to the *numerus*), how could he solve these questions which he now sent, seeing that certain of them involved operations much more complicated than that of the rule above written ? If he understood the questions which he now sent for solution, he could not want to be taught this rule. Then Juan Antonio moderated his demand still farther, and said he would be satisfied with a copy of the questions which Fiore had put to Tartaglia, adding that the favour would be much greater if Tartaglia's own questions were also given. He probably felt that it would be mere waste of breath to beg again for Tartaglia's answers. The end of the matter was that Tartaglia handed over to the messenger the questions which Fiore had propounded in the Venetian contest, and authorized Juan Antonio to get a copy of his own from the notary who had drawn up the terms of the disputation with Fiore. The date of this communication is January 2, 1539, and on February 12 Cardan writes a long letter to Tartaglia, complaining in somewhat testy spirit of the reception given to his request. He is aggrieved that Tartaglia should have sent him nothing but the questions put to him by Fiore, thirty in number indeed, but only one in substance, and that he should have dared to hint that those which he (Cardan) had sent for solution were not his own, but

the property of Giovanni Colla. Cardan had found
Colla to be a conceited fool, and had dragged the
conceit out of him—a process which he was now about
to repeat for the benefit of Messer Niccolo Tartaglia.
The letter goes on to contradict all Tartaglia's assertions
by arguments which do not seem entirely convincing,
and the case is not made better by the abusive passages
interpolated here and there, and by the demonstration
of certain errors in Tartaglia's book on Artillery. In
short a more injudicious letter could not have been
written by any man hoping to get a favour done to him
by the person addressed.

In the special matter of the problems which he sent
to Tartaglia by the bookseller Juan Antonio, Cardan
made a beginning of that tricky and crooked course
which he followed too persistently all through this
particular business. In his letter he maintains with a
show of indignation that he had long known these
questions, had known them in fact before Colla knew
how to count ten, implying by these words that he
knew how to solve them, while in reality all he knew
about them was the fact that they existed. Tartaglia
in his answer is not to be moved from his belief, and
tells Cardan flatly that he is still convinced Giovanni
Colla took the questions to Milan, where he found no
one able to solve them, not even Messer Hieronimo
Cardano, and that the mathematician last-named sent
them on by the bookseller for solution, as has been
already related.

This letter of Tartaglia's bears the date of February
13, 1539, and after reading it and digesting its contents,
Cardan seems to have come to the conclusion that he
was not working in the right way to get possession of
this secret which he felt he must needs master, if he

wanted his forthcoming book to mark a new epoch in
this History of Mathematics, and that a change of
tactics was necessary. Alfonso d'Avalos, Cardan's
friend and patron, was at this time the Governor of
Milan. D'Avalos was a man of science, as well as a
soldier, and Cardan had already sent to him a copy of
Tartaglia's treatise on Artillery, deeming that a work of
this kind would not fail to interest him. In his first
letter to Tartaglia he mentions this fact, while picking
holes in the writer's theories concerning transmitted
force and views on gravitation. This mention of the
name of D'Avalos, the master of many legions and of
many cannons as well, to a man who had written a
Treatise on the management of Artillery, and devised
certain engines and instruments for the management of
the same, was indeed a clever cast, and the fly was
tempting enough to attract even so shy a fish as Niccolo
Tartaglia. In his reply to Jerome's scolding letter of
February 12, 1539, Tartaglia concludes with a description
of the instruments which he was perfecting : a square to
regulate the discharge of cannon, and to level and
determine every elevation ; and another instrument for
the investigation of distances upon a plane surface. He
ends with a request that Cardan will accept four copies
of the engines aforesaid, two for himself and two for the
Marchese d'Avalos.

The tone of this letter shows that Cardan had at
least begun to tame the bear, who now seemed disposed to dance *ad libitum* to the pleasant music of words
suggesting introductions to the governor, and possible
patronage of these engines for the working of artillery.
Cardan's reply of March 19, 1539, is friendly—too
friendly indeed—and the wonder is that Tartaglia's
suspicions were not aroused by its almost sugary polite-

ness. It begins with an attempt to soften down the asperities of their former correspondence, some abuse of Giovanni Colla, and an apology for the rough words of his last epistle. Cardan then shows how their misunderstanding arose chiefly from a blunder made by Juan Antonio in delivering the message, and invites Tartaglia to come and visit him in his own house in Milan, so that they might deliberate together on mathematical questions; but the true significance of the letter appears in the closing lines. " I told the Marchese of the instruments which you had sent him, and he showed himself greatly pleased with all you had done. And he commanded me to write to you forthwith in pressing terms, and to tell you that, on the receipt of my letter, you should come to Milan without fail, for he desires to speak with you. And I, too, exhort you to come at once without further deliberation, seeing that this said Marchese is wonted to reward all men of worth in such noble and magnanimous and liberal fashion that none of them ever goes away dissatisfied."

The receipt of this letter seems to have disquieted Tartaglia somewhat; for he has added a note to it, in which he says that Cardan has placed him in a position of embarrassment. He had evidently wished for an introduction to D'Avalos, but now it was offered to him it seemed a burden rather than a benefit. He disliked the notion of going to Milan; yet, if he did not go, the Marchese d'Avalos might take offence. But in the end he decided to undertake the journey; and, as D'Avalos happened then to be absent from Milan on a visit to his country villa at Vigevano, he stayed for three days in Cardan's house. As a recorder of conversations Tartaglia seems to have had something of Boswell's gift. He gives an abstract of an eventful dialogue with his

host on March 25, 1539, which Cardan begins by a
gentle reproach anent his guest's reticence in the matter
of the rule of the *cosa* and the *cubus* equal to the *numerus*.
Tartaglia's reply to this complaint seems reasonable
enough (it must be borne in mind that he is his own
reporter), and certainly helps to absolve him from the
charge sometimes made against him that he was nothing
more than a selfish curmudgeon who had resolved to
let his knowledge die with him, rather than share it
with other mathematicians of whom he was jealous.
He told Cardan plainly that he kept his rules a secret
because, for the present, it suited his purpose to do so.
At this time he had not the leisure to elaborate farther
the several rules in question, being engaged over a
translation of Euclid into Italian; but, when this work
should be completed, he proposed to publish a treatise
on Algebra in which he would disclose to the world all
the rules he already knew, as well as many others which
he hoped to discover in the course of his present work.
He concludes : "This is the cause of my seeming dis-
courtesy towards your excellency. I have been all the
ruder, perhaps, because you write to me that you are
preparing a book similar to mine, and that you propose
to publish my inventions, and to give me credit for the
same. This I confess is not to my taste, forasmuch as
I wish to set forth my discoveries in my own works,
and not in those of others." In his reply to this, Cardan
points out that he had promised, if Tartaglia so desired,
that he would not publish the rules at all; but here
Messer Niccolo's patience and good manners gave way,
and he told Messer Hieronimo bluntly that he did not
believe him. Then said Cardan : "I swear to you by
the Sacred Evangel, and by myself as a gentleman, that
I will not only abstain from publishing your discoveries

—if you will make them known to me—but that I will promise and pledge my faith of a true Christian to set them down for my own use in cypher, so that after my death no one may be able to understand them. If you will believe this promise, believe it; if you will not, let us have done with the matter." " If I were not disposed to believe such oaths as these you now swear," said Tartaglia, " I might as well be set down as a man without any faith at all. I have determined to go forthwith to Vigevano to visit the Signor Marchese, as I have now been here for three days and am weary of the delay, but I promise when I return that I will show you all the rules." Cardan replied : " As you are bent on going to Vigevano, I will give you a letter of introduction to the Marchese, so that he may know who you are; but I would that, before you start, you show me the rule as you have promised." " I am willing to do this," said Tartaglia, " but I must tell you that, in order to be able to recall at any time my system of working, I have expressed it in rhyme; because, without this precaution, I must often have forgotten it. I care naught that my rhymes are clumsy, it has been enough for me that they have served to remind me of my rules. These I will write down with my own hand, so that you may be assured that my discovery is given to you correctly." Then follow Tartaglia's verses :

" Quando chel cubo con le cose apresso
Se agualia à qualche numero discreto
Trouan dui altri differenti in esso
Dapoi terrai questo per consueto
Ch'el lor' produtto sempre sia eguale
Al terzo cubo delle cose neto
El residuo poi suo generale
Delli lor lati cubi ben sottratti
Varra la tua cosa principale.
In el secondo de cotesti atti

Quando chel cubo restasse lui solo
Tu osseruarai quest' altri contratti
Del numer farai due tal part 'à uolo
Che luna in l'altra si produca schietto
El terzo cubo delle cose in stolo
Delle qual poi, per commun precetto
Torrai li lati cubi insieme gionti
Et cotal summa sara il tuo concetto
Et terzo poi de questi nostri conti
Se solve col recordo se ben guardi
Che per natura son quasi congionti
Questi trouai, et non con passi tardi
Nel mille cinquecent' e quatro è trenta
Con fondamenti ben sald' è gagliardi
Nella citta del mar' intorno centa."

Having handed over to his host these rhymes, with the precious rules enshrined therein, Tartaglia told him that, with so clear an exposition, he could not fail to understand them, ending with a warning hint to Cardan that, if he should publish the rules, either in the work he had in hand, or in any future one, either under the name of Tartaglia or of Cardan, he, the author, would put into print certain things which Messer Hieronimo would not find very pleasant reading.

After all Tartaglia was destined to quit Milan without paying his respects to D'Avalos. There is not a word in his notes which gives the reason of this eccentric action on his part. He simply says that he is no longer inclined to go to Vigevano, but has made up his mind to return to Venice forthwith; and Cardan, probably, was not displeased at this exhibition of petulant impatience on the part of his guest, but was rather somewhat relieved to see Messer Niccolo ride away, now that he had extracted from him the coveted information. From the beginning to the end of this affair Cardan has been credited with an amount of subtle cunning which he assuredly did not manifest at other times when his wits were pitted for contest with those of other men. It has been advanced to his disparagement that he walked in deceitful ways from the very beginning ; that he dangled before Tartaglia's eyes the prospect of gain and preferment simply for the purpose of enticing him to Milan, where he deemed he might use more efficaciously his arguments for the accomplishment of the purpose which was really in his mind ; that he had no intention of advancing Tartaglia's fortunes when he suggested the introduction to D'Avalos, but that the Governor of Milan was brought into the business merely that he might be used as a potent ally in the attack upon Tartaglia's obstinate silence. Whether this may have been his line of action or not, the issue shows that he was fully able to fight his battle alone, and that his powers of persuasion and hard swearing were adequate when occasion arose for their exercise. It is quite possible that Tartaglia, when he began to reflect over what he had done by writing out and handing over to Cardan his mnemonic rhymes, fell into an access of suspicious anger—at Cardan for his wheedling persistency, and at himself for yielding thereto—and packed himself off in a rage with the determination to have done with Messer Hieronimo and all his works. Certainly his carriage towards Cardan in the weeks ensuing, as exhibited in his correspondence, does not picture him in an amiable temper. On April 9 Jerome wrote to him in a very friendly strain, expressing regret that his guest should have left Milan without seeing D'Avalos, and fear lest he might have prejudiced his fortunes by taking such a step. He then goes on to describe to Tartaglia the progress he is making in his work with the Practice of Arithmetic, and to ask him for help in solving one of the cases in Algebra, the rule for which was indeed contained in Tartaglia's verses, but expressed somewhat obscurely, for which reason Cardan had missed its meaning.[1]   In his reply, Tartaglia ignores Jerome's courtesies altogether, and tells him that what he especially desires at the present moment is a sight of that volume on the Practice of Arithmetic, "for," says he, "if I do not see it soon, I shall begin to suspect that this work of yours will probably make manifest some breach of faith; in other words, that it will contain as interpolations certain of the rules I taught you." Niccolo then goes on to explain the difficulty which had puzzled Cardan, using terms which showed plainly that he had as poor an opinion of his correspondent's wit as of his veracity.

Cardan was an irascible man, and it is a high tribute to his powers of restraint that he managed to keep his temper under the uncouth insults of such a letter as the foregoing. The more clearly Tartaglia's jealous, suspicious nature displays itself, the greater seems the wonder that a man of such a disposition should ever have disclosed such a secret. He did not believe Cardan when he promised that he would not publish the rules in question without his (the discoverer's) consent—why then did he believe him when he swore by the Gospel? The age was one in which the binding force of an oath was not regarded as an obligation of any particular sanctity if circumstances should arise which made the violation of the oath more convenient than its observance.   However, the time was not yet come for Jerome

---

[1] Cardan writes: "Vi supplico per l'amor che mi portati, et per l'amicitia ch'è tra noi, che spero durara fin che viveremo, che mi mandati sciolta questa questione. I cubo piu 3. cose egual à 10." Cardan had mistaken $(\frac{1}{3} b)^3$ for $\frac{1}{3} b^3$, or the cube of $\frac{1}{3}$ of the co-efficient for $\frac{1}{3}$ of the cube of the co-efficient.—*Quesiti et Inventioni* p. 124. ·

to begin to quibble with his conscience. On May 12, 1539, he wrote another letter to Tartaglia, also in a very friendly tone, reproaching him gently for his suspicions, and sending a copy of the *Practice of Arithmetic* to show him that they were groundless. He protested that Tartaglia might search from beginning to end without finding any trace of his jealously-guarded rules, inasmuch as, beyond correcting a few errors, the writer had only carried Algebra to the point where Fra Luca had left it. Tartaglia searched, and though he could not put his finger on any spot which showed that Messer Hieronimo had broken his oath, he found what must have been to him as a precious jewel, to wit a mistake in reckoning, which he reported to Cardan in these words:

"In this process your excellency has made such a gross mistake that I am amazed thereat, forasmuch as any man with half an eye must have seen it—indeed, if you had not gone on to repeat it in divers examples, I should have set it down to a mistake of the printer." After pointing out to Cardan the blunders aforesaid, he concludes: "The whole of this work of yours is ridiculous and inaccurate, a performance which makes me tremble for your good name."[1]

Every succeeding page of Tartaglia's notes shows more and more clearly that he was smarting under a sense of his own folly in having divulged his secret. Night and day he brooded over his excess of confidence, and as time went by he let his suspicions of Cardan grow into savage resentment. His ears were open to every rumour which might pass from one class-room to another. On July 10 a letter came to him from one Maphio of Bergamo, a former pupil, telling how Cardan

[1] *Quesiti et Inventioni*, p. 125.

was about to publish certain new mathematical rules in
a book on Algebra, and hinting that in all probability
these rules would prove to be Tartaglia's, whereupon he
at once jumped to the conclusion that Maphio's gossip
was the truth, and that this book would make public
the secret which Cardan had sworn to keep. He left
many of Cardan's letters unanswered; but at last he
seems to have found too strong the temptation to say
something disagreeable; so, in answer to a letter from
Cardan containing a request for help in solving an
equation which had baffled his skill, Tartaglia wrote
telling Cardan that he had bungled in his application of
the rule, and that he himself was now very sorry he had
ever confided the rule aforesaid to such a man. He ends
with further abuse of Cardan's *Practice of Arithmetic*,
which he declares to be merely a confused farrago of
other men's knowledge,[1] and with a remark which he
probably intended to be a crowning insult. "I well
remember when I was at your house in Milan, that you
told me you had never tried to discover the rule of the
cosa and the *cubus* equal to the *numerus* which was
found out by me, because Fra Luca had declared it to be
impossible;[2] as if to say that, if you had set yourself to
the task you could have accomplished it, a thing which
sets me off laughing when I call to mind the fact that it

---

[1] "Non ha datta fora tal opera come cose composto da sua testa
ma come cose ellette raccolte e copiate de diverse libri a penna."
—*Quesiti et Inventioni*, p. 127.

[2] Cardan repeats the remark in the first chapter of the *Liber
Artis Magnæ* (*Opera*, tom. iv. p. 222). "Deceptus enim ego verbis
Lucæ Paccioli, qui ultra sua capitula, generale ullum aliud esse posse
negat (quanquam tot jam antea rebus a me inventis, sub manibus
esset) desperabam tamen invenire, quod quærere non audebam."
Perhaps he wrote them down as an apology or a defence against the
storm which he anticipated as soon as Tartaglia should have seen
the new Algebra.

is now two months since I informed you of the blunders you made in the extraction of the cube root, which process is one of the first to be taught to students who are beginning Algebra. Wherefore, if after the lapse of all this time you have not been able to find a remedy to set right this your mistake (which would have been an easy matter enough), just consider whether in any case your powers could have been equal to the discovery of the rule aforesaid."[1]

In this quarrel Messer Giovanni Colla had appeared as the herald of the storm, when he carried to Milan in 1536 tidings of the discovery of the new rule which had put Cardan on the alert, and now, as the crisis approached, he again came upon the scene, figuring as unconscious and indirect cause of the final catastrophe. On January 5, 1540, Cardan wrote to Tartaglia, telling him that Colla had once more appeared in Milan, and was boasting that he had found out certain new rules in Algebra. He went on to suggest to his correspondent that they should unite their forces in an attempt to fathom this asserted discovery of Colla's, but to this letter Tartaglia vouchsafed no reply. In his diary it stands with a superadded note, in which he remarks that he thinks as badly of Cardan as of Colla, and that, as far as he is concerned, they may both of them go whithersoever they will.[2]

Colla propounded divers questions to the Algebraists

---

[1] Subsequently Tartaglia wrote very bitterly against Cardan, as the latter mentions in *De Libris Propriis*. " Nam etsi Nicolaus Tartalea libris materna lingua editis nos calumniatur, impudentiæ tamen ac stultitiæ suæ non aliud testimonium quæras, quam ipsos illius libros, in quibus nominatim splendidiorem unumquemque e civibus suis proscindit : adeò ut nemo dubitet insanisse hominem aliquo infortunio."—*Opera*, tom. i. p. 80.

[2] *Quesiti et Inventioni*, p. 129.

of Milan, and amongst them was one involving the equation $x^4 + 6x^2 + 36 = 60x$, one which he probably found in some Arabian treatise. Cardan tried all his ingenuity over this combination without success, but his brilliant pupil, Ludovico Ferrari, worked to better purpose, and succeeded at last in solving it by adding to each side of the equation, arranged in a certain fashion, some quadratic and simple quantities of which the square root could be extracted.[1] Cardan seems to have been baffled by the fact that the equation aforesaid could not be solved by the recently-discovered rules, because it produced a bi-quadratic. This difficulty Ferrari overcame, and, pursuing the subject, he discovered a general rule for the solution of all bi-quadratics by means of a cubic equation. Cardan's subsequent demonstration of this process is one of the masterpieces of the *Book of the Great Art*. It is an example of the use of assuming a new indeterminate quantity to introduce into an equation, thus anticipating by a considerable space of time Descartes, who subsequently made use of a like assumption in a like case.

How far this discovery of Ferrari's covered the rules given by Tartaglia to Cardan, and how far it relieved Cardan of the obligation of secresy, is a problem fitted for the consideration of the mathematician and the casuist severally.[2] An apologist of Cardan might affirm that he cannot be held to have acted in bad faith in publishing the result of Ferrari's discovery. If this

---

[1] Montucla, *Histoire de Math.* i. 596, gives a full account of Ferrari's process.

[2] In the *De Vita Propria*, Cardan dismisses the matter briefly: " Ex hoc ad artem magnam, quam collegi, dum Jo. Colla certaret nobiscum, et Tartalea, à quo primum acceperam capitulum, qui maluit æmulum habere, et superiorem, quam amicum et beneficio devinctum, cum alterius fuisset inventum."—ch. xlv. p. 175.

discovery included and even went beyond Tartaglia's, so much the worse for Tartaglia. The lesser discovery (Tartaglia's) Cardan never divulged before Ferrari unravelled Giovanni Colla's puzzle; but it was inevitable that it must be made known to the world as a part of the greater discovery (Ferrari's) which Cardan was in no way bound to keep a secret. The case might be said to run on all fours with that where a man confides a secret to a friend under a promise of silence, which promise the friend keeps religiously, until one day he finds that the secret, and even more than the secret, is common talk of the market-place. Is the obligation of silence, with which he was bound originally, still to lie upon the friend, even when he may have sworn to observe it by the Holy Evangel and the honour of a gentleman ; and is the fact that great renown and profit would come to him by publishing the secret to be held as an additional reason for keeping silence, or as a justification for speech? In forming a judgment after a lapse of three and a half centuries as to Cardan's action, while having regard both to the sanctity of an oath at the time in question, and to the altered state of the case between him and Tartaglia consequent on Ludovico Ferrari's discovery, an hypothesis not overstrained in the direction of charity may be advanced to the effect that Cardan might well have deemed he was justified in revealing to the world the rules which Tartaglia had taught him, considering that these isolated rules had been developed by his own study and Ferrari's into a principle by which it would be possible to work a complete revolution in the science of Algebra.

In any case, six years were allowed to elapse before Cardan, by publishing Tartaglia's rules in the *Book of the Great Art*, did the deed which, in the eyes of many, branded him as a liar and dishonest, and drove Tartaglia almost wild with rage. That his offence did not meet with universal reprobation is shown by negative testimony in the *Judicium de Cardano*, by Gabriel Naudé.[1] In the course of his essay Naudé lets it be seen how thoroughly he dislikes the character of the man about whom he writes. No evil disposition attributed to Cardan by himself or by his enemies is left unnoticed, and a lengthy catalogue of his offences is set down, but this list does not contain the particular sin of broken faith in the matter of Tartaglia's rules. On the contrary, after abusing and ridiculing a large portion of his work, Naudé breaks out into almost rhapsodical eulogy about Cardan's contributions to Mathematical science. "Quis negabit librum de Proportionibus dignum esse, qui cum pulcherrimis antiquorum inventis conferatur? Quis in Arithmetica non stupet, eum tot difficultates superasse, quibus explicandis Villafrancus, Lucas de Burgo, Stifelius, Tartalea, vix ac ne vix quidem pares esse potuissent?" It seems hard to believe, after reading elsewhere the bitter assaults of Naudé,[2] that he would have neglected so tempting an opportunity of darkening the shadows, if he himself had felt the slightest offence, or if public opinion in the learned world was in any perceptible degree scandalized by the disclosure made by the publication of the *Book of the Great Art*.

This book was published at Nuremberg in 1545, and in its preface and dedication Cardan fully acknowledges his obligations to Tartaglia and Ferrari, with respect to the rules lately discussed, and gives a catalogue of the

---

[1] Prefixed to the *De Vita Propria*.

[2] In a question of broken faith, Cardan laid himself open especially to attack by reason of his constant self-glorification in the matter of veracity.

former students of the Art, and attributes to each his particular contribution to the mass of knowledge which he here presents to the world. Leonardo da Pisa,[1] Fra Luca da Borgo, and Scipio Ferreo all receive due credit for their work, and then Cardan goes on to speak of " my friend Niccolo Tartaglia of Brescia, who, in his contest with Antonio Maria Fiore, the pupil of Ferreo, elaborated this rule to assure him of victory, a rule which he made known to me in answer to my many prayers." He goes on to acknowledge other obligations to Tartaglia :[2] how the Brescian had first taught him that algebraical discovery could be most effectively advanced by geometrical demonstration, and how he himself had followed this counsel, and had been careful to give the demonstration aforesaid for every rule he laid down.

The *Book of the Great Art* was not published till six years after Cardan had become the sharer of Tartaglia's secret, which had thus had ample time to germinate and bear fruit in the fertile brain upon which it was cast. It is almost certain that the treatise as a whole—leaving out of account the special question of the solution of cubic equations—must have gained enormously in completeness and lucidity from the fresh knowledge revealed to the writer thereof by Tartaglia's reluctant disclosure, and, over and beyond this, it must be borne in mind that Cardan had been working for several years at Giovanni Colla's questions in conjunction

[1] Leonardo knew that quadratic equations might have two positive roots, and Cardan pursued this farther by the discovery that they might also have negative roots.

[2] " Caput xxviii. De capitulo generali cubi et rerum æqualium numero, Magistri Nicolai Tartagliæ, Brixiensis—Hoc capitulum habui à prefato viro ante considerationem demonstrationum secundi libri super Euclidem, et æquatio hæc cadit in ℞. cu v binomii ex genere binomii secundi et quinti m̄. ℞. cuba universali recisi ejusdem binomii."—*Opera*, tom. iv. p. 341.

with Ferrari, an algebraist as famous as Tartaglia or himself. The opening chapters of the book show that Cardan was well acquainted with the chief properties of the roots of equations of all sorts. He lays it down that all square numbers have two different kinds of root, one positive and one negative,[1] *vera* and *ficta :* thus the root of 9 is either 3. or -3. He shows that when a case has all its roots, or when none are impossible, the number of its positive roots is the same as the number of changes in the signs of the terms when they are all brought to one side. In the case of $x^3 + 3bx = 2c$, he demonstrates his first resolution of a cubic equation, and gives his own version of his dealings with Tartaglia. His chief obligation to the Brescian was the information how to solve the three cases which follow, *i. e.* $x^3 + bx = c$. $x^3 = bx + c$. and $x + {}^3c = bx$, and this he freely acknowledges, and furthermore admits the great service of the system of geometrical demonstration which Tartaglia had first suggested to him, and which he always employed hereafter. He claims originality for all processes in the book not ascribed to others, asserting that all the demonstrations of existing rules were his own except three which had been left by Mahommed ben Musa, and two invented by Ludovico Ferrari.

With this vantage ground beneath his feet Cardan raised the study of Algebra to a point it had never reached before, and climbed himself to a height of fame to which Medicine had not yet brought him. His name as a mathematician was known throughout Europe, and the success of his book was remarkable. In the *De*

[1] Montucla, who as a historian of Mathematics has a strong bias against Cardan, gives him credit for the discovery of the *ficta radices*, but on the other hand he attributes to Vieta Cardan's discovery of the method of changing a complete cubic equation into one wanting the second term.—Ed. 1729, p. 595.

Libris Propriis there is a passage which indicates that he himself was not unconscious of the renown he had won, or disposed to underrate the value of his contribution to mathematical science. "And even if I were to claim this art (Algebra) as my own invention, I should perhaps be speaking only the truth, though Nicomachus, Ptolemæus, Paciolus, Boetius, have written much thereon. For men like these never came near to discover one-hundredth part of the things discovered by me. But with regard to this matter—as with divers others— I leave judgment to be given by those who shall come after me. Nevertheless I am constrained to call this work of mine a perfect one, seeing that it well-nigh transcends the bounds of human perception." [1]

[1] *Opera*, tom. i. p. 66.

CHAPTER VI

IT has been noted that Cardan quitted Pavia at the end of 1544 on account of the bankruptcy of the University, and that in 1546 a generous offer was made to him on condition of his entering the service of Pope Paul III.; an offer which after some hesitation he determined to refuse. In the autumn of this same year he resumed his teaching at Pavia, a fact which sanctions the assumption that this luckless seat of learning must have been once more in funds. In the year following, in 1547, there came to him another offer of employment accompanied by terms still more munificent than the Pope's, conveyed through Vesalius [1] and the ambassador of the King of Denmark. "The emolument was to be a salary of three hundred gold crowns per annum of the Hungarian currency, and in addition to these six hundred more to be paid out of the tax on skins of price. This last-named money differed in value by about an eighth from the royal coinage, and would be somewhat slower in coming in. Also the security for its payment was not so solid, and would in a measure be subject to risk. To this was farther added maintenance for myself and

---

[1] Vesalius had certainly lectured on anatomy at Pavia, but it would appear that Cardan did not know him personally, seeing that he writes in *De Libris Propriis* (*Opera*, tom. i. p. 138) : "Brasavolum . . . nunquam vidi, ut neque Vesalium quamquam intimum mihi amicum."

five servants and three horses. This offer I did not accept because the country was very cold and damp, and the people well-nigh barbarians ; moreover the rites and doctrines of religion were quite foreign to those of the Roman Church." [1]

Cardan was now forty-six years of age, a mathematician of European fame, and the holder of an honourable post at an ancient university, which he might have exchanged for other employment quite as dignified and far more lucrative. In dealing with a character as bizarre as his, it would be as a rule unprofitable to search deeply for motives of action, but in this instance it is no difficult matter to detect upon the surface several causes which may have swayed him in this decision to remain at Pavia. However firmly he may have set himself to win fame as a physician, he was in no way disposed to put aside those mathematical studies in which he had already made so distinguished a name, nor to abandon his astrology and chiromancy and discursive reading of all kinds. At Pavia he would find leisure for all these, and would in addition be able to make good any arrears of medical and magical knowledge into which he might have fallen during the years so largely devoted to the production of the *Book of the Great Art.* Moreover, the time in question was one of the prime epochs in the history of the healing art. A new light had just arisen in Vesalius, who had recently published his book, *Corporis Humani Fabrica*, and was lecturing in divers universities on the new method of Anatomy, the actual dissection of the human body. He went to Pavia in the course of his travels and left traces of his visit in the form of a revived and re-organized school of Anatomy. This fact alone would

[1] *De Vita Propria*, ch. xxxii. p. 99.

have been a powerful attraction to Cardan, ever greedy as he was of new knowledge, but there was another reason which probably swayed him more strongly still, to wit, the care of his eldest son's education and training. Gian Battista Cardano was now in his fourteenth year, and, according to the usages of the time, old enough to make a beginning of his training in Medicine, the profession he was destined to follow. It is not recorded whether or not he chose this calling for himself; but, taking into account the deep and tender affection Jerome always manifested towards his eldest son, it is not likely that undue compulsion was used in the matter. The youth, according to his father's description, strongly favoured in person his grandfather Fazio.[1] He had come into the world at a time when his parents' fortunes were at their lowest ebb, during those terrible months spent at Gallarate,[2] and in his adolescence he bore divers physical evidences of the ill nurture—it would be unjust to call it neglect—which he had received. At one time he was indeed put in charge of a good nurse, but he had to be withdrawn from her care almost immediately through her husband's jealousy, and he was next sent to a slattern, who fed him with old milk, and not enough of that; or more often with chewed bread. His body was swollen and unhealthy, he suffered greatly from an attack of fever, which ultimately left him deaf in one ear. He gave early evidence of a fine

[1] In describing Fazio, Jerome writes: "Erat Euclidis operum studiosus, et humeris incurvis : et filius meus natu major ore, oculis, incessu, humeris, illi simillimus."—*De Vita Propria*, ch. iii. p. 8. In the same chapter Fazio is described as "Blæsus in loquendo ; variorum studiorum amator: ruber, oculis albis et quibus noctu videret."

[2] "At uxor mea imaginabatur assidue se videre calvariam patris, qui erat absens dum utero gereret Jo : Baptistam."—*Paralipomenon*, lib. iii. c. 21.

taste in music, an inheritance from his father, and was, according to Cardan's showing, upright and honest in his carriage, gifted with talents which must, under happier circumstances, have placed him in the first rank of men of learning, and in every respect a youth of the fairest promise. The father records that he himself, though well furnished by experience in the art of medicine, was now and again worsted by his son in disputation, and alludes in words of pathetic regret to divers problems, too deep for his own powers of solution, which Gian Battista would assuredly have mastered in the course of time. He does not forget to notice certain of the young man's failings; for he remarks that he was temperate of speech, except when he was angered, and then he would pour forth such a torrent of words that he scarce seemed in his right mind. Cardan professes to have discerned a cause for these failings, and the calamities flowing therefrom, in the fact that Gian Battista had the third and fourth toes of his right foot united by a membrane; he declares that, if he had known of this in time, he would have counteracted the evil by dividing the toes.[1] Gian Battista eventually gained the *baccalaureat* in his twenty-second year, and two years after became a member of the College.

The life which Cardan planned to lead at Pavia was unquestionably a full one. He had several young men under his care as pupils besides his son, amongst them being a kinsman of his, Gasparo Cardano, a youth of sterling virtue and a useful coadjutor in times to come. He was at this time engaged on his most important works in Medicine and Physical Science. He worked hard at his profession, practising occasionally and reading voraciously all books bearing on his studies. He

---

[1] *De Utilitate*, p. 832.

wrote and published several small works during the four years—from 1547 to 1551—of his Professorship at Pavia; the most noteworthy of which were the Book of Precepts for the guidance of his children, and some Treatises on the Preservation of Health. He also wrote a book on Physiognomy, or as he called it Metoposcopy, an abstract of which appears as a chapter in *De Utilitate* (lib. iii. c. 10), but the major part of his time must have been consumed in collecting and reducing to form the huge mass of facts out of which his two great works, *De Subtilitate* and *De Varietate Rerum*, were built up.

A mere abstract of the contents of these wonderful books would fill many pages, and prove as uninteresting and unsuggestive as abstracts must always be; and a commentary upon the same, honestly executed, would make a heavy draft on the working life-time of an industrious student. In reference to each book the author has left a statement of the reasons which impelled him to undertake his task, the most cogent of which were certain dreams.[1] Soon after he had begun to write the *De Astrorum Judiciis* he dreamt one night that his soul, freed from his body, was ranging the vault of heaven near to the moon, and the soul of his father was there likewise. But he could not see this spirit, which spake to him saying, "Behold, I am given to you as a comrade." The spirit of the father then went on to tell the son how, after various stages of probation, he would attain the highest heaven, and in the terms of this discourse Cardan professed to discern the scheme of his more important works.

The *De Subtilitate* represents Cardan's original con-

---

[1] "Post ex geminatis somniis, scripsi libros de Subtilitate quos impressos auxi et denuo superauctos tertio excudi curavi."—*De Vita Propria*, ch. xlv. p. 175.

ception of a treatise dealing with the Cosmos, but
during the course of its preparation a vast mass of
subsidiary and contingent knowledge accumulated in
his note-books, and rendered necessary the publication
of a supplementary work, the *De Varietate*,[1] which, by
the time it was finished, had grown to a bulk exceeding
that of the original treatise. The seminal ideas which
germinated and produced such a vast harvest of printed
words, were substantially the same which had possessed
the brains of Paracelsus and Agrippa. Cardan postu-
lates in the beginning a certain sympathy between the
celestial bodies and our own, not merely general, but
distributive, the sun being in harmony with the heart,
and the moon with the animal humours. He considers
that all organized bodies are animated, so that what we
call the Spirit of Nature is present everywhere. Beyond
this everything is ruled by the properties of numbers.[2]
Heat and moisture are the only real qualities in Nature,
the first being the formal, and the second the material,
cause of all things; these conceptions he gleaned
probably from some criticisms of Aristotle on the
archaic doctrines of Heraclitus and Thales as to the
origin of the universe.

It is no marvel that a writer, gifted with so bizarre and
imaginative a temper, so restless and greedy of knowledge, sitting down to work with such a projection
before him, should have produced the richest, and at

---

[1] " Libros de Rerum varietate anno MDLVIII edidi : erant enim
reliquiæ librorum de subtilitate."—*De Vita Propria*, p. 176. "Rever-
sus in patriam, perfeci libros XVII de Rerum varietate quos jampri-
dem inchoaveram."—*Opera*, tom. i. p. 110. He had collected much
material during his life at Gallarate.

[2] Aristotle, *Metaphysics*, book I. ch. v., contains an examination
of the Pythagorean doctrine which maintains Number to be the
substance of all things:—ἀλλ' αὐτὸ τὸ ἄπειρον καὶ αὐτὸ τὸ ἓν οὐσίαν
εἶναι τούτων ὧν κατηγοροῦνται.

the same time the most chaotic, collection of the facts of
Natural Philosophy that had yet issued from the press.
The erudition and the industry displayed in the gathering together of these vast masses of information, and in
their verification by experiment, are indeed amazing ;
and, in turning over his pages, it is impossible to stifle
regret that Cardan's confused method and incoherent
system should have rendered his work comparatively
useless for the spread of true knowledge, and qualified it
only for a place among the *labores ineptiarum*.

Cardan begins with a definition of Subtilty. "By
subtilty I mean a certain faculty of the mind by which
certain phenomena, discernible by the senses and
comprehensible by the intellect, may be understood,
albeit with difficulty." Subtilty, as he understood it,
possesses a threefold character: substance, accident, and
manifestation. With regard to the senses he admits but
four to the first rank : touch, sight, smell, and hearing ;
the claims of taste, he affirms, are open to contention.
He then passes on to discuss the properties of matter:
fire, moisture, cold, dryness, and vacuum. The last-
named furnishes him with a text for a discourse on a
wonderful lamp which he invented by thinking out the
principle of the vacuum. This digression on the very
threshold of the work is a sample of what the reader
may expect to encounter all through the twenty-one
books of the *De Subtilitate* and the seventeen of the *De
Varietate*. Regardless of the claims of continuity, he
jumps from principle to practice without the slightest
warning. Intermingled with dissertations on abstract
causes and the hidden forces of Nature are to be found
descriptions of taps and pumps and syphons, and
of the water-screw of Archimedes, the re-invention of
which caused poor Galeazzo Rosso, Fazio's blacksmith

friend, to go mad for joy. There are diagrams of furnaces, of machinery for raising sunken ships, and of the common steelyard. Cardan finds no problem of the universe too recondite to essay, and in like manner he sets down information as to the most trivial details of every-day economy: how to kill mice, why dogs bay the moon, how to make vinegar, why a donkey is stupid, why flint and steel produce fire, how to make the hands white, how to tell good mushrooms from bad, and how to mark household linen. He treats of the elements, Earth, Air, and Water, excluding Fire, because it produces nothing material; of the heavens and light: metals, stones, plants, and animals. Marvellous stories abound, and the most whimsical theories are advanced to account for the working of Nature. He tells how he once saw a man from Porto Maurizio, pallid, with little hair on his face, and fat in person, who had in his breasts milk enough to suckle a child. He was a soldier, and this strange property caused him no slight inconvenience. Sages, he affirms, on account of their studious lives, are little prone to sexual passion. With them the vital power is carried from the heart to a region remote from the genitals, *i. e.* to the brain, and for this reason such men as a rule beget children weak and unlike themselves. Diet has a valid effect on character, as the Germans, who subsist chiefly on the milk of wild cows, are fierce and bold and brutal. Again, the Corsicans, who eat young dogs, wild as well as domestic, are notably fierce, cruel, treacherous, fearless, nimble, and strong, following thus the nature of dogs. He argues at length to show that man is neither an animal nor a plant, but something between the two. A man is no more an animal than an animal is a plant. The animal has the *anima sensitiva* which the plant lacks, and man transcends the animal through the gift of the *anima intellectiva*, which, as Aristotle testifies, differs from the *sensitiva*. Some maintain that man and the animals must be alike in nature and spirit, because it is possible for man to catch certain diseases from animals. But animals take certain properties from plants, and no one thinks of calling an animal a plant. Man's nature is threefold : the Divine, which neither deceives nor is deceived ; the Human, which deceives, but is not deceived ; the Brutish, which does not deceive, but is deceived. Dissertations on the various sciences, the senses, the soul and intellect, things marvellous, demons and angels, occupy the rest of the chapters of the *De Subtilitate*.

At the end of the last book of *De Varietate*, Cardan gives a table showing the books of the two works arranged in parallel columns so as to exhibit the relation they bear to each other. A comparison of the treatment accorded to any particular branch of Natural Philosophy in the *De Subtilitate* with that given in the *De Varietate*, will show that in the last-named work Cardan used his most discursive and anecdotic method. Mechanics are chiefly dealt with in the *De Subtilitate*, and all through this treatise he set himself to observe in a certain degree the laws of proportion, and kept more or less to the point with which he was dealing, a system of treatment which left him with a vast heap of materials on his hands, even after he had built up the heavy tome of the *De Subtilitate*. Perhaps when he began his work upon the fresh volume he found this *ingens acervus* too intractable and heterogeneous to be susceptible of symmetrical arrangement, and was forced to let it remain in confusion. Few men would sit down with a light heart to frame a well-ordered treatise out of the *débris* of a heap of note-books, and it would be unjust

to censure Cardan's literary performance because he
failed in this task. Probably no other man living in his
day would have achieved a better result. It is certain
that he expended a vast amount of labour in attempting
to reduce his collected mass of facts even to the imperfect form it wears in the *De Varietate Rerum*.[1]

Considering that this book covers to a great extent
the same ground as its predecessor, Cardan must be
credited with considerable ingenuity of treatment in
presenting his supplementary work without an undue
amount of repetition. In the *De Varietate* he always con-
trives to bring forward some fresh fact or fancy to illustrate whatever section of the universe he may have under
treatment, even though this section may have been
already dealt with in the *De Subtilitate*. The characteristic most strongly marked in the later book is the
increased eagerness with which he plunges into the
investigation of certain forces, which he professes to
appreciate as lying beyond Nature, and incapable of
scientific verification in the modern sense, and the fabled
manifestations of the same. He loses no opportunity
of trying to peer behind the curtain, and of seeking—
honestly enough—to formulate those various pseudo-
sciences, politely called occult, which have now fallen
into ridicule and disrepute with all except the charlatan
and the dupe, who are always with us. Where he
occupies in the *De Subtilitate* one page in considering
those things which lie outside Nature—demons, ghosts,

---

[1] "Sed nullus major labor quam libri de Rerum Varietate quem
cum sæpius mutassem, demum traductis quibuscunque insignio-
ribus rebus in libros de Subtilitate, ita illum exhausi, ut totus denuo
conscribendus fuerit atque ex integro restituendus."—*Opera*, tom.
i. p. 74.
· He seems to have utilized the services of Ludovico Ferrari in
compiling this work.—*Opera*, tom. i. p. 64.

incantations, succubi, incubi, divinations, and such like
—he spends ten in the *De Varietate* over kindred
subjects.   There is a wonderful story[1] told by his
father of a ghost or demon which he saw in his
youth while he was a scholar in the house of Giovanni
Resta at Pavia.   He searches the pages of Hector
Boethius, Nicolaus Donis, Rugerus, Petrus Toletus,
Leo Africanus, and other chroniclers of the marvellous,
for tales of witchcraft, prodigies, and monstrous men
and beasts, and devotes a whole chapter to chiromancy,[2] a subject with which he had occupied his
plenteous leisure when he was waiting for patients at
Sacco.   The diagram of the human hand given by him
does not differ greatly from that of the contemporary
hand-books of the " Art," and the leading lines are
just the same.   The heavenly bodies are as potent here
as in Horoscopy.   The thumb is given to Mars, the
index finger to Jupiter, the middle finger to Saturn, the
ring finger to the Sun, and the little finger to Venus.
Each finger-joint has its name, the lowest being called
the procondyle, the middle the condyle, and the upper
the metacondyle.   He passes briefly over as lines of
little import, the *via combusta* and the *Cingulus
Orionis*, but lays some stress on the character of the
nails and the knitting together of the hand, declaring
that hands which can be bent easily backward denote
effeminacy or a rapacious spirit.   He teaches that lines
are most abundant in the hands of children, on account
of the tenderness of the skin, and of old men on account
of the dryness, a statement which might suggest the
theory that lines come into existence through the opening and closing of the hand.   But the adoption of this
view would have proved more disastrous to chiromancy

[1] *De Varietate*, p. 661.   [2] Book XV. ch. lxxix.

than ridicule or serious criticism; so he straightway finds an explanation for this fact in the postulate that lines in young people's hands speak as to the future, and in old men's as to the past. Later he goes on to affirm that lines in the hand cannot be treated as mere wrinkles arising from the folding of the skin, unless we are prepared to admit that wrinkled people are more humorous than others, alluding no doubt to the lines in the face caused by laughter, a proposition which does not seem altogether convincing or consequential, unless we also postulate that all humorous men laugh at every joke. There is a line in the hand which he calls the *linea jecoraria*, and the triangle formed by this and the *linea vitæ* and the *linea cerebri*, rules the disposition of the subject, due consideration being given to the acuteness or obtuseness of the angles of this triangle. Cardan seems to have based his treatise on one written by a certain Ruffus Ephesius, and it is without doubt one of the dullest portions of his work.[1]

It is almost certain that Cardan purposed to let the *De Varietate* come forth from the press immediately after the *De Subtilitate*, but before the MS. was ready, it came to pass that he was called to make that memorable journey to Scotland in order to find a remedy for the ailment which was troubling the Archbishop of St. Andrews, a journey which has given to Britons

---

[1] He gives one example of his skill as a palmist in the *De Vita Propria:* "Memini me dum essem adolescens, persuasum fuisse cuidam Joanni Stephano Biffo, quod essem Chiromanticus, et tamen nil minus : rogat ille, ut prædicam ei aliquid de vita ; dixi delusum esse a sociis, urget, veniam peto si quicquam gravius prædixero : dixi periculum imminere brevi de suspendio, intra hebdomadam capitur, admovetur tormentis : pertinaciter delictum negat, nihilominus tandem post sex menses laqueo vitam finivit.' —ch. xlii. p. 156.

a special interest in his life and work. In dealing with the Cosmos in the *De Subtilitate* he had indeed made brief mention of Britain; but, writing then, he had no personal relations with either England or Scotland, or the people thereof; and, but for his subsequent visit, he would not have been able to set down in the pages of his second book so many interesting and suggestive notes of what he had seen and heard, and his ideas of the politics of the time. Again, if he had not been urged by the desire all men feel to read what others may have to say about places they have visited, it is not likely that he would have searched the volumes of Hector Boethius and other early writers for legends and stories of our island. Writing of Britain [1] in the *De Subtilitate* he had praised its delicate wool and its freedom from poisonous beasts : a land where the wolf had been exterminated, and where the sheep might roam unvexed by any beast more formidable than the fox. The inordinate breeding of rooks seems even in those days [2] to have led to a war of extermination against them, carried on upon a system akin to that which was waged against the sparrow in the memory of

---

[1] "Ergo nunc Britannia inclyta vellere est. Nec mirum cum nullū animal venenatū mittat, imò nec infestum præter vulpem, olim et lupum : nunc vero exterminatis etiam lupis, tutò pecus vagat. Rore cœli sitim sedant greges, ab omni alio potu arcentur, quod aquæ ibi ovibus sint exitiales : quia tamen in pabulo humido vermes multi abundant, cornicū adeo multitudo crevit, ut ob frugum damna nuper publico consilio illas perdentibus proposita præmia sint : ubi enim pabulum, ibi animalia sunt quæ eo vescuntur, atque immodicè tunc multiplicantur cum ubique abundaverit. Caret tamen ut dixi, serpentibus, tribus ex causis : nam pauci possunt generari ob frigus immensum."—*De Subtilitate*, p. 298.

[2] Æneas Sylvius in describing his visit to Britain a century earlier says that rooks had been recently introduced, and that the trees on which they roosted and built belonged to the King's Exchequer.

men yet living. But besides this one, he records, in the *De Subtilitate*, few facts concerning Britain. He quotes the instances of Duns Scotus and Suisset in support of the view that the barbarians are equal to the Italians in intellect,[1] and he likewise notices the use of a fertilizing earth—presumably marl—in agriculture,[2] and the longevity of the people, some of whom have reached their hundred and twentieth year.[3] The first notice of us in the *De Varietate* is in praise of our forestry, forasmuch as he remarked that the plane tree, which is almost unknown in Italy through neglect, thrives well in Scotland, he himself having seen specimens over thirty feet high growing in the garden of the Augustinian convent near Edinburgh. The lack of fruit in England he attributes rather to the violence of the wind than to the cold ; but, in spite of our cruel skies, he was able to eat ripe plums in September, in a district close to the Scottish border. He bewails the absence of olives and nuts, and recommends the erection of garden-walls in order to help on the cultivation of the more delicate fruits.

In a conversation with the Archbishop of St. Andrews he was told that the King of Scots ruled over one hundred and sixty-one islands, that the people of the Shetland Islands lived for the most part on fish prepared by freezing or sun-drying or fire, and had no other wealth than the skins of beasts. Cardan pictures

---

[1] " Ejusdem insulæ accola fuit Ioannes, ut dixi, Suisset [Richard Swineshead] cognomēto Calculator : in cujus solius unius argumenti solutione, quod contra experimentū est de actione mutua tota laboravit posteritas ; quem senem admodum, nec inventa sua dum legeret intelligentem, flevisse referunt. Ex quo haud dubium esse reor, quod etiam in libro de animi immortalite scripsi, barbaros ingenio nobis haud esse inferiores : quandoquidem sub Brumæ cælo divisa toto orbe Britannia duos tam clari ingenii viros emiserit."—*De Subtilitate*, p. 444.

[2] *Ibid.*, p. 142.   [3] p. 369.

I

the Shetlanders of that time as leading an ideal life, unvexed by discord, war, or ambition, labouring in the summer for the needs of winter, worshipping Christ, visited only once a year by a priest from Orkney, who came over to baptize the children born within the last twelve months, and was remunerated by a tenth of the catch of fish. He speaks of the men of Orkney as a very lively, robust, and open-hearted crew, furnished with heads strong enough to defy drunkenness, even after swallowing draughts of the most potent wine. The land swarms with birds, and the sheep bring forth two or even three lambs at a time. The horses are a mean breed, and resemble asses both as to their size and their patience. Some one told him of a fish, often seen round about the islands, as big or even bigger than a horse, with a hide of marvellous toughness, and useful for the abundance of oil yielded by its carcase. He attributes the bodily strength of these northerners to the absence of four deleterious influences—drunkenness, care, heat, and dry air. Cardan seems to have been astonished at the wealth of precious stones he found in Scotland— dark blue stones, diamonds, and carbuncles [1]—" maxime juxta academiam Glaguensis oppidi in Gludisdalia regione," and he casts about to explain how it is that England produces nothing of the kind, but only silver and lead. He solves the question by laying down an axiom that the harder the environment, the harder the stone produced. The mountains of Scotland are both higher and presumably harder than those of England, hence the carbuncles.

[1] The fame of Scots as judges of precious stones had spread to Italy before Cardan's time. In the *Novellino* of Masuccio, which was first printed in 1476, there is a passage in the tenth novel of the first part, in which a rogue passes as "grandissimo cognoscitore" of gems because he had spent much time in Scotland.

He was evidently fascinated with the wealth of local legend and story which haunted the misty regions he visited. In dealing with demons and familiar spirits he cites the authority of Merlin, "whose fame is still great in England," and tells a story of a young woman living in the country of Mar.[1] This damsel was of noble family and very fair in person, but she displayed a great unwillingness to enter the marriage state. One day it was discovered that she was pregnant, and when the parents went to make inquisition for the seducer, the girl confessed that, both by day and night, a young man of surpassing beauty used to come and lie with her. Who he was and whence he came she knew not. They, though they gave little credit to her words, were informed by her handmaid, some three days afterwards, that the young man was once more with her; wherefore, having broken open the door, they entered, bearing lights and torches, and beheld, lying in their daughter's arms, a monster, fearsome and dreadful beyond human belief. All the neighbours ran quickly to behold the grisly sight, and amongst them a good priest, well acquainted with pagan rites. When he had come anear, and had said some verses of the Gospel of Saint John, the fiend vanished with a terrible noise, bearing away the roof of the chamber, and leaving the bed in flames. In three days' time the girl gave birth to a monstrous child, more hideous than anything heretofore seen in Scotland, wherefore the nurses, to keep off disgrace from the family, caused it to be burnt on a pile of wood. There is another story of a youth living about fourteen miles from Aberdeen, who was visited every night by a demon lady of wonderful loveliness, though he bolted and locked his chamber-door; but by fasting and praying and keep-

[1] *De Varietate*, p. 636.

ing his thoughts fixed on holy things he rid himself at last of the unclean spirit.[1] He quotes from Boethius the whole story of Macbeth,[2] and tells how "Duffus rex" languished and wasted under the malefic arts of certain witches who made an image of the king in wax and, by using various incantations, let the same melt slowly away before the fire. The unhappy king came near to die, but, as soon as these nefarious practices were discovered, the image was destroyed, whereupon the king was restored to health.[3]

When Cardan received the first letter from Scotland the manuscript of the *De Varietate* must have been ready or nearly ready for the printer ; but, for some reason or other, he determined to postpone the publication of the work until he should have finished with the Archbishop, and took his manuscript with him when he set forth on his travels. In 1550 there came another break in Cardan's life as Professor at Pavia, the reason being the usual one of dearth of funds.[4] In 1551 he went back for a short time, but the storms of war were rising on all sides, and the luckless city of Pavia was in the very centre of the disturbance. The French once more crossed the Alps, pillaging and devastating the country, their ostensible mission being the vindication of the rights of Ottavio Farnese to the Duchy of Parma. Ottavio had quarrelled with Pope Julius III., who called upon the Emperor for assistance. War was declared, and Charles set to work to annex Parma and Piacenza as well to the Milanese. Cardan withdrew to Milan at the end of the year. Gian Battista had now completed his medical course, so there was now no reason why he should continue to live

---

[1] *De Varietate*, p. 637.   [2] *Ibid.*, p. 637.   [3] *Ibid.*, p. 565.
[4] " Peracto L anno quod stipendium non remuneraretur mansi Mediolani."—*De Vita Propria*, ch. iv. p. 15.

permanently at Pavia. Moreover at this juncture he seems to have been strongly moved to augment the fame which he had already won in Mathematics and Medicine by some great literary achievement, and he worked diligently with this object in view.[1]

At the beginning of November 1551, a letter came to him from Cassanate,[2] a Franco-Spanish physician, who was at that time in attendance upon the Archbishop of St. Andrews, requesting him to make the journey to Paris, and there to meet the Archbishop, who was suffering from an affection of the lungs. The fame of Cardan as a physician had spread as far as Scotland, and the Archbishop had set his heart on consulting him. Cassanate's letter is of prodigious length. After a diffuse exordium he proceeds to praise in somewhat fulsome terms the *De Libris Propriis* and the treatises *De Sapientia*[3] and *De Consolatione*, which had been given to him by a friend when he was studying at Toulouse in 1549. He had just read the *De Subtilitate*, and was inflamed with desire to become acquainted with everything which Cardan had ever written. But what struck Cassanate more than anything was a passage in the *De Sapientia* on a medical question, which he extracts and incorporates in his epistle. Cardan writes there : " But if my profession itself will not give me a living, nor open out an avenue to some other career, I must needs set my brains to work, to find therein something unknown hitherto, for the charm of novelty is unfailing, something which would prove of the highest utility in a particular case. In Milan,

---

[1] About this time he wrote the *Liber Decem Problematum*, and the treatise *Delle Burle Calde*, one of his few works written in Italian.—*Opera*, tom. i. p. 109.

[2] Cassanate's letter is given in full (*Opera*, tom. i. p. 89).

[3] The quotation from the *De Sapientia* differs somewhat from the original passage which stands on p. 578 of the same volume.

while I was fighting the battle against hostile prejudice, and was unable to earn enough to pay my way (so much harder is the lot of manifest than of hidden merit, and no man is honoured as a prophet in his own country), I brought to light much fresh knowledge, and worked my hardest at my art, for outside my art there was naught to be done. At last I discovered a cure for phthisis, which is also known as Phthœ, a disease for many centuries deemed incurable, and I healed many who are alive to this day as easily as I have cured the *Gallicus morbus*. I also discovered a cure for intercutaneous water in many who still survive. But in the matter of invention, Reason will be the leader, but Experiment the Master, the stimulating cause of work in others. If in any experiment there should seem to be an element of danger, let it be performed gently, and little by little."[1] It is not wonderful that the Archbishop, who doubtless heard all about Cardan's asserted cure of phthisis from Cassanate, should have been eager to submit his asthma to Cardan's skill. After acknowledging the deep debt of gratitude which he, in common with the whole human race, owed to Cardan in respect to the two discoveries aforesaid, Cassanate comes to the business in hand, to wit, the Archbishop's asthma. Not content with giving a most minute description of the symptoms, he furnishes Cardan also with a theory of the operations of the distemper. He writes : " The disease at first took the form of a distillation from the brain into the lungs, accompanied with hoarseness, which, with the help of the physician in attendance, was cured for a time, but the temperature of the brain continued unfavourable, being too cold and too moist, so that certain unhealthy humours were collected in the head and there remained,

[1] *Opera*, tom. i. p. 89.

because the brain could neither assimilate its own nutriment, nor disperse the humours which arose from below, being weakened through its nutriment of pituitous blood. After an attack of this nature it always happened that, whenever the body was filled with any particular matter, which, in the form of substance, or vapour, or quality, might invade the brain, a fresh attack would certainly arise, in the form of a fresh flow of the same humour down to the lungs. Moreover these attacks were found to agree almost exactly with the conjunctions and oppositions of the moon."[1]

Cassanate goes on to say that his patient had proved somewhat intractable, refusing occasionally to have anything to do with his medical attendants, and that real danger was impending owing to the flow of humour having become chronic. Fortunately this humour was not acrid or salt; if it were, phthisis must at once supervene. But the Archbishop's lungs were becoming more and more clogged with phlegm, and a stronger effort of coughing was necessary to clear them. Latterly much of the thick phlegm had adhered to the lungs, and consequently the difficulty of breathing was great. Cassanate declares that he had been able to do no more than to keep the Archbishop alive, and he fears no one would be able to work a complete cure, seeing that the air of Scotland is so moist and salt, and that the Archbishop is almost worried to death by the affairs of State. He next urges Cardan to consent to meet the Archbishop in Paris, a city in which learning of all sorts flourishes exceedingly, the nurse of many great philosophers, and one in which Cardan would assuredly meet the honour and reverence which is his

---

[1] In a subsequent interview with Cardan, Cassanate modifies this statement.—*Opera*, tom. ix. p. 124.

due. The Archbishop's offer was indeed magnificent in its terms. Funds would be provided generous enough to allow the physician to travel post the whole of the journey, and the goodwill of all the rulers of the states *en route* would be enlisted in his favour. Cassanate finishes by fixing the end of January 1552 as a convenient date for the *rendezvous* in Paris, and, as time and place accorded with Cardan's wishes, he wrote to Cassanate accepting the offer.

The Archbishop of St. Andrews was John Hamilton, the illegitimate brother of James, Earl of Arran, who had been chosen Regent of the kingdom after the death of James V. at Flodden, and the bar sinister, in this case as in many others, was the ensign of a courage and talent and resource in which the lawful offspring was conspicuously wanting. Any student taking a cursory glance at the epoch of violence and complicated intrigue which marked the infancy of Mary of Scotland, may well be astonished that a man so weak and vain and incompetent as James Hamilton—albeit his footing was made more secure by his position as the Queen's heir-presumptive—should have held possession of his high dignities so long as he did. Alternately the tool of France and of England, he would one day cause his great rival Cardinal Beatoun to be proclaimed an enemy of his country, and the next would meet him amicably and adopt his policy. After becoming the partisan of Henry VIII. and the foe of Rome, he finally put the coping-stone to his inconsistencies by becoming a convert to Catholicism in 1543. But in spite of his indolence and weakness, he was still Regent of Scotland, when his brother, the Archbishop, was seized with that attack of periodic asthma which threatened to change vitally the course of Scottish politics. A very slight study of contemporary records will show that Arran had been largely, if not entirely, indebted to the distinguished talents and to the ambition of his brother for his continued tenure of the chief power of the State. If confirmation of this view be needed, it will be found in the fact that, as soon as the Archbishop was confined to a sick-room, Mary of Guise, the Queen Mother, supported by her brothers in France and by the Catholic party at home, began to undermine the Regent's position by intrigue, and ultimately, partly by coaxing, partly by threats, won from him a promise to surrender his power into her hands.

In the meantime Cardan was waiting for further intelligence and directions as to his journey. The end of January had been fixed as the date of the meeting at Paris, and it was not until the middle of February that any further tidings came to him. Then he received a letter from Cassanate and a remittance to cover the expenses of his journey.[1] He set out at once on February 22, undaunted by the prospect of a winter crossing of the Simplon, and, having travelled by way of Sion and Geneva, arrived at Lyons on March 13. In Cassanate's first letter Paris had been named as the place of meeting ; but, as a concession to Cardan's convenience, Lyons was added as an alternative, in case he should find it impossible to spare time for a longer journey. Cardan accordingly halted at Lyons, but neither Archbishop nor physician was there to meet him. After he had waited for more than a month, Cassanate appeared alone, and brought with him a heavy purse of money for the cost of the long journey to Scotland, which he now begged Cardan to undertake, and a letter

[1] "Accepique antequam discederem aureos coronatos Gallicos 500 et M.C.C. in reditu."—*De Vita Propria*, ch. iv. p. 16.

from the Archbishop himself, who wrote word that, though he had fully determined in the first instance to repair to Paris, or even to Lyons, to meet Cardan, he found himself at present mastered by the turn of circumstances, and compelled to stay at home. He promised Cardan a generous reward, and a reception of a nature to convince him that the Scots are not such Scythians as they might perchance be deemed in Milan.[1] Cardan's temper was evidently upset by this turn of affairs, and his suspicions aroused ; for he sets down his belief that patient and physician had from the first worked with the intention of dragging him all the way to Scotland, but that they had waited till he was across the Alps before showing their hand, fearing lest if the word Scotland should have been used at the outset, he would never have moved from Milan.[2]   In describing his journey he writes:—" I tarried in Lyons forty-six days, seeing nothing of the Archbishop, nor of the physician whom I expected, nevertheless I gained more than I spent. I met there Ludovico Birago, a gentleman of Milan, and commander of the King's foot-soldiers, and with him I contracted a close friendship, so much so that, had I been minded to take service under Brissac, the King's lieutenant, I might have enjoyed a salary of one thousand crowns a year. Shortly afterwards Guglielmo Cassanate, the Archbishop's physician, arrived in Lyons and brought with him three hundred other golden crowns, which he handed to me, in order that I might make the journey with him to Scotland, offering in addition to pay the cost of travel, and promising me divers gifts in addition. Thus, making part of our

---

[1] " Difficillimis causis victus venire non potui." The Archbishop's letter is given in *Opera*, tom. i. p. 137.

[2] *Geniturarum Exempla*, p. 469.

journey down the Loire, I arrived at Paris. While I was there I met Orontius; but he for some reason or other refused to visit me. Under the escort of Magnienus [1] I inspected the treasury of the French Kings, and the Church of Saint Denis. I saw likewise something there, not so famous, but more interesting to my mind, and this was the horn of a unicorn, whole and uninjured. After this we met the King's physicians, and we all dined together, but I declined to hold forth to them during dinner, because before we sat down they were urgent that I should begin a discussion. I next set forth on my journey, my relations with Pharnelius and Silvius, and another of the King's physicians, [2] whom I left behind, being of a most friendly nature, and travelled to Boulogne in France, where, by the command of the Governor of Sarepont, an escort of fourteen armed horsemen and twenty foot-soldiers was assigned to me, and so to Calais. I saw the tower of Cæsar still standing. Then having crossed the narrow sea I went to London, and at last met the Archbishop at Edinburgh

[1] He mentions this personage in *De Varietate*, p. 672: "Johannes Manienus medicus, vir egregius et mathematicaram studiosus." He was physician to the monks of Saint Denis.

[2] The reception given to Cardan in Paris was a very friendly one. Orontius was a mechanician and mathematician; and jealousy of Cardan's great repute may have kept him away from the dinner, but the physicians were most hospitable. Pharnelius [Fernel] was Professor of Medicine at the University, and physician to the Court. Sylvius was an old man of a jocular nature, but as an anatomist bitterly opposed to the novel methods of Vesalius, who was one of Cardan's heroes. With this possibility of quarrelling over the merits of Vesalius, it speaks well for the temper of the doctors that they parted on good terms. Ranconet, another Parisian who welcomed Cardan heartily, was one of the Presidents of the Parliament of Paris. He seems to have been a man of worth and distinguished attainments, and Cardan gives an interesting account of him in *Geniturarum Exempla*, p. 423.

on the twenty-ninth of June. I remained there till the thirteenth of September. I received as a reward four hundred more gold crowns; a chain of gold worth a hundred and twenty crowns, a noble horse, and many other gifts, in order that no one of those who were with me should return empty-handed."[1]

The Archbishop's illness might in itself have supplied a reason for his inability to travel abroad and meet Cardan as he had agreed to do; but the real cause of his change of plan was doubtless the condition of public affairs in Scotland at the beginning of 1552. In the interval of time between Cassanate's first letter to Cardan and the end of 1551, the Regent had half promised to surrender his office into the hands of the Guise party in Scotland, wherefore it was no wonder that the Primate, recognizing how grave was the danger which threatened the source of his power, should have resolved that, sick or sound, his proper place was at the Scottish Court.

---

[1] *De Vita Propria*, ch. xxix. p. 75. Cardan refers more than once to the generosity of the Archbishop. He computes (*Opera*, tom. i. p. 93) that his visit must have cost Hamilton four talents of gold; that is to say, two thousand golden crowns.

CHAPTER VII

CARDAN, as he has himself related, arrived at Edinburgh on June 29, 1552. The coming of such a man at such a time must have been an event of extraordinary interest. In England the Italy of the Renaissance had been in a measure realized by men of learning and intellect through the reports of the numerous scholars —John Tiptoft, Earl of Worcester, Henry Parker, Lord Morley, Howard Earl of Surrey, and Sir Thomas Wyat, may be taken as examples—who had wandered thither and come back with a stock of histories setting forth the beauty and charm, and also the terror and wickedness, of that wonderful land. Some echoes of this legend had doubtless drifted down to Scotland, and possibly still more may have been wafted over from France. Ascham had taken up his parable in the *Schoolmaster*, describing the devilish sins and corruptions of Italy, and now the good people of Edinburgh were to be given the sight of a man coming thence, one who was fabled to have gathered together more knowledge, both of this world and of that other hidden one which was to them just as real, than any mortal man alive. Under these circumstances it is not surprising that Cardan should have been regarded rather as a magician than as a doctor, and in the *Scotichronicon* [1] it is recorded

[1] *Scotichronicon*, vol. i. p. 286 [ed. G. F. S. Gordon, Glasgow, 1867]. Naudé, in his *Apologie pour les grands hommes soupçonnez*

that the Primate was cured of a lingering asthma by the
incantations of an astrologer named Cardan, from Milan.
Cardan in his narrative speaks of Edinburgh as the
place where he met his patient, and does not mention
any other place of sojourn, but the record just quoted
goes on to say that he abode with the Primate for eleven
weeks at his country residence at Monimail, near Cupar,
Fife, where there is a well called to this day Cardan's
Well.

Cardan, as it has been noticed already, refused to
commit himself to any opinion as to the character of
the Archbishop's distemper over the dinner-table where
he and Cassanate had been entertained by the French
King's physicians. Cassanate had set forth his views
in full as to the nature of the asthma which had to be
dealt with in his letter to Cardan, and it is highly probable that he would again bring forward these views in
the hearing of the Paris doctors. It is certain that some
of the French physicians had, previous to this, prescribed
a course of treatment for the Archbishop, probably
without seeing him, and that the course was being tried
when Cardan arrived in Edinburgh.[1] For the first six
weeks of his stay he watched the case, and let the treatment aforesaid go on—whether it differed from that which
Cassanate recommended or not there is no evidence to
show. But no good result came of it. The Archbishop
wasted in body and became fretful and disturbed in

de Magie, writes: " Ceux qui recherchoiant les Mathématiques et
les Sciences les moins communes étoient soupçonnez d'être enchan-
teurs et Magiciens."—p. 15.

[1] " Curam agebat Medicus ex constituto Medicorum Lutetian-
orum."—*De Vita Propria*, ch. xl. p. 137. Cardan makes no direct
mention of any other physician in Scotland besides Cassanate ; but
the Archbishop would certainly have a body physician in attendance during Cassanate's absence.

mind, and, at last, Cardan was obliged to let his opinion of the case be known ; and, as this was entirely hostile to the treatment which was being pursued, the inevitable quarrel between the doctors burst forth with great violence. The Archbishop was irate with his ordinary medical attendant, probably the physician who was left in charge during Cassanate's absence—and this man retaliated upon Cardan for having thus stirred up strife. Cardan's position was certainly a very uneasy one. The other physicians were full of jealousy and malice, and the Archbishop began to accuse him of dilatory conduct of the case, redoubling his complaints as soon as he found himself getting better under the altered treatment. So weary did Cardan become of this bickering that he begged leave to depart at once, but this proposition the Primate took in very ill part.

Cassanate in his first diagnosis had traced the Archbishop's illness to an excess of coldness and humidity in the brain. Now Cardan, on the other hand, maintained that the brain was too hot. He found Cassanate's treatment too closely fettered by his theory as to the causes of periodic asthma, but he did not venture to exhibit his own course of treatment till after he had gained some knowledge of the Archbishop's temper and habits. He came to the conclusion that his patient was overwrought with the cares of State, that he ate too freely, that he did not sleep enough, and that he was of a temper somewhat choleric. Cardan set forth this view of the case in a voluminous document, founding the course of treatment he proposed to pursue upon the aphorisms of Galen. He altogether rejected Cassanate's view as to the retention of the noxious humours in the head. The Archbishop had the ruddy complexion of a man in good health, a condition which could scarcely co-exist with the loading of the brain with matter which would certainly putrify if retained for any long time. Cardan maintained that the serous humour descended into the lungs, not by the passages, but by soaking through the membranes as through linen.[1] After describing the origin and the mode of descent of this humour, he goes on to search for an auxiliary cause of the mischief, and this he finds in the imperfect digestive powers of the stomach and liver. If the cause lay entirely in the brain, how was it that all the cerebral functions were not vitiated? In fine, the source of the disease lay, not in the weakness of the brain, but in an access of heat, caused possibly by exposure to the sun, by which the matter of the brain had become so rarefied that it showed unhealthy activity in absorbing moisture from the other parts. This heat, therefore, must be reduced.

To accomplish this end three lines of treatment must be followed. First, a proper course of diet; second, drugs; and third, certain manual operations. As to diet, the Archbishop was ordered to take nothing but light and cooling food, two to four pints of asses' milk in the early morning, drawn from an ass fed on cooling herbs, and to use all such foods as had a fattening tendency; tortoise or turtle-soup,[2] distilled snails, barley-water and chicken-broth, and divers other rich edibles. The purging of the brain was a serious business; it was to be compassed by an application to the coronal suture of an ointment made of Greek pitch, ship's tar, white mustard, euphorbium, and honey of anathardus: the

---

[1] "Per totam tunicam sicut in linteis."—*Opera*, tom. ix. p. 128.
[2] "Accipe testudinem maximam et illam incoque in aqua, donec dissolvatur, deinde abjectis corticibus accipiantur caro, et ossa et viscera omnia mundata."—*Opera*, tom. ix. p. 140.

compound to be sharpened, if necessary, by the addition of blister fly, or rendered less searching by leaving out the euphorbium and mustard. Cardan adds, that, by the use of this persuasive application, he had sometimes brought out two pints of water in twenty-four hours. The use of the shower-bath and plentiful rubbing with dry cloths was also recommended.

The purging of the body was largely a question of diet. To prevent generation of moisture, perfumes were to be used ; the patient was to sleep on raw silk and not upon feathers, and to let an hour and a half come between supper and bed-time. Sleep, after all, was the great thing to be sought. The Archbishop was counselled to sleep from seven to ten hours, and to subtract time from his studies and his business and add the same to sleep.[1]

Cardan's treatment, which seems to have been suggested as much by the man of common-sense as by the physician, soon began to tell favourably upon the Archbishop. He remained for thirty-five days in charge of his patient, during which time the distemper lost its virulence and the patient gained flesh. In the meantime the fame of his skill had spread abroad, and wellnigh the whole nobility of Scotland flocked to consult him,[2] and they paid him so liberally that on one day he made nineteen golden crowns. But when winter began to draw near, Cardan felt that it was time to move

[1] Another piece of advice runs as follows : "De venere certe non est bona, neque utilis, ubi tamen contingat necessitas, debet uti ea inter duos somnos, scilicet post mediam noctem, et melius est exercere eam ter in sex diebus pro exemplo ut singulis duobus diebus semel, quam bis in una die, etiam quod staret per decem dies." —*Opera*, tom. ix. p. 135.

[2] "Interim autem concurrebant multi, imo pené tota nobilitas." —*Opera*, tom. l. p. 93.

southward. He feared the cold ; he longed to get back to his sons, and he was greatly troubled by the continued ill-behaviour of one of the servants he had brought with him—"maledicus, invidus, avarissimus, Dei contemptor ;" but he found his patient very loth to let him depart. The Archbishop declared that his illness was alleviated but not cured, and only gave way unwillingly when Cardan brought forward arguments to show what dangers and inconveniences he would incur through a longer stay. Cardan had originally settled to return by way of Paris, but letters which he received from his young kinsman, Gasparo Cardano, and from Ranconet, led him to change his plans. The country was in a state of anarchy, the roads being infested with thieves, and Gasparo himself had the bad fortune to be taken by a gang of ruffians. In consequence of these things Cardan determined to return by way of Flanders and the Empire.

It was not in reason that Cardan would quit Scotland and resign the care of his patient without taking the stars into his counsel as to the future. He cast the Archbishop's horoscope, and published it in the *Geniturarum Exempla*. It was not a successful feat. In his forty-eighth year, *i.e.* in 1560, the astrologer declared that Hamilton would be in danger of poison and of suffering from an affection of the heart. But the time of the greatest peril seemed to lie between July 30 and September 21, 1554. The stars gave no warning of the tragic fate which befell Archbishop Hamilton in the not very distant future. For the succeeding six years he governed the Church in Scotland with prudence and leniency, but in 1558 he began a persecution of the reformers which kindled a religious strife, highly embarrassing to the Catholic party then holding the reins of

power. His cruelties were borne in mind by the reformers when they got the upper hand. In 1563 he
was imprisoned for saying mass. In 1568 Mary, after
her escape from Loch Leven, gave the chief direction of
her affairs into the hands of the Archbishop, who was
the bitter foe of the Regent Murray. Murray having
defeated the Queen's forces at Langside, Hamilton took
refuge in Dumbarton Castle, which was surprised and
captured in 1571, when the Archbishop was taken to
Stirling and hanged. In the words of the *Diurnal of
Occurrants :* "as the bell struck six hours at even, he
was hangit at the mercat cross of Stirling upon a
jebat."[1] His enemies would not let him rest even
there, for the next day, fixed to the tree, were found the
following verses :

> " Cresce diu, felix arbor, semperque vireto
> Frondibus ut nobis talia poma feras."

To return to Cardan. Having at last won from his
patient leave to depart, he set forth laden with rich gifts.
In Scotland, Cardan found the most generous pay-
masters he had ever met. In recording the niggard
treatment which he subsequently experienced at the
hands of Brissac, the French Viceroy, he contrasts it
with the liberal rewards granted to him in what must
then have been the poorest of the European kingdoms;[2]
and in the Preface of the *De Astrorum Judiciis* (Basel,

---

[1] *Scotichronicon*, vol. i. p. 234. Larrey in his *History of England*
seems to have given currency to the legend that Cardan foretold
the Archbishop's death. " S'il en faut croire ce que l'Histoire nous
dit de ce fameux Astrologe, il donna une terrible preuve de sa science
à l'Archevêque qu'il avoit gueri, lorsque prenait congé de lire, il lui
tint ce discours : ' Qu'il avoit bien pu le guerir de sa maladie ; mais
qu'il n'étoit pas en son pouvoir de changer sa destinée, ni d'empêcher
qu'il ne fût pendu.'"—Larrey, *Hist. d'Angleterre*, vol. ii. p. 711.

[2] *De Vita Propria*, ch. xxxii. p. 101.

1554) he writes in sympathetic and grateful terms of the kind usage he had met in the North.[1]   It must have been a severe disappointment to him that he was unable to revisit Paris on his way home, for letters from his friend Ranconet told him that a great number of illustrious men had proposed to repair to Paris for the sake of meeting him ; and many of the nobles of France were anxious to consult him professionally, one of them offering a fee of a thousand gold crowns.   But Cardan was so terrified by the report given by Gasparo of the state of France, that he made up his mind he would on no account touch its frontiers on his homeward journey.

Before he quitted Scotland there had come to him letters from the English Court entreating him to tarry there some days on his way home to Italy, and give his opinion on the health of Edward VI., who was then slowly recovering from an attack of smallpox and measles.   The young King's recovery was more apparent than real, for he was, in fact, slowly sinking under the constitutional derangement which killed him a few months later.   Cardan could hardly refuse to comply with this request, nor is there any evidence to show that he made this visit to London unwillingly.   But he soon found out that those about the Court were anxious to hear from him something more than a statement of his opinion as to Edward's health.   They wanted, before all else, to learn what the stars had to say as to the probable duration of the sovereign's life.   During his stay in Scotland Cardan would certainly have gained some

---

[1] " Scoticū nomen antea horruerā, eorum exemplo qui prius cœperunt odisse quam cognoscere. Nunc cum ipsa gens per se humanissima sit atque supra existimationem civilis, tu tamen tantum illi addis ornamenti, ut longe nomine tuo jam nobilior evadat."—*De Astrorum Judiciis*, p. 3.

intelligence of the existing state of affairs at the English Court; how in the struggle for the custody of the regal power, the Lord High Admiral and the Lord Protector, the King's uncles, had lost their heads; and how the Duke of Northumberland, the son of Dudley, the infamous minion of Henry VII. and the destroyer of the ill-fated Seymours, had now gathered all the powers and dignities of the kingdom into his own hands, and was waiting impatiently for the death of Edward, an event which would enable him to control yet more completely the supreme power, through the puppet queen whom he had ready at hand to place upon the throne. An Italian of the sixteenth century, steeped in the traditions of the bloody and insidious state-craft of Milan and the Lombard cities, Cardan would naturally shrink from committing himself to any such perilous utterance: all the more for the reason that he had already formed an estimate of the English as a fierce and cruel people. With his character as a magician to maintain he could scarcely keep entire silence, so he wrote down for the satisfaction of his interrogators a horoscope: a mere perfunctory piece of work, as we learn afterwards. He begins by reciting the extraordinary nature of the King's birth, repeating the legend that his mother was delivered of him by surgical aid, and only lived a few hours afterwards; and declares that, in his opinion, it would have been better had this boy never been born at all. "Nevertheless, seeing that he had come into this world and been duly trained and educated, it would be well for mankind were he to live long, for all the graces waited upon him. Boy as he was, he was skilled in divers tongues, Latin, English, and French, and not unversed in Greek, Italian, and Spanish; he had likewise knowledge of dialectics, natural philosophy, and music. His culture is the reflection of our mortal nature; his gravity that of kingly majesty, and his disposition is worthy of so illustrious a prince. Speaking generally, it was indeed a strange experience to realize that this boy of so great talent and promise was being educated in the knowledge of the affairs of men. I have not set forth his accomplishments, tricked out with rhetoric so as to exceed the truth; of which, in sooth, my relation falls short." Cardan next draws a figure of Edward's horoscope, and devotes several pages to the customary jargon of astrologers; and, under the heading "De animi qualitatibus," says: "There was something portentous about this boy. He had learnt, as I heard, seven languages, and certainly he knew thoroughly his own, French, and Latin. He was skilled in Dialectic, and eager to be instructed in all subjects. When I met him, he was in his fifteenth year, and he asked me (speaking Latin no less perfectly and fluently than myself), 'What is contained in those rare books of yours, *De rerum varietate?*' for I had dedicated these manuscripts to his name.[1] Whereupon I began by pointing out to him what I had written in the opening chapter on the cause of the comets which others had sought so long in vain. He was curious to hear more of this cause, so I went on to tell him that it was the collected light of the wandering stars. 'Then,' said he, 'how is it, since the stars are set going by various impulses, that this light is not scattered, or carried along with the stars in their courses?' I replied: 'It does indeed move with them, but at a speed vastly greater on account of the difference of our point of view; as, for

---

[1] Cardan evidently carried the MS. with him, for he writes (*Opera*, tom. i. p. 72): "Hoc fuit quod Regi Angliæ Edoardo sexto admodum adolescenti dum redirem a Scotia ostendi."

instance, when the prism is cast upon the wall by the sun and the crystal, then the least motion of the crystal will shift the position of the reflection to a great distance.' The King said: 'But how can this be done when no *subjectum* is provided? for in the case you quote the wall is the *subjectum* to the reflection.' I replied: 'It is a similar effect to that which we observe in the Milky Way, and in the reflection of light when many candles are lighted in a mass; these always produce a certain clear and lucent medium. *Itaque ex ungue leonem.*'

" This youth was the great hope of good and learned men everywhere, by reason of his frankness and the gentleness of his manners. He began to take an interest in the Arts before he understood them, and to understand them before he had full occasion to use them. The production of such a personality was an effort of humanity; and, should he be snatched away before his time, not only England, but all the world must mourn his loss.

"When he was required to show the gravity of a king, he would appear to be an old man. He played upon the lyre; he took interest in public affairs; and was of a kingly mind, following thus the example of his father, who, while he was over-careful to do right, managed to exhibit himself to the world in an evil light. But the son was free from any suspicion of such a charge, and his intelligence was brought to maturity by the study of philosophy."

Cardan next makes an attempt to gauge the duration of the King's life, and when it is considered that he was a skilled physician, and Edward a sickly boy, fast sinking into a decline, it is to be feared that he let sincerity give way to prudence when he proclaimed that, in his fifty-sixth year the King would be troubled with divers illnesses. "Speaking generally of the whole duration of his life he will be found to be steadfast, firm, severe, chaste, intelligent, an observer of righteousness, patient under trouble, mindful both of injuries and benefits, one demanding reverence and seeking his own. He would lust as a man, but would suffer the curse of impotence. He would be wise beyond measure, and thereby win the admiration of the world ; very prudent and high-minded; fortunate, and indeed a second Solomon."

Edward VI. died on July 6, 1553, about six months after Cardan had returned to Milan ; and, before the publication of the *Geniturarum Exempla* in 1554, the author added to the King's horoscope a supplementary note, explaining his conduct thereanent and shedding some light upon the tortuous and sinister intrigues which at that time engaged the ingenuity of the leaders about the English Court. Now that he was safe from the consequences of giving offence, he wrote in terms much less guarded as to the state of English affairs. It must be admitted that his calculations as to the King's length of days, published after death, have no special value as calculations ; but his impressions of the probable drift of events in England are interesting as the view of a foreigner upon English politics, and moreover they exhibit in strong light the sinister designs of Northumberland. Cardan records his belief that, in the fourth month of his fifteenth year, the King had been in peril of his life from the plottings of those immediately about him. On one occasion a particular disposition of the sun and Mars denoted that he was in danger of plots woven by a wicked minister, nay, there were threatenings even of poison.[1] He does not shrink from affirming that this unfortunate boy met his death by the treachery of those

---

[1] "Cumque ibi esset nodus etiā venenum, quod utinā abfuerit."
—*Geniturarum Exempla*, p. 411.

about him. As an apology for the horoscope he drew
when he was in England, he lays down the principle
that it is inexpedient to give opinions as to the duration
of life in dealing with the horoscopes of those in feeble
health, unless you shall beforehand consult all the
directions and processes and ingresses of the ruling
planets, "and if I had not made this reservation in the
prognostic I gave to the English courtiers, they might
justly have found fault with me."

He next remarks that he had spent much time in
framing this horoscope—albeit it was imperfect—according to his usual practice, and that if he had gone on
somewhat farther, and consulted the direction of the sun
and moon, the danger of death in which the King stood
would straightway have manifested itself. If he had
still been distrustful as to the directions aforesaid, and
had gone on to observe the processes and ingresses, the
danger would have been made clear, but even then
he would not have dared to predict an early death
to one in such high position : he feared the treacheries
and tumults and the transfer of power which must
ensue, and drew a picture of all the evils which might
befall himself, evils which he was in no mood to face.
Where should he look for protection amongst a strange
people, who had little mercy upon one another and would
have still less for him, a foreigner, with their ruler a mere
boy, who could protect neither himself nor his guest ? It
might easily come about that his return to Italy would
be hindered ; and, supposing the crisis to come to the
most favourable issue, what would he get in return for
all this danger and anxiety ? He calls to mind the
cases of two soothsayers who were foolish enough to
predict the deaths of princes, Ascletarion, and a certain
priest, who foretold the deaths of Domitian and Galeazzo

Sforza ; and describes their fate, which was one he did not desire to call down upon himself. Although his forecast as to Edward's future was incomplete and unsatisfactory, he foresaw what was coming upon the kingdom from the fact that all the powers thereof, the strong places, the treasury, the legislature, and the fleet, were gathered into the hands of one man (Northumberland). "And this man, forsooth, was one whose father [1] the King's father had beheaded ; one who had plunged into confusion all the affairs of the realm ; seeing that he had brought to the scaffold, one after the other, the two maternal uncles of the King. Wherefore he was driven on both by his evil disposition and by his dread of the future to conspire against his sovereign's life. Now in such a season as this, when all men held their tongues for fear (for he brought to trial whomsoever he would), when he had gained over the greater part of the nobles to his side by dividing amongst them the spoil of the Church ; when he, the most bitter foe of the King's title and dignity, had so contrived that his own will was supreme in the business of the State, I became weary of the whole affair ; and, being filled with pity for the young King, proved to be a better prophet on the score of my inborn common-sense, than through my skill in Astrology. I took my departure straightway, conscious of some evil hovering anigh, and full of tears." [2]

The above is Cardan's view of the machinations of the statesmen in high places in the English Court during the last months of Edward's life. Judged by the subsequent action of Northumberland it is in the main correct ; and, taking into consideration his associations and environment during his stay in London, this view bears evident

[1] Edmund Dudley, the infamous minister of Henry VII.
[2] *Geniturarum Exempla*, p. 412.

traces of independent judgment. Sir John Cheke, the King's former preceptor, and afterwards Professor of Greek at Cambridge, had received him with all the courtesy due to a fellow-scholar, and probably introduced him at Court. Cheke was a Chamberlain of the Exchequer, and just about this time was appointed Clerk to the Privy Council, wherefore he must have been fully acquainted with the aims and methods of the opposing factions about the Court. His fellow-clerk, Cecil, was openly opposed to Northumberland's designs, and prudently advanced a plea of ill health to excuse his absence from his duties : but Cheke at this time was an avowed partisan of the Duke, and of the policy which professed to secure the ascendency of the anti-Papal party. Cardan, living in daily intercourse with Cheke, might reasonably have taken up the point of view of his kind and genial friend ; but no, — he evidently rated Northumberland, from beginning to end, as a· knave and a traitor, and a murderer at least in will.

When he quitted England in the autumn of 1552 Cardan did not shake himself entirely free from English associations. In an ill-starred moment he determined to take back to Italy with him an English boy.[1] He was windbound for several days at Dover, and the man with whom he lodged seems to have offered to let him take his son, named William, aged twelve years, back to Italy. Cardan was pleased with the boy's manner and appearance, and at once consented ; but the adventure proved a disastrous one. The boy and his new

[1] In the prologue to *Dialogus de Morte*, Opera, tom. i. p. 673, he gives a full account of this transaction. Of the boy himself he writes : "hospes ostendit mihi filium nomine Guglielmum, ætatis annorum duodecim, probum, scitulum, et parentibus obsequentem. Avus paternus nomine Gregorius adhuc vivebat, et erat Ligur : pater Laurentius, familia nobili Cataneorum."

protector could not exchange a word, and only managed to make each other understand by signs, and that very imperfectly. The boy was resolute to go on while Cardan wanted to be rid of him; but his conscience would not allow him to send him home unless he should, of his own free will, ask to be sent, and by way of giving William a distaste for the life he had chosen, he records that he often beat him cruelly on the slightest pretext. But the boy was not to be shaken off. He persisted in following his venture to the end, and arrived in Cardan's train at Milan, where he was allowed to go his own way. The only care for his training Cardan took was to have him taught music. He chides the unhappy boy for his indifference to learning and for his love of the company of other youths. What with his literary work and the family troubles which so soon fell upon him, Cardan's hands were certainly full; but, all allowance being made, it is difficult to find a valid excuse for this neglect on his part. William grew up to be a young man, and was finally apprenticed to a tailor at Pavia, but his knavish master set him to work as a vinedresser, suspecting that Cardan cared little what happened so long as the young man was kept out of his sight. William seems to have been a merry, good-tempered fellow; but his life was a short one, for he took fever, and died in his twenty-second year.[1]

Besides chronicling this strange and somewhat pathetic incident, Cardan sets down in the *Dialogus de Morte* his general impressions of the English people. Alluding to the fear of death, he remarks that the English, so far as

[1] *Opera*, tom. i. p. 119. Cardan here calls him "Gulielmus *Lataneus* Anglus adolescens mihi charissimus." In the *De Morte*, however, he speaks of him as "ex familia Cataneorum" (see last page).

he has observed, were scarcely at all affected by it, and he commends their wisdom, seeing that death is the last ill we have to suffer, and is, moreover, inevitable. " And if an Englishman views his own death with composure, he is even less disturbed over that of a friend or kinsman : he will look forward to re-union in a future state of immortality. People like these, who stand up thus readily to face death and mourn not over their nearest ones, surely deserve sympathy, and this boy (William) was sprung from the same race. In stature the English resemble Italians, they are fairer in complexion, less ruddy, and broad in the chest. There are some very tall men amongst them : they are gentle in manner and friendly to travellers, but easily angered, and in this case are much to be dreaded. They are brave in battle, but wanting in caution ; great eaters and drinkers, but in this respect the Germans exceed them, and they are prone rather than prompt to lust. Some amongst them are distinguished in talent, and of these Scotus and Suisset[1] may be given as examples. They dress like Italians, and are always fain to declare that they are more nearly allied to us than to any others, wherefore they try specially to imitate us in habit and manners as closely as they can. They are trustworthy, freehanded, and ambitious ; but in speaking of bravery, nothing can be more marvellous than the

---

[1] Cardan writes (*De Subtilitate*, p. 444) that Suisset [Richard Swineshead], who lived about 1350, was known as the Calculator ; but Kästner [*Gesch. der Math.* 1. 50] maintains that the title Calculator should be applied to the book rather than to the author, and hints that this misapprehension on Cardan's part shows that he knew of Suisset only by hearsay. The title of the copy of Suisset in the British Museum stands " Subtilissimi Doctoris Anglici Suiset. Calculationes Liber," Padue [1485]. Brunet gives one, " Opus aureum calculationum," Pavia, 1498.

conduct of the Highland Scots, who are wont to take
with them, when they are led to execution, one playing
upon the pipes, who, as often as not, is condemned likewise, and thus he leads the train dancing to death."
Like as the English were to Italians in other respects,
Cardan was struck with the difference between the two
nations as soon as the islanders opened their mouths to
speak.   He could not understand a single word, but
stood amazed, deeming them to be Italians who had
lost their wits.   " The tongue is curved upon the palate;
they turn about their words in the mouth, and make a
hissing sound with their teeth."   He then goes on to
say that all the time of his absence his mind was full of
thoughts of his own people in Italy, wherefore he sought
leave to return at once.

CHAPTER VIII

CARDAN travelled southward by way of the Low Countries. He stayed some days at Antwerp, and during his visit he was pressed urgently to remain in the city and practise his art. A less pleasant experience was a fall into a ditch when he was coming out of a goldsmith's shop. He was cut and bruised about the left ear, but the damage was only skin-deep. He went on by Brussels and Cologne to Basel, where he once more tarried several days. He had a narrow escape here of falling into danger, for, had he not been fore-warned by Guglielmo Gratarolo, a friend, he would have taken up his quarters in a house infected by the plague. He was received as a guest by Carlo Affaidato, a learned astronomer and physicist, who, on the day of departure, made him accept a valuable mule, worth a hundred crowns. Another generous offer of a similar kind was made to him shortly afterwards by a Genoese gentle-man of the family of Ezzolino, who fell in with him accidentally on the road. This was the gift of a very fine horse (of the sort which the English call Obinum), but, greatly as Cardan desired to have the horse, his sense of propriety kept him back from accepting this gift.[1]

He went next to Besançon, where he was received by Franciscus Bonvalutus, a scholar of some note, and then

[1] *De Vita Propria*, ch. xxxii. p. 100.

by Berne to Zurich. He must have crossed the Alps
by the Splugen Pass, as Chur is named in his itinerary,
and he also describes his voyage down the Lake of Como
on the way to Milan, where he arrived on January 3,
1553. Cardan was a famous physician when he set out
on his northward journey; but now on his return he
stood firmly placed by the events of the last few months
at the head of his profession. Writing of the material
results of his mission to Scotland, he declares that he is
ashamed to set down the terms upon which he was
paid, so lavishly was he rewarded for his services. The
offers made to him by so many exalted personages to
secure his permanent and exclusive attention would
indeed have turned the heads of most men. There was
the offer from the King of Denmark; another, in 1552,
from the King of France at a salary of thirteen hundred
crowns a year; and yet another made by the agents of
Charles V., who was then engaged in his disastrous
attack upon Metz. All of them he refused: he had no
inclination to share the perils of the leaguer of Metz,
and his sense of loyalty forbad him to join himself to
the power which was at that time warring against his
sovereign. He speaks also of another offer made to him
by the Queen of Scotland of a generous salary if he
would settle in Scotland; but the country was too
remote for his taste. There is no authority for this
offer except the *De Vita Propria*, and it is there set
down in terms which render it somewhat difficult to
identify the Queen aforesaid.[1]

As soon as he entered Milan, Ferrante Gonzaga, the

---

[1] *De Vita Propria*, ch. iv. p. 16: "cum Scotorum Regina cujus
levirum curaveram." Cardan had probably prescribed for a brother
of the Duc de Longueville, the first husband of Mary of Guise,
during his sojourn in Paris.

Governor, desired to secure his services as physician to the Duke of Mantua, his brother, offering him thirty thousand gold crowns as honorarium ; but, in spite of the Governor's persuasions and threats, be would not accept the office. When the news had come to Paris that Cardan was about to quit Britain, forty of the most illustrious scientists of France repaired to Paris in order to hear him expound the art of Medicine ; but the disturbed state of the country deterred him from setting foot in France. He refers to a letter from his friend Ranconet as a testimony of the worship that was paid to him, and goes on to say that, in his journeying through France and Germany, he fared much as Plato fared at the Olympic games.

In a passage which Cardan wrote shortly after his return from Britain, he lets it be seen that he was not ill-satisfied with the figure he then made in the world. He writes—"Therefore, since all those with whom I am intimate think well of me for my truth and probity, I can let my envious rivals indulge themselves as they list in the shameful habit of evil-speaking. With regard to folly, if I now utter, or ever have uttered, foolish words, let those who accuse me show their evidence. I, who was born poor, with a weakly body, in an age vexed almost incessantly by wars and tumults, helped on by no family influence, but forced to contend against the bitter opposition of the College at Milan, contrived to overcome all the plots woven against me, and open violence as well. All the honours which a physician can possess I either enjoy, or have refused when they were offered to me. I have raised the fortunes of my family, and have lived a blameless life. I am well known to all men of worship, and to the whole of Europe. What I have written has been lauded ; in

L

sooth, I have written of so many things and at such length, that a man could scarcely read my works if he spent his life therewith. I have taken good care of my domestic affairs, and by common consent I have come off victor in every contest I have tried. I have refused always to flatter the great; and over and beyond this I have often set myself in active opposition to them. My name will be found scattered about the pages of many writers. I shall deem my life long enough if I come in perfect health to the age of fifty-six. I have been most fortunate as the discoverer of many and important contributions to knowledge, as well as in the practice of my art and in the results attained; so much so that if my fame in the first instance has raised up envy against me, it has prevailed finally, and extinguished all ill-feeling."[1]

These words were written before the publication of the *Geniturarum Exempla* in 1554. Cardan's life for the six years which followed was busy and prosperous, but on the whole uneventful. The Archbishop of St. Andrews wrote to him according to promise at the end of two years to give an account of the results of his treatment. His letter is worthy of remark as showing that he, the person most interested, was well satisfied with Cardan's skill as a physician. Michael, the Archbishop's chief chamberlain, was the bearer thereof, and as Hamilton speaks of him as "epistolam vivam," it is probable that he bore likewise certain verbal messages which could be more safely carried thus than in writing. A sentence in the *De Vita Propria*,[2] mixed up with the account of Hamilton's cure, seems to refer to this embassy, and to suggest that Michael was authorized to promise Cardan a liberal salary if he would accept

---

[1] *Geniturarum Exempla*, p. 459.
[2] *De Vita Propria*, ch. xl. p. 137.

permanent office in the Primate's household. Moreover, Hamilton writes somewhat querulously about Cassanate's absence abroad on a visit to his family, a fact which would make him all the more eager to secure Cardan's services. His letter runs as follows—" Two of your most welcome letters, written some months ago, I received by the hand of an English merchant; others came by the care of the Lord Bishop of Dunkeld, together with the Indian balsam. The last were from Scoto, who sent at the same time your most scholarly comments on that difficult work of Ptolemy.[1] To all that you have written to me I have replied fully in three or four letters of my own, but I know not whether, out of all I have written, any letter of mine has reached you. But now I have directed that a servant of mine, who is known to you, and who is travelling to Rome, shall wait upon

---

[1] *Commentaria in Ptolemæi de Astrorum Judiciis* (Basil, 1554). He wrote these notes while going down the Loire in company with Cassanate on his way from Lyons to Paris in 1552.—*De Vita Propria*, ch. xlv. p. 175.

He gives an interesting account (*Opera*, tom. i. p. 110) as to how the book first came under his notice. The day before he quitted Lyons with Cassanate, a school-master came to ask for advice, which Cardan gave gratis. Then the patient, knowing perhaps the physician's taste for the marvellous, related how there was a certain boy in the place who could see spirits by looking into an earthen vessel, but Cardan was little impressed by what he saw, and began to talk with the school-master about Archimedes. The school-master brought out a work of the Greek philosopher with which was bound up the *Ptolemæi Libri de Judiciis*. Cardan fastened upon it at once, and wanted to buy it, but the school-master insisted that he should take it as a gift. He declares that his Commentaries thereupon are the most perfect of all his writings. The book contains his famous Nativity of Christ. A remark in *De Libris Propriis* (cf. *Opera*, tom. i. p. 67) indicates that there was an earlier edition of Ptolemy, printed at Milan at Cardan's own cost, because when he saw the numerous mistakes made by Ottaviano Scoto in printing the *De Malo Medendi* and the *De Consolatione*, he determined to go to another printer.

you and salute you in my name, and bear to you my gratitude, not only for the various gifts I have received from you, but likewise because my health is well-nigh restored, the ailment which vexed me is driven away, my strength increased, and my life renewed. Wherefore I rate myself debtor for all these benefits, as well as this very body of mine. For, from the time when I began to take these medicines of yours, selected and compounded with so great skill, my complaint has afflicted me less frequently and severely; indeed, now, as a rule, I am not troubled therewith more than once a month; sometimes I escape for two months."[1]

In the following year (1555) Cardan's daughter Chiara, who seems to have been a virtuous and well-conducted girl, was married to Bartolomeo Sacco, a young Milanese gentleman of good family, a match which proved to be fortunate. Cardan had now reached that summit of fame against which the shafts of jealousy will always be directed. The literary manners of the age certainly lacked urbanity, and of all living controversialists there was none more truculent than Julius Cæsar Scaliger, who had begun his career as a man of letters by a fierce assault upon Erasmus with regard to his *Ciceronianus*, a leading case amongst the quarrels of authors. Erasmus he had attacked for venturing to throw doubts upon the suitability of Cicero's Latin as a vehicle of modern thought; this quarrel was over a question of form; and now Scaliger went a step farther, and, albeit he knew little of the subject in hand, published a book of *Esoteric Exercitations* to show that the *De Subtilitate* of Cardan was nothing but a tissue of nonsense.[2] The book

[1] *Opera*, tom. i. p. 93.

[2] Cardan notices the attack in these words—" His diebus quidam conscripserat adversus nostrum de Subtilitate librum, Opus ingens. Adversus quem ego Apologiam scripsi."—*Opera*, tom. i. p. 117.

was written with all the heavy-handed brutality he was accustomed to use, but it did no hurt to Cardan's reputation, and, irritable as he was by nature, it failed to provoke him to make an immediate rejoinder, a delay which was the cause of one of the most diverting incidents in the whole range of literary warfare.

Scaliger sat in his study, eagerly expecting a reply, but Cardan took no notice of the attack. Then one day some tale-bearer, moved either by the spirit of tittle-tattle or the love of mischief, brought to Julius Cæsar the news that Jerome Cardan had sunk under his tremendous battery of abuse, and was dead. It is but bare charity to assume that Scaliger was touched by some stings of regret when he heard what had been the fatal result of his onslaught; still there can be little doubt that his mind was filled with a certain satisfaction when he reflected that he was in sooth a terrible assailant, and that his fist was heavier than any other man's. In any case, he felt that it behoved him to make some sign, wherefore he sat down and penned a funeral oration over his supposed victim, which is worth giving at length.[1]

"At this season, when fate has dealt with me in a fashion so wretched and untoward that it has connected my name with a cruel public calamity, when a literary essay of mine, well known to the world, and undertaken at the call of duty, has ensued in dire misfortune, it seems to me that I am bound to bequeath to posterity

---

Scaliger absurdly calls his work the *fifteenth* book of *Exercitations*, and wished the world to believe that he had written, though not printed, the fourteen others.

[1] It was not printed until many years after the deaths of both disputants, and appeared for the first time in a volume of Scaliger's letters and speeches published at Toulouse in 1621, and it was afterwards affixed to the *De Vita Propria*.

a testimony that, sharp as may have been the vexation brought upon Jerome Cardan by my trifling censures, the grief which now afflicts me on account of his death is ten times sharper. For, even if Cardan living should have been a terror to me, I, who am but a single unit in the republic of letters, ought to have postponed my own and singular convenience to the common good, seeing how excellent were the merits of this man, in every sort of learning. For now the republic is bereft of a great and incomparable scholar, and must needs suffer a loss which, peradventure, none of the centuries to come will repair. What though I am a person of small account, I could count upon him as a supporter, a judge, and (immortal gods) even a laudator of my lucubrations; for he was so greatly impressed by their weighty merits, that he deemed he would best defend himself by avoiding all comment on the same, despairing of his own strength, and knowing not how great his powers really were. In this respect he was so skilful a master, that he could assuredly have fathomed the depths of every method and every device used against him, and would thereby have made his castigation of myself to serve as an augmentation of his own fame. He, in sooth, was a man of such quality that, if he had deemed it a thing demanded of him by equity, he would never have hesitated to point out to other students the truth of those words which I had written against him as an accusation, while, on the other hand, this same constancy of mind would have made him adhere to the opinions he might have put forth in the first instance, so far as these opinions were capable of proof. I, when I addressed my *Exercitations* to him during his life—to him whom I knew by common report to be the most ingenious and learned of mortal men—was in good hope

that I might issue from this conflict a conqueror; and is
there living a man blind enough not to perceive that
what I looked for was hard-earned credit, which I should
certainly have won by finding my views confirmed by
Cardan living, and not for inglorious peace brought
about by his death? And indeed I might have been
suffered to have share in the bounty and kindliness of
this illustrious man, whom I have always heard described as a shrewd antagonist and one full of confidence
in his own high position, for it was an easy task to win
from him the ordinary rights of friendship by any
trifling letter, seeing that he was the most courteous of
mankind. It is scarcely likely that I, weary as I was,
one who in fighting had long been used to perils of all
sorts, should thus cast aside my courage; that I, worn
out by incessant controversies and consumed by the
daily wear and tear of writing, should care for an inglorious match with so distinguished an antagonist; or
that I should have set my heart upon winning a bare
victory in the midst of all this dust and tumult. For
not only was the result which has ensued unlooked for
in the nature of things and in the opinion of all men
qualified to judge in such a case; it was also the last
thing I could have desired to happen, for the sake of
my good name. My judgment has ever been that all
men (for in sooth all of us are, so to speak, little less
than nothing) may so lose their heads in controversy
that they may actually fight against their own interests.
And if such a mischance as this may happen to any
man of eminence—as has been my case, and the case of
divers others I could recall—it shall not be written down
in the list of his errors, unless in aftertimes he shall
seek to justify the same. It is necessary to advance
roughness in the place of refinement, and stubborn

tenacity for steadfastness. No man can be pronounced guilty of offence on the score of some hasty word or other which may escape his lips; such a charge should rather be made when he defends himself by unworthy methods. Therefore if Cardan during his life, being well advised in the matter, should have kept silent over my attempts to correct him, what could have brought me greater credit than this? He would have bowed to my opinion in seemly fashion, and would have taken my censures as those of a father or a preceptor. But supposing that he had ventured to engage in a sharper controversy with me over this question, is there any one living who would fail to see that he might have gone near to lose his wits on account of the mental agitation which had afflicted him in the past? But as soon as his superhuman intellect had thoroughly grasped the question, it seemed to him that he must needs be called upon to bear what was intolerable. He could not pluck up courage enough to bear it by living, so he bore it by dying. Moreover, what he might well have borne, he could not bring himself to bear, to wit that he and I should come to an agreement and should formulate certain well-balanced decisions for the common good. For this reason I lament deeply my share in this affair, I who had most obvious reasons for engaging in this conflict, and the clearest ones for inventing a story as to the victory I hoped to gain; reasons which a man of sober temper could never anticipate, which a brave man would never desire.

"Cardan's fame has its surest foundation in the praise of his adversaries. I lament greatly this misfortune of our republic : the causes of which the parliament of lettered men may estimate by its particular rules, but it cannot rate this calamity in relation to the excellences of this illustrious personality. For in a man of learning three properties ought to stand out pre-eminently—a spotless and gentle rule of life; manifold and varied learning; and consummate talent joined to the shrewdest capacity for forming a judgment. These three points Cardan attained so completely that he seemed to have been made entirely for himself, and at the same time to have been the only mortal made for mankind at large. No one could be more courteous to his inferiors or more ready to discuss the scheme of the universe with any man of mark with whom he might chance to foregather. He was a man of kingly courtesy, of sympathetic loftiness of mind, one fitted for all places, for all occasions, for all men and for all fortunes. In reference to learning itself, I beg you to look around upon the accomplished circle of the learned now living on the earth, in this most fortunate age of ours; here the combination of individual talent shows us a crowd of illustrious men, but each one of these displays himself as occupied with some special portion of Philosophy. But Cardan, in addition to his profound knowledge of the secrets of God and Nature, was a consummate master of the humaner letters, and was wont to expound the same with such eloquence that those who listened to him would have been justified in affirming that he could have studied nothing else all his life. A great man indeed! Great if he could lay claim to no other excellence than this; and forsooth, when we come to consider the quickness of his wit, his fiery energy in everything he undertook, whether of the least or the greatest moment, his laborious diligence and unconquerable steadfastness, I affirm that the man who shall venture to compare himself with Cardan may well be regarded as one lacking in all due modesty. I forsooth feel no hostility

towards one whose path never crossed mine, nor envy of
one whose shadow never touched mine ; the numerous
and weighty questions dealt with in his monumental
work urged me on to undertake the task of gaining
some knowledge of the same. After the completion of
the Commentaries on Subtlety, he published as a kind of
appendix to these that most learned work the *De Rerum
Varietate*. And in this case, before news was brought
to me of his death, I followed my customary practice,
and in the course of three days compiled an Excursus
in short chapters. When I heard that he was dead I
brought them together into one little book, in order that
I also might lend a hand in this great work of his,
and this thing I did after a fashion which he himself
would have approved, supposing that at some time
or other he might have held discourse with me, or
with some other yet more learned man, concerning his
affairs." [1]

[1] " Si Scaliger avoit eu un peu moins de démangeaison de
contre dire, il auroit acquis plus de gloire, qu'il n'a fait dans ce
combat : mais, ce que les Grecs ont apellé ἀμετρία τῆς ἀνθολκῆς, une
passion excessive de prendre le contrepied des autres, a fait grand
tort à Scaliger. C'est par ce principe qu'il a soutenu que le perro-
quet est une très laide bête. Si Cardan l'eût dit, Scaliger lui eût
opposé ce qu'on trouve dans les anciens Poètes touchant la beauté
de cet oiseau. Vossius a fait une Critique très judicieuse de cette
humeur contrariante de Scaliger, et a marqué en même temps en
quoi ces deux Antagonistes étoient supérieurs et inférieures, l'un à
l'autre."—(Scaliger, in *Exercitat.*, 246.) " Quia Cardanus psittacum
commendarat a colorum varietate ac præterea fulgore, quod et Appu-
leius facit in secundo Floridorum, contra contendit esse deformem,
non modo ob fœditatem rostri, ac crurum, et linguæ, sed etiam quia
sit coloris fusci ac cinericii, qui tristis. Quid faciamus summo
Viro ? Si Cardanus ea dixisset, provocasset ad judicia poëtarum,
atque adeo omnium hominum. Nunc quia pulchri dixit coloris,
ille deformis contendit. Hoc contradictionis studium, quod ubique
in hisce exercitationibus se prodit, sophista dignius est, quamque
philosopho."—Bayle : Article " Cardan." (Sir Thomas Browne, in
one of his Commonplace Books, observes—" If Cardan saith a

It is a matter of regret that this cry of *peccavi* was not published till all the chief literary contemporaries of Scaliger were in their graves. As it did not appear till 1621, the men of his own time were not able to enjoy the shout of laughter over his discomfiture which would surely have gone up from Paris and Strasburg and Basel and Zurich. Estienne and Gessner would hardly have felt acute sorrow at a flout put upon Julius Cæsar Scaliger. Crooked-tempered as he was, Cardan, compared with Scaliger, was as a rose to a thistle, but there were reasons altogether unconnected with the personalities of the disputants which swayed the balance to Cardan's advantage. The greater part of Scaliger's criticism was worthless, and the opinion of learned Europe weighed overwhelmingly on Cardan's side. Thuanus,[1] who assuredly did not love him, and Naudé, who positively disliked him, subsequently gave testimony in his favour. He did not follow the example of Erasmus, and let Scaliger's abuse go by in silence, but he took the next wisest course. He published a short and dignified reply, *Actio prima in Calumniatorem*, in which, from title-page

---

parrot is a beautiful bird, Scaliger will set his wits on work to prove it a deformed animal.")

Naudé (*Apologie*, ch. xiii.) says that of the great men of modern times Scaliger and Cardan each claimed the possession of a guardian spirit, and hints that Scaliger may have been moved to make this claim in order not to be outdone by his great antagonist. It should, however, be remembered that Cardan did not seriously assert this belief till long after his controversy with Scaliger. Naudé sums up thus : " D'où l'on peut juger asseurement, que lui et Scaliger n'ont point eu d'autre Genie que la grande doctrine qu'ils s'étoient acquis par leurs veilles, par leurs travaux, et par l'expérience qu'ils avoient des choses sur lesquelles venant à élever leur jugement ils jugeoint pertinemment de toutes matières, et ne laissoient rien échapper qui ne leur fust conneu et manifeste."

[1] Thuanus, ad Annum MDLXXVI, part of the Appendix to the *De Vita Propria*.

to colophon, Scaliger's name never once occurs. The gist of the book may best be understood by quoting an extract from the criticism of Cardan by Naudé prefixed to the *De Vita Propria*. He writes : " This proposition of mine will best be comprehended by the man who shall set to work to compare Cardan with Julius Cæsar Scaliger, his rival, and a man endowed with an intellect almost superhuman. For Scaliger, although he came upon the stage with greater pomp and display, and brought with him a mind filled with daring speculation, and adequate to the highest flights, kept closely behind the lattices of the humaner letters and of medical philosophy, leaving to Cardan full liberty to occupy whatever ground of argument he might find most advantageous in any other of the fields of learning. Moreover, if any one shall give daily study to these celebrated *Exercitations*, he will find therein nothing to show that Cardan is branded by any mark of shame which may not be removed with the slightest trouble, if the task be undertaken in a spirit of justice. For, in the first place, who can maintain that Scaliger was justified in publishing his *Exercitations* three years after the issue of the second edition of the *Libri de Subtilitate*, without ever having taken the trouble to read this edition, and without exempting from censure the errors which Cardan had diligently expunged from his book in the course of his latest revision, lest he (Scaliger) should find that all the mighty labour expended over his criticisms had been spent in vain ? Besides, who does not know that Cardan, in his *Actio prima in Calumniatorem*, blunted the point of all his assailant's weapons, swept away all his objections, and broke in pieces all his accusations, in such wise that the very reason of their existence ceased to be ? Cardan, in sooth, was a true man, and held all humanity as akin to him. There is small reason why we should marvel that he erred now and again ; it is a marvel much greater that he should only have gone astray so seldom and in things of such trifling moment. Indeed I will dare to affirm, and back my opinion with a pledge, that the errors which Scaliger left behind him in these *Exercitations* were more in number than those which he so wantonly laid to Cardan's charge, having sweated nine years over the task. And this he did not so much in the interests of true erudition as with the desire of coming to blows with all those whom he recognized as the chiefs of learning."

During the whole dispute Cardan kept his temper admirably. Scaliger was a physician of repute ; and it is not improbable that the spectacle of Cardan's triumphal progress back to Milan from the North may have aroused his jealousy and stimulated him to make his ill-judged attack. But even on the ground of medical science he was no match for Cardan, while in mathematics and philosophy he was immeasurably inferior. Cardan felt probably that the attack was nothing more than the buzzing of a gadfly, and that in any case it would make for his own advantage and credit, wherefore he saw no reason why he should disquiet himself ; indeed his attitude of dignified indifference was admirably calculated to win for him the approval of the learned world by the contrast it furnished to the raging fury of his adversary.[1]

After the heavy labour of editing and issuing to the world the *De Rerum Varietate,* and of re-editing the

---

[1] Cardan does not seem to have harboured animosity against Scaliger. In the *De Vita Propria,* ch. xlviii. p. 198, he writes : " Julius Cæsar Scaliger plures mihi titulos ascribit, quam ego mihi concedi postulassem, appellans *ingenium profundissimum, felicissimum, et incomparabile.*"

first issue of the *De Subtilitate*, Cardan might well have
given himself a term of rest, but to a man of his temper,
idleness, or even a relaxation of the strain, is usually
irksome. The *De Varietate* was first printed at Basel
in 1553, and, as soon as it was out of the press, it
brought a trouble—not indeed a very serious one—
upon the author. The printer, Petrus of Basel (who
must not be confused with Petreius of Nuremberg)
took it upon him to add to Chapter LXXX of the work
some disparaging remarks about the Dominican brother-
hoods, making Cardan responsible for the assertion that
they were rapacious wolves who hunted down reputed
witches and despisers of God, not because of their
offences, but because they chanced to be the possessors
of much wealth. Cardan remonstrated at once—he
always made it his practice to keep free from all theo-
logical wrangling,—but Petrus treated the whole question
with ridicule,[1] and it does not seem that Cardan could
have had any very strong feeling in the matter, for the
obnoxious passage is retained in the editions of 1556
and 1557. The religious authorities were however fully
justified in assuming that the presence of such a passage
in the pages of a book so widely popular as the *De
Varietate* would necessarily prove a cause of scandal,

---

[1] "Quid tua interest quod quatuor verba adjecerim? an hoc
tantum crimen est! quid facerem absens absenti?" Cardan writes
on in meditative strain : "Cœterum cum non ignorem maculatos
fuisse codices B. Hieronimi, atque aliorum patrum nostrorum, ab his
qui aliter sentiebant, erroremque suum auctoritate viri tegere volue-
runt: ut ne quis in nostris operibus hallucinetur vel ab aliis decipiatur,
sciant omnes me nullibi Theologum agere, nec velle in alienam
messem falcem ponere."—*Opera*, tom. i. p. 112.

Johannes Wierus, one of the first rationalists on the subject of
witchcraft, has quoted largely from Chapter LXXX of *De Varietate*
in his book *De Præstigiis Dæmonum*, in urging his case against
the orthodox view.

and give cause to the enemy to blaspheme. For Reginald Scot, in the eighth chapter of *Discoverie of Witchcraft*, alludes to the passage in question in the following terms : " Cardanus writeth that the cause of such credulitie consisteth in three points : to wit in the imagination of the melancholike, in the constancie of them that are corrupt therewith, and in the deceipt of the Judges; who being inquisitors themselves against heretikes and witches, did both accuse and condemne them, having for their labour the spoile of their goods. So as these inquisitors added many fables hereunto, least they should seeme to have doone injurie to the poore wretches, in condemning and executing them for none offense. But sithens (said he) the springing up of Luther's sect, these priests have tended more diligentlie upon the execution of them ; bicause more wealth is to be caught from them ; insomuch as now they deale so looselie with witches (through distrust of gaines) that all is seene to be malice, follie, or avarice that hath beene practised against them. And whosoever shall search into this cause, or read the cheefe writers hereupon, shall find his words true."

In 1554 Cardan published also with Petrus of Basel the *Ptolemæi de astrorum judiciis* with the *Geniturarum Exempla*, bound in one volume, but he seems to have written nothing but a book of fables for the young, concerning which he subsequently remarks that, in his opinion, grown men might read the same with advantage. It is a matter of regret that this work should have disappeared, for it would have been interesting to note how far Cardan's intellect, acute and many-sided as it was, was capable of dealing with the literature of allegory and imagination. He has set down one fact concerning it, to wit that it contained " multa de futuris arcana." The next year he produced only a few medical trifles, but in 1557 he brought out two other scientific works which he characterizes as admirable—one the *Ars parva curandi*, and the other a treatise *De Urinis*. In the same year he published the book which, in forming a judgment of him as a man and a writer, is perhaps as valuable as the *De Vita Propria* and the *De Utilitate*, to wit the *De Libriis Propriis*. This work exists in three forms : the first, a short treatise, " cui titulus est ephemerus," is dedicated to " Hieronymum Cardanum medicum, affinem suum," and has the date of 1543. The second has the date of 1554, and, according to Naudé, was first published "apud Gulielmum Rovillium sub scuto Veneto, Lugduni, 1557." The third was begun in 1560,[1] and contains comments written in subsequent years. The first is of slight interest, the second is a sort of register of his works, amplified from year to year, while the third has more the form of a treatise, and presents with some degree of symmetry the crude materials contained in the first. Having finished with his writings up to the year 1564, Cardan lapses into a philosophizing strain, and opens his discourse with the ominous words, " Sed jam ad institutum revertamur, déque ipso vitæ humanæ genere aliquo dicamus." He begins with a disquisition on the worthlessness of life, and repeats somewhat tediously the story of his visit to Scotland. He gives a synopsis of all the sciences he had ever studied—Theology, Dialectics, Arithmetic, Music, Optics, Astronomy, Astrology, Geometry, Chiromancy, Agriculture, Medicine, passing on to treat of Magic, portents and warnings, and of his own experience of the same at the crucial moments of his

---

[1] *Opera*, tom. i. p. 96. " Annus hic est Salutis millesimus quingentesimus ac sexagesimus."

life. He ends by a reference to an incident already chronicled in the *De Vita Propria*,[1] how he escaped death or injury from a falling mass of masonry by crossing the street in obedience to an impulse he could not explain, and speculates why God, who was able to save him on this occasion with so little trouble, should have let him rush on and court the overwhelming stroke which ultimately laid him low.

[1] *De Vita Propria*, ch. xxx. p. 78.

M

THE year 1555 may be held to mark the point of time at which Cardan reached the highest point of his fortunes. After a long and bitter struggle with an adverse world he had come out a conqueror, and his rise to fame and opulence, if somewhat slow, had been steady and secure. He longed for wealth, not that he might figure as a rich man, but so that he might win the golden independence which permits a student to prosecute the task which seems to subserve the highest purposes of true learning, and frees him from the irksome battle for daily bread. He loved, indeed, to spend money over beautiful things, and there are few more attractive touches in the picture he draws of himself than the confession of his passion for costly penholders, gems, rare books, vessels of brass and silver, and painted spheres.[1] In this brief season of ease and security, there were no flaming portents in the sky to foretell the cruel stroke of evil fortune which was destined so soon to fall upon him.

Cardan has left a very pathetic sketch of his own miserable boyhood in the strangely ordered home in Milan, with his callous, tyrannical father, his quick-tempered mother, and the superadded torment of his Aunt Margaret's presence. Fazio Cardano was a man

[1] *De Vita Propria*, p. 57.

of rigorous sobriety, and he seems moreover to have atoned for his early irregularities by the practice of that austere piety which Jerome notices more than once as a characteristic of his old age.[1] The discipline was hard, and the life unlovely, but the home was at least decent and orderly, and no opportunities or provocations to loose manners or ill doing existed therein. In Cardan's own case it is to be feared that, after Lucia's death, the affairs of his household fell into dire confusion, in spite of the presence of his mother-in-law, Thadea, who had come to him as housekeeper—her husband, Altobello, having died soon after the marriage of his daughter with Cardan. He was an ardent lover of music, and, as a consequence, his house would be constantly filled with singing men and boys, a tribe of somewhat sinister reputation.[2] Then, when he was not engaged with music, he would be gambling in some fashion or other.

---

[1] "In ore illud semper ei erat : Omnis spiritus laudet Dominum, qui ipse est fons omnium virtutum."—*De Vita Propria*, ch. iii. p. 7. Reginald Scot, in the *Discoverie of Witchcraft*, says that the aforesaid exclamation of Fazio was the Paracelsian charm to drive away spirits that haunt any house. There is a passage in *De Consolatione* (*Opera*, tom. i. p. 600) which gives Fazio's view of happiness after death :—"Memineram patrem meum, Facium Cardanum, cum viveret, in ore semper habuisse, se mortem optare, quod nullum suavius tempus experiretur, quā id in quo profundissime dormiens omnium quæ in hac vita fiunt expers esset."

[2] Cardan gives his impressions of musicians :—"Unde nostra ætate neminem ferme musicum invenias, qui non omni redundat vitiorum genere. Itaque hujusmodi musica maximo impedimento non solum pauperi et negotioso viro est, sed etiam omnibus generaliter. Quin etiam virorum egregiorum nostræ ætatis neminem musicum agnovimus, Erasmum, Alciatum, Budæum, Jasonem, Vesalium, Gesnerum. At vero quod domum everterit meam, si dicam, vera fatebor meo more. Nam et pecuniæ non levem jacturam feci, et quod majus est, filiorum mores corrupi. Sunt enim plerique ebrii, gulosi, procaces, inconstantes, impatientes, stolidi, inertes, omnisque libidinis genere coinquinati. Optimi quique inter illos stulti sunt."—*De Utilitate*, p. 362.

After lamenting the vast amount of time he has wasted over the game of chess, he goes on : " But the play with the dice, an evil far more noxious, found its way into my house ; and, after my sons had learned to play the same, my doors always stood open to dicers. I can find no excuse for this practice except the trivial one, that, what I did, I did in the hope of relieving the poverty of my children."[1] In a home of this sort, ruled by a father who was assuredly more careful of his work in the study and class-room than of his duties as paterfamilias, it is not wonderful that the two young men, Gian Battista and Aldo, should grow up into worthless profligates. It has been recorded how Cardan, during a journey to Genoa, wrote a Book of Precepts for his children,[2] a task the memory of which afterwards wrung from him a cry of despair. There never was compiled a more admirable collection of maxims ; but, excellent as they were, it was not enough to write them down on paper; and the young men, if ever they took the trouble to read them, must have smiled as they called to mind the difference between their father's practices and the precepts he had composed for their guidance. Furthermore, he had written at length, in the *De Consolatione*, on the folly which parents for the most part display in the education of their children. " They show their affection in such foolish wise, that it would be nearer the mark to say they hate, rather than love, their offspring. They bring them up not to follow virtue, but to occupy themselves with all manner of hurtful things ; not to learning, but to riot ; not to the worship of God, but to foster in them the

---

[1] *De Vita Propria*, ch. xiii. p. 45.

[2] " Quid profuit hæc tua industria, quis infelicior in filiis? quorum alter male periit : alter nec regi potest nec regere ? "—*Opera*, tom. i. p. 109.

desire to drain the cup of lustful pleasure ; not for the life eternal, but to the enticements of lechery."[1]

At this time Gian Battista had gained the doctorate of medicine at Pavia, and had made his contribution to medical knowledge by the publication of an insignificant tract, *De cibis fœtidis non edendis.* Cardan was evidently full of hope for his elder son's career, but Aldo seems to have been a trouble from the first. Yet, in casting Aldo's horoscope (probably at the time of his birth) Cardan predicts for him a flourishing future.[2] Never was there made a worse essay in prophecy. Aldo's childhood had been a sickly one. He had well-nigh died of convulsions, and later on he had been troubled with dysentery, abscesses of the brain, and a fever which lasted six months. Moreover, he could not walk till he was three years old. With a weakly body, his nature seems to have put forth all sorts of untoward growths. There is a story which Naudé brings forward as part of his indictment against Cardan, that the father being irritated beyond endurance by some ill conduct of his younger son during supper, cut off his ear by way of punishment. It was a most barbarous act ; one going far beyond the range of any tradition of the early *patria potestas,* which may have yet lingered in Italy; and scarcely calculated to bring about reformation in the youth thus punished. In any case, Aldo went on from bad to worse; at one time his father found it necessary to place him under restraint, and the last record of him is that one in Cardan's testament, by which he was disinherited.

Gian Battista's failings were doubtless grave and

---

[1] *Opera,* tom. i. p. 614.

[2] " In cæteris erit elegans, splendidus, humanus, gravis et qui ab omnibus, potentioribusque, præsertim probetur."—*Geniturarum Exempla,* p. 464.

numerous, but he had at least sufficient industry to
qualify himself as a physician. He was certainly
his father's favourite child, and on this account the
eulogies written of him in those dark hours when
Cardan's reason was reeling under the accumulated
blows of private grief and public disgrace, must be
accepted with caution. There is no evidence to show
he was in intellect anything like the budding genius
his father deemed him; as to conduct and manner of
life, his carriage was exactly what the majority of
youths, brought up in a similar fashion, would have
adopted. There must have been something in the
young man's humours which from the first made his
father apprehensive as to the future, for Cardan soon came
to see that an early marriage would be the surest safeguard for Gian Battista's future. With his mind bent on
this scheme, he pointed out to his son various damsels
of suitable station, any one of whom he would be ready
to welcome into his family, but Gian Battista always
found some excuse for declining matrimony. He declared that he was too closely engaged with his work ;
and, over and beyond this, it would not be seemly to
bring home a bride into a house like their own, full of
young men, for Cardan, as usual, had several pupils
living with him. It was at the end of 1557 that the
first forebodings of misfortune appeared. To Cardan,
according to custom, they came in the form of a portent,
for he records how he lay awake at midnight on December
20, and was suddenly conscious that his bed was shaking.
He at once attributed this to a shock of an earthquake,
and in the morning he demanded of the servant, Simone
Sosia, who occupied the truckle bed in the room, whether
he had felt the same. Simone replied that he had,
whereupon Cardan, as soon as he arose, went to the

piazza and asked of divers persons he met there, whether they had also been disturbed, but no one had felt anything of the shock he alluded to. He went home, and while the family were at table, a messenger, sent, as he afterwards records, by a certain woman of the town,[1] entered the room, and told him that his son was going to be married immediately after breakfast. Cardan asked who the bride might be, but the messenger said he knew not, and departed. It is not quite clear whether Gian Battista was present or not, but as soon as ever the messenger had departed, Cardan let loose an indignant outburst over his son's misconduct, reproaching him with undutiful secresy, and setting forth how he had introduced to him four young ladies of good family, of whom two were certainly enamoured of him. Any one of the four would have been acceptable as a daughter-in-law, but he declared that now he would insist upon having full information as to the antecedents of any other bride his son might have selected, before admitting her to the shelter of his roof. Over and over again had he counselled Gian Battista that he must on no account marry in haste, or without his advice, or without making sure that his income would be sufficient to support the responsibilities of the married state; rather than this should happen, he would willingly allow the young man to keep a mistress in the house for the sake of offspring, for he desired beyond all else to rear grandchildren from Gian Battista, because he nursed the belief that, as the son resembled his grandfather Fazio, so the son's children would resemble their grand-father—himself. When he was questioned, Gian Battista declared he knew nothing about the report, and was fully as astonished as his father ; but two days later Gian Battista's own servant came to the house, and announced

---

[1] " A scorto nuntius venit."—*De Utilitate*, p. 833.

that his master had been married that same morning,[1] but that he knew not the name of the bride. Cardan now ascertained that Gian Battista's disinclination for matrimony had arisen from the fact that he had been amusing himself with a girl who was nothing else than an attractive and finely-dressed harlot, named Brandonia Seroni, the last woman in all Milan whom he could with decency receive into his house. And the pitiful story was not yet complete. In marrying her the foolish youth had burdened himself with her mother, two or more sisters, and three brothers, the last-named being rough fellows without any calling but that of common soldiers. The character of the girl herself may be judged by the answer given by her father Evangelista Seroni to Cardan during the subsequent trial. When Seroni was asked whether he had given his daughter as a virgin in marriage, he answered frankly in the negative.

Cardan at once made up his mind to shut his door upon the newly-married pair; but the unconquerable tenderness he felt for Gian Battista urged him on to send to the young man all the ready money he had saved. After two years of married life, two children, a boy and a girl, were born: husband and wife alike were in ill health, and every day brought its domestic quarrel. In the meantime sinister whispers were heard, set going in the first instance by the mother and sister of Brandonia, that Gian Battista was the father neither of the first nor of the second child. They even went so far as to designate the men to whom they rightly belonged,

---

[1] This incident is taken from the *De Utilitate*, which was written soon after the events chronicled. The account given in the *De Vita Propria*, written twenty years later, differs in some details. "Venio domum, accurrit famulus admodum tristis, nunciat Johannem Baptistam duxisse uxorem Brandoniam Seronam." — *De Vita Propria*, ch. xli. p. 147.

and contrived that this rumour should come to the ears of the injured husband. The consequence of their malignant tale-bearing was a quarrel more violent than ever, and the rise of a resolution in Gian Battista's mind to rid himself at all hazard of the accursed burden he had bound upon his shoulders.

Until the end of 1559 Cardan continued to live in Milan, vexed no doubt by the ever-present spectacle of the wretched case into which his beloved son had fallen. He records how the young wife, unknown to her husband, handed over to her father the wedding-ring which he (Cardan) had given to his son, along with a piece of silken stuff, in order to pledge them for money. This outrage, joined to the certain conviction that his wife was false to him, proved a provocation beyond the limits of Gian Battista's patience, and finally incited him to make a criminal attempt upon Brandonia's life. Hitherto he had been earnest enough in his desire to rid himself of his wife so long as she raged against him; but, on the restoration of peace, his anger against her would vanish. Now he had lost all patience; he laid his plans advisedly, and set to work to execute them by enlisting the co-operation of the servant who had been with him ever since his marriage, and by taking to live with him in his own house Seroni, his wife, and son and daughter.[1] It cannot be said that the would-be murderer displayed at this juncture any of the traditional Italian craft in setting about his deadly task. The day before the attempt was made he took out of pawn the goods which Evangelista Seroni had pledged, and promised his servant a gift of clothes and money if he would compass

---

[1] Cardan in describing this action of Gian Battista, who was then determined to murder his wife, says of him : " Erat enim natura clemens admodum et gratus."—*De Utilitate*, p. 834.

the death of Brandonia, who was still ailing from the effects of her second confinement. To this suggestion the servant, who had also warned Gian Battista of his wife's misconduct, at once assented.

But even on the very day when he had fully determined to make his essay in murder he vacillated again and again, and it seemed likely that Brandonia would once more be reprieved. When he entered her bedchamber, full of his resolve to strike for freedom, he found her lying gravely ill with an attack of fever, shivering violently, and cold at the extremities. His anger forthwith vanished, and his hand was stayed ; but as if urged on by ruthless fate, the mother-in-law, and the sister, and Brandonia herself, ill as she was, attacked Gian Battista with the foulest abuse and reproaches ; this was the last straw. He went out and sought his servant, and told the fellow at once to make a cake and put a poison therein. The date of this fatal action was some day early in 1560.

On October 1, 1559, Cardan had left Milan, and gone back to Pavia to resume his work as professor, taking Aldo with him. He threw himself into the discharge of his office and the life of the city with his customary ardour. Over and above his work of teaching he completed his treatise *De Secretis*, and likewise found time to hold a long disputation on the decisions of Galen with Andrea Camutio, one of the most illustrious physicians of the age. Concerning this episode he writes : " In disputation I showed myself so keen of wit that all men marvelled at the instances I brought forward, but for a long time no one ventured to put me to the proof. Thus I escaped the trouble of any such undertaking until two accidents both unforeseen involved me therein. At Pavia, Branda Porro, my whilom teacher in Philosophy, interrupted me one day when I was disputing with Camutio[1] on some matter of Philosophy, for, as I have said before, my colleagues were wont to lead me on to argue in philosophy because they were well assured that it would be vain to try to get the better of me in Medicine. Now Branda began by advancing Aristotle as an authority, whereupon I, when he brought out his citation, said, ' Take care, you have left out the "*non*" which should stand after "*album.*" ' Then Branda contradicted me, and I, spitting out the phlegm with which I am often troubled, told him quietly that he was in the wrong. He sent for the *Codex* in great rage, and when it was brought I asked that it might be given to me. I then read out the words just as they stood ; but he, as if he suspected that I was reading falsely, snatched the volume out of my hands, and declared that I was puting a cheat upon my hearers. When he came to the word in dispute he held his tongue forthwith, and all the others looked at me in amazement." [2]

It is certain that Cardan was still vexed in mind by the trouble he had left behind him at Milan. If he had not forgiven Gian Battista, he was full of kindly thought

---

[1] " Triduana illa disceptatio Papiæ cum Camutio instituta, publicata apud Senatum : ipse primo argumento primæ diei siluit."— *De Vita Propria*, ch. xii. p. 37. This does not exactly tally with Camutio's version. With regard to Cardan's assertion that his colleagues hesitated to meet him in medical discussion it may be noted that Camutio printed a book at Pavia in 1563, with the following title : " Andreæ Camutii disputationes quibus Hieronymi Cardani magni nominis viri conclusiones infirmantur, Galenus ab ejusdem injuria vindicatur, Hippocratis præterea aliquot loca diligentius multo quam unquam alias explicantur." In his version (*De Vita Propria*, ch. xii. p. 37) Cardan inquires sarcastically : " Habentur ejusdem imagines quædam typis excusæ in Camutii monumentis."

[2] *De Vita Propria*, ch. xii. p. 39. The Third Book of the *Theonoston* (*Opera*, tom. ii. p. 403) is in the form of a disputation, " De animi immortalite," with this same Branda.

of him.   He sent him from Pavia a new silk cloak, such as physicians wear, so that he might make a better show in his calling, and doubtless continued his supplies of money.   Just a week before the quarrel last recorded, Aldo, against his father's wish, left Pavia and returned to Milan.   Cardan used every argument he could bring forward to keep his younger son with him, but in vain ; and, as he was unwilling to put constraint upon him, Aldo departed.   Cardan says that he was within an ace of going with him, for the University was then in vacation : then the crowning catastrophe might have been averted, but the same fate which was driving on the son to destruction, kept the father at Pavia.   Thus it happened that Aldo was an inmate of his brother's house when the poisoned cake was made.   Cardan has written down a detailed account of the perpetration of this squalid tragedy, and no clearer presentation can be given than the one which his own words supply.

He writes : " Thus my son and the servant went together to make the cake, and the servant put therein secretly some of the poison which had been given him. After the cake had been made, a small piece was given to my son's wife, who was very ill at the time, but her stomach rejected it at once.   Her mother ate some of it, and likewise vomited after taking it.   Though Gian Battista saw what happened he did not believe that the cake was really poisoned, for two reasons.   First, because he had not, in truth, ordered that the poison should be mixed therewith ; and second, because his brother-in-law (Bartolomeo Sacco) had said to him, before the cake was finished, ' See that you make it big enough, for I also am minded to taste it.'   Next he gave some to his father-in-law, who straightway vomited, and complained of a pricking of the tongue.   He warned my son ; but he, still holding that the cake was harmless, ate thereof somewhat greedily; and, after having been sick, had to lie by for some time. On the second day after this Gian Battista, and his brother, and the servant as well were taken in hold: and on the Sunday following I, having been informed of what had happened, went to Milan in great anxiety as to what I should do."

The news which had been brought to Cardan at Pavia told him, over and beyond what is written above, that his son's wife was dead, poisoned as every one believed through having eaten the cake, which had caused nausea and pain to every one else who had tasted it.[1] The catastrophe was accompanied by the usual portents. Some weeks previous to the attempt Gian Battista had chanced to walk out to the Porta Tonsa, clad in the smart silk gown which his father had recently given him, and as he was passing a butcher's shop, a certain pig, one of a drove which was there, rose up out of the mud and attacked the young physician and befouled his gown. The butcher and his men, to whom the thing seemed portentous, drove off the hog with staves, but this they could only do after the beast had wearied itself, and after Gian Battista had gone away. Again, at the beginning of February following, while Cardan was in residence as a Professor at Pavia, he chanced to look at the palm of his hand, and there, at the root of the third finger of the right hand, he beheld a mark like a bloody sword. That same evening a messenger

---

[1] In his defence at the trial Cardan affirmed that, while Brandonia was lying sick from eating the cake, her mother and the nurse quarrelled and fought, and finally fell down upon the sick woman. When the fight was over Brandonia was dead. In *Opera*, tom. ii. p. 311 (*Theonoston*, lib. i.) he writes: "Obiit illa non veneno, sed vi morbi atque Fato quo tam inclytus juvenis morte sua, omnia turbare debuerat."

arrived from Milan with the news of his son's arrest, and a letter from his son-in-law, begging him to come at once. The mark on his hand grew and grew for fifty-three days, gradually mounting up the finger, until the last fatal day, when it extended to the tip of the finger, and shone bright like fiery blood. The morning after Gian Battista's execution the mark had almost vanished, and in a day or two no sign of it remained.

Cardan hurried to Milan to hear from Bartolomeo Sacco, his son-in-law, the full extent of the calamity. Probably there were few people in the city who did not regard Gian Battista as a worthless fellow, whose death would be a gain to the State and a very light loss to his immediate friends, but Cardan was not of this mind. He turned his back upon his professional engagements at Pavia, and threw himself, heart and soul, into the fight for his son's life. He could not make up his mind as to Gian Battista's recent conduct; if he ate of the cake, he surely could not have put in poison himself, or directed others to do so ; if, on the other hand, he had poisoned the cake, Cardan feared greatly that, in the simplicity of his nature, he would assuredly let his accusers know what he had done. And his mind was greatly upset by the prodigies of which he had recently had experience. For some reason or other he did not visit the accused in prison, or give him any advice as to what course he should follow, a piece of neglect which he cites as a reproach against himself afterwards ; but certain associates of Gian Battista, and his fellow-captives as well, urged him to assert his innocence, a course which Cardan recognized as the only safe one. At the first examination the accused followed this counsel ; at the second he began to waver when the servant deposed that his master had given him a certain powder to mix with Brandonia's food in order to increase her flow of milk; and, later on, when confronted with the man from whom he had received the poison, he confessed all; and, simpleton as he was, admitted that for two months past his mind had been set upon the deed, and that on two previous occasions he had attempted to administer to her the noxious drug against the advice of his servant. From the first Cardan had placed his hopes of deliverance in the intervention of the Milanese Governor, the Duca di Sessa, who had not long ago consulted him as physician,[1] but the Duke refused to interfere. The intervention of an executive officer in the procedure of a Court of Justice was no rare occurrence at that period, and Cardan was deeply disappointed at the squeamishness or indolence of his whilom patient. He records afterwards how the Duke met his full share of the calamities which fell upon all those who were concerned in Gian Battista's condemnation;[2] and in the *Dialogus Tetim*, a work which he wrote immediately after the trial, he bewails afresh the inaction of this excellent ruler and the consequent loss of his son.[3]

For twenty days and more, while Gian Battista lay in prison, Cardan, almost mad with apprehension and suspense, spent his time studying in the library at Milan. Sitting there one day, he heard a warning voice which told him that the thing he most feared had indeed

[1] "Vocatus sum enim ad Ducem Suessanum ex Ticinensi Academia accepique C. aureos coronatos et dona ex serico."—*De Vita Propria*, ch. xl. p. 138.

[2] *De Vita Propria*, ch. xli. p. 153.

[3] *Opera*, tom. i. p. 671. He cites the names of former Governors of Milan and other patrons, many of them harsh men, and not one as kind and beneficent as the Duca di Sessa; to wit Antonio Leva, Cardinal Caracio, Alfonso d'Avalos, Ferrante Gonzaga, the Cardinal of Trent, and the Duca d'Alba. Yet the rule of his best friend brought him his worst misfortune.

come to pass. He felt that his heart was broken, and, springing up, he rushed out into the court, where he met certain of the Palavicini, the friends with whom he was staying, and cried out, " Alas, alas, he was indeed privy to the death of his wife, and now he has confessed it all, therefore he will be condemned to death and beheaded." Then having caught up a garment he went out to the piazza, and, before he had gone half-way he met his son-in-law, who asked him in sorrowful tones whither he was going. Cardan answered that he was troubled with apprehensions lest Gian Battista should have confessed his crime, whereupon Bartolomeo Sacco told him that what he feared had indeed come to pass. Gian Battista had admitted the truth of the charge against him : he was ultimately put on his trial before the Senate of Milan,[1] the President of the Court being one Rigone, a man whom Cardan afterwards accused of partiality and of a hostile bias towards the prisoner. Cardan himself stood up to defend his son ; but with a full confession staring him in the face, he was sorely puzzled to fix upon a line of defence. This he perceived must of necessity be largely rhetorical; and, after he had grasped the entire situation, he set to work to convince the Court on two main points, first, that Gian Battista was a youth of simple guileless character; and, second, there was no proof that Brandonia had died of poison. A physician of good repute, Vincenzo Dinaldo, swore that she had died of fever (*lipyria*), and not from the effect of poison ; and five others, men of the highest character, declared that she bore no signs of poison, either externally or internally. Her tongue and extremities and her body were not blackened, nor was the stomach swollen,

---

[1] There is a full account of the trial in an appendix to the *De Utilitate ex Adversis Capienda* (Basel, 1561). It is not included in the edition hitherto cited.

nor did the hair and nails show any signs of falling, nor were the tissues eaten away. In the opening of his defence Cardan attempted to discredit the character of Brandonia. He showed how great were the injuries and provocations which Gian Battista had received from her, and that she was a dissolute wanton ; her father himself, when under examination, having refused to say that she was a virgin when she left his house to be married. He claimed justification for the husband who should slay his wife convicted of adultery ; and here, in this case, Brandonia was convicted by her own confession. He maintained that, if homicide is to be committed at all, poison is preferable to the knife, and then he went on to weave a web of ineffectual casuistry in support of his view, which moved the Court to pity and contempt. He cited the *Lex Cornelia*, which doomed the common people to the arena, and the patricians to exile, and claimed the penalty last-named as the one fitting to the present case.[1] Then he proceeded to show that the woman had really died from natural causes; for, even granting that she had swallowed arsenic in the cake, she had vomited at once, and the poison would have no time to do its work ; moreover there was no proof that Gian Battista had given specific directions to anybody to mix poison with the ingredients of the cake. The most he had done was to utter some vague words thereanent to his servant, who forthwith took the matter into his own hands.[2] If Gian Battista

[1] Laudabatur ejus benignitas ac simul factum Io. Petri Solarii tabellionis, qui cum filium spurium convictum haberet de veneficio, in duas sorores legitimas, solum hæreditatis consequendæ causa, satis habuit damnasse illum ad triremes."—*De Vita Propria*, ch. x. p. 33.

[2] " Evasit nuper ob constantiam in tormentis famulus filii mei, qui pretio venenum dederat dominæ sine causa : periit filius meus, qui nec jusserat dari."—*De Utilitate*, p. 339.

N

had known, if he had merely been suspicious that the
cake was poisoned, would he have let a crumb of it pass
his lips ; and if any large quantity of poison had been
present, would he and the other persons who had eaten
thereof have recovered so quickly ? Cardan next went
on to argue that, whatever motive may have swayed
Gian Battista at this juncture, it could not have been
the deliberate intent to kill his wife, because forsooth the
wretched youth was incapable of deliberate action of
any sort. He could never keep in the same mood for
four-and-twenty hours at a stretch. He nursed alternately in his heart vengeance and forgiveness, changing
as discord or peace ruled in his house. Cardan showed
what a life of misery the wretched youth had passed
since his marriage. Had this life continued, the finger of
shame would have been pointed at him, he must have
lost his status as a member of his profession, and have
been cut off from the society of all decent people ; nay,
he would most likely have died by the hand of one
or other of his wife's paramours. This was to show
how powerful was the temptation to which the husband
was exposed, and again he sang the praises of poison as
an instrument of " removal " ; because if effectively
employed, it led to no open scandal.

He next brought forward the simple and unsophisti-
cated character of the accused, and the physical afflictions which had vexed him all his life, giving as
illustrations of his son's folly the headlong haste with
which he had rushed into a marriage, his folly in giving
an ineffectual dose, if he really meant to poison his wife,
in letting his plot be known to his servant, and in
confessing. Lastly, Cardan had in readiness one of his
favourite portents to lay before the Court. When
Brandonia's brother had come into the house and found

his father and sister sick through eating the cake, he suspected foul play and rushed at Gian Battista and at Aldo who was also there, and threatened them with his sword; but before he could harm them he fell down in a fit, his hand having been arrested by Providence. Providence had thus shown pity to this wretched youth, and now Cardan besought the Senate to be equally merciful.

Cardan's pleas were all rejected; indeed such issue was inevitable from the first, if the Senate of Milan were not determined to abdicate the primary functions of a judicial tribunal. Gian Battista was condemned to death, but a strange condition was annexed to the sentence, to wit that his life would be spared, if the prosecutors, the Seroni family, could be induced to consent. But their consent was only to be gained by the payment of a sum of money entirely beyond Cardan's means, their demand having been stimulated through some foolish boasting of the family wealth by the condemned prisoner.[1] Cardan was powerless to arrest the course of the law, and Gian Battista was executed in prison on the night of April 7, 1560.

In the whole world of biographic record it would be hard to find a figure more pathetic than that of Cardan fighting for the life of his unworthy son. No other episode of his career wins from the reader sympathy half so deep. The experience of these terrible days certainly shook still further off its balance a mind not over steady in its calmest moments. Cardan wrote

---

[1] Gian Battista seems to have boasted about the family wealth, and thus stirred up the Seroni to demand an excessive and impossible sum. " Hæc et alia hujusmodi cum protulissem, non valere, nisi eousque, ut decretum sit, si impetrare pacem potuissem vitæ parceretur. Sed non potuit filii stultitia, qui dum jactat opes quæ non sunt, illi quod non erat exigunt."—*De Vita Propria*, ch. x. p. 34.

voluminously and laboriously over Gian Battista's fate, but in his dirges and lamentations he never lets fall an expression of detestation or regret with regard to the crime itself: all his soul goes out in celebrating the charm and worth of his son, and in moaning over the ruin of mind, body, and estate which had fallen upon him through this cruel stroke of adverse fate. When he sat down to write the *De Vita Propria*, Cardan was strongly possessed with the belief that all through his career he had been subject to continuous and extraordinary persecution at the hands of his enemies. The entire thirtieth chapter is devoted to the description of these plots and assaults. In his earlier writings he attributes his calamities to evil fate and the influences of the stars ; his wit was indeed great, and assuredly it was allied to madness, so it is not impossible that these personal foes who dogged his steps were largely the creatures of an old man's monomaniacal fancies. The persecution, he affirms, began to be so bitter as to be almost intolerable after the condemnation of Gian Battista. "Certain members of the Senate afterwards admitted (though I am sure they would be loth that men should hold them capable of such a wish) that they condemned my son to death in the hope that I might be killed likewise, or at least might lose my wits, and the powers above can bear witness how nearly one of these ills befell me. I would that you should know what these times were like, and what practices were in fashion. I am well assured that I never wrought offence to any of these men, even by my shadow. I took advice how I might put forward a defence of some kind on my son's behalf, but what arguments would have prevailed with minds so exasperated against me as were theirs ? "[1]

[1] *De Vita Propria*, ch. x. p. 33.

CHAPTER X

CARDAN had risen to high and well-deserved fame, and this fact alone might account for the existence of jealousy and ill-feeling amongst certain of those whom he had passed in the race. Some men, it is true, rise to eminence without making more than a few enemies, but Cardan was not one of these. His foes must have been numerous and truculent, the assault they delivered must have been deadly and overwhelming to have brought to such piteous wreck fortunes which seemed to rest upon the solid ground of desert. The public voice might accuse him of folly, but assuredly not of crime; he was the victim and not the culprit; his skill as a physician was as great as ever, but these considerations weighed little with the hounds who were close upon his traces. Now that the tide of his fortune seemed to be on the ebb they gathered around him. He writes: "And this, in sooth, was the chief, the culminating misfortune of my life: forasmuch as I could not with any show of decency be kept in my office, nor could I be dismissed without some more valid excuse, I could neither continue to reside in Milan with safety, nor could I depart therefrom. As I walked about the city men looked askance at me; and whenever I might be forced to exchange words with any one, I felt that I was a disgraced man. Thus, being conscious that my company was unacceptable, I shunned my friends. I had no notion what I should do, or whither I should go. I cannot say whether I was more wretched in myself than I was odious to my fellows."[1]

Cardan gathered a certain amount of consolation from meditating over the ills which befell all those who were concerned in Gian Battista's fate. The Senator Falcutius, a man of the highest character in other respects, died about four months later, exclaiming with his dying breath that he was undone through the brutal ignorance of a certain man, who had been eager for the death sentence. One Hala shortly afterwards followed Falcutius to the grave, having fallen sick with phthisis immediately after the trial. Rigone, the President of the Court, lost his wife, and gave her burial bereft of the usual decencies of the last rite, a thing which Cardan says he could not have believed, had he not been assured of the same by the testimony of many witnesses. It was reported too, that Rigone himself, though a man of good reputation, was forced to feign death in order to escape accusation on some charge or other. His only son had died shortly before, so it might be said with reason that his house was as it were thrown under an evil spell by the avenging Furies of the youth whom he had sent to die in a dungeon. Again, within a few days the prosecutor himself, Evangelista Seroni, the man who was the direct cause of his son-in-law's death, was thrown into prison, and, having been deprived of his office of debt collector, became a beggar. Moreover, the son whom he specially loved was condemned to death in Sicily, and died on the gallows. Public and private calamity fell upon the Duca di Sessa,[2] the Governor of

---

[1] *De Vita Propria*, ch. xxvii. p. 71.

[2] "Quin etiam dominus ac Princeps alioquin generosus et humanus, cum ipsum ob invidiam meam et accusatorum multitudinem dese-

Milan, doubtless because he had allowed the law to take
its course. Indeed every person great or small who had
been concerned in Gian Battista's condemnation, was,
by Cardan's showing, overtaken by grave misfortune.

Cardan still held his Professorship at Pavia, and in
spite of the difficulties and embarrassments of his position he went back to resume his work of teaching a few
days after the fatal issue of his son's trial and condemnation. By the pathetic simplicity of its diction the
following extract gives a vivid and piteous picture of
the utter desolation and misery into which he was cast :
it shows likewise that, after a lapse of fifteen years, the
memory of his shame and sorrow was yet green, and
that a powerful stimulus had been given to his superstitious fancies by the events lately chronicled. " In
the month of May, in the year MDLX, a time when
sleep had refused to come to me because of my grief for
my son's death: when I could get no relief from fasting
nor from the flagellation I inflicted upon my legs when
I rode abroad, nor from the game of chess which I then
played with Ercole Visconti, a youth very dear to me,
and like myself troubled with sleeplessness, I prayed
God to have pity upon me, because I felt that I must
needs die, or lose my wits, or at least give up my work
as Professor, unless I got some sleep, and that soon.
Were I to resign my office, I could find no other means
of earning my bread : if I should go mad I must become
a laughing-stock to all. I must in any case lavish what

---

ruisset, et ipse multis modis conflictatus est gravibus morbis, cæde
propriæ neptis à conjuge suo, litibus gravibus: tum etiam subsecuta
calamitas publica, Zotophagite insula amissa, classe regia dissipata."
—*De Vita Propria*, ch. xli. p. 153. The island alluded to must
have been *Lotophagites insula*, an island near the Syrtes Minor
on the African coast, and the loss of the same probably refers to
some disaster during the Imperialist wars against the Moors.

still remained of my patrimony, for at my advanced age I could not hope to find fresh employment. Therefore I besought God that He would send me death, which is the lot of all men. I went to bed: it was already late, and, as I must needs rise at four in the morning, I should not have more than two hours' rest. Sleep, however, fell upon me at once, and meseemed that I heard a voice speaking to me out of the darkness. I could discern naught, so it was impossible to say what voice it was, or who was the speaker. It said, 'What would you have?' or 'What are you grieving over?' and added, 'Is it that you mourn for your son's death?' I replied, 'Can you doubt this?' Then the voice answered, 'Take the stone which is hanging round your neck and place it to your mouth, and so long as you hold it there you will not be troubled with thoughts of your son.' Here I awoke, and at once asked myself what this beryl stone could have to do with sleep, but after a little, when I found no other means of escape from my trouble, I called to mind the words spoken of a certain man: 'He hoped even beyond hope, and it was accounted to him as righteousness' (spoken of Abraham), and put the stone in my mouth, whereupon a thing beyond belief came to pass. In a moment all remembrance of my son faded from my mind, and the same thing happened when I fell asleep a second time after being aroused."[1]

The record of Cardan's life for the next two years is a meagre one. His rest was constantly disturbed either by the machinations of his foes or by the dread thereof, the evil last-named being probably the more noxious of the two. As long ago as 1557 he had begun the treatise *De Utilitate ex Adversis Capienda,* a work giving evidence

[1] *De Vita Propria,* ch. xliii. p. 160.

of careful construction, and one which, as a literary performance, takes the first rank.[1]   This book had been put
aside, either through pressure of other work or family
troubles, but now the circumstances in which he found
himself seemed perfectly congenial for the elaboration
of a subject of this nature, so he set to work to finish it,
concluding with the chapter *De Luctu*, which has been
used largely as the authority for the foregoing narrative
of Gian Battista's crime and death.   At this period, when
his mind was fully stored and his faculties adequately
disciplined for the production of the best work, he seems
to have realized with sharp regret that the time before
him was so short, and that whatever fresh fruit of knowledge he might put forth would prove of very slight
profit to him, as author.   Writing of his replies given to
certain mathematical professors, who had sent him
problems for solution, he remarks that, although he may
have a happy knack of dispatching with rapidity any
work begun, he always begins too late.   In his fifty-
eighth year he answered one of these queries, involving
three very difficult problems, within seven days ; a feat
which he judges to be a marvel : but what profit will it
bring him now ?   If he had written this treatise when he
was thirty he would straightway have risen to fame and
fortune, in spite of his poverty, his rivals, and his
enemies.   Then, in ten years' space, he would have
finished and brought out all those books which were now
lying unfinished around him in his old age ; and moreover would have won so great gain and glory, that no

[1] Cardan rates it as his best work on an ethical subject.—*Opera*,
tom i. p. 146. And on p. 115 he writes : " Utinam contigisset absol-
vere ante errorem filii ; neque enim ille errasset, nec errandi causam
aliquam habuisset : nec, etiamsi errasset, periisset."   He also
quotes a letter full of sound and loving counsels which he had sent
to Gian Battista six months before he fell into the snare.

farther good fortune would have remained for him to ask for. Another work which he had begun about the same time (1558) was the treatise on *Dialectic,* illustrated by geometrical problems and theorems, and likewise by the well-known logical catch lines *Barbara Celarent.* During the summer vacation of 1561 he returned to Milan, and began a *Commentary on the Anatomy of Mundinus,* the recognized text-book of the schools up to the appearance of Vesalius. In the preface to this work he puts forward a vigorous plea for the extended use of anatomy in reaching a diagnosis.[1] He had likewise on hand the *Theonoston,* a set of essays on Moral subjects written something in the spirit of Seneca; and, after Gian Battista's death, he wrote the dialogue *Tetim, seu de Humanis Consiliis.* In the year following, 1561, a farther sorrow and trouble came upon him by the death of the English youth, William. If he was guilty of neglect in the case of this young man— and by his own confession he was—he was certainly profoundly grieved at his death. In the Argument to the *Dialogus de Morte* he laments that he ever let the youth leave his house without sending him back to England, and tells how he was cozened by Daldo, the crafty tailor, out of a premium of thirty-one gold crowns, in return for which William was to be taught a trade. " But during the summer, Daldo, who had a little farm in the country, took the youth there and let him join in the village games, and by degrees made him into a vine-dresser. But if at any time it chanced that William's services were also wanted at the tailor's shop, his master would force him to return thereto in the evening (for the farm was two miles distant), and sit sewing all the night. Besides this the boy would go dancing with the villagers,

[1] *Opera,* tom. x. p. 129.

and in the course of their merry-making he fell in love
with a girl. While I was living at Milan he was taken
with fever, and came to me ; but, for various reasons, I
did not give proper attention to him, first, because he
himself made light of his ailment ; second, because I
knew not that his sickness had been brought on by excessive toil and exposure to the sun ; and third, because,
when he had been seized with a similar distemper on
two or three occasions before this, he had always got
well within four or five days. Besides this I was then
in trouble owing to the running away of my son Aldo
and one of my servants. What more is there to tell?
Four days after I had ordered him to be bled, messengers came to me in the night and begged me to go
and see him, for he was apparently near his end. He
was seized with convulsions and lost his senses, but I
battled with the disease and brought him round. I was
obliged to return to Pavia to resume my teaching, and
William, when he was well enough to get up, was forced
to sleep in the workshop by his master, who had been
bidden to a wedding. There he suffered so much from
cold and bad food that, when he was setting out for
Pavia to seek me, he was again taken ill. His unfeeling
master caused him to be removed to the poor-house, and
there he died the following morning from the violence
of the distemper, from agony of mind, and from the cold
he had suffered. Indeed I was so heavily stricken by
mischance that meseemed I had lost another son."

It was partly as a consolation in his own grief, and
partly as a monument to the ill-fated youth, that Cardan
wrote the *Dialogus de Morte*, a work which contains
little of interest beyond the record of Cardan's impressions of Englishmen already quoted. But it was beyond
hope that he should find adequate solace for the gnawing

grief and remorse which oppressed him in this, or any
other literary work. He was ill looked upon at Milan,
but his position at Pavia seems to have been still more
irksome. He grew nervous as to his standing as a physician, for, with the powerful prejudice which had been
raised against him both as to his public and his private
affairs, he felt that a single slip in his treatment of any
particular case would be fatal to him. In Milan he did
meet with a certain amount of gratitude from the
wealthier citizens for the services he had wrought them;
but in Pavia, his birthplace, the public mind was strongly
set against him; indeed in 1562 he was subjected to so
much petty persecution at the hands of the authorities
and of his colleagues, that he determined to give up his
Professorship at all cost. He describes at great length
one of the most notable intrigues against him. " Now
in dealing with the deadly snares woven against my life,
I will tell you of something strange which befell me.
During my Professorship at Pavia I was in the habit of
reading in my own house. I had in my household at
that time a woman to do occasional work, the youth
Ercole Visconti, two boys, and another servant. Of the
two boys, one was my amanuensis and well skilled in
music, and the other was a lackey. It was in 1562 that
I made up my mind to resign my office of teaching and
quit Pavia, a resolution which the Senate took in ill part,
and dealt with me as with a man transported with rage.
But there were two doctors of the city who strove with
all their might to drive me away: one a crafty fellow who
had formerly been a pupil of mine; the other was the
teacher extraordinary in Medicine, a simple-minded man,
and, as I take it, not evil by nature; but covetous and
ambitious men will stop at nothing, especially when the
prize to be won is an office held in high esteem. Thus,

when they despaired of getting rid of me through the action of the Senate—what though I was petitioning to be relieved of my duties—they laid a plot to kill me, not by the dagger for fear of the Senate and of possible scandal, but by malignant craft. My opponent perceived that he could not be promoted to the post of principal teacher unless I should leave the place, and for this reason he and his allies spread their nets from a distance. In the first place, they caused to be written to me, in the name of my son-in-law [1] and of my daughter as well, a most vile and filthy letter telling how they were ashamed of their kinship with me; that they were ashamed likewise for the sake of the Senate, and of the College; and that the authorities ought to take cognizance of the matter and pronounce me unworthy of the office of teacher and cause me to be removed therefrom forthwith. Confounded at receiving such an impudent and audacious reproof at the hands of my own kindred, I knew not what to do or say, or what reply I should make; nor could I divine for what reason this unseemly and grievous affront had been put upon me. It afterwards came to light that the letter was written in order to serve as an occasion for fresh attacks; for, before many days had passed, another letter came to me bearing the name of one Fioravanti, written in the following strain. This man was likewise shocked for the sake of the city, the college, and the body of professors, seeing that a report had been spread abroad that I was guilty of abominable offences which cannot be named. He would call upon a number of his friends to take steps to compel me to consider the public scandal I was causing, and would see that the houses where these offences were committed should be pointed out. When I read this

---

[1] Bartolomeo Sacco was evidently living at Pavia at this date.

letter I was as one stupefied, nor could I believe it was the work of Fioravanti, whom I had hitherto regarded as a man of seemly carriage and a friend. But this letter and its purport remained fixed in my mind and prompted me to reply to my son-in-law; for I believed no longer that he had aught to do with the letter which professed to come from him; indeed I ought never to have harboured such a suspicion, seeing that both then and now he has always had the most kindly care for me; nor has he ever judged ill of me.

"I called for my cloak at once and went to Fioravanti, whom I questioned about the letter. He admitted that he wrote it, whereupon I was more than ever astonished, for I was loth to suspect him of crooked dealing, much more of any premeditated treachery. I began to reason with him, and to inquire where all these wonderful plans had been concocted, and then he began to waver, and failed to find an answer. He could only put forward common report, and the utterances of the Rector of the Gymnasium, as the source of them."[1]

Cardan goes on to connect the foregoing incident, by reasoning which is not very clear, with what he maintained to have been a veritable attempt against his life. "The first act of the tragedy having come to an end, the second began, and this threw certain light upon the first. My foes made it their special care that I, whom they held up as a disgrace to my country, to my family, to the Senate, to the Colleges of Milan and Pavia, to the Council of Professors, and to the students, should become a member of the Accademia degli Affidati, a society in which were enrolled divers illustrious theologians, two Cardinals, and two princes, the Duke of Mantua, and the Marquis Pescara. When they perceived how loth I

---

[1] *De Vita Propria*, ch. xxx. p. 83.

was to take this step they began to threaten. What was I to do, broken down by the cruel fate of my son, and suffering every possible evil? Finally I agreed, induced by the promise they made me, that, in the course of a few days, I should be relieved of my duties as Professor; but I did not then perceive the snare, or consider how it was that they should now court the fellowship of one whom, less than fifteen days ago, all ranks of the College had declared to be a monster not to be tolerated. Alas for faith in heaven, for the barbarity of men, for the hatred of false friends, for that shamelessness and cruelty more fell than serpent's bite! What more is there to tell? The first time I entered the room of the Affidati I saw that a heavy beam had been poised above in such fashion that it might easily fall and kill whatsoever person might be passing underneath. Whether this had been done by accident or design I cannot say. But hereafter I attended as rarely as possible, making excuses for my absence; and, when I did go, I went when no one looked for me, and out of season, taking good heed of this trap the while. Wherefore no evil befell me thereby, either because my foes deemed it unwise to work such wickedness in public, or because they had not finally agreed to put their scheme in operation, or because they were plotting some fresh evil against me. Another attempt was made a few days later, when I was called to the ailing son of one Piero Trono, a surgeon; they placed high over the door a leaden weight which might easily be made to fall, pretending that it had been put there to hold up the curtain. This weight did fall; and, had it struck me, it would certainly have killed me: how near I was to death, God knows. Wherefore I began to be suspicious of something I could not define, so greatly was my mind upset. Then a third attempt was made, which was evident enough. A few days later, when they were about to sing a new Mass, the same rascally crew came to me, asking me whether I would lend them the services of my two singing boys, for my enemies knew well enough that these boys acted as my cup-bearers, and over and beyond this they made an agreement with my hired woman that she should give me poison. They first went to Ercole and tried to persuade him to go to the function ; and he, suspecting nothing, at first promised his help ; but when he heard that his fellow was to go likewise, he began to smell mischief and said, 'Only one of us knows music.' Then Fioravanti, a blunt fellow, was so wholly set on getting them out of the house that he said, 'Let us have both of you, for we know that the other is also a musician ; and, though he may not be one of the best, still he will serve to swell the band of choristers.' Then Ercole said somewhat vaguely that he would ask his master. He came to me, having fathomed and laid bare the whole intention of the plot, so that, if I had not been stark mad and stupid, I might easily have seen through their design. Fifteen days or so had passed when the same men once more sought me out and begged me to let them have the two boys to help them in the performance of a comedy. Then Ercole came to me and said, 'Now in sooth the riddle is plain to read ; they are planning to get all your people away from your table, so that they may kill you with poison ; nor are they satisfied with plotting your death merely by tricks of this sort ; they are determined to kill you by any chance which may offer." [1]

How far these plots were real, and how far they sprang from monomania it is impossible to say. Car-

[1] *De Vita Propria*, ch. xxx. p. 86.

dan's relations with his brother physicians had never been of the happiest, and it is quite possible that a set may have been made in the Pavian Academy to get rid of a colleague, difficult to live with at the best, and now cankered still more in temper by misfortune, and likewise, in a measure, disgraced by the same. Surrounded by annoyances such as these, and tormented by the intolerable memories and associations of the last few years, it is not wonderful that he should seek a way out of his troubles by a change of scene and occupation.

As early as 1536 Cardan had had professional relations with certain members of the Borromeo family, which was one of the most illustrious in Milan, and in 1560 Carlo Borromeo was appointed Archbishop of Milan. There is no record of the date when Cardan first made acquaintance with this generous patron, who was the nephew of the reigning Pope, Pius IV., himself a Milanese, but it is certain that Cardan had at an earlier date successfully treated the mother of the future Cardinal,[1] wherefore it is legitimate to assume that the physician was *persona grata* to the whole family. As soon as Cardan had determined to withdraw from Pavia he applied to the Cardinal, who had just made a magnificent benefaction to Bologna in the form of the University buildings. He espoused Cardan's interests at once, and most opportunely, for the protection of a powerful personage was almost as needful at Bologna, as the sequel shows, as it would have been at Pavia. It was evident that Cardan had foes elsewhere than in Pavia; indeed the early stages of the negotiation, which went on in reference to his transfer to Bologna, suggest a doubt whether the change would bring him any advantage other than the substitution of one set of enemies for another. He

[1] *De Vita Propria*, ch. xvii. p. 55.

o

writes: "When I was about to be summoned to teach at Bologna, some persons of that place who were envious of my reputation sent a certain officer (a getter-up of petitions) to Pavia. Now this fellow, who never once entered the class-room, nor had a word with any one of my pupils, wrote, on what authority I know not, a report in these words: 'Concerning Girolamo Cardano, I am told that he taught in this place, but got no pupils, always lecturing to empty benches: that he is a man of evil life, ill regarded by all, and little less than a fool, repulsive in his manners, and entirely unskilled in medicine. After he had promulgated certain of his opinions he found no one in the city who would employ him, nor did he practise his art.'

"These words were read to the Senate by the messenger on his return in the presence of the illustrious Borromeo, the Pope's Legate to the city. The Senate were upon the point of breaking off all further negotiations, but while the man was reading his report, some one present heard the words in which he declared that I did not practise medicine. 'Hui!' he cried, 'I know that is not true, for I myself have seen divers men of the highest consideration going to him for help, and I—though I am not to be ranked with them—have often consulted him myself.' Then the Legate took up the parole and said, 'I too bear witness that he cured my own mother when she was given up by every one else.' Then the first speaker suggested that probably the rest of the tale was just as worthy of belief as this one statement, the Legate agreeing thereto; whereupon the messenger aforesaid held his tongue and blushed for shame. Ultimately the Senate determined to appoint me Professor for one year, 'for,' they said, 'if he should prove to be the sort of man the officer describes, or if his teaching should profit us nothing, we can let him go ; but if it be otherwise, the contract may be ratified.' With regard to the salary, over which a dispute had already arisen, the Legate gave his consent, and the business came to an end.

"But, disregarding this settlement, my opponents urged one of their number to wait upon me as a delegate from the Senate, and this man would fain have added to the terms already sanctioned by the Senate, others which I could not possibly accept. He offered me a smaller stipend, no teaching room was assigned to me, and no allowance for travelling expenses. I refused to treat with him, whereupon he was forced to depart, and to return to me later on with the terms of my engagement duly set forth."[1]

It was in June 1562 that Cardan finally resigned his position at Pavia, but it was not until some months after this date that the final agreement with the Bolognese Senate, lately referred to, was concluded, and in the interim he was forced to suffer no slight annoyance and persecution at the hands of his adversaries in Pavia, in Bologna, and in Milan as well. Just before he resigned his Professorship he was warned by the portentous kindling of a fire, seemingly dead,[2] that fresh mischief was afoot, and he at once determined in his mind that his foes had planned destruction against him afresh. So impressed was he at this manifestation that he swore he would not leave home on the day following. "But early in the morning there came to my house four or five of my pupils bidding me to a feast, where all the chief Professors of the Gymnasium and the Academy proposed to be present. I replied

---

[1] *De Vita Propria*, ch. xvii. p. 54.

[2] *Ibid.*, ch. xxx. p. 88. There is also a long account of this occurrence in *Opera*, tom. x. p. 459.

that I could not come, whereupon they, knowing that it was not my wont to dine in the middle of the day, and deeming that it was on this score that I refused to join them, said, 'Then for your sake we will make the feast a supper.' I answered that I could not on any account make one of their party, and then they demanded to know the cause of my refusal. I replied it was because of a strange event which had befallen me, and of a vow I had made thereanent. At this they were greatly astonished, and two of them exchanged significant glances, and they urged me again and again that I should not be so firmly set upon marring so illustrious a gathering by my absence, but I gave back the same answer as before."[1] They came a second time, but Cardan was not to be moved. He records, however, that he did break his vow after all by going out after dusk to see a poor butcher who was seriously ill.

It is hard to detect any evidence of deadly intent in what seems, by contemporary daylight, to have been a complimentary invitation to dinner; but to the old man, possessed as he was by hysterical terrors, this episode undoubtedly foreshadowed another assault against his life. He finds some compensation, however, in once more recording the fact that all these disturbers of his peace—like the men who were concerned in Gian Battista's condemnation—came to a bad end. His rival, who had taken his place as Professor, had not taught in the schools more than three or four times before he was seized with disease and died after three months' suffering. "Upon him there lay only the suspicion of the charge, but I heard afterwards that a friend of his was certainly privy to the deed of murder which they had resolved to work upon me by giving me a cup

[1] *De Vita Propria*, ch. xxx. p. 89.

of poisoned wine at the supper. In the same year died Delfino, and a little while after Fioravanti." [1]

In July Cardan withdrew to Milan, where, to add to his other troubles, he was seized with an attack of fever. He was now thoroughly alarmed at the look of his affairs. Many of his fears may have been imaginary, but the burden of real trouble which he had to carry was one which might easily bring him to the ground, and, when once a man is down, the crowd has little pity or scruple in trampling him to death. He set about to review his position, and to spy out all possible sources of danger. He writes : " I called to mind all the books I had written, and, seeing that in them there were many obscure passages upon which an unfavourable meaning might be put by the malice of my enemies, I wrote to the Council, submitting all my writings to its judgment and will and pleasure. By this action I saved myself from grave danger and disgrace in the future." [2] The Council to which Cardan here refers was probably the Congregation of the Index appointed by the Council at Trent for the authoritative examination of all books before allowing them to be read by the faithful. Before the close of the Council (1563) these duties had been handed over to the Pope (Pius IV.), who published the revised and definite Roman Index in 1564.

---

[1] *De Vita Propria*, ch. xxx. p. 90.   [2] *Opera*, tom. x. p. 460.

CHAPTER XI

WHILE Cardan was lying sick at Milan, a messenger came from Pavia, begging him to hasten thither to see his infant grandson, who had been ailing when he left Pavia, and was now much worse. The journey under the burning sun of the hottest summer known for many years aggravated his malady, but he brought the child out of danger. He caught erysipelas in the face, and to this ailment succeeded severe trouble with the teeth. If it had not been for the fact that the time of the new moon had been near, he says that he must have submitted to blood-letting; but after the new moon his health mended, and thus he escaped the two-fold danger—that of the disease, and that of the lancet. He tells of an attempt made against his life by a servant for the sake of robbery, an attempt which came very near success; and of a severe attack of gout in the knee. After a month's confinement to his house he began to practise Medicine; and, finding patients in plenty, he nourished a hope that Fortune had done her worst, and that he might be allowed to repair his shattered fortunes by the exercise of his calling, but the activity of his adversaries—which may or may not have been provoked solely by malignity—was unsleeping. He hints at further attempts against his good name and his life, and gives at length some painful details of another charge made against him of an infamous character. It is almost certain that his way was made all the harder for him from the complaints which he had put in print about the indifference of the Duca di Sessa to his interests at the time of Gian Battista's trial. The Milanese doctors had no love for him, and every petulant word he might let fall would almost surely be brought to the Governor's ears. By Cardan's own admission it appears that utterances of this sort were both frequent and acrid. There was a certain physician of the city who wished to place his son gratis in Cardan's household. Cardan, however, refused, whereupon the physician in question called attention to a certain book in which Cardan had made some remarks to the effect that the friendship of the Duca di Sessa had been a fatal one to him, inasmuch as, having trusted too entirely to this friendship for his support, he had let go other interests which might have served him better. The physician aforesaid made a second application to Cardan to receive his son, offering this time to intercede with the Governor on his behalf. This proposition roused the old man's anger, and he exclaimed that he had no need of such friendship or protection; that in fact the interruption of their good understanding had come about more by his own act than the Governor's, who had been either unable or unwilling to save Gian Battista's life. The doctor replied, in the presence of divers persons, that Gian Battista had perished through his own foolishness: if he had not confessed he would never have been condemned; that the Senate had condemned him and not the Duca di Sessa, and that Cardan was now slandering this prince most unjustly. A lot of busy-bodies had by this time been attracted by the wrangle, and these heard the doctor's accusations in full, but gathered a very imperfect notion of Cardan's reply. He indignantly denied this charge, and in his own account of the scene he affirms that he won the approbation of all who listened, by the moderation of his bearing and speech.

Four days after this occurrence he again met this physician, who declared he knew for certain that a kinsman of the Duca di Sessa, a hot-tempered man, had just read some slanders written by Cardan about the Duke, and had declared he would cut the writer in half and throw his remains into the jakes; the physician went on to say that he had appeased this gentleman's resentment, and that Cardan had now no cause for fear. Cardan at once saw through the dishonesty of the fellow, who was not content with bringing forward an unjust accusation, but must likewise subject him to these calumnies and the consequent dangers. After a bout of wrangling, in which the physician sought vainly to win from him an acknowledgment of the service he had wrought, the malicious fellow shouted out to the crowd which had gathered around them that Cardan persisted in his infamous slanders against the Governor. Wanton as the charge was, Cardan felt that with his present unpopularity it might easily grow into a fatal danger. Might was right in Milan as far as he was concerned, but he determined that he must make a stand against this pestilent fellow. By good luck he met some friends, to whom he told the adventure ; and while he was speaking, the gentleman who was said to have threatened him, and the slanderous physician as well, joined the gathering ; whereupon one of Cardan's friends repeated the whole story to the gentleman ; who, as he was quite unversed in letters, was hugely diverted at hearing himself set down as a student, and told the physician that he was a fool, thereby delivering Cardan at least from this annoyance.

He had refused the terms which the party opposed to him in the Senate at Bologna had sent for his acceptance, and was still waiting to hear whether they would carry out their original propositions. It was during this time of suspense that he was subjected to strange and inexplicable treatment at the hands of the Milanese Senate, treatment which, viewed by the light of his own report—the only one extant—seems very harsh and unjust. He writes: "At the time when I was greatly angered by the action of the Bolognese agent, four of the Senators persuaded me to seek practice once more in Milan, wherefore I, having altered my plans, began to try to earn an honest living, for I reckoned that the Senate of Milan knew that I had rejected the offers from Bologna, since these offers were unjust in themselves, and put before me in unjust fashion. But afterwards, although the same iniquitous terms were offered to me, I accepted them, not indeed because I was satisfied therewith, but because of my necessity, and so that I might be free from those dangers which, as I have before stated, pressed upon me in those days. The reason why I took this step was that the Senate, by most unexpected action, removed my name from the lists of those licensed to teach ; nor was this all. They warned me by a message that they had recently given hearing to a double charge against me of very grave offences, and that nothing but my position, and the interests of the College, kept them back from laying me in hold. Nevertheless, influenced by these considerations, they had been moved to reduce my punishment to that of exile. But neither my good fortune nor God deserted me ; for on the same day certain things came to pass by means of which I was able, with a single word, to free myself from all suspicion upon either charge, and to prove my innocence.   Moreover, I forced them to admit that no mention of this affair had ever been made before the Senate, although two graduates had informed me that it had been discussed." [1]

The Senate, however, was reluctant to stultify its late action, and refused to restore Cardan's name to the list of teachers.   But he was put right in the sight of the world by the sharp censure pronounced by the Senate upon those busy-bodies who had ventured to speak in its name.   Cardan's last days in Milan were cheered with a brief gleam of good fortune.   His foes seem to have overshot the mark, and to have aroused sympathy for the old man, who, whatever his faults, was alike an honour to his country and the victim of fortune singularly cruel.   The city took him under its protection, assured of his innocence as to the widespread charges against him, and pitying his misfortunes.   His friend Borromeo had probably been forwarding his interests at the Papal Court, for he records that, just at this time, certain Cardinals and men of weight wrote to him from Rome in kindly and flattering terms.   On November 16, 1562, the messenger from the Senate of Bologna arrived at Milan, bearing an offer of slightly more liberal terms.   They were not so favourable as Cardan wished for ; but, even had they been worse, he would probably have closed with them.   In spite of the benevolent attitude of his well-wishers in Milan, it irked him to be there ; the faces in the streets, the town gossip, all tended to recall to him the death of his son, so he departed at once to take up his duties.

At Bologna Cardan went first to live in a hired house

[1] *Opera*, tom. x. p. 462.

in the Via Gombru. Aldo was nominally a member of
his household; but his presence must have been a
plague rather than a comfort to his father, and he took
with him likewise his orphan grandson, the son of Gian
Battista and Brandonia, whom he destined to make his
heir on account of Aldo's ill conduct.[1] This young
man seems to have been a hopeless scoundrel from the
first. The ratio in which fathers apportion their affection amongst their offspring is a very capricious one,
and Cardan may have been fully as wide of the mark in
chiding his younger as he was in lauding the talents
and virtues of his elder son. But it is certain that on
several occasions the authorities shared Cardan's view of
Aldo's ill behaviour. More than once he alludes to the
young reprobate's shameful conduct, and the intolerable
annoyance caused by the same. Many of the ancient
rights of parents over their children, which might to-day
be deemed excessive, were still operative in the cities
of Italy, and Cardan readily invoked the help of them
in trying to work reformation of a sort upon Aldo,
whom he caused to be imprisoned more than once, and
finally to be banished.[2] The numerous hitches which
delayed his final call to Bologna were probably due to
the fact that a certain party amongst the teachers there
were opposed to his appointment, and things did not
run too smoothly after he had taken up his residence
in his new home. It was not in Cardan's nature, however much he may have been cowed and broken down
by misfortune, to mix with men inimical to himself
without letting them have a taste of his quality. He
records one skirmish which he had with Fracantiano,

---

[1] " Sed filius minor natu adeò malè se gessit, ut malim transire
in nepotem ex primo filio."—*De Vita Propria*, ch. xxxvi. p. 112.

[2] *De Vita Propria*, ch. xxvii. p. 71.

the Professor of the Practice of Medicine, a skirmish which, in its details, resembles so closely his encounter with Branda Porro, at Pavia, some time before, that it suggests a doubt whether it ever had a separate existence, and was not simply a variant of the Branda legend. "It happened that he (Fracantiano) was giving an account of the passage of the gall into the stomach, and was speaking in Greek before the whole Academy (he was making the while an anatomical dissection), when I cried out, 'There is an "ου" wanting in that sentence.' And as he delayed making any correction of his error, and I kept on repeating my remark in a low voice, the students cried out, 'Let the *Codex* be sent for.' Fracantiano sent for it gladly. It was brought at once, and when he came to read the passage, he found that what I had affirmed was true to a hair. He spake not another word, being overwhelmed with confusion and astonishment. Moreover the students, who had almost compelled me to come to the lecture, were even more impressed by what had happened. But from that day forth my opponent avoided all meeting with me; nay, he even gave orders to his servants that they should warn him whenever they might see me approaching, and thus he contrived that we should never foregather. One day when he was teaching Anatomy, the students brought me, by a trick, into the room, whereupon he straightway fled, and having entangled his feet in his robe, he fell down headlong. This accident caused no little confusion, and shortly afterwards he left the place, being then a man well advanced in years." [1]

He had not lived long in Bologna before he was fated to experience another repetition of one of the untoward

[1] *De Vita Propria*, ch. xii. p. 40.

episodes of his past life, to wit the fall of a house. It was not his own house this time, but it was sufficiently near to induce him to change his abode without delay. Next door to the house he had hired in the Via Gombru stood a palace belonging to a certain Gramigna. " The entire house fell, and was ruined in a single night, and together with the house perished the owner thereof." It was believed that this man had divers powerful enemies, and, in order that he might secure his position, he contrived to bring certain of his foes into his house, having first made a mine of gunpowder under the portico, and set a match thereto. But for some reason or other the plot miscarried the night when he destined to carry it out. Gramigna went to see what was amiss, and at that very moment the mine exploded and brought the house to the ground. After this explosion Cardan moved to a house in the Galera quarter, belonging to the family of Ranucci ; but he did not find this dwelling perfect, as he was forced to vacate the rooms which were most to his taste on account of the bad state of the ceilings, the plaster of which, more than once, fell down upon his head.

In his *Paralipomena*, " the last fruit off an old tree," which he put together about this time, there are numerous stories of prodigies and portents ; of doors which would not close, and doors which opened of their own accord ; of rappings on the walls, and of mysterious thunderings and noises during the night. He tells, at length, the story, already referred to, of the strange thing which happened to him, on the eve of his departure from Pavia in 1562, while he was awaiting tidings from Rome as to his appointment at Bologna. " I wore on the index finger of my right hand a selenite stone set in a ring, and on my left a jacinth, which I never took off my finger, this stone being large and hexagonal in shape. I took the selenite from my finger and put it beneath my pillow, for I fancied it kept off sleep, wearing still the jacinth because it appeared to have the opposite effect. I slept until midnight, when I awoke and missed the ring from my left hand. I called Jacopo Antonio, a boy of fifteen years of age who acted as my servant and slept in a truckle bed, and bade him look for my rings. He found the selenite at once where I had placed it ; but though we both of us sought closely for the jacinth we could not find it. I was sorrowful to death on account of this omen, and despair seized upon my soul when I remembered the dire consequences of similar signs, all of which I had duly noted in my writings. I could scarcely believe this to be a thing happening in the order of nature. After a short delay I collected my thoughts, and told the servant to bring a light from the hearth. He replied that he would rather not do this, that he was afraid of the darkness, and that the fire was always extinguished in the evening. I bade him light a candle with the flint, when he told me that we had neither matches nor tinder nor sulphur. I persisted, and determined that a light should be got by one means or another, for I knew that, if I should go to sleep under so dire an omen, I must needs perish. So I ordered him to get a light as best he could. He went away and raked up the ashes, and found a bit of coal about the bigness of a cherry all alight, and caught hold of it with the tongs. At the same time I had little hope of getting a light, but he applied it to the wick of a lamp and blew thereon. The wick was lighted without any flame issuing from the live coal, which thing seemed to me a further marvel."

After a search with the candle the ring was found on

the floor under the middle of the bed, but the marvel was not yet worked out: the ring could not possibly have got into such a place unless it had been put there by hand. It could not have rolled there, on account of its shape, nor could it have fallen from the bed, because the pillow was closely joined to the head of the bed, round which ran a raised edge with no rift therein. Cardan concludes: "I know that much may be said over this matter, but nothing, forsooth, which will convince a man, ever so little inclined to superstition, that there was no boding sign manifested thereby, foretelling the ruin of my position and good name. Then, having soothed my mind, albeit I was well-nigh hopeless, I consoled myself with the belief that God still protected me." After pondering long and anxiously over the possible significance of this sign he took a more sanguine view of the future. He next put the jacinth ring on his finger and bade the boy try to pull it off, but he tried in vain, so well and closely did the ring fit the finger. From this time forth Cardan laid aside this ring, after having worn it for many years as a safeguard against lightning, plague, wakefulness, and palpitation of the heart.[1]

Many other instances of a like character might be given from the *Paralipomena ;* but the foregoing will suffice to show that the natural inclination of Cardan's temper towards the marvellous had been aggravated by his recent troubles. Also the belief that all men's hands were against him never slumbered, but for this disposition there may well have been some justification. Scarcely had he settled in Bologna before an intrigue was set in motion against him. "After the events aforesaid, and after I had gone to teach in Bologna, my adversaries,

[1] *Opera,* tom. x. p. 459.

by a trick, managed to deprive me of the use of a class-room, that is to say they allotted to me an hour just about the time of dinner, or they gave the class-room at the very same hour, or a little earlier, to another teacher. When I perceived that the authorities were unwilling to accede to three distinct propositions which I made to them, namely, that this other teacher should begin his lecture sooner and leave off sooner: or that he should teach alternately with me: I so far got my own way at the next election that the other lecturer had to do his teaching elsewhere."[1]

It would appear that the intrigues, of which Cardan gives so many instances, must have been the work of certain individuals, jealous of his fame and perhaps smarting under some caustic speech or downright insult, rather than of the authorities; the Senate of Bologna showed no hostility to him, but on the other hand procured for him the privileges of citizenship. While the negotiations were going on at Bologna for the further regulation of his position as a teacher, he tells a strange story how, on three or four different occasions, certain men came to him by night, in the name of the Senate and of the Judicial officers, and tried to induce him to recommend that a certain woman, who had been condemned for blasphemy, and for poisoning or witchcraft as well, should be pardoned, both by the temporal and spiritual authorities, bringing forward specially the argument that, in the sight of philosophers, such things as demons and spirits did not exist. They likewise urged him to procure the release from prison of another woman, who had not yet been condemned, because a certain sick man had died under the hands of some other doctors. They brought also a lot of nativities for him to read, as

[1] *De Vita Propria*, ch. xvii. p. 56.

if he had been a soothsayer, and not a teacher of medicine, but he would have nothing to say to them.[1]

It is somewhat strange that Cardan should have detected no trace of the snare of the enemy in this manœuvre. Bearing in mind the character of the request made, and the fact that Cardan was by no means a *persona grata* to the petitioners, it seems highly probable that they might have been more anxious to draw from Cardan a profession of his disbelief in witch-craft, than to procure the enlargement of the accused persons whose cause they had nominally espoused. At this period it was indeed dangerous to be a wizard, but it was perhaps still more dangerous to pose as an avowed sceptic of witchcraft. At the end of the fifteenth century the frequency of executions for sorcery in the north of Italy had provoked a strong outburst of popular feeling against this wanton bloodshed ; but Spina, writing in the interest of orthodox religion, deplores that disbelief in the powers of Evil and their manifestations, always recognized by the Church, should have led men on to profess by their action any doubt as to the truth of witchcraft. But in spite of the fulminations of men of this sort, from this time onwards the more enlightened scholars of Europe began to modify their opinions on the subject of demoniac possession, and of witchcraft in general. The first book in which the new views were enunciated was the treatise *De Præstigiis Dæmonum*, by Johann Wier, a physician of Cleves, published in 1563. The step in advance taken by this reformer was not a revolutionary one. He simply denied that witches were willing and conscious instruments of the malefic powers, asserting that what evil they wrought came about by reason of the delusions with which the evil

---

[1] *De Vita Propria*, ch. xxiii. p. 104.

P

spirits infected the persons said to be possessed.   The
devil afflicted his victims directly, and then threw
the suspicion of the evil deed upon some old woman.
Wier's book was condemned and denounced by the
clergy—he himself was a Protestant—but the most
serious counterblast against it came from the pen of
Jean Bodin, the illustrious French philosopher and jurist.
He held up Wier to execration as an impious blasphemer,
and asserted that the welfare of Christendom must needs
suffer great injury through the dissemination of doctrines
so detestable as those set forth in his book.[1]

Seeing that such a spirit was dominant in the minds
of men like Bodin, it will be evident that a charge of
impiety or atheism might well follow a profession of
disbelief, or even scepticism, as to the powers of witches
or of evil spirits.   A maxim familiar as an utterance of
Sir Thomas Browne, " Ubi tres medici duo athei," was,
no doubt, in common use in Cardan's time; and he, as a
doctor, would consequently be ill-looked upon by the
champions of orthodoxy, who would certainly not be
conciliated by the fact that he was the friend of Cardinal
Morone.   This learned and enlightened prelate had
been imprisoned by the savage and fanatical Paul IV.,
on a charge of favouring opinions analogous to Pro-
testantism, but Pius IV., the easy-going Milanese jurisconsult, turned ecclesiastic, enlarged him by one of the
first acts of his Papacy, and restored him to the charge
of the diocese of Modena.

Besides enjoying at Bologna the patronage of princes
of the Church like Borromeo and Morone, Cardan found

[1] This opinion prevailed with men of learning far into the next
century. Sir Thomas Browne writes : " They that doubt of these, do
not only deny them, but spirits ; and are obliquely and upon consequence a sect not of infidels, but atheists."—*Religio Medici*, *Works*,
vol. ii. p. 89.

there an old friend in Ludovico Ferrari, who was at this time lecturing on mathematics. He also received into his house a new pupil, a Bolognese youth named Rodolfo Sylvestro, who was destined hereafter to bring as great credit to his teacher's name in Medicine as Ferrari had already brought thereto in Mathematics. Rodolfo proved to be one of the most faithful and devoted of friends; he remained at Bologna as long as Cardan continued to live there, sharing his master's ill-fortune, and ultimately accompanied him to Rome in 1571. He gives the names of two other Bolognese students, Giulio Pozzo and Camillo Zanolino, but of all his surviving pupils he rates Sylvestro as the most gifted.

The records of Cardan's life at this period are scant and fragmentary, few events being chronicled except dreams and portents. In giving an account of one of these manifestations, which happened in September 1563, he incidentally lets light upon certain changes and vicissitudes in his own affairs. He was at this time living in an apartment in the house of the Ranucci, next door to a half-ruined palace of the Ghislieri. One night he awoke from sleep, and found that the neck-band of his shirt had become entangled with the cord by which he kept his precious emerald and a written charm suspended round his neck. He tried to disentangle the knot, but in vain, so he left the complication as it was, purposing to unravel it by daylight. He did not fall asleep; but, after lying quiet for a little, he determined to attempt once more whether he could undo the knot, when he found that everything was clear, and the stone under his armpit. "This sign showed me an unhoped-for solution of certain weighty difficulties, and at the same time proved, as I have often said elsewhere, that there must have been present something else unperceived by me. For my affairs were in this condition: my son-in-law at Milan had the administration of the scant remains of my property, and I received no rents therefrom for a whole year. My literary work was lying at the printer's, but it was not printed. Here, at Bologna, I was forced to lecture without having a fixed hour assigned to me. A crowd of enemies were intriguing against me. My son Aldo was in prison, and of little profit to me. But immediately after this portent I learned that my two chief opponents were either dying or about to retire. The question of the lecture-room was settled amicably, so that for the next year I was able to live in quiet. These two matters having come to an issue, I will next describe what came to pass with regard to the others.

"During the next July (1564), through the help of Francesco Alciati,[1] the secretary of Pope Pius IV., a man to whom I am indebted for almost every benefit I have received since 1561, I began to enjoy my own again. On August 26 I received from the printer my books all printed with the greatest care, and by reason of the dispatch of this business my income was greatly increased. The next day my chief opponent resigned his office, and left vacant a salary of seven hundred gold crowns. The only manifestation of adverse fortune left to trouble me was the conspiracy of the doctors against me, but there were already signs that this would disappear before long, and in sooth it came to an end after the lapse of another year."[2]

During this portion of his life at Bologna, Cardan seems to have lived comparatively alone, and to have

---

[1] This was the Cardinal, the nephew of Andrea the great jurist, who was also a good friend of Cardan.

[2] *Opera*, tom. x. p. 463.

spent his weary leisure in brooding over his sorrows.
He began his long rambling epilogue to the *De Libris
Propriis*, and, almost on the threshold, pours out his
sorrow afresh over Gian Battista's unhappy fate. After
affirming that Death must necessarily come as a friend
to those whose lives are wretched, he begins to speculate
whether, after all, he ought not to rejoice rather than
mourn over his son's death. "Certes he is rid of this
miserable life of danger and difficulty, vain, sorrowful,
brief, and inconstant; these times in which the major
part of the good things of the world fall to the trickster's
share, and all may be enjoyed by those who are backed
up by wealth or power or favour. Power is good when
it is in the hands of those who use it well, but it is a
great evil when murderers and poisoners are allowed to
wield it. To the ill-starred, to the ungodly, and to the
foolish, death is a boon, freeing them from numberless
dangers, from heavy griefs, from fatal troubles, and from
infamy; wherefore in such cases it ought not to be
spoken of as something merely good or indifferent, but
rated as the best of fortune. Shall I not declare to God
(for He willed the deed), to myself, and to my surviving
family, that my son's death was a thing to be desired,
for God does all justly, wisely, and lovingly? He lets
me stand as an example to show others that a good and
upright man cannot be altogether wretched. I am poor,
infirm, and old; bereaved by a cruel wrong of my best-
loved son, a youth of the fairest promise, and left only
with the faintest hope of any ray of future good fortune,
or of seeing my race perpetuated after my death, for my
daughter, who has been nine years married, is barren.

"At one time I was prosperous in every relation of
life: in my friendships, in my children, and in my health
In my youth I seemed to be one raised up to realize the

highest hopes. I was accustomed to all the good things —nay, to all the luxuries of life. Now I am wretched, despised, with foes swarming around me; I not only count myself miserable, I feel I am far more miserable now than I was happy aforetime. Yet I neither lose my wits nor make any boast, as my actions prove. I do my work as a teacher with my mind closely set on the matter in question, and for this reason I attract a large number of hearers. I manage my affairs better than heretofore; and, if .any man shall compare the book which I have lately published with those which I wrote some time ago, he will not fail to perceive how vastly my intellect has gained in richness, in vivacity, and in purity."

Though the note of sorrow or even of despair is perceptible in these sentences, there is no sign that the virile and elastic spirit of the writer is broken. But there are manifest signs of an increasing tendency towards mental detachment from the world which had used him so ill. With the happiest of men the almost certain prospect of extinction at the end of a dozen years usually tends to foster the growth of a conviction that the world after all is a poor affair, and that to quit it is no great evil. How strongly therefore must reflections of a kindred nature have worked upon a man so cruelly tried as Cardan!

CHAPTER XII

AT the beginning of the year 1565 Cardan had a
narrow escape from death by burning, for his bed from
some unknown cause caught fire twice in the same night
while he was asleep. The servant was disturbed by the
smoke, and having aroused his master, told him what
was amiss, whereupon Cardan flew into a violent rage,
for he deemed that the youth must be drunk. But he
soon perceived the danger, and then they both set to
work to extinguish the flames. His own description of
the occurrence is highly characteristic. " Having put
out the fire, I settled myself again to sleep, and, while I
was dreaming of alarms, and that I was flying from
some danger, it happened that either these terrifying
dreams, or the fire and smoke again aroused me, and,
looking around, I found that the bed was once more
alight, and the greater part of it consumed. The vari-
coloured coverlet, the leather hangings, and all the
covering of the bed was unhurt. Thus this great alarm
and danger and serious disturbance caused only a trifling
loss; less than half of the bed-linen was burnt, but the
blankets were entirely consumed. On the first alarm
the flames burnt out twice or thrice with little smoke,
and caused scarcely any damage. The second time the
fire and the mishap forced me to rise just before dawn,
the fire lasting altogether about seven hours."

There was naturally a warning sign to be found in this accident.[1] The smoke, Cardan said, denoted disgrace; the fire, peril and fear; the flame, a grave and pressing danger to his life. The smouldering fire signified secret plots which were to be put into execution against him by his servants while he lay in bed. And the fact that he set fire to the bed himself, denoted that he would be able to meet any coming danger alone and without assistance. The indictment against him was foreshadowed by the fire and the flames and the smoke. Poison and assault were not to be feared. Men might indeed ask questions as to what kind of danger it could be which only arose from those about him, and fell short of poison and violence. The fire, he goes on to say, signifies the Magistrate. More than once it seemed to be extinct, but it always revived. Danger seemed to threaten him less from open hostility than from the cunning flattery of foes, and from over-confidence on his own part. His books, which he had lately caused to be printed, appeared to be in grave peril, but a graver one overhung his life. He deemed that he would quit the tribunal condemned by the empty scandal of the crowd, suffering no slight loss, and worsted chiefly through putting faith in false friends, and through his own instability. On the whole, the loss would prove inconsiderable; the danger moderate, but the vexation exceedingly heavy. These results might have sprung from causes other than natural ones; but, on the other hand, such things often come about through chance. They might prove to be a warning to him to keep clear

---

[1] He mentions this matter briefly in the *De Vita Propria* : "Bis arsisset lectus, prædixi me non permansurum Bononiæ, et prima vice restiti, secunda non potui."—ch. xli. p. 151. A fuller account of it is in *Opera*, tom. x. p. 464.

of hostile prejudice, and to make friends of those in authority, care being taken not to let himself become involved in their private affairs, and not to seek too close an acquaintance.[1]

Up to this date, Cardan, when he visited his patients, had either walked or ridden a mule. In 1562 he began to use a carriage, but this change of habit brought ill ·luck with it, for, in this same year, his horses ran away; he was thrown out of the vehicle, and sustained an injury to one of the fingers of his right hand, and to the right arm as well.[2] The finger soon healed, but the damage to the right arm shifted itself over to the left side, leaving the right arm sound. The foregoing details, taken chiefly from the *Paralipomena* (Book III. ch. xii.), are somewhat significant in respect to the serious trouble which came upon him soon afterwards.

Though he had now secured a class-room for himself, the malice of his enemies was not yet abated. Just before the end of his term, certain of them went to Cardinal Morone and told him that it would be inexpedient to allow Cardan to retain his Professorship any longer, seeing that scarcely any pupils went to listen to him. The terms Cardan used in describing this hostile movement against him,[3] rouse a suspicion that there may

---

[1] *Opera*, tom. x. p. 464.

[2] *De Vita Propria*, ch. xxx. p. 80. He seems to have had many untoward experiences in driving. He tells of another mishap (*Opera*, tom. i. p. 472) in June 1570; how a fellow, some tipstaff of the courts, jumped into his carriage and frightened the mares Cardan was driving, jeering at them likewise because they were rather bare of flesh.

[3] " Demum sub conductionis fine, voces sparserunt, et maxime apud Moronum Cardinalem, me exiguo auditorio profiteri, quod quanquam non omnino verum esset, quinimo ab initio Academiæ multos, et usque ad dies jejunii haberem auditores."—*De Vita Propria*, ch. xvii. p. 56.

have been some ground for the assertion of his adversaries; but he declares that, at any rate, he had a
good many pupils from the beginning of the session up
to the time of Lent. He gives no clue whereby the
date of this intrigue may be exactly ascertained, but it
probably happened near the end of his sojourn at
Bologna, because in his account of it he describes likewise the cessation of his public teaching, and makes no
mention of any resumption of the same. He declares that
he was at last overborne by the multitude of his foes, and
their cunning plots. Under the pretence that, in seeking
Cardan's removal, they were really acting for his benefit,
they succeeded in bringing Cardinal Morone round to
their views. Cardan's final words in dealing with this
matter help to fix the date of this episode as some time
in 1570. Speaking of his enemies, he writes: "Nay
indeed they have given me greater leisure for the codifi-
cation of my books, they have lengthened my days, they
have increased my fame, and, by procuring my removal
from the work which was too laborious for me, they
secured for me the pleasure I now enjoy in the discovery
and investigation of divers of the secrets of Nature.
Therefore I constantly tell myself that I do not hate
these men, nor deem them blameworthy, because they
wrought me an ill turn, but because of the malignancy
they had in their hearts."[1]

It is almost certain that this removal of Cardan from
his office of teacher was part and parcel of a carefully-
devised plot against him, and a prelude to more serious
trouble in the near future. Early in April 1570 he had
occasion to put into writing a certain medical opinion
which was to be sent to Cardinal Morone. He describes
the episode: "It chanced that one of the sheets of my

[1] *De Vita Propria*, ch. xvii. p. 57.

manuscript fell from the table down upon the floor, and then flew by itself up to the cornice of the room, where it hung, fixed to the woodwork. Greatly amazed, I called for Rodolfo, and pointed out to him this marvel. He did not indeed see it fly up, and at that time I was ignorant as to what it might foretell, for I had no foreboding of the many ills which were about to molest me. But now I see that the meaning of this portent must have been that, after the approaching shipwreck of my fortunes, my bark would be sped along with a more favouring breeze. It was during the month following, unless I am mistaken, that, when I was once more writing a letter to Cardinal Morone, I looked for a certain powder-box which had been missing for some long time, and, when I lifted up a sheet of paper in order to powder it with dust gathered up from the floor of the room, there was the powder-box, hidden beneath the sheet. How could it have come there on the level writing-desk? This sign confirmed the hope I had already conceived of the Cardinal's wisdom and humanity; that he would plead with the Pope, the best of men, in such wise that I should find a prosperous end to my toilsome life." [1]

The blow thus foreshadowed fell on October 6, 1570, when he was suddenly arrested and put under restraint. He speaks of a bond which he gave for eighteen hundred gold crowns; and says that, while he was in hold, all his estate was administered by the civil authorities. Rodolfo Sylvestro was constantly with him during his incarceration, and on January 1, 1571, he was released, just at nightfall, and allowed to return to his own house. While he was in prison in the month of October some mysterious knockings at the door supplied him with a

[1] *De Vita Propria*, ch. xliii. p. 163.

fulfilment and explanation of the portents lately chronicled. The knockings appeared furthermore to warn him of approaching death, and he began to bewail his misery; but, having gathered courage, he heartened himself to face his doom, which could be nothing worse than death. Young men, leaders of armies, courted death in battle to win the favour of their sovereigns; wherefore he, a decrepit old man, might surely await his end with calmness. He then wanders off into a long disquisition on the philosophy of Polybius, and forgets entirely to set down further details of his imprisonment, or to explain the cause thereof.

Pius IV. had died at the end of 1565, and had been succeeded by Michele Ghislieri, the Cardinal of Alessandria, as Pius V. Like his predecessor, the new Pope was a Milanese by birth, but in character and aims the two Popes were entirely different. Pius. V. identified himself completely with the work of the Holy Office, and straightway set in operation all its powers for the extirpation of the heretical opinions which, on account of the easy-going character of the late Pope, had made much progress in Italy, and nowhere more than in Bologna. Von Ranke, in the *History of the Popes*, gives an extract (vol. i. p. 97) from the compendium of the Inquisitors, which sets forth that "Bologna was in a very perilous state, because there the heretics were especially numerous; amongst them was a certain Gian Battista Rotto, who enjoyed the friendship and support of many persons of weight, such as Morone, Pole, and the Marchesa Pescara (Vittoria Colonna). Rotto made himself very active in collecting money, which he distributed amongst the poor folk of Bologna who were heretics."

It will be remembered that in 1562, while he was

waiting in Milan for the appointment as Professor at Bologna, Cardan submitted his books to the Congregation of the Index for approval. He was known to be a fellow-citizen and friend of the reigning Pope: the *corpus* of his work had by that time reached a portentous size, wherefore it is quite possible that the official readers may have been lenient, or cursory, over their work; but when Pius V., the strenuous ascetic foe of heresy, stepped into the place of the indolent Pius IV., jurist and politician rather than Churchman, it is more than probable that certain amateur inquisitors at Bologna, fully as anxious to work Cardan's ruin as to safeguard the faith, may have busied themselves in hunting through his various works for passages upon which to base a charge of unorthodoxy. Such passages were not hard to find. There was the horoscope of Jesus Christ, which subsequently affronted the piety of De Thou. There was the passage already noticed in which he said such hard things of the Dominicans (*De Varietate Rerum*, 1557, p. 572). He had indeed disclaimed it, but there it stood unexpunged in the subsequent editions of the book; and, while considering this detail, it may be remarked that Pius V. began his career as a member of the Dominican Order, the practices of which Cardan had impugned. In the first and second editions of the *De Subtilitate* was another passage in which the tenets of Islam and the circumstances of the birth of Christ were handled in a way which caused grave scandal and offence.[1]

---

[1] "Alii multis diebus abstinent cibo, alii igne uruntur, ac ferro secantur, nullum doloris vestigium preferentes; multi sunt vocem e pectore mittentes, qui olim engastrimuthi dicebantur; hoc autem maxime eis contingit cum orgia quædam exercent, atque circumferuntur in orbem. Quæ tria ut verissima sunt et naturali ratione mira tamen constant, cujus superius mentionem fecimus, ita illud confictum nasci pueros e mulieribus absque concubitu."—*De Subtilitate*, p. 353.

This passage indeed was expunged in the edition of 1560. The *Paralipomena* were not in print and available, but what can be read in them to-day doubtless reflects with accuracy the attitude of Cardan's mind towards religious matters in 1570. Though the *Paralipomena* were locked in his desk, it is almost certain that the spirit with which they were inspired would have infected Cardan's brain, and prompted him to repeat in words the views on religion and a future state which he had already put on paper, for he rarely let discretion interfere with the enunciation of any opinion he favoured. In the *Paralipomena* are many passages written in the spirit of universalism, and treating of the divine principle as something which animates wise men alone, wise men and philosophers of every age and every clime, Aristotle being the head and chief. Plato and Socrates and the Seven Sages adorn this illustrious circle, which includes likewise the philosophers of Chaldea and Egypt. Opinions like these were no longer the passport to Papal favour or even toleration. The age of the humanist Popes was past, and the Puritan movement, stimulated into life by the active competition of the Reformers, was beginning to show its strength, so that a man who spoke in terms of respect or reverence concerning Averroes or Plato would put himself in no light peril. Thus for those of Cardan's enemies who were minded to search and listen it must have been an easy task to formulate against him a charge of heresy, specious enough to carry conviction to such a burning zealot as Pius V. This Pope, in his new regulations for the maintenance of Church discipline, requisitioned the services of physicians in the detection of laxity of religious practices, or of unsoundness. "We forbid," he says in one of his bulls, "every physician, who may be.

called to the bedside of a patient, to visit for more than three days, unless he receives an attestation that the sick man has made fresh confession of his sins."[1] Cardan, with his irritable temper, may very likely have treated this regulation as an unwarrantable interference with his profession, and have paid no attention to it. Again, he evidently followed Hippocrates in rejecting the supernatural origin of disease ; a position greatly in advance of that held by certain of the leading physiologists of the time.[2] Thus in more ways than one he may have laid himself open to some charge of disrespect shown to religion or to the spiritual powers. The absence of any other specific accusation and the circumstances of his incarceration, taken in conjunction with the foregoing considerations, almost compel the conclusion that his arrest and imprisonment in 1570 were brought about by a charge of impiety whispered by some envious tongue which will never now be identified. The sanction given by the authorities of the Church to his writings in 1562, operated without doubt to mitigate the punishment which fell upon him, and suffered him, after due purgation of his offences, to enjoy for the residue of his days a life comparatively quiet and prosperous under the patronage of Pius V.

Though he was let out of prison he was not yet a free man. For some twelve weeks longer he remained a prisoner in his own house, the bond for eighteen hundred gold crowns having doubtless been given on this account. Almost his last reflection about his life at Bologna is one in which he records his satisfaction that all the men who plotted against him there met their death soon

---

[1] Ranke, *History of the Popes*, vol. i. p. 246.

[2] Mr. Stephen Paget in his life of Ambroise Paré, the great contemporary French surgeon, gives an interesting account of Paré's beliefs on the divine cause of the plague, p. 269.

after their attempt, thus sharing the fate of his enemies at Milan and Pavia. If he is to be believed in this matter, the Fates, though they might not shield him from attack, proved themselves to be diligent and remorseless avengers of his wrongs. At the end of September he turned his back upon Bologna and the cold hospitality it had given him, and set forth on his last journey. He travelled by easy stages, and entered Rome on October 7, 1571, the day upon which Don John of Austria annihilated the Turkish fleet at Lepanto.

There are evidences in his later writings beyond those already cited, that Cardan's views on religion had undergone change during his sojourn at Bologna. It was the custom, even with theologians of the time, to illustrate freely from the classics, wherefore the spectacle of the names of the great men of Greek and Roman letters, scattered thickly about the pages of any book, would not prove or even suggest unorthodoxy. Cardan quotes Plato or Aristotle or Plotinus twenty times for any saint in the Calendar. He does not mention the Virgin more than once or twice in the whole of the *De Vita Propria ;* and, in discoursing on the immortality of the soul, he cites the opinion of Avicenna, but makes no mention of either saint or father.[1] The world of classic thought was immeasurably nearer and more real to Cardan than it can be to any modern dweller beyond the Alps : to him there had been no solution of continuity between classic times and his own. When he sat down to write in the *Theonoston* his meditations on the death of his son, in the vain hope of reaping consolation therefrom, he invoked the golden rule of Plotinus, which lays down that the future is foreseen and arranged by the gods. Being thus arranged, it must needs be just, for God is the

[1] *De Vita Propria,* ch. xxii. p. 63.

highest expression of justice. Against a fate thus settled for us we have no right to complain, lest we should seem to be setting ourselves into opposition to God's will. Here, although he writes in the spirit of a Christian, the authority cited is that of a heathen philosopher, and the form of his meditations is taken rather from Seneca than from father or schoolman. The devotional bias of Cardan's nature seems to have been strengthened temporarily by the terrible experiences of Gian Battista's trial and death; but in the course of his residence at Bologna a marked reaction set in, and the fervent religious outburst, in which he sought consolation during his intolerable sorrow, was succeeded by a calmer mood which regarded the necessary evils of life as transitory accidents, and death as the one and certain end of sorrow, and perhaps of consciousness as well. What he wrote during his residence in Rome he kept in manuscript; his recent experience at Bologna warned him that, living under the shadow of the Vatican with Pius V. as the ruler thereof, it behoved him to walk as an obedient son of the Church.

Cardan went first to live in the Piazza di San Girolamo, not far from the Porto del Popolo, but subsequently he lived in a house in the Via Giulia near the church of Santa Maria di Monserrato, where probably he died. He had not long been settled in Rome before he was able to add a fresh supernatural experience to his already overburdened list. In the month of August 1572 he was lying awake one night with a lamp burning, when suddenly he heard a loud noise to the right of the chamber, as if a cart laden with planks was being unloaded. He looked up, and, the door being open at the time, he perceived a peasant

Q

entering the room. Just as he was on the threshold
the intruder uttered the words, "*Te sin casa*," and
straightway vanished. This apparition puzzled him
greatly, and he alludes to it again in chapter xlvii.
of the *De Vita Propria*. Ultimately he dismisses it
with the remark that the explanation of such phenomena is rather the duty of theologians than of philosophers.

With regard to matters of religious belief he seems
to have taken as a rule of conduct the remark above
written, and left them to the care of professional
experts, for very few of his recorded opinions throw
any light upon his views of the dogmas and doctrines
of the Church. Whatever the tenor of these opinions
may have been, he never proclaimed them definitely.
Probably they interested him little, for he was not
the man to keep silent over a subject which he had
greatly at heart. He gave a general assent to the
teaching of the Church, taking up the mental attitude
of the vast majority of the learned men of his time, and
expected that the Church would do all that was necessary for him in its own particular province. If he regarded
Erasmus and Luther as disturbers of the faith and heretics,
he did not say so, nor did he censure their activity.
(Erasmus he praises highly in the opening words of the
horoscope which he drew for him.—*Gen. Ex.*, p. 496.) But
he had certainly no desire to emulate them or give them
his support. The world of letters and science was wide
enough even for his active spirit; the world lying behind
the veil he left to the exploration of those inquirers who
might have a taste for such a venture. Still every page
of his life's record shows how strong was his bent towards
the supernatural; but the phase of the supernatural which
he chose for study was one which Churchmen, as a rule,

had let alone. Spirits wandering about this world were of greater moment to him than spirits fixed in beatitude or bane in the next; and accordingly, whenever he finds an opportunity, he discourses of apparitions, lamiæ, incubi, succubi, malignant and beneficent genii, and the methods of invoking them. Now that old age was pressing heavily upon him and he began to yearn for support, he sought consolation not in the ecstatic vision of the fervent Catholic, but in fostering the belief that he was in sooth under the protection of some guardian spirit like that which had attended his father and divers of the sages of old. Although he had in his earlier days treated his father's belief with a certain degree of respect and credence,[1] there is no evidence that he was possessed with the notion that any such supernatural guardian attended his own footsteps at the time when he put together the *De Varietate;* indeed it would seem that his belief was exactly the opposite. He writes as follows: "It is first of all necessary to know that there is one God, the Author of all good, by whose power all things were made, and in whose name all good things are brought to pass ; also, that if a man shall err he need not be guilty of sin. That there is no other to whom we owe anything or whom we are bound to worship or serve. If we keep these sayings with a pure mind we shall be kept pure ourselves and free from sin. What a demon may be I know not, these beings I neither recognize nor love. I worship one God, and Him alone I serve. And in truth these things ought not to be published in the hearing of unlearned folk ; for, if once this belief in spirits be taken up, it may easily come to pass that they who apply themselves to such arts will attribute

---

[1] " Multa de dæmonibus narrabat, quæ quam vera essent nescio." —*De Utilitate*, p. 348.

God's work to the devil."[1]   And in another place : " I
of a truth know of no spirit or genius which attends
me ; but should one come to me, after being warned
of the same in dreams, if it should be given to me by
God, I will still reverence God alone ; to Him alone will
I give thanks, for any benefit which may befall me, as
the bountiful source and principle of all good.   And, in
sooth, the spirit may rest untroubled if I repay my debt
to our common Master.   I know full well that He has
given to me, for my good genius, reason, patience in
trouble, a good disposition, a disregard of money and
dignities, which gifts I use to the full, and deem them
better and greater possessions than the Demon of
Socrates."[2]

About the Demon of Socrates Cardan has much to
say in the *De Varietate*.   He never even hints a doubt
as to the veracity and sincerity of Socrates.   He is quite
sure that Socrates was fully persuaded of the reality of
his attendant genius, and favours the view that this belief
may have been well founded.   He takes an agnostic
position,[3] confining his positive statement to an assertion of his own inability to realize the presence of
any ghostly minister attendant upon himself.   In the
De Subtilitate he tells an experience of his own by way
of suggesting that some of the demons spoken of by the
retailers of marvels might be figments of the brain.
In 1550 Cardan was called in to see a certain woman
who had long been troubled with an obscure disease of
the bladder.   Every known remedy was tried in vain,

[1] *De Varietate*, p. 351.
[2] *Ibid.*, p. 658.
[3] In his counsel to his children, he writes : " Do not believe that
you hear demons speak to you, or that you behold the dead.   Seek
not to learn the truth of these things, for they are amongst the things
which are hidden from us."

when one day a certain Josephus Niger,[1] a distinguished
Greek scholar, went to see the patient. Niger, according
to Cardan's account, was quite ignorant of medicine, but
he was reputed to be a skilled master of magic arts. The
woman had a son, a boy about ten years old, and Josephus
having handed him a three-cornered crystal, which he
had with him, bade the youth secretly to look into it,
and then declare, in his mother's hearing, that he could
see in the crystal three very terrible demons going on
foot. Then, after Josephus had whispered certain other
words in the boy's ear, the boy went on to say that he
beheld another demon, vastly bigger than the first,
riding on horseback and bearing in his hand a three-
tined fork. This monster overthrew the other demons,
and led them away captive, bound with chains to his
saddlebow. After listening to these words the woman
rapidly got well, and Cardan, in commenting on the
event, declares that she must have been cured either by
the agency of the demons or by the force of the imagination, inasmuch as it would be difficult, if not impossible,
to invent any other reason of her recovery.[2] In another
passage of the *De Subtilitate* he displays judicious reserve
in writing of Demons in general.[3]

During those terrible days, when his son had just died
a felon's death, and when he himself was haunted by the
real dangers which beset him, and almost maddened by
the signs and tokens which seemed to tell of others to
come, the belief which Fazio his father had nourished

---

[1] Cardan alludes to Niger in *De Varietate*, p. 641: "Referebat
aliquando Josephus Niger harum rerum maximé peritus, dæmonem
pueris se sub forma Christi ostendisse, petiisseque ut adoraretur."

[2] *De Subtilitate*, p. 530.

[3] " Nolim ego ad trutinam hæc sectari, velut Porphyrius, Psellus,
Plotinus, Proclus, Jamblicus, qui copiose de his quæ non videre,
velut historiam natæ rei scripserunt."—*De Subtilitate*, p. 540.

easily found a lodgment in his shaken and bewildered brain. In the *Dialogus de Humanis Consiliis*, one of the speakers tells of a certain man who is clearly meant to be Cardan himself. The speaker goes on to say that he is sure this man is attended by a genius, which manifested itself to him somewhat late in his life. "Aforetime, indeed, it had been wont to convey to him warnings in dreams and by certain noises. What greater proof of his power could there be than the cure of this man, without the use of drugs, of an intestinal rupture on the right side? If indeed it had not fared with him thus, after his son's death, he would at once have passed out of this life, whereby many and great evils might have come to pass. He was freed also from another troublesome ailment. In sooth, so many and so mighty are the wonderful things which had befallen him, that I, who am very intimate with him (and he himself thinks the same), am constrained to believe that he is attended by a genius, great and powerful and rare, and that he is not the master of his own actions. What he would have, he has not; and what he has, he would not have chosen, or even wished for. This thing causes him much trouble, but he submits when he reflects that all things are God's handiwork." The speaker ends by saying that he never heard of any others thus attended, save this man, and his father before him, and Socrates.[1]

But it is in chapter xlvii. of the *De Vita Propria*, which must have been written shortly before his death, that he lets the reader see most plainly how strong was the hold which this belief in a guardian spirit of his own had taken upon him. "It is an admitted truth," he writes, "that attendant spirits have protected certain men, to wit, Socrates, Plotinus, Synesius, Dion, Flavius

[1] *Opera*, tom. i. 672.

Josephus, and myself. All of these have enjoyed prosperous lives except Socrates and me, and I, as I have said before, was at one time offered many and favourable opportunities for the achievement of happiness. But C. Cæsar the dictator, Cicero, Antony, Brutus, and Cassius were also attended by mighty spirits, albeit malignant. For a long time I have been persuaded that I too had one, but by what method it gave me intelligence as to events about to happen, I could not exactly ascertain until I reached the seventy-fourth year of my age, the season when I began to write this record of my life. I now perceive that when I was in Milan in 1557, when my genius perceived what was hanging over me—how that my son on that same evening had promised to marry Brandonia Seroni, and that he would complete the nuptials the following day—it produced in me that palpitation of the heart of which I have already made mention, a weakness known to my genius alone, a manifestation which served to simulate a trembling of the bed."

Cardan writes at length to show that the mysterious knocking which he and Rodolfo Sylvestro had heard during his imprisonment at Bologna, the peasant who entered his bed-chamber saying "*Te sin casa,*" and divers other manifestations, going back as far as 1531 —croaking of ravens, barking of dogs, and the ignition of fire-wood—must all have been brought about by the working of this powerful spirit. In 1570 there happened to him one of his everyday experiences of the presence of supernatural powers. In the middle of the night he was conscious of some presence walking about the room. It sat down beside him, and at the same time a loud noise arose from a chest which stood near. This phenomenon, he admits, might well have been the figment of a brain overburdened with thought ; but suddenly his memory flies back to an experience of his twentieth year, upon which he proceeds to build a story, wild and fanciful even for his powers of imagination. " What man was it," he asks, " who sold me that copy of Apuleius when I was in my twentieth year, and forthwith went away ? I indeed, at that time, had made only one essay in the literary arena, and had no knowledge of the Latin tongue; but in spite of this, and because the book had a gilded cover, I was imprudent enough to buy it. The very next day I found myself just as well versed in Latin as I am now. Moreover, almost at the same time I acquired knowledge of Greek and Spanish and French, sufficient for reading books written in these languages."

Cardan was by this time completely possessed by the belief in his attendant genius, and the flash of memory which recalled the purchase of some book or other in his youth, suggested likewise the attribution of certain mystic powers to this guardian genius, and conjured up some fanciful explanation as to the way these powers had been exercised upon himself; he, the person most closely concerned, being entirely unconscious of their operation at the time when they first affected him. This recorded belief in a gift of tongues is one of the most convincing bits of evidence to be gleaned from Cardan's writings of the insanity which undoubtedly afflicted him, at least periodically, at this crisis of his life.

CHAPTER XIII

AFTER the accusation brought against him at Milan in 1562, Cardan had been prohibited from teaching or lecturing in that city, and similar disabilities had followed his recent imprisonment at Bologna. At Rome no duties of this kind awaited him, so he had full time to follow his physician's calling after taking up his residence there. He records the cure of a noble matron, Clementina Massa, and of Cesare Buontempo, a jurisconsult, both of whom had been suffering for nearly two years. The circumstances of his retirement from Bologna would not affect his reputation as a physician, and he seems to have had in Rome as many or even more patients than he cared to treat ; and in writing in general terms concerning his successes as a healer, he says : " In all, I restored to health more than a hundred patients, given up as incurable in Milan, in Bologna, and in Rome." Of all the friends Cardan had in this closing period of his life, none was more useful or benevolent than Cardinal Alciati, who, although he had been secretary to Pius IV., contrived to retain the favour of his successor. This piece of good fortune Alciati owed to the protection of Carlo Borromeo, who had been his pupil at Pavia, and had procured for him from Pius IV. a bishopric, a cardinal's hat, and the secretaryship of Dataria. Another of Cardan's powerful friends was the Prince of Matellica,

of whom he speaks in terms of praise inflated enough
to be ridiculous, were it not for the accompanying note
of pathos. After celebrating the almost divine character of this nobleman, his munificence and his superhuman abilities, he goes on: "What could there be in
me to win the kindly notice of such a patron? Certainly
I had done him no service, nor could he hope I should
ever do him any in the future, I, an old man, an outcast
of fortune, and prostrated by calamity. In sooth, there
was naught about me to attract him; if indeed he found
any merit in me, it must have been my uprightness."

Powerful friends are never superfluous, and Cardan
seems to have needed them in Rome as much as in
Bologna. In 1573 he again hints at plots against his
life, but almost immediately after recording his suspicions
he goes on to suggest that his danger had arisen chiefly
from his ignorance of the streets of Rome, and from the
uncouth manners of the populace. "Many physicians,
more cautious than myself, and better versed in the
customs of the place, have come by their death from
similar cause." The danger, whatever its nature, seems
to have threatened him as a member of the practising
faculty at Rome rather than as the persecuted ex-teacher
of Pavia and Bologna. Rodolfo Sylvestro was not
the only one of his former associates near him in his
old age, for he notes that Simone Sosia, who had been
his *famulus* at Pavia in 1562, was still in his service at
Rome.

In reviewing the machinations of his enemies to bring
about his dismissal from the Professorship at Bologna,
Cardan indulges in the reflection that these men unwillingly did him good service, that is, they procured him
leisure which he might use in the completion of his unfinished works, and in the construction of fresh monu-

ments which he proposed to build up out of the vast
store of material accumulated in his industrious brain.
The literary record of his life in Rome shows that this
was no vain saying. He was at work on the later
chapters of the *De Vita Propria* up to the last weeks
of his life ; and, scattered about these, there are records
of his work of correction and revising. While telling of
the books he has lately been engaged with, he wanders
off in the same sentence to talk of the dream which
urged him to write the *De Subtilitate*, and of the execution of the *Commentarii in Ptolomæum*, during his voyage
down the Loire. In 1573 he seems to have found the
mass of undigested work more than he could bear to
behold ; for, after making extracts of such matter as he
deemed worth keeping, he consigned to the flames no
less than a hundred and twenty of his manuscripts.[1]
Before leaving Bologna he had put into shape the
Proxenata, a lengthy collection of hints, maxims, and reflections as to everyday life ; he had re-edited the *Liber
Artis Magnæ*, and had added thereto the treatise *De
Proportionibus*, and the *Regula Aliza*. He also took
in hand two books on Geometry, and one on Music, and
this last he completed in.1574. On November 16, 1574,
he records that he is at that moment writing an explanation of the more abstruse works of Hippocrates,
but that he is yet far from the end of his task.

In the *De Libris Propriis* he gives a list of all his

---

[1] " Qua causa permotus sim ad scribendum, superius intellexisse
te existimo, quippe somnio monitus, inde bis, terque, ac quater, ac
pluries, ut alias testatus sum ; sed et desiderio perpetuandi nominis.
Bis autem magnam copiam ac numerum eorum perdidi ; primum
circa XXXVII annum, cum circiter IX. libros exussi, quod
vanos ac nullius utilitatis futuros esse intelligerem ; anno autem
MDLXXIII alios CXX libros, cum jam calamitas illa cessasset
cremavi."—*De Vita Propria*, ch. xlv. pp. 174, 175.

published works, and likewise a table of the same arranged in the order in which they ought to be read. He apologizes for the imperfect state in which some of them are left, and declares that the sight of his unfinished tasks never fails to awaken in his breast a bitter sense of resentment over that loss which he had never ceased to mourn. "At one time I hoped," he writes, "that these works would be corrected by my son, but this favour you see has been denied to me. The desire of my enemies was not to make an end of him, but of me; not by gentle means, in sooth, but by cruel open murder; to let me fall in the very blood of my son." It is somewhat remarkable that in this matter Cardan was destined to suffer a disappointment similar to that which he himself brought upon his own father by refusing to qualify himself to become the commentator on Archbishop Peckham's *Perspectiva*. He next gives the names of all those who had commended him in their works, and finds a special cause for gratification in the fact that, out of the long list set down, only four or five were known to him personally, and these not intimately. There is, however, another short list of censors; and of these he affirms that a certain Brodeus alone is worthy of respect. Of Buteon, who criticized the treatise on *Arithmetic*, he says: "*Est plane stultus et elleboro indiget.*" Tartaglia's name is there, and he, according to Cardan, was forced to eat his words; "but he was ashamed to do what he promised, and unwilling to blot out what he had written. He went on in his wrong-headed course, living upon the labour of other men like a greedy crow, a manifest robber of other men's wealth of study; so impudent that he published as his own, in the Italian tongue, that invention for the raising of sunken ships which I had made known four years before. This he did, understanding the subject only imperfectly, and making no mention of my name. But men of real learning also attacked me : Rondeletius, and Julius Scaliger ; and Fuchsius, in the proem of his book, says that my work *Medicinæ Contradictiones* should be avoided like deadly poison. Julius Scaliger has been fully answered in the *Apologia* in the Books on Subtlety."[1]

There is a passage from De Thou's *History of his Own Times*, affixed to all editions of the *De Vita Propria*,[2] in which is given a contemporary sketch of Cardan during his residence at Rome. "His whole life," De Thou writes, " has been as strange as his present manners, and he, in sooth, out of singleness of mind or frankness, has written about himself certain statements, the like of which have never before been heard of a man of letters, and these I do not feel bound to unfold to any one, let him be ever so curious. I, myself, happening to be in Rome a few years before his death, often spoke to him and observed him with astonishment as he took his walks about the city clad in strange garb. When I considered the many writings of this famous man, I could perceive in him nothing to justify his great renown. Wherefore I am all the more inclined to turn to that very acute criticism of Julius Cæsar Scaliger, who exercised his extraordinary genius in making a special examination of the treatise *De Subtilitate Rerum*. He, having carefully noted everywhere the unequal powers of this writer, decided that he was one who, in certain subjects, knew more than a man could know, while in others he seemed more simple than a child. In the science of Arithmetic he worked hard

---

[1] *Opera*, tom. i. p. 122.
[2] *De Vita Propria*, p. 232.

and made many discoveries; but he was subject to strange and excessive aberration of mind, and was guilty of the most impudent blasphemy, in that he was minded to subject to the artificial laws of the stars the Ruler of the stars Himself, for this thing he did in the horoscope of our Saviour which he drew."

Another witness of his life in Rome is François d'Amboise, a young French nobleman, who was engaged on his book *De Symbolis Heroicis*. He says that he saw Cardan, who was living in a spacious house, on the walls of which, in place of elegant paintings or vari-coloured tapestries, were written the words, " *Tempus mea possessio*."

In his later writings there are farther indications that he was wont to conjure up omens and portents chiefly at those times when he was in danger and mental distress. In the case which is given below, the omen showed itself in a season of trouble, but Cardan, in describing it later, treats it as if he were a modern scientist. The distressing memories of the imprisonment had faded, and writing in ease and security at Rome he begins to rationalize. In the dialogue between himself and his father, written shortly before his death, Fazio calls his son's attention to certain of the omens and portents already noticed ; and, after discussing these, Jerome goes on to tell for the first time of another boding event which, as he affirms, distressed him even more than the loss of his office and the prohibition to publish his books. On the day of his incarceration, on two different occasions, he met a cow being driven to the slaughter-house, with much shouting and beating with sticks and barking of dogs. The explanation of this event which he puts in Fazio's mouth is entirely conceived in the spirit of rationalism. What was there to wonder at ? There was

a butcher's shop in the street, and animals going to
slaughter would naturally be met there. Why should
a man fear to meet a cow? If it had been a bull there
might have been something in it. Then with regard to
the shaking of a window-casement; this might easily
have been occasioned by the flight of a bird.[1] He was
certainly less inclined to put faith in the warnings of the
stars and in the lines of his hand. His line of life was
very short and irregular, intersected and bifurcated,
while the rest of the lines were little thicker than hairs.
In his horoscope was a certain malefic influence which
threatened that his life would be cut short before his
forty-fifth year. " But," he writes in the year before his
death, "here I am, living at the age of seventy-five." [2]
The one supernatural idea which seems to have
deepened with old age and remained undisturbed to
the end was his belief in his attendant genius. In
what he wrote during his last years his mood was almost
entirely introspective, contemplative, and didactic, yet
here and there he introduces a sentence which lets in
a little light from his way of life and personal affairs,
and helps to show how he occupied himself, and what
his humour was. He tells how one day, in 1576, he was
writing about the fennel plant in his treatise *De Tuenda
Sanitate*, a plant which he praised highly because it
pleased his palate. But shortly afterwards, when he
was walking one day in the Roman vegetable market,
an old man, shabbily dressed, met him and dissuaded
him from the use of the plant aforesaid, saying: "In
Galen's opinion you may as readily meet your death

[1] *Opera*, tom. i. p. 639. In the *De Varietate* he says that
natural causes may in most cases be found for seeming marvels.
"Ecce auditur strepitus in domo, potest esse mus, felis, ericius,
aut quod tigna subsidant blatta."—p. 624.

[2] *De Vita Propria*, ch. xli. p. 152.

thereby as by eating hemlock." "I answered that I knew well enough the difference between hemlock and fennel, but the old man said, 'Take care, I know what I am saying,' and went on murmuring something about Galen. Whereupon I went home and found in Galen a passage I had not hitherto noticed, and, having changed my former views, I added many fresh excerpts to my treatise."

Although his faith may have been shaken in the ability of the stars to govern his own fortunes, he records a case in which he himself filled the post of *vates*, and which came to a sudden and terrible issue. Cardan was present at a supper-party, and in the course of conversation let fall the remark, "I should like to say something, were I not afraid that my words would disturb the company," to which one of the guests replied, "You mean that you would prophesy death to one of us here present." Cardan replied, "Yes, within the present year," and in the next sentence he tells how on the first day of December in that same year a certain young man, named Virgilius, who had been present at the gathering aforesaid, died, and he sets down this event as a fulfilment of his prophecy.

But in the same chapter he lets the reader into the secret of his system of prophecy, and displays it as simply an affair of common-sense, one recommended by Aristotle as the only trustworthy method of divining future events. Cardan writes: "I used to inquire what might be the exact nature of the business in hand, and began by making myself acquainted with the character of the locality, the ways of the people, and the quality of the chief actors. I unfolded a vast number of historical instances, leading events and secret transactions as well, and then, when I had confirmed the facts set forth by my method of art, I gave my judgment thereupon." [1]

In his latter years Cardan must have been in easy circumstances. The pension from the Pope—no mention is made of its amount—and the fees he received from his patients allowed him to keep a carriage ; and writing in his seventy-fifth year, he says that no fees would tempt him to join any consultation unless he should be well assured what sort of men he was expected to meet. [2]

In the *Norma Vitæ Consarcinata* [3] he relates how in April 1576 there were two inmates of the Xenodochium at Rome, Troilus and Dominicus. It seemed that Troilus exercised some strange and malefic influence over his companion, who was taken with fever. He got well of this, but only to fall into a dropsy, which despatched him in a week. Shortly before his death, at the seventh hour, he cried out to two Spaniards who were standing by the bed that he had suffered such great torture from the working of Troilus, and that he was dying therefrom. "Therefore," he cried, "in your presence I summon him with my dying words to appear before God's tribunal, that he may give an account of all the evil he has wrought against me." On the following day there came a messenger from Corneto, a few miles from Rome, saying that Troilus, who was sojourning there, had fallen sick. The physician inquired at what hour, and the messenger said it was at seven o'clock, a day or two ago. He lay ill some days, an unfavourable case, but not a desperate one, and one night shortly afterwards at seven o'clock, the top of the mosquito curtains fell, and he died at exactly the same hour as Dominicus.

[1] *De Vita Propria*, chapter xlii., *passim.*
[2] *Ibid.*, p. 66.   [3] *Opera*, tom. i. p. 339.

R

He tells another long story of an adventure which befell him in May 1576. One day he was driving in his carriage in the Forum, when he remembered that he wanted to see a certain jeweller who lived in a narrow alley close by. Wherefore he told his coachman, a stupid fellow, to go to the Campo Altoviti, and await him there. The coachman drove off apparently understanding the order; but, instead of going to the place designated, went somewhere else; so Cardan, when he set about to find his carriage, sought in vain. He had a notion that the man had gone to a spot near the citadel, so he walked thither, encumbered with the thick garments he had put on as necessary for riding in the carriage. Just then he met a friend of his, Vincenzio, a Bolognese musician, who remarked that Cardan was not in his carriage as usual. The old man went on towards the citadel, but saw nothing of the carriage; and now he began to be seriously troubled, for there was naught else to be done but to go back over the bridge, and he was wearied with long fasting and his heavy clothes. He might indeed have asked for the loan of a carriage from the Governor of the castle; but he was unwilling to do this, so having commended himself to God, he resolved to use all his patience and prudence in finding his way back. He set out, and when he had crossed the bridge, he entered the banking-house of the Altoviti to inquire as to the alteration in the rate of exchange on Naples, and there sat down to rest. While the banker was giving him this information, the Governor entered the place, whereupon Cardan went out and there he found his carriage, the driver having been informed by Vincenzio, whom he had met, of the mistake he had made. Cardan got into the carriage, and while he was wondering whether or not he had better go home and break his fast, he found three raisins in his pocket, and thus made a fortunate ending of all his difficulties.

All this reads like a commonplace chapter of accidents; but the events recorded did not present themselves to Cardan in this guise. He sits down to moralize over the succession of momentary events: his meeting with Vincenzio; Vincenzio's meeting with the driver, and directions given to the man to drive to the money-changers'; the presence of the Governor, his exit from the bank, his consequent meeting with the carriage, and his discovery of the raisins, seven occurrences in all, any one of which, if it had happened a little sooner or a little later, would have brought about great inconvenience, or even worse. He does not deny that other men may not now and then encounter like experiences, but the experiences of other men were not fraught with such momentous crises, nor did they foreshadow so many or grave dangers.

The chronicling of this episode and the fanciful coincidence of the deaths of Dominicus and Troilus may be taken as evidence that his idiosyncrasies were becoming aggravated by the decay of his faculties. Writing on October 1, 1576, he makes mention of the various testaments he had already made, and goes on to say that he had resolved to make a new and final disposition of his goods. He would fain have let his property descend to his immediate offspring, but with a son like Aldo this was impossible, so he left all to Gian Battista's son, who would now be a youth about eighteen years of age, Aldo getting nothing. He desired, for reasons best known to himself, that all his descendants should remain *in curatela* as long as possible, and that all his property should be held on trust; if the issue of his body should fail, then the succession should pass in perpetuity to his kinsfolk on the father's side. He desired that his works should be corrected and printed, and that, if heirs failed entirely, his house at Bologna should pass to the University, and be styled, after his family, *Collegium Cardanorum.*

There is no authentic record of the exact date of Cardan's death. De Thou, in writing the record of 1576, says that if Cardan's life had been prolonged by three days he would have completed his seventy-fifth year. As Cardan's birthday was September 24, 1501, this would fix his death on September 21, 1576. The exact figures given by De Thou are: "eodem, quo prædixerat, anno et die, videlicet XI. Kalend. VIII.," and he adds by way of information that a belief was current at the time that Cardan, who had foretold how he would die on this day and in this year, had abstained from food for some days previous to his death in order to make the fatal day square with the prophecy.

But the details which Cardan himself has set down concerning the last few weeks of his life are inconsistent with the facts chronicled by De Thou. In the *De Vita Propria*, chapter xxxvi., Cardan records how on October 1, 1576, he set to work to make his last will and testament, wherefore if credit is to be given to his version rather than to that of De Thou, he was alive and active some days after the date of his death as fixed by the chronicler. In cases where the record of an event of his early life given in the *De Vita Propria* differs from an account of the same in some contemporary writing, the testimony of the *De Vita Propria* may justly be put aside; but in this instance he was writing of something which could only have happened a few days past, and the balance of probability is that he was right and De Thou wrong.

Bayle notices this discrepancy, and in the same paragraph taxes De Thou with a mistake of which he is innocent. He states that De Thou placed the date of Cardan's death in 1575, whereas the excerpt cited above runs: "Thuanus ad annum MDLXXVI., p. 136, lib. lxii. tom. 4. Romæ magni nominis sive Mathematicus, sive Medicus Hieronymus Cardanus Mediol. natus hoc anno itidem obiit."

No mention is made of the disease to which Cardan finally succumbed. Had his frame not been of the strongest and most wiry, it must have gone to pieces long before through the havoc wrought by the severe and continuous series of ailments with which it was afflicted; so it seems permissible to assume that he died of natural decay. His body was interred in the church of Sant Andrea at Rome, and was subsequently transferred to Milan to be deposited finally under the stone which covered the bones of his father in the church of San Marco. This tomb, which Jerome had erected after Fazio's death, bore the following inscription:

FACIO CARDANO

I. C.

Mors fuit id quod vixi : vitam mors dedit ipsa,
Mens æterna manet, gloria tuta quies.

Obiit anno MDXXIV. IV. Kalend. Sept. anno Ætatis LXXX.
Hieronymus Cardanus Medicus Parenti posterisque V.P.[1]

---

[1] Tomasinus, *Gymnasium Patavinum.*

CHAPTER XIV

THE estimates hitherto made concerning Cardan's character appear to have been influenced too completely, one way or the other, by the judgment pronounced upon him by Gabriel Naudé, and prefixed to all editions of the *De Vita Propria*. Some writers have been disposed to treat Naudé as a hide-bound pedant, insensible to the charm of genius, and the last man who ought to be trusted as the valuator of a nature so richly gifted, original, and erratic as was Cardan's. Such critics are content to regard as black anything which Naudé calls white and *vice versâ*. Others accept him as a witness entirely trustworthy, and adopt as a true description of Cardan the paragraphs made up of uncomplimentary adjectives—applied by Cardan to himself—which Naudé has transferred from the *De Vita Propria* and the *Geniturarum Exempla* to his *Judicium de Cardano*.

It may be conceded at once that the impression received from a perusal of this criticism is in the main an unfavourable one of Cardan as a man, although Naudé shows himself no niggard of praise when he deals with Cardan's achievements in Medicine and Mathematics. But in appraising the qualifications of Naudé to act as a judge in this case, it will be necessary to bear in mind the fact that he was in his day a leading exponent of liberal opinions, the author of a treatise exposing the mummeries and sham mysteries of the Rosicrucians, and of an "Apologie pour les Grands Hommes soupçonnez de Magie," and a disbeliever in supernatural manifestations of every kind. With a mind thus attuned it is no matter of surprise that Naudé should have been led to speak somewhat severely when called upon to give judgment on a man saturated as Cardan was with the belief in sorcery, witches, and attendant demons.

If Naudé indeed set to work with the intention of drawing a figure of Cardan which should stand out a sinister apparition in the eyes of posterity, his task was an easy one. All he had to do was to place Jerome Cardan himself in the witness-box. Reference to the passages already quoted will show that, in the whole *corpus* of autobiographic literature, there does not exist a volume in which the work of self-dissection has been so ruthlessly and completely undertaken and executed as in Cardan's memoirs. It has all the vices of an old man's book; it is garrulous, vain-glorious, and full of needless repetition; but, whatever portion of his life may be under consideration, the author never shrinks from holding up to the world's gaze the result of his searches in the deepest abysses of his conscience. Autobiographers, as a rule, do not feel themselves subject to a responsibility so deep as this. Memory turns back to the contemplation of certain springs of action, certain achievements in the past, making a judicious selection from these, and excerpting only such as promise to furnish the possible reader with a pleasing impression of the personality of the subject. With material of this sort at hand, the autobiographer sets to work to construct a fair and gracious monument, being easily persuaded that it would be a barbarous act to mar its symmetry by the introduction of loathly and misshapen blocks like those which Cardan, had he been the artist, would have chosen first of all.

Naudé, after he has recorded the fact that, from his first essay in letters, he had been a zealous and appreciative student of Cardan's works, sets down Cardan's picture of himself, taken from his own Horoscope in the *Geniturarum Exempla*, "nugacem, religionis contemptorem, injuriæ illatæ memorem, invidum, tristem, insidiatorem, proditorem, magum, incantatorem, frequentibus calamitatibus obnoxium, suorum osorē, turpi libidini deditum, solitarium, inamœnum, austerum, spontè etiam divinantem, zelotypum, lascivum, obscœnum, maledicum, obsequiosum, senum conversatione se delectantem, varium, ancipitem, impurū, et dolis mulierum obnoxium, calumniatorem, et omnino incognitum propter naturæ et morum repugnantiam, etiam his cum quibus assidue versor." The critic at once goes on to state that in his opinion this description, drawn by the person who ought to know best, is, in the main, a correct one. What better account could you expect, he asks, of a man who put faith in dreams and portents and auguries; who believed fully in the utterances of crazy beldames, who saw ghosts, and who believed he was attended by a familiar demon? Then follows a catalogue of moral offences and defects of character, all taken from Cardan's own confessions, and a pronunciation by Naudé that the man who says he never lies, must be of all liars the greatest; the charge of mendacity being driven home by references to Cardan's alleged miraculous comprehension of the classic tongues in a single night, and his pretended knowledge of a cure for phthisis. There is no need to follow Naudé farther in his diatribe against the faults and imperfections, real and apparent, of Cardan's character; these must be visible enough to the most

cursory student. Passages like these arouse the suspicion that Naudé knew books better than men, that at
any rate he did not realize that men are to be found,
and not seldom, who take pleasure in magnifying their
foibles into gigantic follies, and their peccadilloes into
atrocious crimes ; while the rarity is to come across one
who will set down these details with the circumstantiality
used by Cardan. There is one defect in the *De Vita
Propria*—an artistic one—which Naudé does not notice,
namely, that in his narrative of his early days Cardan
often over-reaches himself. His show of extreme accuracy destroys the perspective of the story, and, in
his anxiety to be minute over the sequence of his
childish ailments, the most trivial details of his uneasy
dreams, and the cuffs he got from his father and his
Aunt Margaret, he confuses the reader with multitudinous particulars and ceases to be dramatic. But
the hallucinations which he nourished about himself
were not all the outcome of senility. In the *De Varietate*,
the work upon which he spent the greatest care, and
the product moreover of his golden prime, he gives an
account of four marvellous properties with which he was
gifted.[1] The first of these was the power to pass, whenever the whim seized him, from sense into a kind of
ecstasy. While he was in this state he could hear but
faintly the sound of voices, and could not distinguish
spoken words. Whether he would be sensitive to any
great pain he could not say, but twitchings and the
sharpest attacks of gout affected him not. When he
fell into this state he felt a certain separation about the
heart, as if his soul were departing from that region and
taking possession of his whole body, a door being opened
for the passage of the same. The sensation would begin

---

[1] *De Varietate*, p. 314.

in the cerebellum, and thence would be diffused along
the spine. The one thing of which he was fully conscious,
was that he had passed out of himself. The second
property was that, when he would, he could conjure up
any images he liked before his eyes, real εἴδωλα, and not
at all to be compared with the blurred processions of
phantoms which he was wont to see when he was a child.
At the time when he wrote, perhaps by reason of his
busy life, he no longer saw them whensoever he would,
nor so perfectly expressed, nor for so long at a time.
These images constantly gave place one to another, and
he would behold groves, and animals, and orbs, and
whatever he was fain to see. This property he attributed to the force of his imaginative power, and his
clearness of vision. The third property was that he
never failed to be warned in dreams of things about to
happen to him; and the fourth was that premonitory
signs of coming events would display themselves in the
form of spots on his nails. The signs of evil were black
or livid, and appeared on the middle finger; white spots
on the same nail portending good fortune. Honours
were indicated on the thumb, riches on the fore-finger,
matters relating to his studies and of grave import on
the third finger, and minor affairs on the little finger.

In putting together the record of his life, Cardan
eschewed the narrative form and followed a method of
his own. He collected the details of his qualities, habits,
and adventures in separate chapters; his birth and
lineage, his physical stature, his diet, his rule of life, his
imperfections, his poverty, the misfortunes of his sons,
his masters and pupils, his travels, his experiences of
things beyond nature, his cures, the persecutions of his
foes, and divers other categories being grouped together
to make up the *De Vita Propria*, which, though it is

the most interesting book he has left behind him, is certainly the most clumsy and chaotic from a literary point of view. The chapters for the most part begin with his early years, and end with some detail as to his life in Rome, each one being a categorical survey of a certain side of his life ; but remarks as to his personal peculiarities are scattered about from beginning to end. He tells how he could always see the moon in broad daylight ;[1] of his passion for wandering about the city by night carrying arms forbidden by the law ; of his practice of self-torture, beating his legs with a switch, twisting his fingers, pinching his flesh, and biting his left arm ; and of going about within doors with naked legs ; how at one time he was possessed with the desire, *heroica passio*, of suicide ; of his habit of filling his house with pets of all sorts—kids, lambs, hares, rabbits, and storks. The chapter in which he records all the maladies which afflicted him, puts upon the reader's credulity a burden almost as heavy as is the catalogue given by another philosopher of the number of authors he mastered before his twelfth year. Two attacks of the plague, agues, tertian and quotidian, malignant ulcers, hernia, hæmorrhoids, varicose veins, palpitation of the heart, gout, indigestion, the itch, and foulness of skin. Relief in the second attack of plague came from a sweat so copious that it soaked the bed and ran in streams down to the floor ; and, in a case of continuous fever, from voiding a hundred and twenty ounces of urine. As a boy he was a sleep-walker, and he never became warm below the knees till he had been in bed six hours, a circumstance which led his mother to predict that his time on earth would be brief.

Cardan lived an abstemious life. He broke his fast

[1] *De Vita Propria*, ch. xxxvii. p. 115.

on bread-and-water and a few grapes. He sometimes dined off bread, the yolk of an egg, and a little wine, and would take for supper a mess of beetroot and rice and a chicory salad. The catalogue of his favourite dishes seems to exhaust every known edible, and it will suffice to remark that he was specially inclined to sound and well-stewed wild boar, the wings of young cockerels and the livers of pullets, oysters, mussels, fresh-water crayfish because his mother ate greedily thereof when she was pregnant with him; but of all dishes he rates the best a carp from three pounds weight to seven, taken from a good feeding-ground. He praises all sweet fruit, oil, olives, and finds in rue an antidote to poison. Ten o'clock was his hour for going to bed, and he allowed himself eight hours' sleep. When wakeful he would walk about the room and repeat the multiplication table. As a further remedy for sleeplessness he would reduce his food by half, and would anoint his thighs, the soles of his feet, the neck, the elbows, the carpal bones, the temples, the jugulars, the region of the heart and of the liver, and the upper lip with ointment of poplars, or the fat of bear, or the oil of water-lilies.

These few extracts will show that an intelligible narrative could scarcely be produced by the methods Cardan used. The book is a collection of facts, classified as a scientific writer would arrange the sections and subsections of his subject. In gathering together and grouping the leading points of his life, a method somewhat similar to his own will suffice, but there will be no need to descend to a subdivision so minute as his own. A task of this sort is never an easy one, and in this instance the difficulties are increased by the diffuse and complicated nature of the subject matter; and because, owing to Cardan's wayward mental habit, there is no saying in what corner of the ten large folios which contain his writings some pregnant and characteristic sentence, picturing effectively some aspect of his nature or perhaps exhibiting the man at a glance, may not be hidden away.

It must not be inferred, because Cardan himself and his critics after him, have laid such great stress upon his vices and imperfections, that he was devoid of virtues. The most striking and remarkable of his merits was his industry, but even in this particular instance, where his excellence is most clearly manifest, he is constantly lamenting his waste of time and idleness. Again and again he mourns over the precious hours he has spent over chess and dice and games of chance. In his counsels to his children, he compares a gambler to a sink of all the vices, and in writing of his early life at Sacco he describes himself as an idle profligate, and tells how he entirely neglected his profession. If indeed such monstrous cantles were cut out of his time through idleness he must, though his life proved a long one, have possessed extraordinary power of rapid production ; for the huge mass of his published work, without taking any account of the many manuscripts he burned from time to time, would, in the case of most men, represent the ceaseless labour of a long life. And the *corpus* is not great by reason of haste or want of finish. He has recorded more than once how it was ever his habit to let his work be polished to the utmost before putting it in type. The citations with which his pages bristle proclaim him to be a reader almost as voracious and catholic as Burton ; and Naudé, with the watchfulness of the hostile critic in his heart and the bookworm's knowledge in his brain, would have been ready and able to convict him of quoting authors he had not read, if the least handle for this charge should have been given, but no accusation of the kind is preferred. The story of his life shows him to be full of rough candour and honesty, and unlikely to descend to subterfuge, while his great love of reading and his accurate retentive memory would make easy for him a task which ordinary mortals might well regard as hopeless.

Those critics who pass judgment on Cardan, taken solely as a Physician or as a Mathematician, will give a presentment more fallacious than imperfect generalizations usually furnish, for in Cardan's case the man, taken as a whole, was incomparably greater than the sum of his parts. Naudé remarks that a man who knows a little of everything, and that little imperfectly, deserves small respect as a citizen of the republic of letters, but Cardan did not belong to this category, as Julius Cæsar Scaliger found to his cost. He was not like the bookmen of the revival of learning—Poliziano, Valla, or Alberti may stand as examples—who after putting on the armour of the learned language and saturating themselves with the *literæ humaniores*, made excursions into some domain of science for the sake of recreation. Cardan might rather be compared with Varro or Theophrastus in classic, and with Erasmus, Pico, Grotius, or Casaubon in modern times. On this point Naudé indulges in something approaching panegyric. He writes—"Investigation will show us that many excelled him in the humanities or in Theology, some even in Mathematics, some in Medicine and in the knowledge of Philosophy, some in Oriental tongues and in either side of Jurisprudence, but where shall we find any one who had mastered so many sciences by himself, who had plumbed so deeply the abysses of learning and had written such ample commentaries on the subjects he studied? Assuredly in Philosophy, in Metaphysics, in History, in Politics, in Morals, as well as in the more abstruse fields of learning, nothing that was worth consideration escaped his notice."

The foregoing eulogy from the pen of an adverse critic gives eloquent testimony to Cardan's industry and the catholicity of his knowledge. As to his industry, the record of his literary production, chronicled incidentally in the course of the preceding pages, will be evidence enough, seeing that, from the time when he "commenced author," scarcely a year went by when he did not print a volume of some sort or other; to say nothing of the production of those multitudinous unpublished MSS., of which some went to build up the pile he burnt in his latter years in Rome, while others, perhaps, are still mouldering in the presses of university or city libraries of Italy. Frequent reference has been made to the more noteworthy of his works. Books like the *De Vita Propria*, the *De Libris Propriis*, the *De Utilitate ex Adversis Capienda*, the *Geniturarum Exempla*, the *Theonoston*, the *Consilia Medica*, the dialogues *Tetim* and *De Morte*, have necessarily been drawn upon for biographical facts. The *De Subtilitate* and the *De Varietate Rerum;* the *Liber Artis Magnæ*, the *Practica Arithmeticæ*, have been noticed as the most enduring portions of his legacy to posterity; wherefore, before saying the final word as to his literary achievement, it may not be superfluous to give a brief glance at those of his books which, although of minor importance to those already cited, engaged considerable attention in the lifetime of the writer.

The work upon which Cardan founded his chief hope of immortality was his *Commentary on Hippocrates*. In

bulk it ranks first easily, filling as it does one of the
large folios of the edition of 1663. Curiously enough,
in addition to a permanent place in the annals of
medicine, Cardan anticipated for this forgotten mass
of type a general and immediate popularity; wider
than any which his technical works could possibly
enjoy, seeing that it dealt with the preservation of
health, the greatest mortal blessing, and must on this
account be of interest to all men. It will be enough to
remark of these commentaries that no portion of
Cardan's work yields less information as to the author's
life and personality; to dilate upon them, ever so super-
ficially, from a scientific point of view, would be waste
of time and paper. Another of his works, which he
rated highly, was his treatise on Music. It was begun
during his tenure of office at Pavia, *circa* 1547, and he
was still at work upon it two years before his death.[1]
It is not difficult to realize, even at this interval of time,
that this book at the date of its publication must have
been welcomed by all musical students as a valuable
contribution to the literature of their subject. It is
strongly marked by Cardan's particular touch, that
formative faculty by which he almost always succeeded
in stimulating fresh interest in the reader, and exhibiting
fresh aspects of whatever subject he might be treating.
This work begins by laying down at length the general
rules and principles of the art, and then goes on to treat
of ancient music in all its forms; of music as Cardan
knew and enjoyed it; of the system of counterpoint
and composition, and of the construction of musical
instruments.

The Commentary on *Ptolemæi de Astrorum Judiciis*,

---

[1] " Musicam, sed hanc anno post VI. scilicet MDLXXIV. correxi
et transcribi curavi."—*De Vita Propria*, ch. xlv. p. 176.

the writing of which beguiled the tedium of his voyage
down the Loire on his journey to Paris in 1552, is a
book upon which he spent great care, and is certainly
worthy of notice. Cardan's gratitude to Archbishop
Hamilton for the liberal treatment and gracious reception he had recently encountered in Scotland, prompted
him to dedicate this volume to his late patient. He
writes in the preface how he had expected to find the
Scots a pack of barbarians, but their country, he affirms,
is cultivated and humanized beyond belief,—"and you
yourself reflect such splendour upon your nation that
now, by the very lustre of your name, it must needs
appear to the world more noble and illustrious than at
any time heretofore. What need is there for me to
speak of the school founded by you at St. Andrews,
of sedition quelled, of your country delivered, of the
authority of your brother the Regent vindicated? These
are merely the indications of your power, and not the
source thereof." In the preface he also writes at length,
concerning the horoscope of Christ,[1] in a strain of
apology, as if he scented already the scandal which the
publication of this injudicious performance was destined
to raise. In estimating the influence of comets he sets
down several instances which had evidently been brought
to his notice during his sojourn in Scotland : how in
1165, within fourteen days of the appearance of a great
comet, Malcolm IV., known on account of his conti-
nence as the virgin king, fell sick and died. Again,
in 1214 two comets, one preceding and the other following
the sun, appeared as fore-runners of the death of King
William after a reign of forty-nine years. Perhaps the
most interesting of his comments on Ptolemy's text are
those which estimate the power of the stellar influences

---

[1] This is on p. 164.

S

on the human frame, an aspect of the question which, by reason of his knowledge of medicine and surgery, would naturally engage his more serious attention. He tells of the birth of a monstrous child—a most loathsome malformation—at Middleton Stoney, near Oxford, during his stay in England,[1] and gives many other instances of the disastrous effects of untoward conjunction of the planets upon infants born under the influence of the same. He accuses monks and nuns of detestable vices in the plainest words, words which were probably read by the emissaries of the spiritual authority when the charge of impiety was being got up against him. In the *Geniturarum Exempla* the horoscopes of Edward VI., Archbishop Hamilton, and Cardan himself have been already noticed ; that of Sir John Cheke comes next in interest to these, and, it must be admitted, is no more trustworthy. It declares that Cheke would attain the age of sixty-one years, that he would be most fortunate in gathering wealth and friends around him, that he would die finally of lingering disease, and involve many in misfortune by his death—a faulty guess, indeed, as to the future of a man who died at forty-three, borne down by the weight of his misfortunes, neglected and forgotten by his former adherents, stripped of his wealth and covered with shame, in that he had abjured his faith to save a life which was so little worth preserving.

Naudé does not neglect to censure Cardan for his maladroit attempts to read the future. He writes :—
" This matter, forsooth, gave a ready handle to Cardan's rivals, and especially to those who were sworn foes of astrology ; so that they were able to jibe at him freely because, neither in his own horoscope, nor in that of his son Giovanni Battista, nor in that of Aymer Ranconet,

1 Page 266.

nor in that of Edward VI., king of England, nor in any other of the schemes that he drew, did he rightly foresee any of the events which followed. He did not divine that he himself was doomed to imprisonment, his son to the halter, Ranconet to a violent death, and Edward to a brief term of life, but predicted for each one of these some future directly contrary." [1]

The treatise *De Consolatione*, probably the best known of Cardan's ethical works, was first published at Venice in 1542 by Girolamo Scoto, but it failed at first to please the public taste. It was not until 1544, when it was re-issued bound up with the *De Sapientia* and the first version of the *De Libris Propriis* from the press of Petreius at Nuremberg, that it met with any success. Perhaps the sober tone and didactic method of this treatise appealed more readily to the mood of the German than of the Italian reader. From internal evidence it is obvious that Cardan was urged to write it by the desire of making known to the world the bitter experience of his early literary and professional struggles. In the opening paragraph he lets it be seen that he intends to follow a Ciceronian model, and records his regret that the lament of Cicero over his daughter's death should have perished in the barbarian wars. The original title of the book was *The Accuser*, to wit, something which might censure the vain passions and erring tendencies of mankind, " at post mutato nomine, et in tres libellos diviso, de Consolatione eum inscripsimus, quod longe magis infelices consolatione, quam fortunati reprehensione, indigere viderentur." The subsequent success of the book was probably due to this change of name, though the author himself preferred to have discovered

----

[1] *Judicium de Cardano.*

a special reason for its early failure.[1]   The plan of the treatise is the same as that of a dozen others of the same nature : an effort to persuade men in evil case that they may find relief by regarding the misfortunes they suffer as transitory accidents in no way affecting the chief end of life, and by seeking happiness alone in trafficking with the riches of the mind.

It is doubtful whether any of the books written with this object have ever served their purpose, save in the case of their originators.   Cardan may have found the burden of his failure and poverty grow lighter as he set down his woes on paper, but the rest of the world must have read the book for some other reason than the hope of consolation.   Read to-day in Bedingfield's quaint English, the book is full of charm and interest.   It is filled with apt illustration from Greek philosophy and from Holy Writ as well, and lighted up by spaces of lively wit.   It was accepted by the public taste for reasons akin to those which would secure popularity for a clever volume of essays at the present time, and was translated into more than one foreign language, Bedingfield's translation being published some thirty years after its first appearance.

The *De Sapientia*, with which it is generally classed, is of far less interest.   It is a series of ethical discourses, lengthy and discursive, which must have seemed dull enough to contemporary students : to read it through now would be a task almost impossible.   It is only remembered because Cardan has inserted therein, somewhat incongruously, that account of his asserted cures of phthisis which Cassanate quoted when he wrote to Cardan about Archbishop Hamilton's asthma, and

[1] Page 57.

which were afterwards seized upon by hostile critics as evidence of his disregard of truth.

Another of his minor works highly characteristic of the author is the *Somniorum Synesiorum*, a collection of all the remarkable dreams he ever dreamt, many of which have been already noticed. To judge from what specimens of his epistles are extant, Cardan seems to have been a good letter-writer. One of the most noteworthy is that which he addressed to Gian Battista after his marriage. It shows Cardan to have been a loving father and a master of sapient exhortation, while the son's fate gives melancholy testimony of the futility of good counsel unaided by direction and example. He tells of his grief at seeing the evil case into which his son had fallen, vexed by poverty, disgrace, and loss of health, how he would gladly even now receive the prodigal into his house (he says nothing about the wife), did he not fear that such a step would lead to his own ruin rather than to his son's restoration. After showing that any fresh misfortune to himself must needs cut away the last hope for Gian Battista, he sketches out a line of conduct for the ill-starred youth which he declared, if rightly pursued, might re-establish his fortunes.

He begins by advising his son to read and lay to heart the contents of the *De Consolatione* and the *De Utilitate*, and then, somewhat more to the purpose, promises him half his earnings of the present and the coming year. Beyond this Gian Battista should have half the salary of any office which his father might get for himself, and half of the piece of silk which he had received from the Venetian Ambassador, supposing that the young man should not be able to get a like piece for himself from the same source.

He next cites the *De Consolatione* to demonstrate the

futility of lamentation over misfortune past or present, or indeed over any decree of fate. He bids Gian Battista reflect that he is human not a brute, a man not a woman, a Christian not a Moslem or Jew, an Italian not a barbarian, sprung from a worthy city and family, and from a father whose name by itself will prove a title to fame. His only real troubles are a weak body and infirm health—one a gift of heredity, the other aggravated by dissolute habits. It may be a vain thing for men to congratulate themselves over their happiness, but it is vainer for them to cry out for solace over past calamity. Contempt of money is foolish, but contempt of God is ten times worse. Cardan concludes this part of his letter by reciting two maxims given him by his father—one, to have daily remembrance of God and of His vast bounty, the other, to pursue with the utmost diligence any task taken in hand.

Cardan then treats the scapegrace to a string of maxims from the *De Utilitate*, maxims which a model son might have read, but which Gian Battista would certainly put aside unnoticed, and finishes with some serviceable practical counsel: "Keep your mind calm, go early to bed, for ours is a hot-blooded race and predisposed to suffer from stone. Take nine hours' sleep, rise at six and visit your patients, being careful to use no speech unconnected with the case before you. Avoid heating your body to perspiration; go forth on horseback, come back on foot; and on your return put on warm clothes. Drink little, break your fast on bread, dried fish, and meat, and then give four hours to study, for studies bring pleasure, relief from care, and mental riches; they are the foundations of renown, and enable a man to do his duty with credit. See your patients again; and, before you sup, take exercise in the woods and fields adjacent. Should you become over-heated or wet with rain, cast off and dry your damp clothes, and don dry ones. Sup heartily, and go to bed at eight; and when, by the brevity of the night, this is not convenient, take a corresponding rest during the day. Abstain from summer fruit, from black wine, from vain overflow of talk, from falsehood and gaming, from trusting a woman or over-indulging her, for she is a foolish animal and full of deceit. Over-fondness towards a woman will surely bring evil upon you. Bleed and purge yourself as little as possible; learn by experience of other men's faults and misfortunes; live frugally; bear yourself suavely to all men; and let study be your main end. All this and more have I set forth in the books I have named. Trust neither promises nor hopes, for these may be vain and delusive; and reckon your own only that which you hold in your hand. Farewell."

From the fact that Cardan took part in an unofficial medical conference in Paris, that he afterwards superseded Cassanate as the Archbishop of St. Andrews' physician, and did not find himself with a dozen or so quarrels on his hands, it may be assumed that he was laudably free from the jealousy attributed by tradition to his profession. This instance becomes all the more noteworthy when his natural irascibility, and the character of the learned controversy of the times comes to be considered. He does not spare his censure in remarking on the too frequent quarrels of men of letters,[1] albeit these quarrels must have lent no little gaiety to the literary world. No one who reads the account of Gian

---

[1] "Ita nostra ætate, lapsi sunt clarissimi alioqui viri in hoc genere. Budæus adversus Erasmum, Fuchsius adversus Cornarium, Silvius adversus Vesalium, Nizolius adversus Maioragium: non tam credo justis contentionum causis, quam vanitate quadam et spe augendæ opinionis in hominibus."—*Opera*, tom. i. p. 135.

Battista's fate can doubt the sincerity of Cardan's remorse for that neglect of the boy's youthful training which helped to bring him to ruin, and the care which he bestowed upon his grandson Fazio proved that his regret was not of that sort which exhales itself in empty words. The zeal with which he threw himself into the struggle for his son's life, and his readiness to strip himself of his last coin as the fight went on, show that he was capable of warm-hearted affection, and afraid of no sacrifice in the cause of duty.

The brutal candour which Cardan used in probing the weaknesses of his own nature and in displaying them to the world, he used likewise in his dealings with others. If he detected Branda Porro or Camutio in a blunder he would inform them they were blockheads without hesitation, and plume himself afterwards on the score of his blunt honesty. Veracity was not a common virtue in those days, but Cardan laid claim to it with a display of insistence which was not, perhaps, in the best taste. Over and over again he writes that he never told a lie ;[1] a contention which seems to have roused especially the bile of Naudé, and to have spurred him on to make his somewhat clumsy assault on Cardan's veracity.[2] His citation of the case of the stranger who came with the volume of Apuleius for sale, and of the miraculous gift of classic tongues, has already been referred to ; but these may surely be attributed to an exaggerated activity of that particular side of Cardan's

---

[1] He writes in this strain in *De Vita Propria*, ch. xiv. p. 49, in *De Varietate Rerum*, p. 626, and in *Geniturarum Exempla*, p. 431.

[2] On the subject of dissimulation Cardan writes : "Assuevi vultum in contrarium semper efformare ; ideo simulare possum, dissimulare nescio."—*De Vita Propria*, ch. xiii. p. 42. Again in *Libellus Præceptorum ad filios* (*Opera*, tom. i. p. 481), "Nolite unquam mentiri, sed circumvenire [circumvenite ?]."

imagination which was specially prone to seize upon some figment of the brain, and some imperfectly apprehended sensation of the optic nerve, and fashion from these materials a tale of marvel. Delusions of this sort were common in reputed witches, as Reginald Scot writes—"They learne strange toongs with small industrie (as Aristotle and others affirme)."[1] The other charge preferred by Naudé as to the pretended cure of consumption, and the consequent quibbling and tergiversation, is a more valid one. It has been noted how Cardan, previous to his journey to Scotland, had posed as the discoverer of a cure for this malady. In the list of his cures successfully treated he includes several in which he restored patients suffering from blood-spitting, fever, and extreme emaciation to sound health, the most noteworthy of these being that of Girolamo Tiboldo, a sea-captain. When the sick man had risen from his bed and had become fat and healthy, Cardan deemed that the occasion justified a certain amount of self-gratulation, but the physicians, out of envy, declared that Tiboldo had never suffered from true phthisis. In his account of the case Cardan says that he, and the physicians as well, were indeed untruthful over the matter, his own falsehood having been the result of over-sanguine hope, and theirs the outcome of spiteful envy. Tiboldo died after all of chest disease, but not till five years later, and then from a chill caught through sitting in wet garments.[2] The term consumption has always been applied somewhat loosely, and Cardan probably would have been allowed the benefit of this

[1] *Discoverie of Witchcraft*, ch. xi.

[2] Donato Lanza, the druggist, who had been his first introducer to Sfondrato, was equally perverse. After Cardan had cured him of phthisis, he jumped out of a window to avoid arrest, and fell into a fish-pond, and died of the cold he took.—*Opera*, tom. i. p. 83.

usage if he had not, in an excess of candour, set down
the workings of his mind and conscience with regard to
this matter. Writing of his treatment of Archbishop
Hamilton, he says : " And in truth I cured scarcely any
patients of phthisic disease, though I did find a remedy
for many who were suffering from similar maladies,
wherefore that boast of mine, that proclamation of merit
to which I had no right, worked no small profit to me, a
man very little given to lying. For the people about
the Archbishop, urged on by these and other considerations, persuaded him that he had no chance of regaining
his health except by putting himself under my care, and
that he should fly to me as his last hope."[1] It has
already been noted that Cardan's claim to some past
knowledge in the successful treatment of chest diseases
had weight with the Archbishop and Cassanate, and the
result of his visit surely proved that their confidence was
not ill-placed ; his boasting may have been a trifle excessive, but it was based on hope rather than achievement ; and if proof can be adduced that it was not
prompted by any greed of illegitimate fame or profit, it
may justly be ranked as a weakness rather than as a
serious offence. To these two instances of falsehood
Naudé adds a third, to wit, Cardan's claim to the
guidance of a familiar spirit. He refuses to let this rank
as a delusion ; and, urged no doubt by righteous indignation against the ills springing from kindred super-
stitions, he writes down as a liar rather than a dupe the
man who, after mastering the whole world of science,
could profess such folly.

Considering the catholicity of Cardan's achievements,
and the eager spirit of inquiry he displayed in fields of
learning remote from his own particular one, it is worthy

[1] *Opera*, tom. i. p. 136.

of notice that he did not allow this discursive humour, which is not seldom a token of instability, to hold him back from pursuing the supreme aim of his life, that is, eminence in the art of Medicine. In his youth the threats and persuasions of his father could not induce him to take up Jurisprudence with an assured income and abandon Medicine. At Sacco, at Gallarate, and afterwards in Milan he was forced by the necessity of bread-winning to use his pen in all sorts of minor subjects that had no real fascination for him, but all his leisure was devoted to the acquisition of Medical knowledge. Prudence as well as inclination had a share in directing his energies into this channel, for a report, for which no doubt there was some warrant, was spread abroad that what skill he had lay entirely in the knowledge of Astrology ; and, as this rumour operated greatly to his prejudice,[1] he resolved to perfect himself in Medicine and free his reputation from this aspersion. He had quarrelled violently with the physicians over the case of Count Borromeo's child which died, and with Borromeo himself, and, almost immediately after this, he published his book, *De Astrorum Judiciis*, a step which tended to identify him yet more closely with Astrology, and to raise a cry against him in Milan, which he declares to be the most scandal-mongering city in the Universe. But it is clear that in this instance scandal was not far wrong, and that Cardan himself was right in purging himself of the quasi science he ought never to have taken up.

Medicine, when Cardan began his studies, was beginning to feel the effects of the revival of Greek learning. With the restored knowledge of the language of Greece there arose a desire to investigate the storehouses of science, as well as those of literature, and the extravagant

---

[1] *De Vita Propria*, ch. x. p. 32.

assumption of the dogmatists, and the eccentricities of the Arabic school gave additional cogency to the cry for more light. The sects which Galen had endeavoured to unite sprang into new activity within a century after his death. The Arabian physicians, acute and curious as they were, had exercised but a very transient influence upon the real progress of the art, the chief cause of their non-success being their adhesion to arbitrary and empirical tradition. At the end of the fifteenth century, Leonicinus, a professor at Ferrara, recalled the allegiance of his pupils to the authority of Hippocrates by the ability and eloquence of his teaching ; and, by his translation of Galen's works into Latin, he helped still farther to confirm the ascendency of the fathers of Medicine. The Arabians, sprung from the East, the storehouse of drugs and simples, and skilled in Chemistry, were the founders of the Pharmacopœia,[1] but with this exception they did nothing to advance Medicine beyond the point where the Greeks had left it. The treatises of Haly, Avicenna, and Maimonides were little better than faint transcriptions of the writings of the great forerunners. Their teaching was random and spasmodic, whereas the system of Hippocrates was conceived in the spirit of Greek philosophy, moving on by select experience, always observant and cautious, and ascending by slow and certain steps to the generalities of Theory. Indeed the science of Medicine in the hands of Hippocrates and his school seems, more than any other, to have presented to the world a rudimentary essay, a faint foreshadowing of the great fabric of inductive process, subsequently formulated by the genius of Bacon. At various epochs

---

[1] The Materia Medica of Mesua, dating from the eleventh century, was used by the London College of Physicians in framing their Pharmacopœia in 1618.

Medicine had been specially stimulated by the vivifying spirit of Greek science ; in the Roman school in the days of Celsus, and in the Arabian teaching likewise. Fuller acknowledgment of the authority of Greek Medicine came with the Renaissance,[1] but even this long step in advance did not immediately liberate the art from bondage. A new generation of professors arose who added fresh material to the storehouses, already overflowing, of pedantic erudition, and showed the utmost contempt for any fruit of other men's labour which might not square exactly with the utterances of the founders. This attitude rendered these professors of Medicine the legitimate objects of ridicule, as soon as the leaven of the revival began to work, and the darts of satire still fly, now and then, at the same quarry. Paracelsus, disfigured as his teaching was by mysticism, the arts of the charlatan, and by his ignorant repudiation of the service of Anatomy, struck the first damaging blows at this illegitimate ascendency, by the frequent success of his empirical treatment, by the contempt he heaped upon the scholastic authorities, and by the boldness with which he assailed every thesis which they maintained. Men of more sober intellect and weighty learning soon followed in his track. Fernelius, one of the physicians Cardan met in Paris, boldly rejected what he could not approve by experience in the writings of Hippocrates and Galen, and stood forth as the advocate for free inquiry, and Joubert of Montpelier, Argentier of Turin, and Botal of Asti subsequently took a similar course.

When Cardan went to study at Pavia in 1519 this tradition was unshaken. It was not until the advent of Vesalius that the doom of the ancient system was

[1] In 1443 a copy of Celsus was found at Milan ; Paulus Ægineta was discovered a little later.

sounded. Then, when Anatomy sprang to the front as the potent ally of Medicine, the science of healing entered upon a fresh stage, but this new force did not make itself felt soon enough to seduce Cardan from the altars of the ancients to the worship of new gods. As long as he lived he was a follower of the great masters, though at the same time his admiration of the teaching of Vesalius was enthusiastic and profound. His love of truth and sound learning forbade him to give unreflecting adhesion to the precepts of any man, however eminent, and when he found that Galen was a careless commentator on Hippocrates,[1] and failed to elucidate the difficulties with which he professed to deal, he did not spare his censure.[2] In the *De Subtilitate* he speaks of him as "Verbosus et studio contradicendi tædulus ut alterum vix ferre queas, in reliquo gravis jactura artium posita sit, quam nostræ ætatis viri restituere conati sunt."[3] But as Galen's name is quoted as an authority on almost every page of the *Consilia Medica*, it may be assumed that Cardan's faith in his primary theories was unshaken. In his Commentaries on Hippocrates, Galen professes a profound respect for his master, but the two great men must be regarded as the leaders of rival schools ; indeed it could hardly be otherwise, seeing how vast was the mass of knowledge which Galen added to the art during his lifetime.

Hippocrates, by denying the supernatural origin of disease, by his method of diagnosis, by the importance he attached to air and diet, by his discriminating use of drugs, and by the simplicity of his system generally,

---

[1] *Opera*, tom. ix. p. 1.

[2] *De Immortalitate Animorum* (Lyons, 1545), p. 73. *De Varietate*, p. 77. *Opera*, tom. i. p. 135.

[3] *De Subtilitate*, p. 445.

had placed Medicine on a rational basis. In the six
hundred years' space which elapsed before the appearance of Galen, Medicine was broken up into many rival
schools. The Dogmatici and the Empirici for many
years wrangled undisturbed, but shortly after the
Christian era the Methodici entered the field, to be
followed later on by the Eclectici and a troop of other
sects, whose wranglings, and whose very names, are now
forgotten. In his *History of Medicine*, Dr. Bostock
gives a sketch of the attitude of Galen towards the rival
schools. " In his general principles he may be considered as belonging to the Dogmatic sect, for his
method was to reduce all his knowledge, as acquired by
the observation of facts, to general theoretical principles.
These principles he indeed professed to deduce from
experience and observation,[1] and we have abundant
proofs of his diligence in collecting experience and his
accuracy in making observations ; but still, in a certain
sense at least, he regards individual facts and the details
of experience as of little value, unconnected with the
principles which he laid down as the basis of all medical
reasoning. In this fundamental point, therefore, the
method pursued by Galen appears to have been directly
the reverse of that which we now consider as the correct
method of scientific investigation ; and yet, such is the
force of actual genius, that in most instances he attained
the ultimate object in view, although by an indirect
path. He was an admirer of Hippocrates, and always
speaks of him with the most profound respect, pro-
fessing to act upon his principles, and to do little more

[1] "Galen's great complaint against the Peripatetics or Aristo-
telians, was that while they discoursed about Anatomy they could
not dissect. He met an argument with a dissection or an experiment. Come and see for yourselves, was his constant cry."—
Harveian Oration, Dr. J. F. Payne, 1896.

than expound his doctrines and support them by new facts and observations. Yet in reality we have few writers whose works, both as to substance and manner, are more different from each other than those of Hippocrates and Galen, the simplicity of the former being strongly contrasted with the abstruseness and refinement of the latter."

The antagonism between these two great men was not perhaps more marked than might have been expected, considering that an interval of six hundred years lay between them. However loyal he may have been to his master, Galen, with his keen, catholic, and subtle intellect, was bound to fall under the sway of Alexandrian influence while he studied in Alexandria as the pupil of Heraclianus. The methods of the contemporary school of philosophy fascinated him; and, in his endeavour to bring Medicine out of the chaotic welter in which he found it, he attempted—unhappily for the future of science—to use the hyper-idealistic Platonism then dominant in Alexandria, rather than the gradual and orderly induction of Hippocrates, as a bond of union between professional and scientific medicine ; a false step for which not even his great services to anatomy and physiology can altogether atone. Yet most likely it was this same error, an error which practically led to the enslavement of Medicine till the seventeenth century, which caused Cardan to regard him, and not Hippocrates, as his master. The vastness and catholicity of Galen's scheme of Medicine must have been peculiarly attractive to a man of Cardan's temper ; and that Galen attempted to reconcile the incongruous in the teleological system which he devised, would not have been rated as a fault by his Milanese disciple.

Galen taught as a cardinal truth the doctrine of the

Hippocratic elements, heat, cold, moisture, and dryness, and a glance at the Consilium which Cardan wrote out on Archbishop Hamilton's illness, will show how completely he was under the sway of this same teaching. The genius of Hippocrates was perhaps too sober and orderly to win his entire sympathy; the encyclopædic knowledge, the literary grace, and the more daring flights of Galen's intellect attracted him much more strongly. Hippocrates scoffed at charms and amulets, while Galen commended them, and is said to have invented the anodyne necklace which was long known and worn in England. There is no need to specify which of the masters Cardan would swear by in this matter. The choice which Cardan made, albeit it was exactly what might have been anticipated, was in every respect an unfortunate one. He put himself under a master whose teaching could have no other effect than to accentuate the failings of the pupil, whereas had he let his mind come under the more regular discipline of Hippocrates' method, it is almost certain that the mass of his work, now shut in dusty folios which stand undisturbed on the shelves for decade after decade, would have been immeasurably more fruitful of good. With all his industry in collecting, and his care in verifying, his medical work remains a heap of material, and nothing more valuable. Learning and science would have profited much had he put himself under the standard of the Father of Medicine, and still more if fate had sent him into being at some period after the world of letters had learned to realize the capabilities of the inductive system of Philosophy.

It may readily be conceded that Cardan during his career turned to good account the medical knowledge which he had gathered from the best attainable sources,

. T

and that he was on the whole the most skilful physician of his age. He likewise foreshadowed the system of deaf mute instruction. A certain Georgius Agricola, a physician of Heidelberg who died in 1485, makes mention of a deaf mute who had learnt to read and write, but this statement was received with incredulity. Cardan, taking a more philosophic view, declared that people thus afflicted might easily be taught to hear by reading, and to speak by writing; writing was associated with speech, and speech with thought, but written characters and ideas might be connected without the intervention of sounds.[1] This view, put forward with all the authority of Cardan's name, would certainly rouse fresh interest in the question, and, whether stimulated by his words or not, an attempt to teach deaf mutes was made by Pedro de Ponce, a Spanish Dominican, about 1560. But it would not be permissible to claim for Cardan any share in the epoch-making discoveries in Medicine. Galen as an experimental physiologist had brought diagnosis to a level unattained before. His methods had been abandoned by his successors, and practice had in consequence suffered deterioration, but Cardan, studying under the revived Galenism, called into life by the teaching of Vesalius, went to deal with his cures under conditions more favourable than those offered by any previous period of the world's history. His cure of Archbishop Hamilton's asthma, over which Cassanate and the other doctors had failed, was due to a more careful diagnosis and a more judicious application of existing rules, rather than to the working of any new discoveries of his own. Viewed as a soldier in the service of Hygeia, how transient and slender is the fame of Cardan compared with that of Linacre, Vesalius, or

[1] *Opera*, tom. x. p. 462.

Harvey! Were his claims to immortality to rest entirely on his contribution to Medicine, his name would have gone down.to oblivion along with that of Cavenago, Camutio, Della Croce, and the multitude of jealous rivals who, according to his account, were ever plotting his downfall. But it was rescued from this fate by his excellence as a mathematician, by the interest clinging to his personality, by the enormous range of his learning, by his picturesque reputation as a dreamer of dreams, and a searcher into the secrets of the hidden world. In an age when books were few and ill-composed, his works became widely popular; because, although he dealt with abstruse subjects, he wrote—as even Naudé admits—in a passably good style, and handled his subject with a lightness of touch which was then very rare. This was the reason why men went on reading him long after his works had ceased to have any scientific value; which induced writers like Burton and Sir Thomas Browne to embroider their pages freely with quotations from his works, and thus make his name familiar to many who have never handled a single one of his volumes.

It is somewhat strange to find running through the complex web of Cardan's character a well-defined thread of worldly wisdom and common-sense; to find that a man, described by almost every one who has dealt with his character as a credulous simpleton, one with disordered wits, or a down-right madman, should, when occasion demanded, prove himself to be a sharp man of business. When Fazio died he left his son with a number of unsettled law-suits on hand, concerning which he writes: " From my father's death until I was forty-six, that is to say for a space of twenty-three years, I was almost continually involved in law-suits. First with Alessandro

Castillione, surnamed Gatico, with respect to certain plantations, and afterwards with his kinsfolk. Next with the Counts of Barbiani, next with the college, next with the heirs of Dominico de Tortis, who had held me in his arms when I was baptized. Out of all these suits I came victorious. It was indeed a matter for surprise that I should have got the better of Alessandro Castillione, seeing that his uncle sat as judge. Moreover, he had already got a decision against me, a decision which, as the jurisconsults declared, helped my case as the trial went on, and I was able to force him to pay me all the money which was in dispute. A like good fortune attended me while my claims were considered by the heads of the Milanese College, and finally rejected by several votes. Then afterwards, when they had decided to admit me, and when they tried to subject me to certain rules which placed me on a footing inferior to their own, I compelled them to grant me full membership. In the case of the Barbiani, after long litigation and many angry words and much trouble, I came to terms with them ; and, having received the sum of money covenanted by agreement, I was entirely freed from vexation of the law."[1] Writing generally of his monetary dealings, Cardan says : "Whenever I may have incurred a loss, I have never been content merely to retrieve the same, I have always contrived to seize upon something extra."[2] Or again: "If at any time I have lost twenty crowns, I have never rested until I have succeeded in getting back these and twenty more in addition."[3]

Cardan left in his *Dicta Familiaria* and *Præcep-*

---

[1] *De Vita Propria*, ch. xxviii. p. 73. [2] *Ibid.*, ch. xxiii. p. 64.

[3] *De Utilitate*, p. 309. He also writes at length in the Proxenata on Domestic Economy.—Chapter xxxvii. *et seq. Opera*, tom. i. p 377.

torum ad filios Libellus a long list of aphorisms and counsels, many of which give evidence of keen insight and busy observation of mankind, while some are distinguished by a touch of humour rare in his other writings. He bids his children to be careful how they offend princes, and, offence being given, never to flatter themselves that it has been pardoned; to live joyfully as long as they can, for men are for the most part worn out by care; never to take a wife from a witless stock or one tainted with hereditary disease; to refrain from deliberating when the mind is disturbed; to learn how to be worsted and suffer loss; and to trust a schoolmaster to teach children, but not to feed them. One of the dicta is a gem of quaint wisdom. "Before you begin to wash your face, see that you have a towel handy to dry the same." If all the instances of prodigies, portents, visions, and mysterious warnings which Cardan has left on record were set down in order, a perusal of this catalogue would justify, if it did not compel, the belief that he was little better than a credulous fool, and raise doubts whether such a man could have written such orderly and coherent works as the treatise on Arithmetic, or the book of the Great Art. But Cardan was beyond all else a man of moods, and it would be unfair to figure as his normal mental condition those periods of overwrought nervousness and the hallucinations they brought with them. In his old age the nearness of the inevitable stroke, and the severance of all earthly ties, led him to discipline his mind into a calmer mood, but early and late during his season of work his nature was singularly sensitive to the wearing assaults of cares and calamities. In crises of this kind his mind would be brought into so morbid a condition, that it would fall entirely under the sway of any single idea then dominant; such idea would master him entirely, or even haunt him like one of those unclean spectres he describes with such gusto in the *De Varietate*. What he may have uttered when these moods were upon him must not be taken seriously; these are the moments to which the major part of his experiences of things *supra naturam* may be referred. But there are numerous instances in which he describes marvellous phenomena with philosophic calm, and examines them in the true spirit of scepticism. In his account of the trembling of the bed on which he lay the night before he heard of Gian Battista's marriage, he goes on to say that a few nights after the first manifestation, he was once more conscious of a strange movement; and, having put his hand to his breast, found that his heart was palpitating violently because he had been lying on his left side. Then he remembered that a similar physical trouble had accompanied the first trembling of the bed, and admits that this manifestation may be referred to a natural cause, *i. e.* the palpitation. He tells also how he found amongst his father's papers a record of a cure of the gout by a prayer offered to the Virgin at eight in the morning on the first of April, and how he duly put up the prayer and was cured of the gout, but he adds: "Sed in hoc, auxiliis etiam artis usus sum."[1] Again with regard to the episode of the ignition of his bed twice in the same night, without visible cause, he says that this portent may have come about by some supernatural working; but that, on the other hand, it may have been the result of mere chance. He tells another story of an experience which befell him when he was in Belgium.[2] He was aroused early in the morning by the noise made outside his door by a dog catching fleas. Having got

[1] *De Vita Propria*, ch. xxxvii. p. 118.   [2] *De Varietate*, p. 589.

out of bed to see to this, he heard the sound as of a key being softly put into the lock. He told this fact to the servants, who at once took up the tale, and persuaded themselves that they had heard many noises of the same kind, and others vastly more wonderful; in short, the whole house was swarming with apparitions. The next night the noise was repeated, and a second observation laid bare the real cause thereof. The scratching of the dog had caused the bolt to fall into the socket, and this produced the noise which had disquieted him. He writes in conclusion: "Thus many events which seem to defy all explanation have really come to pass by accident, or in the course of nature. Out of such manifestations as these the unlettered, the superstitious, the timorous, and the over-hasty make for themselves miracles."[1] Again, after telling a strange story of a boy who beheld the image of a thief in the neck of a phial, and of some incantations of Josephus Niger, he concludes: "Nevertheless I am of opinion that all these things were fables, and that no one could have had any real knowledge thereof, seeing that they were nothing else than vain triflings."[2]

In a nature so complex and many-sided as Cardan's, strange resemblances may be sought for and discovered, and it certainly is an unexpected revelation to find a mental attitude common to Cardan, a man tied and bound by authority and the traditions of antiquity, and such a daring assailant of the schools and of Aristotle as Doctor Joseph Glanvil. The conclusions of Cardan as to certain obscure phenomena recently cited show that, in matters lying beyond sensual cognition, he kept an open mind. In summing up the case of the woman said to have been cured by the incantations of Josephus

---

[1] *De Varietate*, p. 589.   [2] *Ibid.*, p. 640.

Niger, he says that she must have been cured either by the power of the imagination, or by the agency of the demons. Here he anticipates the arguments which Glanvil sets forth in *Sadducismus Triumphatus.* Writing on the belief in witchcraft Glanvil says, " We have the attestation of thousands of eye and ear witnesses, and these not of the easily-deceivable vulgar only, but of wise and grave discerners ; and that when no interest could oblige them to agree together in a common Lye. I say, we have the light of all these circumstances to confirm us in the belief of things done by persons of despicable power and knowledge, beyond the reach of Art and ordinary Nature. Standing public Records have been kept of these well-attested Relations, and Epochas made of those unwonted events. Laws in many Nations have been enacted against those vile practices ; those amongst the Jews and our own are notorious ; such cases have often been determined near us by wise and reverend Judges, upon clear and convictive Evidence ; and thousands of our own Nation have suffered death for their vile compacts with Apostate spirits. All these I might largely prove in their particular instances, but that 'tis not needful since these did deny the being of Witches, so it was not out of ignorance of these heads of Argument, of which probably they have heard a thousand times ; but from an apprehension that such a belief is absurd, and the things impossible. And upon these presumptions they condemn all demonstrations of this nature, and are hardened against conviction. And I think those that can believe all Histories and Romances; That all the wiser would have agreed together to juggle mankind into a common belief of ungrounded fables, that the sound senses of multitudes together may deceive them,

and Laws are built upon Chimeras; That the greatest
and wisest Judges have been Murderers, and the sagest
persons Fools, or designing Impostors; I say those
that can believe this heap of absurdities, are either
more credulous than those whose credulity they repre-
hend; or else have some extraordinary evidence of their
perswasion, viz.: That it is absurd and impossible that
there should be a Witch or Apparition."[1] Cardan's argument in the case of the sick woman, that it would be difficult if not impossible to invent cause for her cure, other
than the power of imagination or Demoniac agency, if
less emphatic and lengthy than Glanvil's, certainly runs
upon parallel lines therewith, and suggests, if it does not
proclaim, the existence of such a thing as the credulity
of unbelief; in other words that those who were disposed
to brush aside the alternative causes of the cure as set
down by him, and search for others, and put faith in
them, would be fully as credulous as those who held the
belief which he recorded as his own.

[1] *Sadducismus Triumphatus* (Ed. 1682), p. 4.

CHAPTER XV

WHEN dealing with Cardan's sudden incarceration in 1570, in the chronicle of his life, it was assumed that his offence must have been some spoken or written words upon which a charge of impiety might have been fastened. Leaving out of consideration the fiery zeal of the reigning Pope Pius V., it is hard to determine what plea could have been found for a serious charge of this nature. Cardan's work had indeed passed the ecclesiastical censors in 1562; but in the estimation of Pius V. the smallest lapse from the letter of orthodoxy would have seemed grave enough to send to prison, and perhaps to death, a man as deeply penetrated with the spirit of religion as Cardan assuredly was. One of his chief reasons for refusing the King of Denmark's generous offer was the necessity involved of having to live amongst a people hostile to the Catholic religion; and, in writing of his visit to the English Court, he declares that he was unwilling to recognize the title of King Edward VI., inasmuch as by so doing he might seem to prejudice the rights of the Pope.[1] In spite of this positive testimony, and the absence of any utterances of manifest heresy, divers writers in the succeeding century classed him with the unbelievers. Dr. Samuel Parker in his *Tractatus de Deo*, published in 1678,

[1] *De Vita Propria*, ch. xxix. p. 76.

includes him amongst the atheistical philosophers; but a perusal of the Doctor's remarks leaves the reader unconvinced as to the justice of such a charge. The term Atheism, however, was at this time used in the very loosest sense, and was even applied to disbelievers in the apostolical succession.[1] Dr. Parker writes, "Another cause which acted, together with the natural disposition of Cardan, to produce that odd mixture of folly and wisdom in him, was his habit of continual thinking by which the bile was absorbed and burnt up; he suffered neither eating, pleasure, nor pain to interrupt the course of his thoughts. He was well acquainted with the writings of all the ancients—nor did he just skim over the heads and contents of books as some do who ought not to be called learned men, but skilful bookmongers. Every author that Cardan read (and he read nearly all) he became intimately acquainted with, so that if any one disputing with him, quoted the authority of the ancients, and made any the least slip or mistake, he would instantly set them right." Dr. Parker is as greatly amazed at the mass of work he produced, as at his powers of accumulation, and maintains that Cardan believed he was endowed with a faculty which he calls *repræsentatio*, through which he was able to apprehend things without study, "by means of an interior light shining within him. From which you may learn the fact that he had studied with such enduring obstinacy that he began to persuade himself that the visions which appeared before him in these fits and transports of the mind, were the genuine inspirations of the Deity." This is evidently Dr. Parker's explanation of the attendant demon, and he ends by declaring that Cardan was rather fanatic than infidel.

[1] Dugald Stewart, *Dissertations*, p. 378.

Mention has been made of the list of his vices and imperfections which Cardan wrote down with his own hand. Out of such a heap of self-accusation it would have been an easy task for some meddlesome enemy to gather up a plentiful selection of isolated facts which by artful combination might be so arranged as to justify a formal charge of impiety. The most definite of these charges were made by Martin del Rio,[1] who declares that Cardan once wrote a book on the Mortality of the Soul which he was wont to exhibit to his intimate friends. He did not think it prudent to print this work, but wrote another, taking a more orthodox view, called *De Immortalitate Animorum.* Another assailant, Theophile Raynaud, asserts that certain passages in this book suggest, if they do not prove, that Cardan did not set down his real opinions on the subject in hand. Raynaud ends by forbidding the faithful to read any of Cardan's books, and describes him as " Homo nullius religionis ac fidei, et inter clancularios atheos secundi ordinis ævo suo facile princeps." Of all Cardan's books the *De Immortalitate Animorum* is the one in which materials for a charge of impiety might most easily be found. It was put together at a time when he had had very little practice in the Greek tongue, and it is possible that many of his conclusions may be drawn from premises only imperfectly apprehended. Scaliger in his Exercitations seizes upon one passage[2] which, according to his ren-

---

[1] The writer, a Jesuit, says in *Disquisitionum Magicarum* (Louvanii, 1599), tom. i.:—" In Cardani de Subtilitate et de Varietate libris passim latet anguis in herba et indiget expurgatione Ecclesiasticæ limæ." Del Rio was a violent assailant of Cornelius Agrippa.

[2] " Quoniam intellectus intrinsecus est homini, belluis extrinsecus collucet: unus etiam satisfacere omnibus, quæ in una specie sunt potest, hominibus plures sunt necessarii: tertia est quod hominis anima tanquam speculum est levigata, splendida, solida, clara: belluarum autem tenebrosa nec levis ; atque ideo in nostra anima lux mentis

dering, implied that Cardan reckoned the intelligence of men and beasts to be the same in essence, the variety of operation being produced by the fact that the apprehensive faculty was inherent in the one, and only operative upon the other from without. But all through this book it is very difficult to determine whether the propositions advanced are Cardan's own, or those of the Greek and Arabian writers he quotes so freely: and this charge of Scaliger, which is the best supported of all, goes very little way to convict him of impiety. In the *De Vita Propria* there are several passages [1] which suggest a belief akin to that of the Anima Mundi; he had without doubt made up his mind that this work should not see the light till he was beyond the reach of Pope or Council. The origin of this charge of impiety may be referred with the best show of probability to his attempt to cast the horoscope of Jesus Christ.[2] This, together with a diagram, is given in the Commentaries on Ptolemy, and soon after it appeared it was made the occasion of a fierce attack by Julius Cæsar Scaliger, who declared that such a scheme must be flat blasphemy, inasmuch as the author proved that all the actions of Christ necessarily followed the position of the stars at the time of His nativity. If Scaliger had taken the trouble to glance at the Commentary he would have discovered that Cardan especially guarded himself against any accusation of this sort, by setting down

---

refulget multipliciter confracta, inde ipse Intellectus intelligit. Ceteris autem potentiis, ut diximus, nullus limes prescriptus est : at belluarum internis facultatibus tantum licet agnoscere, quantum per exteriores sensus accesserit."—*De Imm. Anim.*, p. 283.

[1] "Deum debere dici immensum : omnia quæ partes habent diversas ordinatas animam habere et vitam."—p. 167.

[2] In the last edition of *De Libris Propriis* he calls it "Christique nativitas admirabilis."—*Opera*, tom. i. p. 110.

that no one was to believe he had any intention of asserting that Christ's divinity, or His miracles, or His holy life, or the promulgation of His laws were in any way influenced by the stars.[1] Naudé, in recording the censures of De Thou, "Verum extremæ amentiæ fuit, imo impiæ audaciæ, astrorum commentitiis legibus verum astrorum dominum velle subjicere. Quod ille tamen exarata Servatoris nostri genitura fecit," and of Joseph Scaliger, "impiam dicam magis, an 'jocularem audaciam quæ et dominum stellarum stellis subjecerit, et natum eo tempore putarit, quod adhuc in lite positum est, ut vanitas cum impietate certaret,"[2] declares that it was chiefly from the publication of this horoscope that Cardan incurred the suspicion of blasphemy; but, with his free-thinking bias, abstains from adding his own censure. He rates Scaliger for ignorance because he was evidently under the impression that Cardan was the first to draw a horoscope of Christ, and attacks Cardan chiefly on the score of plagiary. He records how divers writers in past times had done the same thing. Albumasar, one of the most learned of the Arabs, whose *thema natalium* is quoted by Roger Bacon in one of his epistles to Clement V., Albertus Magnus, Peter d'Ailly the Cardinal of Cambrai, and Tiberius Russilanus who lived in the time of Leo X., all constructed nativities of Christ, but Cardan makes no mention of these horoscopists, and, according to the view of Naudé, poses as the inventor of this form of impiety, and is consequently guilty of literary dishonesty, a worse sin, in his critics' eyes, than the framing of the horoscope itself.

That there was in Cardan's practice enough of curiosity and independence to provoke suspicion of his

[1] *Ptolemæi de Astrorum Judiciis,* p. 163.
[2] *Præfatio in Manilium.*

orthodoxy in the minds of the leaders of the post-Tridentine revival, is abundantly possible; but there is nothing in all his life and works to show that he was, according to the standard of every age, anything else than a spiritually-minded man.[1] It would be hard to find words more instinct with the true feeling of piety, than the following taken from the fifty-third chapter of the *De Vita Propria*,—" I love solitude, for I never seem to be so entirely with those who are especially dear to me as when I am alone. I love God and the spirit of good, and when I am by myself I let my thoughts dwell on these, their immeasurable beneficence; the eternal wisdom, the source and origin of clearest light, that true joy within us which never fears that God will forsake us; that groundwork of truth; that willing love; and the Maker of us all, who is blessed in Himself, and likewise the desire and safeguard of all the blessed. Ah, what depth and what height of righteousness, mindful of the dead and not forgetting the living. He is the Spirit who protects me by His commands, my good and merciful counsellor, my helper and consoler in misfortune."

Two or three of Cardan's treatises are in the *materna lingua*, but he wrote almost entirely in Latin, using a style which was emphatically literary.[2] His Latin is probably above the average excellence of the age, and if the classic writers held the first place in his estimation —as naturally they would—he assuredly did not neglect the firstfruits of modern literature. Pulci was his favourite poet. He evidently knew Dante and Boc-

---

[1] A proof of his liberal tone of mind is found in his appreciation of the fine qualities of Edward VI. as a man, although he resented his encroachments as a king upon the Pope's rights.

[2] In the *De Vita Propria*, ch. xxxiii. p. 106, he fixes into his prose an entire line of Horace, "Canidia afflasset pejor serpentibus Afris."

caccio well, and his literary insight was clear enough to perceive that the future belonged to those who should write in the vulgar tongue of the lands which produced them.[1]

Perhaps it was impossible that a man endowed with so catholic a spirit and with such earnest desire for knowledge, should sink into the mere pedant with whom later ages have been made acquainted through the farther specialization of science. At all events Cardan is an instance that the man of liberal education need not be killed by the man of science. For him the path of learning was not an easy one to tread, and, as it not seldom happens, opposition and coldness drove him on at a pace rarely attained by those for whom the royal road to learning is smoothed and prepared. For a long time his father refused to give him instruction in Latin, or to let him be taught by any one else, and up to his twentieth year he seems to have known next to nothing of this language which held the keys both of letters and science. He began to learn Greek when he was about thirty-five, but it was not till he had turned forty that he took up the study of it in real earnest ;[2] and, writing some years later, he gives quotations from a Latin version of Aristotle.[3] In his commentaries on Hippocrates he used a Latin text, presumably the translation of Calvus printed in Rome in 1525, and quotes Epicurus in Latin in the *De Subtilitate* (p. 347), but in works like the *De Sapientia* and the *De Consolatione* he quotes Greek freely, supplying in nearly every case a Latin version of the passages cited. These treatises

---

[1] "At Boccatii fabulæ nunc majus virent quam antea : et Dantis Petrarchæque ac Virgilii totque aliorum poemata sunt in maxima veneratione."—*Opera*, tom. i. p. 125.

[2] *Ibid.*, tom. i. p. 59. [3] *De Vita Propria*, ch. xii.—xiii. pp. 39, 44.

bristle with quotations, Horace being his favourite author. " Vir in omni sapientiæ genere admirandus." [1] As with many moderns his love for Horace did not grow less as old age crept on, for the *De Vita Propria* is perhaps fuller of Horatian tags than any other of his works. It would seem somewhat of a paradox that a sombre and earnest nature like Cardan's should find so great pleasure in reading the elegant *poco curante* triflings of the Augustan singer, were it not a recognized fact that Horace has always been a greater favourite with serious practical Englishmen than with the descendants of those for whom he wrote his verses.

It was a habit with Cardan to apologize in the prefaces of his scientific works for the want of elegance in his Latin, explaining that the baldness and simplicity of his periods arose from his determination to make his meaning plain, and to trouble nothing about style for the time being; but the following passage shows that he had a just and adequate conception of the necessary laws of literary art. " That book is perfect which goes straight to its point in one single line of argument, which neither leaves out aught that is necessary, nor brings in aught that is superfluous: which observes the rule of correct division; which explains what is obscure; and shows plainly the groundwork upon which it is based." [2]

The *De Vita Propria* from which this extract comes is in point of style one of his weakest books, but even in this volume passages may here and there be found of considerable merit, and Cardan was evidently studious to let his ideas be presented in intelligible form, for he records that in 1535 he read through the whole

---

[1] *Opera*, tom. i. p. 505.   [2] *De Vita Propria*, ch. xxvii. p. 72.

of Cicero, for the sake of improving his Latin. His style, according to Naudé, held a middle place between the high-flown and the pedestrian, and of all his books the *De Utilitate ex Adversis Capienda*, which was begun in 1557, shows the nearest approach to elegance, but even this is not free from diffuseness, the fault which Naudé finds in all his writings. Long dissertations entirely alien from the subject in hand are constantly interpolated. In the Practice of Arithmetic he turns aside to treat of the marvellous properties of certain numbers, of the motion of the planets, and of the Tower of Babel ; and in the treatise on Dialectic he gives an estimate of the historians and letter-writers of the past. But here Cardan did not sin in ignorance ; his poverty and not his will consented to these literary outrages. He was paid for his work by the sheet, and the thicker the volume the higher the pay.[1]

When he made a beginning of the *De Utilitate* Cardan was at the zenith of his fortunes. He had lately returned from his journey to Scotland, having made a triumphant progress through the cities of Western Europe. Thus, with his mind well stored with experience of divers lands, his wits sharpened by intercourse with the *élite* of the learned world, and his hand nerved by the magnetic stimulant of success, he sat down to write as the philosopher and man of the world, rather than as the man of science. He was, in spite of his prosperity, inclined to deal with the more sombre side of life. He seems to have been specially drawn to write of

---

[1] " Eo tantum fine, quemadmodum alicubi fatetur, ut plura folia Typographis mitteret, quibuscum antea de illorum pretio pepigerat ; atque hoc modo fami, non secus ac famæ scriberet."—Naudæus, *Judicium.*

death, disease, and of the peculiar physical misfortune which befell him in early manhood. Like Cicero he goes on to treat of Old Age, but in a spirit so widely different that a brief comparison of the conclusions of the two philosophers will not be without interest. Old age, Cardan declares to be the most cruel and irreparable evil with which man is cursed, and to talk of old age is to talk of the crowning misfortune of humanity. Old men are made wretched by avarice, by dejection, and by terror. He bids men not to be deceived by the flowery words of Cicero,[1] when he describes Cato as an old man, like to a fair statue of Polycleitus, with faculties unimpaired and memory fresh and green. He next goes on to catalogue the numerous vices and deformities of old age, and instances from Aristotle what he considers to be the worst of all its misfortunes, to wit that an old man is well-nigh cut off from hope ; and by way of comment grimly adds, " If any man be plagued by the ills of old age he should blame no one but himself, for it is by his own choice that his life has run on so long." He vouchsafes a few words of counsel as to how this hateful season may be robbed of some of its horror. Our bodies grow old first, then our senses, then our minds. Therefore let us store our treasures in that part of us which will hold out longest, as men in a beleaguered city are wont to collect their resources in the citadel, which, albeit it must in the end be taken, will nevertheless be the last to fall into the foeman's hands. Old men should avoid society, seeing that they can bring nothing thereto worth having : whether they speak

---

[1] In *De Consolatione* (*Opera*, tom. i. p. 604) he writes :— " Quantum diligentiæ, quantum industriæ Cicero adjecit, quo conatu nixus est ut persuaderet senectutem esse tolerandam."

or keep silent they are in the way, and they are as irksome to themselves when they are silent, as they are to others when they speak. The old man should take a lesson from the lower animals, which are wont to defend themselves with the best arms given them by nature: bulls with their horns, horses with their hoofs, and cats with their claws ; wherefore an old man should at least show himself to be as wise as the brutes and maintain his position by his wisdom and knowledge, seeing that all the grace and power of his manhood must needs have fled.[1]

In another of his moral treatises he has formulated a long indictment against old age, that hateful state with its savourless joys and sleepless nights. Did not Zeno the philosopher strangle himself when he found that time refused to do its work. The happiest are those who earliest lay down the burden of existence, and the Law itself causes these offenders who are least guilty to die first, letting the more nefarious and hardened criminals stand by and witness the death of their fellows. There can be no evil worse than the daily expectation of the blow that is inevitable, and old age, when it comes, must make every man regret that he did not die in infancy. "When I was a boy," he writes, "I remember one day to have heard my mother, Chiara Micheria—herself a young woman—cry out that she wished it had been God's will to let her die when she was a child. I asked her why, and she answered: 'Because I know I must soon die, to the great peril of my soul, and besides this, if we shall diligently weigh and examine all our experiences of life, we shall not light upon a single one which will not have brought us

---

[1] *De Utilitate*, book ii. ch. 4.

more sorrow than joy. For afflictions when they come mar the recollection of our pleasures, and with just cause; for what is there in life worthy the name of delight, the ever-present burden of existence, the task of dressing and undressing every day, hunger, thirst, evil dreams? What more profit and ease have we than the dead? We must endure the heat of summer, the cold of winter, the confusion of the times, the dread of war, the stern rule of parents, the anxious care of our children, the weariness of domestic life, the ill carriage of servants, lawsuits, and, what is worst of all, the state of the public mind which holds probity as silliness; which practises deceit and calls it prudence. Craftsmen are counted excellent, not by their skill in their art, but by reason of their garish work and of the valueless approbation of the mob. Wherefore one must needs either incur God's displeasure or live in misery, despised and persecuted by men.'"[1] These words, though put into his mother's mouth, are manifestly an expression of Cardan's own feelings.

Cardan was the product of an age to which there had recently been revealed the august sources from which knowledge, as we understand the term, has flowed without haste or rest since the unsealing of the fountain. He counts it rare fortune to have been born in such an age, and rhapsodizes over the flowery meadow of knowledge in which his generation rejoices, and over the vast Western world recently made known. Are not the artificial thunderbolts of man far more destructive than those of heaven? What praise is too high for the magnet which leads men safely over perilous seas, or for the art of printing? Indeed it needs but little

[1] *De Consolatione* (*Opera*, tom. i. p. 605).

more to enable man to scale the very heavens. With
his mind thus set upon the exploration of these new
fields of knowledge ; with the full realization how vast
was the treasure lying hid therein ; it was only natural
that a spirit so curious and greedy of fresh mental food
should have fretted at the piteous brevity of the earthly
term allowed to man, and have rated as a supreme evil
that old age which brought with it decay of the faculties
and foreshadowed the speedy and inevitable fall of the
curtain.   Cicero on the other hand had been nurtured in
a creed and philosophy alike outworn.   The blight
of finality had fallen upon the moral world, and the
physical universe still guarded jealously her mighty
secrets.   To the eyes of Cicero the mirror of nature was
blank void and darkness, while Cardan, gazing into the
same glass, must have been embarrassed with the
number and variety of the subjects offered, and may
well have felt that the longest life of man ten times
prolonged would rank but as a moment in that Titanic
spell of work necessary to bring to the birth the teeming
burden with which the universe lay in travail.   Here is
one and perhaps the strongest reason of his hatred of
old age ; because through the shortness of his span of
time he could only deal with a grain or two of the sand
lying upon the shores of knowledge.   Cicero, with his
more limited vision, conscious that sixty years or so of
life would exhaust every physical delight, and blunt and
mar the intellectual ; ignorant both of the world of new
light lying beyond the void, and of the rapture which
the conquering investigator of the same must feel in
wringing forth its secrets, welcomed the gathering
shades as friendly visitants, a mood which has asserted
itself in later times with certain weary spirits, sated with

knowledge as Vitellius was sated with his banquets of nightingales' tongues.

Cardan with all his curiosity and restless mental activity was hampered and restrained in his explorations by the bonds which had been imposed upon thought during the rule of authority. These bonds held him back—acting imperceptibly—as they held back Abelard and many other daring spirits trained in the methods of the schoolmen, and allowed him to do little more than range at large over the fields of fresh knowledge which were destined to be reaped by later workers trained in other schools and under different masters. Learning was still subject to authority, though in milder degree, than when Thomas of Aquino dominated the mental outlook of Europe, and the great majority of the men who posed as Freethinkers, and sincerely believed themselves to be Freethinkers, were unconsciously swayed by the associations of the method of teaching they professed to despise. Their progress for the most part resembled the movement of a squirrel in a rotatory cage, but though their efforts to conquer the new world of knowledge were vain, it cannot be questioned that the restrictions placed around them, while nullifying the result of their investigations, stimulated enormously the activity of the brain and gave it a formal discipline which proved of the highest value when the real literary work of Modern Europe began. The futilities of the problems upon which the scholastic thinkers exercised themselves gave occasion for the satiric onslaught both of Rabelais and Erasmus. " Quæstio subtilissima, utrum Chimæra in vacuo bombinans possit comedere secundas intentiones ; et fuit debatuta per decem hebdomadas in Consilio Constantiensi," and " Quid consecrasset Petrus, si consecrasset eo tempore, quo corpus Christi pendebet in cruce?" are samples which will be generally familiar, but the very absurdity of these exercitations serves to prove how strenuous must have been the temper of the times which preferred to exhaust itself over such banalities as are typified by the extracts above written, rather than remain inactive. The dogmas in learning were fixed as definitely as in religion, and the solution of every question was found and duly recorded. The Philosopher was allowed to strike out a new track, but if he valued his life or his ease, he would take care to arrive finally at the conclusion favoured by authority.

Cardan may with justice be classed both with men of science and men of letters. In spite of the limitations just referred to it is certain that as he surveyed the broadening horizon of the world of knowledge, he must have felt the student's spasm of agony when he first realized the infinity of research and the awful brevity of time. His reflections on old age give proof enough of this. If he missed the labour in the full harvest-field, the glimpse of the distant mountain tops, suffused for the first time by the new light, he missed likewise the wearing labour which fell upon the shoulders of those who were compelled by the new philosophy to use new methods in presenting to the world the results of their midnight research. Such work as Cardan undertook in the composition of his moral essays, and in the Commentary on Hippocrates put no heavy tax on the brain or the vital energies ; the Commentary was of portentous length, but it was not much more than a paraphrase with his own experiences added thereto. Mathematics were his pastime, to judge by the ease and rapidity with which he solved the problems sent to him by Francesco

Sambo of Ravenna and others.[1] He worked hard no doubt, but as a rule mere labour inflicts no heavier penalty than healthy fatigue. The destroyer of vital power and spring is hard work, combined with that unsleeping diligence which must be exercised when a man sets himself to undertake something more complex than the mere accumulation of data, when he is forced to keep his mental powers on the strain through long hours of selection and co-ordination, and to fix and concentrate his energies upon the task of compelling into symmetry the heap of materials lying under his hand. The *De Subtilitate* and the *De Varietate* are standing proofs that Cardan did not overstrain his powers by exertion of this kind.

Leaving out of the reckoning his mathematical treatises, the vogue enjoyed by Cardan's published works must have been a short one. They came to the birth only to be buried in the yawning graves which lie open in every library. At the time when Spon brought out his great edition in ten folio volumes in 1663, the mists of oblivion must have been gathering around the author's fame, and in a brief space his words ceased to have any weight in the teaching of that Art he had cultivated with so great zeal and affection. The mathematician who talked about " Cardan's rule " to his pupils was most likely ignorant both of his century and his birthplace. Had it not been for the references made by writers like Burton to his dabblings in occult learning, his claims to read the stars, and to the guidance of a

---

[1] *Opera*, tom. i. p. 113. On the same page he adds:—" Fui autem tam felix in cito absoluendo, quam infelicissimus in sero inchoando. Cœpi enim illum anno ætatis meæ quinquagesimo octavo, absolvi intra septem dies ; pene prodigio similis."

peculiar spirit, his name would have been now unknown, save to a few algebraists; and his desire, expressed in one of the meditative passages of the *De Vita Propria*, would have been amply fulfilled : " Non tamen unquam concupivi gloriam aut honores : imo sprevi, cuperem notum esse quod sim, non opto ut sciatur qualis sim." [1]

[1] *De Vita Propria*, ch. ix. p. 30.

INDEX